EBERHARDT'S GHOST

Allan Clark Morgan

Eberhardt's Ghost

ISBN: 0983703221
ISBN-13: 978-0983703228

Acknowledgment

Many thanks are due my wife Alice
for her inspiration and encouragement.

Books by Allan Clark Morgan

EBERHARDT'S GHOST

LIKE FATHER LIKE SON

NO END IN SIGHT

THE BABY PHOENIX

**These books are available in Paper back
copy and Electronic copy via Kindle
on Amazon and other retailers**

About the Author

Allan Clark Morgan is a retired Chemical Engineer. This is his fourth book on high tech terrorism. He is a military history buff. His hobbies include reading, writing, cooking, bridge and all sorts of puzzles.

He divides his time between Cape Ann in the summer and the Florida Keys in the winter.

EBERHARDT'S GHOST

Nazi machinations aimed at producing a super race continue. Karl Eberhardt, the genius physicist who led the Nazi nuclear weapons development and Wilfried Baumgartner, a gifted neurosurgeon, achieved some success in electroencephalographically educating a few men and women. Siegfried Bachmeier their genius 'subject' won the Physics Prize at Heidelberg University for his doctoral dissertation on subatomic particles. Eberhardt is gone now, or is he?

Bachmeier's work has alarmed Guenther Reinhardt, an eminent Los Alamos physicist and Randolph Biggs, perhaps the world's preeminent expert on particle beam weaponry. They turn to DCAC to stop any further work by Bachmeier. He is dangerously close to achieving the ability to destroy satellites. Henry Magnuson is the tip of the DCAC spear.

Bachmeier has ample resources in his native Argentina as well as Germany. His grandfather was the head of the Nazi community in Argentina. His uncle is now the head. A highly intelligent, beautiful and rich woman from Saudi Arabia is close to his uncle and finances his development work. Bachmeier moves swiftly and the weapon he develops is used against a British Petroleum oil platform. The American and British Navies enter the fray....

Neurosurgery Institute

Herbertshausen, Germany

May 1942

Herr Doctor Professor Wilfried Baumgartner is on the telephone with Heinrich Himmler.

"Yes Reichsfuhrer we had almost ninety percent retention. The Subject lived for nearly two days after the procedure."

"How do you know that you achieved such a high retention level?"

"We tested the Subject before and after the session. He was able to hum most of the music in the order it was fed to his brain through the transmitter."

"Have you done this with anything besides music?"

"We have been able to transmit a few words but we have to send them one letter at a time."

"But you can transmit letters?"

"Yes Reichsfuhrer."

"There were no wires?"

"There were no wires on the Source but of course we had wires on the Subject to transmit the carrier frequency. The actual information was sent through the transmitter."

"This does not damage the Source in any way?"

"That is correct Reichsfuhrer. The compound the Source drinks does not appear to do any harm whatsoever."

"Are you able to record anything?"

"We have the electroencephalograms from the Subject but these are relatively low frequency. We can see the carrier frequency. I don't know for sure but I suspect the frequency of the transmission is beyond the capabilities of our instruments."

"You are certain that there is no damage to the Source."

"Yes."

"We need more men like Eberhardt on the project. Do you think we are ready to try this on someone who we don't want dead in a few days?"

"Please send me another five subjects from Dachau. It would be preferable if they were reasonably intelligent to start with. Heil Hitler."

"Heil Hitler."

Reichsfuhrer Himmler is ecstatic. They are getting close to being able to transfer thought across great distances. This will provide an ultra-secure form of communication and possibly even mind control.

Siegfried Bachmeier's apartment

Heidelberg, Germany

May 4, 1993 Tuesday 1700

Siegfried Bachmeier managed to reach his telephone on the seventh ring. He is a graduate student in Physics at the University and is nearing the end of his Doctoral studies.

"Hello."

"Siegfried, this is Grandpa."

This is somewhat unusual. His grandfather Wilhelm Bachmeier usually calls him on Saturdays.

"Yes Grandpa. How are you?"

"That is what I am calling about. I can not talk about this in detail over this phone but I wanted to tell you that your father is missing. I think it would be wise for you to not come back to Argentina until you hear from me again."

"I was planning on coming home to see you in July and doing some skiing In Bariloche."

"Please stay where you are and finish up as soon as you are able. You said you thought you could finish later this year didn't you?"

"Yes Grandpa, I expect to finish in August."

"I will contact you in a month or two. I love you."

"I love you too Grandpa."

Aeropuerto Internacional Ministro Pistarini
Ezeiza, Argentina
June 28, 1993 Monday 1300

The South African Airways Johannesburg to Buenos Aires flight landed on time. Captain Oskar Brandt and Commander Hermann Schliefenbaum are dressed in civilian clothes and have only small carry-on bags. They pass through immigration and customs at Ezeiza without any problems. Oskar's son Raphael embraces his father as soon as he is through the door out of the customs hall.

"Welcome home Dad. I am very happy to see you."

He warmly shakes Hermann's hand.

"Welcome back Hermann."

"I am glad to be here."

When they exit the terminal there is the usual mob scene. Oskar's driver has managed to park the ten seat Mercedes van less than forty meters from the terminal door. When they pass through the door he runs over and embraces Oskar and Hermann. He grabs their bags and puts them in the back. They are soon on their way to Zarate. Oskar and Hermann both live there about two kilometers apart. As soon as they are underway, Oskar and Hermann relate the parts of the story that Raphael does not know.

"The weapon aimed at Tel Aviv detonated prematurely. It had a magnetic homing feature. I can only speculate that there was a ship between us and the shore and that the thing found it."

"There has been some speculation in the press about that Dad. You are probably right. The weapon detonated about twelve kilometers off shore."

"The SASC *(Southern Arabian Shipping Company)* container ship was right where it was supposed to be. We rendezvoused with it about seventy miles north of Port Said. We scuttled your grandfather's boat in 1250 meters of water. We got through the Suez Canal but then there was a little excitement. Somehow, the Americans must have been able to "see" the rendezvous on their satellite radar. It was pitch black and raining heavily when we met the container ship. I was certain we could not be seen by their satellites. Captain Bihari told me they saw a submarine on radar just as they were entering the northern approach to the canal. Two days later we were torpedoed about one hundred miles north of Jeddah. The Saudi Coast Guard picked us up about six hours later. They took us to the SASC dock in Jeddah. Captain Ridwan got us home from there. All our people made it. There were two crewmen on the Duha Ali that did not make it. I think they were in the engine room and the second torpedo killed them."

"We have had a little excitement around here also Dad. The Americans raided Rancho Don Martinez the day you left Bahia Blanca. We think they captured Gerbert Bachmeier, Helmut Vogel, Fritz Wexler and Werner Runkel."

"What were those guys doing out there Monday night?"

"I heard that Gerbert was a little m ffed about not being able to go to Wilhelm's send-off dinner Saturday and was determined to have his own party. Tuesday morning those guys did not show up at the yard so Benno Weber went looking for them. He found a real mess at Don Martinez. They destroyed the machine tools and took any and all records they could find."

"None of the guys were there?"

"Benno said the chef was shot dead and the only people he found were four hookers who were handcuffed and blindfolded. Apparently Wilhelm ordered the hookers be killed and buried so they wouldn't be talking about what happened."

"Two weeks later the Americans raided Rancho de Mil Robles. Wilhelm and Klaus escaped literally as the Americans were descending on the ranch house. Apparently they have some sort of Vertical Take Off and Landing (VTOL) aircraft that they can launch from a submarine. Wreckage of two of them was found at the ranch. As best we can figure they launched these aircraft offshore of Mar del Plata. That is four hundred kilometers from the ranch."

"Where is Wilhelm?"

"He said you would know where to find him. He wouldn't tell me. He also said that you would need to get in touch with Siegfried. He was much more worried about his grandson than his son."

"Yes, it has been that way for quite a few years."

"Dad, we must assume that the Americans have captured Gerbert and Helmut. Presumably they will find out what those two know about our operations – which is almost everything."

"Neither of them knew the targets. Even our crew did not know the target until we surfaced off New York to launch the V-1500."

"They are after Wilhelm and Prince Rashid. I don't think they will bother CCM (Construcciones Centrales Marinas), but I am sure that they know that you commanded the boat. There are more than 300,000 people dead in New York City as a result of the bombing. The bomb ruptured a subway tunnel under New York harbor and the whole system was filled up with seawater. I think they will seek retribution until they get it."

"We can't do anything about that."

"What happened in Haifa?"

"The Jews have not released any casualty figures. They did however drop three thermonuclear weapons on the Iranians. Apparently they thought that Iran is where the bombs intended for Haifa and Tel Aviv came from."

"Yes, we heard about that as soon as we reached the dock in Jeddah. I didn't know that the Jews had thermonuclear weapons."

"Neither did the Iranians. They are saying that the Americans gave the Jews the thermonuclear weapons."

"Yes, we also heard that when we got to Jeddah."

"Has there been anything unusual at either yard?"

"Yes. About a week after you left we found a cut in the canvas on the water side of the drydock in Bahia Blanca. There were some scratch marks on the top of the door which we think were made by a grappling hook. We think the Americans managed to get up there and take a look inside the drydock."

"Hmm. They did the same thing in Belen."

"Yes."

"They were a little late both times."

Traffic is relatively light and they are home in Zarate in a little over an hour.

Rancho de Mil Robles
San Pablo de Arno, Argentina
August 25, 1993 Wednesday

Siegfried Bachmeier completed his Doctoral work at Heidelberg the twentieth of August. He and his girlfriend celebrated that weekend in Rudesheim. Late Monday afternoon Oskar Brandt called him and told him that his grandfather was in all likelihood dead at the hands of the Americans and that his grandfather left instructions that he should come home immediately. He got a straight shot from Frankfurt to Buenos Aires on a Lufthansa 747-400 Tuesday evening. Oskar met him at Ezeiza Wednesday and they drove to the ranch. Most of the damage caused by the Americans had been cleaned up although there were still pockmarks in the outside stone wall of the ranch house. Oskar relates how his father and Siegfried's grandfather were life-long friends. Each of them was appointed trustee of the other's worldly goods in the event one of them died. The responsibility of trustee devolved to Oskar following Otto's death a few years ago. Oskar opened the safe in the ranch house where Siegfried's grandfather kept his will. Then they went to one of the barns and Oskar opened the safe beneath the floor of a horse stall. The Americans did not find this safe and in fact they apparently were unable to open the safe in the ranch house either. Oskar had other things to attend to so he left right after lunch.

Siegfried has taken a cursory look at the contents of these safes. He found two other properties which he had never heard of. He also found some correspondence between his grandfather and a Herr Albert Debbinck in the 1968 to 1977 time frame. Something about this caught his eye so he started reading it rather carefully. Debbinck is writing in Dutch so it is slow going. He finally deciphers that Debbinck is a Nazi sympathizer who is working in the South African nuclear weapons develop-ment program. The South Africans are shipping ben-eficiated uranium to Argentina for use in the Argentine nuclear power reactors. His grandfather and Debbinck have an arrangement whereby some of this uranium never leaves South Africa but is instead diverted to a nuclear pile that Professor Eberhardt built in South Africa in the late 1930's. He has heard his grandfather mention Eberhardt but he never met the man until he went to graduate school in Heidelberg. Late in the after-noon he calls Oskar.

"Uncle Oskar, I looked at some of the papers in Grandpa's safe. You were right about the property. There are two properties I never heard of. Do you know Professor Eberhardt?"

"Yes, why do you ask?"

"Do you know that Professor Eberhardt visited me several times while I was at Heidelberg?"

"No, I did not."

"There is some correspondence between grandpa and this Debbinck guy that mentions a nuclear pile in South Africa. It says Eberhardt built this thing in the late 1930's."

(This gets Oskar to thinking. Did Wilhelm get Plutonium from this pile? I know my father knew he had some on the boat but I am not sure he knew how much.)

"Where are the two properties that you didn't know about Siegfried?"

"One is in Rio Negro and the other is in Córdoba."

"The one in Rio Negro is where the Americans killed your grandfather. Siegfried, I suggest that you take these papers and put them back in the safe under the horse stall. I don't know how the Americans found the ranch in Rio Negro. No one up here in the north besides me, your grandfather and Klaus knew about this ranch. Klaus was killed at the ranch in Rio Negro. Now, you and I are the only ones up north that know about this place. I did not know about either of these locations until my father died nine years ago. You know that my father and your grandfather were very close. Even your father did not know about this ranch. Your grandfather had another organization to handle things with these two ranches. He used a different name in Rio Negro and the other one was nominally the property of a family named Stauffer. I would like to see the correspondence concerning South Africa. You are the second person today to mention Plutonium to me and the second person today to mention South Africa."

"We could have supper together in Zarate if you like Uncle."

"That will be fine. You can stay here tonight. I don't want you driving around after you have too much wine."

They eat at El Toro Rugiente (The Roaring Bull) and they do have a little too much wine. No matter, Oskar's driver does not drink when he needs to drive. They go back to his home and Oskar pours a couple of snifters of Ramefort. They go over the correspondence. Oskar can read Dutch much better than Siegfried so it doesn't take very long for him to get the gist of this. It looks like there may be some Plutonium around that only Wilhelm and Eberhardt knew about. Getting hold of this Plutonium will likely be difficult. Wilhelm and Eberhardt are dead. Who knows if this Debbinck guy is still alive? Then he remembers that Captain Ridwan is in South Africa. Maybe he can find out. Siegfried interrupts his train of thought.

"Oskar, I have a strange feeling that I have heard of this Debbinck guy before."

"Of course, you were looking at your grandfather's notes this afternoon."

"No, I mean before that. He is a big Dutchman and he went to Heidelberg. He was in the SS with my grandfather."

Oskar doesn't know what to make of this. How can Siegfried have any clue about the Dutchman? He said some things on the way out from the airport that sounded like flashbacks to times before he was born.

Siegfried completed his Doctoral work in Nuclear Physics and may have discovered a new sub-atomic particle. He finished in three years. His faculty was very impressed. He found out that Karl Eberhardt obtained his entrance to the graduate school at Heidelberg with one simple word-of-mouth recommendation. Somehow, he is associating Karl and Debbinck and the photolinos. Karl stopped by several times a year to check and see how he was doing. He introduced Siegfried to Professor Emeritus Wilfried Baumgartner the first month he was at Heidelberg. Baumgartner was a renowned Molecular Biologist and neuro-surgeon specializing in the study of the human brain. At Karl's suggestion he volunteered to participate in a study that Baumgartner was doing on the measurement of brain activity. This involved sessions where he was often sedated while the Professor generated electroencephalograms. The Professor often took blood samples as well when he did the electroencephalograms. Several of these sessions occurred while Karl was visiting Heidelberg.

Defense Contractor Assistance Corporation receives considerable funding from various government agencies, primarily the Defense Department and the CIA, but is not in any way connected to the United States Government. The name suggests that they help defense contractors but that is only a small part of their function. The head of the organization is John Carpenter. He is a former SEAL and graduate of Annapolis. He also has a master's degree in Electrical Engineering from MIT. He is in his early fifties and in very good shape at 6'5" and 255 pounds. He has a few more gray hairs than he did a few years ago and does not use shoe polish to alter this situation. The intelligence business runs in his genes. His father was in the OSS and worked for Bill Donovan during the Second World War.

He has a dozen employees, all of whom have technical backgrounds. Henry Magnuson is the one who probably contributes most to his expanding population of gray hairs. Henry is ten years younger and two inches shorter. He is still a pretty good sized guy at 6'3" and 215 pounds. Henry has been at DCAC for nearly three years. He was in the CIA for the previous eight and in Army Intelligence before that. There are rumors to the effect that Henry is a professional assassin. If there is any merit to these, it should be noted, with few exceptions, that he has been involved in the premature demises of people who he has been instructed to 'take care of'. In fact, the most recent assassination or killing he was involved in was at a remote hunting lodge in southern Argentina and he didn't kill anyone. This raid was launched from the special ops boat USS Georgia and resulted in the deaths of Wilhelm Bachmeier and Prince Rashid Aziz Al Saud, amongst others. These two terrorists are believed to have been the masterminds of the attacks on New York, Haifa and Tel Aviv. Henry was just there to see if he could recognize any of the folks who the CIA terminated that day. Their bodies were brought to the US Naval Base at Kings Bay Georgia where it is presumed that they are still residing at forty below zero. Prince Rashid presents something of a problem. The President of France declared him dead in the middle of July but that turned out to be one of his doubles that got dead. The CIA actually dispatched him the eighteenth of August. The USS Georgia didn't return to Kings Bay until late last Wednesday night and Henry didn't depart for Boston until Friday. John wasn't in the office yesterday so this morning is the first time they have had a cup of coffee together since the eleventh of the month.

"So we finally got him."

"Yes."

"What did Henri Drouhin have to say?"

"I think he is satisfied that this is the real deal. He reminded me that we are to tell no one about this."

"Of course. There is an excellent chance that this will remain quiet for a while, certainly as long as the guys running the show here and in France are still in office."

"What about Bachmeier?"

"They ran a DNA test on him and Gerbert. They are father and son with something like five nines probability. I brought back a snap shot of Wilhelm. This was taken after he was cleaned up. The grenades didn't do a thing for the appearances of those guys in the ranch house."

"That was pretty clever how Guenther figured out where the ranch was."

"Guenther is pretty clever."

'Pretty clever' is an understatement of the first magnitude. Guenther Reinhardt is a very unusual man who is highly instrumental in the development of new weaponry at Los Alamos and elsewhere. He is intimately involved in things nuclear and thermonuclear and Lord knows what else. He is seventy three years old and no longer a regular employee of the US Government but he still has government supplied offices and staffs in both Los Alamos and Fort Meade and the use of any sort of government transport whenever he wants to wherever he wants. He prefers the relative solitude of Los Alamos so one is more likely to find him there than Fort Meade. He has the ear of the President of the United States, the NSA Secretary and the Director of the CIA as well as the people at the Los Alamos Lab. He is well connected with the upper echelons of the Defense Department. He is something like a US Marshal and Senior Scientist rolled into one. He still stands 6'3" and at 270 pounds is carrying a bit more around than he should. His IQ is off the charts and he has a photographic memory. He has spent the last forty years doing pretty much whatever takes his fancy and for the past two years he has spent a good part of his time helping deal with the Saudi Princes and the old Nazis they have linked up with. There is no likelihood that Guenther Reinhardt is his real name. His wife and family were killed twenty eight years ago by some Russian agents. That was in reprisal for a particularly successful screwing that he gave the Russian weapons research effort on neutron bombs. DCAC works closely with Guenther.

"Did anything more transpire about the crew of the submarine while I was wandering around Chile and Argentina and the depths of the Atlantic?"

"No. When I was at NSA yesterday they showed me some satellite evidence that the Saudi Coast Guard picked them up and took them to Jeddah. All they really know is that a couple of Saudi Coast Guard boats were in the vicinity where the Duha Ali got torpedoed. They could 'see' the boats with the radar satellites but it was night, they have no photographic evidence. We think Prince Rashid or one of his minions got them back to Buenos Aires via Bahrain and Johannesburg. Nobody named Brandt or Schleifenbaum showed up on any passenger manifest out of Bahrain so they probably used aliases. There are enough people going that way that there is no good way to sort out what is happening. Fred has been having 'Charlie' (a Cray 3 computer with a few goodies added by Fred) look but I am not optimistic."

"So they got away with it."

"At least for now."

"What's Mitch think about that?"

"He says that there is no stomach in Washington for yet another search and destroy mission in Argentina. After the third raid, they kicked practically everyone in the US Embassy out of the country – that includes all the CIA folks. I heard they are down to a dozen US citizens total, including four Marine guards. It is probably a pretty good bet that the locals working in the Embassy are probably all also employees of the Argentine Intelligence folks. We are essentially blind and deaf there now. The Argentines are making life difficult for us. They are photographing every American arriving at Ezeiza and, starting today, they are insisting that every American must have a visa in order to enter the country. They are harassing American owned businesses there with all manner of bureaucratic bullshit, safety inspections, passport inspections, driver license inspections – you name it. The State Department is blam ng the CIA and NSA for all of this."

"They don't care that we finally got those bastards?"

"They don't know and nobody is going to tell them either."

"What about Eberhardt?"

"We don't know a thing. He completely disappeared sometime in early May."

Lunchtime

John Carpenter and Henry Magnuson are playing half-dollar-a-point backgammon on John's desk while they eat lunch. His phone rings.

"Carpenter here."

"Good afternoon Monsieur Carpenter. This is Henri Drouhin."

"Good evening Henri. I am playing backgammon with a reprobate I think you know. I will put you on the speakerphone. What can we do for you?"

"Good afternoon Henry."

"Bonsoir Henri."

Henri Drouhin is the head of French Internal Security for all of France south of a line running approximately from Nantes to Geneva. He has worked closely with DCAC and Henry Magnuson in particular for the past few years in their continued struggle with Prince Rashid. He is one of a very few people who know that Rashid is dead.

"Siegfried Bachmeier's abrupt departure from Heidelberg has us somewhat disturbed. I would rather not say exactly why at this moment. You may recall that we had a little problem with our neighbors recently because of an unrelated matter. It would be best if we don't stir them up any more than we already have. I was hoping that you folks might be able to find out what you can about Siegfried by nosing around Heidelberg."

"We might. Let me make a few phone calls. I will get back to you tomorrow."

They each have a stack of fifty cent coins in front of them. When they finish the game four of those coins migrate to Henry's side of the table. This is a strictly cash transaction. There are no notebooks with a running score.

John calls Guenther Reinhardt. Guenther is very concerned that Henri Drouhin called John. It has got to have something to do with Siegfried's work at CERN. Possibly the French have recognized the link between Siegfried's Doctoral Dissertation and the kind of work he and Randy Biggs are doing in Tennessee. Apparently they know a lot more about this sort of thing than he thought. He will put some of the considerable assets he has at Los Alamos on this. He wants Henry to go to Heidelberg.

Basima's Residence

San Isidro, Argentina

September 1, 1993 Wednesday morning

Rashid has been gone for two weeks. He said he was going to talk to Wilhelm Bachmeier and make some plans for later in the year. He was flying to Bahia Blanca where one of Wilhelm's people would meet him. He said it was a long drive from Bahia Blanca. They had a number of discussions about the wisdom of continuing to associate with Wilhelm. Basima has argued repeatedly that since the United States found his place in Pelicura, they probably can find any other of his properties if they look hard enough. Rashid gave her several safe deposit box keys and told her that if something did go wrong, she should examine the contents of these boxes.

She has refrained from calling CCM because she does not want to be seen as an alarmist but she is very concerned about Rashid's safety. She has Oskar Brandt's number at CCM.

"Hello, this is Prince Rashid's secretary. May I speak with Captain Brandt please?"

"This is Captain Brandt."

"Captain, this is Basima Karim. Do you know where Prince Rashid is?"

"Basima, I am very sorry to tell you that I think Rashid and Wilhelm are either dead or have been captured by the Americans."

"What?'

"As best we can determine, the Americans raided Wilhelm's property down south around the eighteenth of the month. I was invited to this meeting but I had pressing matters at the shipyard and Wilhelm said it could wait. I didn't find out that this happened until the twenty third. I went there immediately to see what was happening first hand. I am satisfied that the Americans must have used very similar equipment to that which they used to raid Rancho de Mil Robles in May when I was not here. With Wilhelm's death or capture I have become the leader of our organization here in Argentina. When I had spoken to the Prince, he always called me from the TASA office. I did hot have the number that you are calling from. I am very sorry."

Her premonition was correct. This is devastating news.

"Thank you Captain. This is shocking news. I need to try to calm down. May I call you again?"

"Yes, of course. I am very sorry Basima."

Basima quickly recognizes that this event has changed her whole life. If and when Rashid's half brother finds out that Rashid is dead, it is certain that he will simply assume Rashid's share of the businesses they now hold together. She is merely Rashid's mistress. She has no rights whatsoever in Saudi Arabia. She might even be put to death for adultery if she ever went back there.

Avenida Florida 99

Buenos Aires, Argentina

September 9, 1993 Thursday 1015

Basima is in the safe deposit vault of Banco de Boston. She has the keys to several safe deposit drawers. The first one she opens has more than twenty jewelry boxes in it. She opens one of these boxes and finds twenty very large diamonds. She opens another one and finds the same thing. There are hundreds of millions of dollars worth of diamonds in this drawer. She puts one of them in her purse. Another of the drawers has fifty coin rolls of South African Krugerrands. When she started to pull this out she quickly concluded that the drawer was so heavy she would not be able to carry it to the table in the privacy cubby five meters away. The third drawer had one hundred dollar bills in it. She knows that a one centimeter stack of these is roughly $10,000. There must be close to two million dollars in cash here. The fourth drawer has two kilos of FPI fibrils in two hundred gram packages. The last drawer has several floppy disks and many papers. There is an envelope addressed in Rashid's hand that simply reads 'Basima'. She opens this and it contains several sheets of paper and a key for a safety deposit box in another bank. The hand written note tells her to please get this key to Wilhelm Bachmeier's grandson. This was Karl's last wish. She put the disks and the envelope in her large purse and locked everything else up.

One of the largest electronics stores in Argentina was only fifty meters from the bank. She purchased an IBM Thinkpad® and a floppy disk drive as well as a *printer. It came to nearly $12000 US including the one hundred percent tariff and the sales tax.*

That afternoon she copied the floppy disks onto her hard drive. The disks were a farewell gift from Professor Eberhardt to Prince Rashid. Rashid told her of Karl's last moments and he told her that Karl gave him the disks two days before. He must have known it was coming.

The contents of some of the disks are in English – no doubt that Karl intended Rashid as the recipient of this information. There is a lengthy section dealing with the specifics of Pakistani Plutonium production. She does not understand the technical parts of this but she does understand that Eberhardt is making very specific recommendations to fix the production operation so that it will make Plutonium suitable for more powerful bombs. He goes on to point out that the Pakis are spending over four percent of their GNP on their weapons development effort.

Then there is a section dealing with the construction of the weapons they used against New York, Haifa and Tel Aviv. In this section there is a lengthy explanation of how the Plodamax works. She notices that Karl refers to Aldrich Kessler several times in this section. He also refers to a company called Advanced Opti-Maser Transmission. She remembers that AOMT was the largest purchaser of the fibrils that they thought were going into Plodamax. That may warrant further investigation. She will talk with Kessler about this. It seems that Karl thought the Plodamax was really the key to making reliable weapons.

Another disk has plans for a number of devices and brief explanations of what they could do. It looks like a toy store catalog for weapons.

She studies this material for hours. Rashid often mentioned that Eberhardt was a veritable walking encyclopedia of exotic weaponry. Now she is beginning to see why. Rashid said that Kessler was very good and would have continued his research on the fibrils in Saudi Arabia. Rashid told him that he thought he would be in danger anyplace that the Americans found out about. Rashid thought that Kessler was going to hide in South Africa. That will be very convenient. He will be able to fly back and forth between Johannesburg and Buenos Aires, if he agrees to continue his work. On the other hand, the French and the Americans have both tried to kill her on separate occasions. So far they have two dead doubles to show for their efforts – but it's like they say – "It's the thought that counts." It is likely that given the opportunity they will kill her.

She reads the notes that Rashid left in the envelope he addressed. Apparently he anticipated that there would be trouble with respect to his business holdings if he were to decease. He has given her the particulars of his voice disguising equipment including a few phone numbers of people who can make this equipment useful to her. The equipment she will need is in the TASA office. As soon as she has the new phone line in San Isidro, she will be able to have this equipment installed. She will be able to impersonate Rashid with this equipment. She will sound the same as he did when he used this equipment. He has gone to the trouble of detailing certain idiosyncrasies in his speech that she might want to incorporate into her way of talking when she uses this equipment. It is not likely that anyone will be so familiar with the timing of his speech as to notice there is any difference, but just in case. Of course, she is free to live out a peaceful life here in Argentina. He certainly does not want to ask her to continue this struggle against the Americans and the Jews. She must decide for herself.

September 3, 1993 Friday

Basima called Oskar at CCM Belen around 0900. They talk a little more about the disaster at Lake Huramento. She guides the conversation around in such a way as to try to get Oskar to reveal his innermost feelings about the deaths of his associates. She mentions that she has some information about the details of the weapons. Oskar does not think they should talk about this on the Argentine telephone system. He offers to buy her lunch at a shorefront restaurant and then continue the conversation at her place this afternoon.

That is what happens. Oskar tells her the story about U-1241. His father captained the submarine on its only voyage. He was supposed to take the Nazi weaponry and some nuclear physicists to Japan so that they could continue the struggle against the Marxists and the Americans. The U-boat was damaged within an hour of leaving the sub pen in Hamburg. His father nursed the boat along for over two months before reaching Argentina. The German community here in Argentina had a modest shipyard where they were able to hide the U-boat for forty eight years. His father had the boat meticulously maintained all this time. His father died several years ago. Oskar relates how he was the captain of the only Argentine submarine to participate in the Maldivas war with Britain and took over the shipyard from his father shortly after he returned from the war. He continued to maintain the submarine. They obtained a competitor's shipyard in Bahia Blanca last year and they were able to move the U-boat there and fix the damage caused by the bombing years ago. The submarine was totally refitted and armed with three nuclear weapons which it eventually delivered to New York and Israel. Oskar scuttled the boat in June in the Mediterranean somewhat north of the Suez Canal. Oskar has no love for the Americans or the Jews. It turns out that he lives alone. His wife died ten years ago and both of his sons have their own families. His elder son Raphael is the manager of CCM. Running the Nazi organization here will take up most of his time. She finds out that Wilhelm had massive land holdings. Oskar is now in control of these. Most of this land was acquired using a small portion of the gold that Oskar's father brought to Argentina. Wilhelm and his father were very close friends.

She printed out some of the weapons related material in the morning. After two hours of conversation she goes to her desk and produces a folder with some of the details of the bombs that Wilhelm made at Rancho Don Martinez. Oscar has not concerned himself with this in the past. He knows how to Captain a submarine and he knows how to run a shipyard. He is not sure that he can do anything with this information.

"If you had another submarine could you strike at the Americans and French again?"

"I don't have a submarine."

"Suppose I could help you get one."

"I am not following you Basima."

"The day after the Americans tried to kill me and Prince Rashid in Switzerland Rashid told Professor Fassbinder he thought it would be a good time to leave Germany. You may not have known that Professor Fassbinder was our neighbor of sorts. He lived about six kilometers from us on the German side of Lake Constance. We could see his house with binoculars. We sailed over there twice in our boat to say hello. He took Rashid's advice and went to South Africa. Apparently he has relatives there."

"I do remember that Abbo was concerned that the Americans were going to find out he was involved in refitting our submarine. He talked about South Africa a few times."

"You remember Captain Ridwan?"

"Yes, fondly I might add. He did a great job getting me and my crew back home from Saudi Arabia. I think most of us thought we would not see Argentina again."

"Captain Ridwan is now in South Africa running a shipyard in Durban. Rashid bought this shipyard shortly after you were able to successfully bomb New York. He knew that your submarine was going to be scuttled after you bombed the Jews. Abbo said that he learned a lot refitting U-1241 and that he thought he could build a submarine which could cruise completely submerged for five or six thousand miles."

"Yes, I remember that distinctly. He said that gold plating of the surfaces around the LOX tanks had been so effective at reducing the boil off that we could do much better the next time."

"The shipyard in Durban can build ships up to one hundred twenty meters. Would you be willing to Captain another submarine Oskar?"

"I would have to think about that a while Basima. My first inclination is to say no. I have too many responsibilities here now."

"Do you know someone else who might?"

"My friend Hermann Schleifenbaum might. But, I don't believe that we can make any more nuclear weapons – we are out of material."

"We might be able to persuade them to part with some of their plutonium. I have a small amount of FPI fibrils. Karl said that Kessler can make enough of his version of Plodamax to make seven or eight weapons. The Pakis are very short of Kessler's version of Plodamax. Karl also stated that we now know how to build a submarine that has a six thousand mile range completely submerged. This is much better than anything the Pakis have. We are not without cards to play."

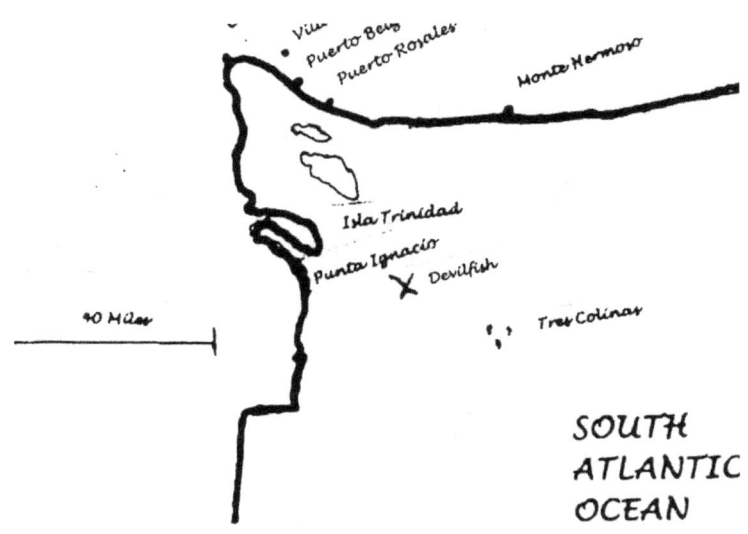

Both Siegfried and Basima wanted to see the lodge on Lake Huramento. Oskar drove from Buenos Aires to Rancho Don Martinez in Pelicura last Monday. They left Buenos Aires very early and arrived at the ranch about 1400 hours. There was enough time for him to give them a thorough tour of the ranch and the bunker complex where the parts for the bombs were made. He showed them the dining room where it is suspected that Siegfried's father Gerbert was captured by the Americans. A year ago practically no one in the Buenos Aires area knew of the existence of this ranch much less the bunker complex. Now, after the American raid showed that they knew where it was and what it was used for, Oskar did not hesitate to show Basima and Siegfried.

They checked into the Tamarisces around 1800 and sat down at the dinner table an hour later. Siegfried had been very quiet on the ride from Pelicura to Villa del Mar. Now shortly after the appetizers appeared on the table he wonders.

"I had the strangest feeling when we were at the ranch like I had been there before but the closest I have ever been to this place is Bariloche. That's as far away as Buenos Aires."

Basima takes note of that remark but says nothing.

Tuesday morning they have a substantial breakfast at the hotel and then Oskar gives them a tour of CCM Bahia Blanca. He shows them the drydock where

U-1241 was refit. Again, Siegfried says he thinks he has seen this place before. They eat lunch at a local seafood restaurant and spend the afternoon sightseeing. Oskar takes them to Puerto Rosales. The Don Martinez is in her slip. They sit down in the main cabin and chat a while.

"I have good memories of his old boat Uncle Oskar. I was never on this one."

"I too have good memories of the old boat Siegfried. This boat, or more precisely your father's decision to name this boat after the ranch, may have led to your father's undoing. In late March, three Norteamericanos posing as Columbian drug dealers showed up at CCM Bahia Blanca ostensibly to buy a boat for smuggling drugs. We later found out that these three men were in the San Isidro Marlin tournament. They were CIA spies. Your father was in that tournament also with this boat. While they were visiting our yard here, one of the people working at the ranch came by the yard to pick up some hardware. He had one of the ranch pick-up trucks which have "Don Martinez, Pelicura" painted on both doors. We think the Americans noticed this and decided to take a more careful look. They found the ranch. Your grandfather was furious....That is water over the dam. The point is that little things sometimes turn out to be important. It probably won't do any harm to tell you this boat was highly instrumental in CCM acquiring the use of the drydock in Bahia Blanca."

Oskar goes on to relate the story about the sinking of the Maria Morales. They eliminated everyone in CCM Bahia Blanca in a single stroke. This enabled them to then replace the people in Bahia Blanca with people from Belen. Siegfried listens in wide-eyed amazement. Oskar tells of the episode with the American submarine which they sank. Don Martinez played an important part here as well. Siegfried confesses that he hasn't seen his father much in the past four years. They had a strained relationship and he has spent his time in Argentina at his grandfather's ranch in San Pablo de Arno or skiing in Bariloche.

Wednesday morning they set out for Lake Huramento. They arrived at the Lake House around noon. Apparently Oskar had called the day before and asked the local police chief, Manfred Weiss, to meet them. The Chief was extremely deferential to Oskar. Oskar told him to speak freely in front of Siegfried and Basima, which he did, somewhat reluctantly. He did most of the explaining in Spanish but after he found out that Basima spoke German also he switched to German. It turned out that Chief Weiss was a direct report to Wilhelm here in the South. He now was a direct report to Oskar. The Chief explained how he had treated the whole Lake House area as a crime scene as soon as he found it. He gave them a guided tour of the area including many photographs taken earlier. He pointed out the footprints where the American aircraft landed. He even had plaster casts of these back at the station. Oskar had given him photographs of the footprints left at Rancho de Mil Robles in San Pablo de Arno. As best anyone could tell the same machines made both sets of footprints. The Chief had impounded the rental vehicle the Norteamericanos left at the fishing lodge as well as the boat they used.

Nobody says anything directly but Siegfried is getting a crash course on the extent of his grandfather's and now Oskar's influence. The broken windows in the lodge have been replaced but numerous grenade fragments are still embedded in much of the woodwork on the first floor. Chief Weiss determined that the fingerprints in the vehicle and on the boat from the fishing lodge two kilometers down the lake were those of the same three men who visited CCM Bahia Blanca in April. The paper work in the Toyota Land Cruiser which the three men used was totally bogus. The rent car company did not exist and there was no record of the vehicle ever even having been imported into Chile. It was a reminder that the Americans have not forgotten what happened in New York – nor are they likely to.

It is nearly a four hour drive from Lake Huramento to Villa Del Mar. Siegfried is stunned by what he has seen and heard in the past day. They stayed in the Tamarisces Friday evening and returned to San Isidro and Zarate Saturday.

Basima was able to get through to Captain Ridwan this morning. The conversation is in Arabic.

"Good afternoon Captain."

"I have not heard from you in a while Basima. How are you and Prince Rashid doing?"

"We believe the Prince is dead. He went to visit Wilhelm Bachmeier at a hunting lodge far south of Buenos Aires last month and he disappeared. There was evidence of a commando raid. This is almost certainly the Americans doing. The five other men who were there in the lodge were killed by grenades and gunfire. He and Wilhelm Bachmeier were not there. We believe that the Americans took their bodies. We found evidence that Henry Magnuson was there."

The captain has heard this name before. He shakes his head.

"I am very sorry Basima."

"I am too Abdul. We can not do anything about that. I do have something I would like you to look into."

She relates the story about Albert Debbinck. The Captain says he will see what he can find out.

Oskar picks her up around noon and they have lunch at the same seaside restaurant they did two weeks ago. When they enter La Ostra Sonriendo (The Smiling Oyster) she notices that a number of the patrons are looking at them as they are lead to their table. It seems that Oskar is well known in these parts and apparently the locals take note of the beautiful woman there with him. She is nearly 5'9" and nicely proportioned while he is a big boned 6'1" carrying a trim ninety kilos.

They linger over the last of the wine for a while. When they get back to Basima's place, Oskar brings up the subject he wants to talk about.

"Basima, you must have noticed that S egfried keeps having these flash-backs. Do you have any idea about what that is all about?"

"I don't know. I have started looking into that. At the moment I am fully occupied trying to salvage as many of Rashid's assets as I can. I have to be rather discreet in my contact with the remnants of SASC because if Rashid's half brother finds out that he is dead that will be the end of my association with any of Rashid's businesses."

"What will you do?"

"I have assets sufficient to sustain me for many lifetimes. That will not be a problem. As you probably know, Prince Rashid was an extremely wealthy man. He left me a great deal of money."

"You are quite a bit older than Rashid aren't you?"

"Yes, I am forty two and he was twenty nine."

La Ostra Sonriendo
San Isidro, Argentina
September 22, 1993 Wednesday

Oskar has invited Basima for lunch at The Smiling Oyster for the third time. This is the best known shellfish restaurant on Rio de la Plata and Oskar is a well known patron. He is somewhat of a celebrity here because of his contributions to the Argentine effort to regain Islas Maldivas. His submarine sank a British destroyer one hundred miles north of Port Howard during the Falklands War. There are a number of regular patrons to this establishment and his third appearance with the same tall beautiful woman is attracting some attention as the Maitre' d leads them to their table.

While dessert is on the way, Basima goes to the Ladies Room. Shortly after she enters she is accosted by a rather stout woman.

"Hello, my name is Irma Nunez. I am Oskar's sister. My husband owns this restaurant so I knew he had reservations today. You know he is a very good man. You are not from around here are you?"

Basima is taken aback by this impromptu monologue. She dries her hands and hurries back to their table.

"Oskar, some woman who introduced herself as your sister accosted me in the Ladies Room."

"I apologize for that Basima. My sister spends an inordinate amount of time trying to get me remarried to some of her girlfriends. She no doubt sees you as a threat to her schemes. Her husband owns this place. She probably had him watching for any reservations I made. The food is excellent here so I frequent the place but maybe we shouldn't if this is going to happen."

"I think she didn't like the idea that I was a foreigner."

"She doesn't like foreigners in general and she particularly does not like beautiful slender women. Her girlfriends don't fit either category."

The churros with the dulce de leche arrive. Basima is thinking if she eats very much of this stuff she will be looking like Irma shortly. Oskar smiles when she confines herself to nursing one churro and some espresso while he downs the other five.

It is only a short drive back to her place. She wants to know what has happened with the safe deposit box.

"I took Siegfried to the bank this morning. It turned out to be much easier than I thought it might be. Ernst Drechsler is the manager there and he met us practically as soon as we walked inside. He took Siegfried aside. They were too far away from me for me to hear what they said. It looked like Ernst took a paper out of his pocket and read some questions to Siegfried. Siegfried answered them satisfactorily I presume. They came back to me and Ernst apologized for the rigmarole but said he had strict orders from Professor Eberhardt that this was the way it was to be done. We had coffee in his office while one of his assistants took Siegfried off to the safe deposit vault. A few minutes later Siegfried was back with a large envelope."

"Did he say what was in there Oskar?"

"I did not presume to ask him Basima. It looked to me like the envelope was still sealed."

Siegfried was anxious to see what was in the envelope and declined an invitation to join Oskar and Basima at the Smiling Oyster. He arrived back at the ranch around noon.

The contents of the envelope were fascinating. He had often wondered why Professor Eberhardt had visited him so often while he was at Heidelberg.

June 10, 1993

Dearest Siegfried,

You probably wonder how I came into your life when you arrived at Heidelberg. I actually came into your life many years before that. Professor Wilfried Baumgartner has been investigating brainwaves and intelligence since the 1930's. This started about the same time that our people were embarked on a program to produce supermen by traditional genetics. This was slow going and it became apparent especially after the catastrophe at Stalingrad that the Third Reich might not be around for one thousand years.

Reichsfuhrer Himmler was a great believer in many things that might be euphemistically described as "occult". He believed that clairvoyance and extra sensory perception were intertwined. Baumgartner was a gifted neuro-surgeon who was focused on finding a cure for epilepsy. He had demonstrated that he could guide rats through a maze if he sent signals to them via minute wires embedded in some parts of their brains. Himmler seized on this work and said that if Baumgartner could transfer intelligence to rats then he should be able to transfer intelligence to people. Wilfried may have only found which places to stimulate the rat's brain so that it turned left of right but there was no stopping Himmler. He set Baumgartner up with a research institute to do this. They were soon experimenting on prisoners from Dachau. There were many false starts. There were nearly 300 deaths because the insertion of the wires did something damaging to the subjects. Finally, in the latter part of 1943 they managed to put some information into a subject's brain without the subject dying in less than a week. This is when I got involved. Himmler wanted to more or less copy the brains of the scientists working at Peenemunde where our advanced weapons technology was being developed. He wanted to use them as 'Sources' to improve the brains of lesser lights. I was one of the 'Sources'. After the war Baumgartner continued his work while teaching at Heidelberg. By the late 1940's he had succeeded in raising the intelligence (at least as judged by the IQ tests we were using at the time) of several young women – without killing them. For reasons no one understood, the technique did not work on men very well – if at all. For some reason or other I was the only Source that it seemed to work with at all. Now, the problem was to find out if this intelligence would be passed on to the woman's offspring. Wilfried and I picked a very bright young woman as our subject. We were able to transmit into her brain a passable knowledge of nuclear physics although she had never been exposed to this in her education. We established this beyond doubt. We were able to do this with no apparent ill effects on that woman. We raised her already very high IQ by roughly thirty percent as best we could measure. We coined the term "electroencephalographically educated" (EEE) to describe her. Wilhelm and I arranged for her to go to Argentina and marry your father. Unfortunately you are her only child. She died giving birth. She produced an extraordinarily intelligent child. We knew that you were a genius by the time you were two. Only Wilfried Baumgartner, your grandfather and I know this. Wilfried succeeded in transferring (copying might be a more accurate term) my thoughts to you. We tested you after the transfer sessions and you knew as much about nuclear physics in the spring of 1993 as I did when I was eighty years old. My friends at Heidelberg say that you should be teaching them not them trying to teach you.

I hope this gives you some understanding of why you have 'flashbacks'. Naturally, my every waking thought is not technical. Thoughts of places I have been and people I have met are constantly wandering around my head just the same as they do in everyone else's. I know some of these have been transferred to you. I am sorry for any inconvenience this may cause.

During the last two sessions with Professor Baumgartner, we tried using you as a Source. Wilfried is very encouraged. He told me that you are only the second man besides me who has been able to act as a Source. I hope you keep in touch with Wilfried and carry on this work.

My kindest regards,

Karl

Siegfried is astounded. He is thinking back to his childhood. No wonder he didn't fit in very well with the other children. They were just normal kids but he was not. He might be the superman that Himmler was trying to produce. Then he starts wondering about the timing of this information. Why did Karl wait until now to tell me this and why didn't he tell me while I was in Germany.

As if on cue he gets a wave of flashbacks. He "sees" U-1241. It is in the Bahia Blanca drydock that Oskar took him to last week. He "sees" the inside of the boat. He "sees" the LOX tanks. He was never within five thousand kilometers of Bahia Blanca while U-1241 was there. He "sees" Basima with a young dark haired man. The man's name is Rashid or Prince Rashid. Karl has a high opinion of him.

He snaps out of this trance. He must talk to Oskar about this. He catches Oskar at CCM Belen around 1730. Oskar says he will buy him his supper if he comes to Zarate.

They eat at a roadside grill not far from Oskar's home and return there for a few brandies.

"That is amazing Siegfried."

"You did not know?"

"I knew you were a very intelligent young man but not anything about what you just told me."

"I told you that I "saw" the interior of your U-boat but you know I was never in the boat. I must have seen an image that came from Karl. When was he on the boat?"

"He was inside the boat on the twenty seventh of April. That is the day we gave Professor Eberhardt and Prince Rashid the tour."

"Professor Eberhardt visited me at school after that. He must have transmitted the images to me then."

"Can you summon up these images at will Siegfried?"

"I don't think I can Oskar but maybe if I were hypnotized I might be able to. I know that some people studying Psychiatry were often in Professor Baumgartner's lab when I was there. They were grad students too and they were into hypnotism as an aid to psychoanalysis. I think they used some kinds of psychoactive drugs as well."

"Basima has a Doctorate in Psychology. I wonder if she knows anything about this sort of thing."

It is getting late and Oskar does not want Siegfried driving back to the ranch with a few brandies in him. They will try to see Basima tomorrow.

Oskar called Basima fairly early and asked whether he and Siegfried could come by. He thought that it might be useful to let Siegfried look at some of the information that Eberhardt left for Rashid. They talked about the mechanics of this a while and decided that the best way to do this was to copy some of the floppy disks and let Siegfried look at the copies. Basima does not have facilities to do this but Oskar says he will take care of that. He and Siegfried show up at Basima's around noon with the equipment necessary to make copies of the floppy disks.

Basima's home is on a one hectare (about 2 1/2 acres) lot which is on one of the canals in this very nice section of San Isidro not far from the college. It is a beautiful spring day and they sit and have coffee and pastries on her veranda.

"Yesterday, Siegfried showed me the letter which was in the security box. This is a most amazing letter which Karl Eberhardt wrote to Siegfried. While he was there at Heidelberg, a Professor Baumgartner was able to copy information from Professor Eberhardt's brain to Siegfried's brain. I do not pretend to understand this but the letter helps to explain Siegfried's frequent flashbacks that both you and I have observed. It is conceivable that he may have most everything Karl saw in his life in his brain – much of it may be in his subconscious. I was wondering whether you know anything about this sort of thing. Siegfried thinks that he might be able to summon this information up under hypnosis. What do you think?"

"My Doctorate is in Psychology which is different than Psychiatry where one would be more likely to find people using hypnosis trying to alter behavior. I do know that there are some drugs around that may be useful for this purpose. There is some evidence that people hallucinating under the influence of psychoactive drugs such as LSD have enhanced memories but that is a very dangerous drug with completely unpredictable effects. I am sure that the people at your university know much more about this than I do Siegfried."

Siegfried recounts his experiences with Eberhardt and Baumgartner. The way Eberhardt encouraged him to participate in the encephalographic studies Baumgartner was doing. It appears that Eberhardt was really interested in seeing whether he could download his brain's content to Siegfried. He relates how after the very first session, he suddenly had an excellent understanding of nuclear fission as well as a much better understanding of quantum theory. He says he keeps thinking about Plodamax. It is some kind of super explosive.

"That is a super explosive made in America Siegfried. Rashid retained a man named Kessler to try to develop this explosive. I know that there was something to do with little fibers in the material that was very important. Karl left a great deal of information for Rashid. I only scanned through it and I understand very little of what I read. I do remember that there was a lengthy explanation of how the Plodamax worked. I will make a copy of the disk where Karl explained this."

Siegfried interjects.

"That will be very interesting. I 'see' Karl explaining this business about the little fibers to Prince Rashid. I am not getting all of it but it all depends on the little fibers. They are small − less than one micron in diameter.

Nobody knows how to make them except some company in Massachusetts."

Basima is awestruck. How can he know that? Karl knew that and Kessler knew that but Oskar did not. She wants to satisfy her curiosity.

"Siegfried, did you ever meet Professor Aldrich Kessler?"

"No. Was he at Heidelberg?"

"I think so."

"What department?"

"I think he was in the Chemistry Department."

"I really only know a few of the Physics people. It is a big university. I spent several months at the CERN facility five hundred kilometers from Heidelberg and much of the rest of my time in another physics lab a few kilometers away from the main part of the University."

"Where was Professor Baumgartner's laboratory?"

"Next to the Biology building. His lab was associated with the Primate Research Center."

Crown Plaza

Heidelberg, Germany

September 25, 1993 Saturday

Henry is traveling as Robert Hartwell, a salesman for Cerebrionics, a little known American manufacturer specialized in developing instrumentation that measures brain waves and other electrical signals generated by living tissue. He landed in Frankfurt late this morning and drove his rented Mercedes to Heidelberg in the early afternoon. He has just finished unpacking his suitcase when there is a knock on his door. He looks through the peephole and much to his amazement there is Christina Miller smiling at him. It has been two years since they shared a wonderful weekend together. He thought he would never see her again. She looks as good as ever. He opens the door and she enters with her suitcase in tow. They embrace and then she backs away a little and starts unbuttoning his shirt...somewhat later.

"How did you know I was here?"

"Your 'father' *(a thinly veiled reference to Guenther)* told me."

"I take it that you are my 'sales trainee'."

"You take it correctly. No one will give it a second thought. It seems like there is almost an epidemic of 'sales trainees' accompanying instrumentation salesmen."

"Are they all as beautiful as you are?"

"Many of them are."

Heidelberg University
Monday September 27, 1993

Henry and Christina had an appointment with Professor Schmidt in the Biology Department for

0900. Emil Schmidt is the head of the depart-
ment and a protégé of Professor Emeritus Wilfried
Baumgartner. He is a renowned scientist in the field of
Psychopharmacology.

"Good morning Herr Hartwell and Fraulein Grunwald."

"Good morning Professor Schmidt. Thank you for
seeing us on such short notice and thank you for your
interest in our latest instrument. This instrument is still
in the development stage but it is showing great promise. As you know, a normal electroencephalogram has
some of the features of an AM radio broadcast signal but
the background or carrier frequency is not as steady as
the radio broadcast. We have an instrument which can
compensate to some extent for this lack of steadiness of
the carrier frequency. We have also developed software
which can process the entire EEG session and almost
completely compensate for this lack of steadiness. We
can then subtract out the variable carrier frequency and
be left with the information-containing parts of the signal. We would like to have your people evaluate this
machine for us. We will pay reasonable amounts to your
faculty and any grad students you feel will help in this
effort and of course we will make a modest contribution
to your building fund. In return, we want you to provide
us any results you obtain six months prior to publishing
them in the open literature."

"This is a perfectly reasonable request Herr Hartwell.
We can live with that."

After some further discussion Professor Schmidt
takes them to the building housing the department's lab-
oratory that is devoted to Primate Research. A gradu-
ate student greets them in English when they arrive at
Professor Baumgartner's laboratory.

"Professor Schmidt, I am sorry that Professor
Baumgartner is not here. He said he would be in later

if he feels up to it. He asked me to show the visitors our prize pupil."

"This is Manfred Bauer one of our most gifted graduate students. He is working with Professor Baumgartner. Manfred, this is Herr Hartwell and Fraulein Grunwald."

He shakes Henry's and Christina's hands and leads them through the door.

When they enter the lab, there is a Chimpanzee holding up a sign that says "Wilkommen". The chimp puts the sign down and walks on his hind legs across the room and shakes hands with Henry and Christina.

"Danke Enos"

"Herr Hartwell, do you by any chance play Backgammon?"

"Yes, I do. Why do you ask?"

Manfred beckons Henry to follow him and turns to the chimp.

"Mitkommen Enos."

The chimp tags along while they cross the large lab to a modest office. There is a Backgammon board set up on a low table with six chairs around it. Manfred gestures for Henry to sit down at the table and for Enos to sit opposite him. It is amazing. They roll the dice to see who will go first and the chimp sees that his die is higher than Henry's so he makes the first roll. The chimp takes about fifteen to twenty seconds to make each move but he makes decent moves. Henry has a slight edge as they start bearing men off but then he throws two big doubles in a row and gets all his men off about two rolls ahead of the chimp. The chimp goes to a nearby file cabinet and pulls out a sign "danke für das spiel". Then he doffs his cap to the visitors and leaves.

"We are trying to teach him to speak but there are some structural differences in the mouth that make this quite difficult. He does understand nearly two hundred words of German. He also knows 'yes', 'no' and 'okay' in English, and, he plays a decent game of Backgammon, as you just saw."

"That is very impressive Professor Schmidt."

"We know that they are doing similar things at Harvard University. We are wondering why you want to choose Heidelberg for your development work."

"One of our competitors already has an arrangement with Harvard."

"We are certainly interested in your new instrument and would like to help you."

Henry is looking around the large laboratory. In addition to the EEG equipment, they have Philips and Toshiba MRI machines. He notices there is a recent issue of the University Alumni magazine on a desk nearby the Toshiba. It is opened to a page where there is a photograph of a young man. He does a double take. The man's name is Siegfried Bachmeier. Manfred notices his interest.

"That is my friend Siegfried Bachmeier. He was probably the best physicist here. He finished his Doctoral work last month and went home to Argentina. He will probably be back for the graduation ceremony or before. He won the Physics Prize this year. He used to visit our lab a few times a year. Professor Baumgartner made many encephalograms of him. He is a genius. Professor Baumgartner was trying to see if there was any correlation between his encephalograms and his intelligence. He had a reference point in Professor Eberhardt who everyone knows is a genius. He has several of Eberhardt's encephalograms. He actually made recordings of them both at the same time on several occasions."

Now, Henry is beginning to understand why Guenther often seemed to shiver when Eberhardt's name was mentioned. Last week, Guenther spent several hours telling Henry what they knew about Baumgartner. There were rumors that he may have achieved some success in transferring intelligence to humans but they have never been verified. Henry has just seen it done with a chimp. Could he possibly have succeeded in transferring Eberhardt's intelligence to Bachmeier? The presence of two MRIs in the lab fascinates Henry.

"Manfred, I could not help but notice that you have two MRIs in your laboratory."

"Yes Henry, we have had some success in modifying these instruments so that they can detect some of the same kinds of electrical activity that a traditional EEG does but without the need to have all these electrodes on the source's head."

"We might be able to contribute something to that effort as well if the signals are similar to those from the EEG instruments."

"I can't speak for Professor Baumgartner but I think he would welcome this effort if it can help us."

Henry makes a note to follow up on this when he gets back to Randy. They thank Manfred for his tour and return to Professor Schmidt's office. They tell Professor Schmidt that someone from their R&D department will probably be accompanying the machine when it gets here about a month from now. They mention the possibility that their machine might also be helpful for the MRI associated work. Professor Schmidt says he will talk with Professor Baumgartner about this. They offer to take Professor Schmidt to lunch but he declines. There is always a department seminar at lunchtime on Mondays. He is the head of the department. He has to go.

Henry and Christina have the rest of the day to themselves. They eat at the same restaurant high up the hill overlooking the city that they ate at two years ago. They have a long talk. Henry has feelings that he has not had in twenty years. He is falling in love with this woman. It's crazy. She is an assassin just like him. Her employers have used her as sexual bait for gaining information on various people they have been interested in. Who knows what she does. No matter. Henry wants her to come back to Boston with him. She thanks him for the offer. She says she will have to clear that with her employers. (At least she didn't say 'no way.)

About 1500, after a little additional sightseeing they are back in their room. Henry dials a number in the US and punches in a three digit number when the answering machine asks him to. He hangs up and then he inserts his scrambler between the phone and the phone jack. Three minutes later the phone rings. It is John.

"Well?"

"They bought it. Now what?"

"Guenther and Randy have something cooked up. There will be some kind of equipment there next month. I think Randy is going to go there."

(Dr. Randolph Biggs is arguably the world's foremost expert on radar and some other forms of wave and particle transmission technology. He has a Doctor's degree in Physics from Princeton and a Doctor's degree from MIT in Electrical Engineering. He has a day job running Memphis Targeting Incorporated. MTI is the company that invented the guidance system for the shoulder fired radar guided Stinger missile – the so called 'Baby Phoenix'. This company does a great deal of classified work for the US Military. He also participates in some highly secretive development work with Los Alamos (that probably means Guenther et al). They have two laboratories. The one in New Mexico is inside a hill and

the one in Tennessee is six hundred feet underground and less than five miles from AOMT's plant.)

"You think it is okay for Randy to come here?"

"Sure, nobody knows anything about him there."

"I think that Eberhardt must know about Randy because Rashid must have told him about Memphis Targeting."

"We don't know where Eberhardt is."

"Well, one thing we found out was that Eberhardt was in this lab we visited this morning on several occasions. There was a grad student there for the tour we got. I happened to see a picture of one Siegfried Bachmeier (from Argentina, no less) in some school publication lying on a desk here. The grad student proceeded to tell me that they did simultaneous encephalograms on Eberhardt and Bachmeier at least three times."

"So?"

"They had a chimp here that they said had a two hundred word vocabulary."

"So, a smart dog probably has a twenty or thirty word vocabulary. A chimp is a lot smarter than a dog. You could probably teach them that."

"The damned thing played a decent game of Backgammon."

"What!"

"John, this is God's truth the critter knew how to play Backgammon. You can talk to Christina if you don't believe me."

John knows that Henry is not above pulling his leg from time to time.

"Let me do that."

Henry hands her the phone.

"John, there is a lot of evidence around there that they have been able to teach this animal to think. I watched the grad student and Professor Schmidt while Henry was playing. There was no evidence of them giving the chimp any signals at all. If the animal wasn't reasoning his moves out himself, then they must have had some other means to transmit instructions to him."

"Did the chimp have an earpiece?"

"No, they showed us that before the game started. There was nothing in either ear."

She hands the phone back to Henry.

"John, the critter apparently knew how to read a few words of German. They had a bunch of small posters in a file cabinet. After the game he went to the cabinet and produced a sign that said 'Thanks for the game.' It was really very impressive. I am beginning to understand why Eberhardt spooks Guenther. This stuff is scary.

There is another thing that we noticed that you might want to fly by the technical gurus. They had two MRIs in the EEG lab. The grad student who showed us around said they were specially modified to produce information somehow akin to that coming from the electroencephalographs without any electrodes attached to the patient's head. I volunteered that the machine Randy and Guenther are going to build might be of some use here as well."

"Before you go anywhere, let me check with Guenther. I will get back to you."

Two hours later, John does get back to them. Somehow, they (John et al and/or Guenther et al) have discovered where Siegfried Bachmeier lived when he was going to school in Heidelberg. He gives Henry an address in the Kirchheim district of Heidelberg. He tells them to attempt to rent the apartment. Christina knows where this place is. It is not far from her apartment but she does not reveal that fact to Henry. When they get there they notice a small 'For Rent' sign in a second floor window. It is in a garden apartment complex. The manager's office is not far. They walk into his office at 1645. He is just about ready to knock off for the day but grudgingly assents to showing them the place now as opposed to tomorrow. He apologizes that they haven't cleaned it up thoroughly yet. It turns out that it is a furnished apartment that they usually rent to wealthy graduate students. The previous resident left abruptly so he is still getting his rent until the end of November. He only decided to try to rent it two weeks ago when he found out that the young man would not be back before the present lease ran out. He notes that Henry and Christina might be happier in one of his larger places that cater to an older crowd. Almost everyone in this building is under thirty. They get the tour of the two bedroom apartment. This quick look around indicates that there is every chance that they will find some of Siegfried Bachmeier's DNA somewhere. Henry says he will take it and hands the Manager a two thousand Deutsche Marks deposit. They will sign all the papers tomorrow morning. The Manager wants to clean the place up but Henry insists that they will take care of that when they buy some new furniture.

Henry and Christina's apartment
Kirchheim district Heidelberg, Germany
September 28, 1993 Tuesday late morning

The rental arrangements were completed by 1000. At 1100 the first group of CIA agents showed up at the apartment. They were masquerading as a used furniture store crew. They removed the contents of the apartment into their truck but not before finding some hair in the nooks and crannies of the couches and gathering finger-prints from many items. There were also some clothes in the closet of one bedroom as well as several video game disks. They found half a case of Riesling in the refrigerator as well as two bottles of Jack Daniels® in the liquor cabinet. Apparently, Siegfried left in a hurry.

Around 1300, the second furniture truck showed up. This one was the real deal. By1500 the apartment was completely refurnished including towels and linens and king sized beds for both bedrooms. It was going to take another day before there was telephone service but the CIA contingent brought them a cellular telephone to use for the time being.

Guenther and Henry are in John's office. The results of the examination of the contents of Siegfried's apartment are on a few sheets of paper. They have Mitch Rogerston the CIA director on the speaker phone. Mitch is the youngest man to ever hold this position. He is forty seven and despite three failed marriages is considered one of the most eligible bachelors in town. Guenther is doing the talking.

"Thanks for providing the moving truck Mitch."

"We had some good luck. Siegfried's finger prints were everywhere and we know they are his because we were able to get a copy of his prints from the University. Apparently they fingerprint everyone who works at CERN. Siegfried spent several months there while he was working on his Dissertation. We used some of these prints from his apartment to get his DNA as well. We also had some DNA samples from the clothing and they matched those of the fingerprints. Now we are going to get into something which is very interesting. Siegfried Bachmeier's DNA indicates that there is no chance that Gerbert Bachmeier is his father. There is also no chance that he is related to Wilhelm Bachmeier either. We are trying to find out what Gerbert knows about the circumstances of his son's birth. Of course we haven't told him of our suspicions yet. We did take some more blood from him and over the weekend this was analyzed at Walter Reed. He has a very low testosterone level for a man his age and we also determined that he has a very low sperm count. We can only speculate about why. You know he had a mild case of the DTs when he first arrived at East Gorham. It might be that he rendered himself sterile by hitting the sauce a bit too hard or maybe he had some ill effects from the mumps – who knows. One can only speculate about what might have happened."

Henry interjects.

"That business about who is his father is interesting. The picture I saw of him, he had blond hair. Gerbert's hair is dark. Isn't dark hair dominant?"

Guenther answers.

"Good point Henry. It usually is. You saw Wilhelm. What color was his hair?"

"It was gray. I wouldn't have a clue to what color it was to begin with, the guy was seventy one I think."

This provokes a chuckle from Guenther. He is seventy three and his hair is white as snow.

"Mitch, can your guys or the FBI find out what color hair Wilhelm started with?"

"I think that has already been done. They can tell all sorts of stuff from the DNA analysis. I wil get Ellen to check on this right now."

Henry continues.

"When I wasn't spying in the lab I visited Professor Baumgartner's home Thursday about midnight. There were several very old wooden file cabinets in his study that I didn't touch because I was afraid that there might have had an alarm system. I got all the numbers off his desktop and his modem. Fred said that was all he needed to hack into the desktop. The files stored in his desktop go back to 1948 when he started teaching at Heidelberg. I wouldn't be surprised if the files in those old cabinets I didn't touch antedate that.

Fred found reference to a 'female subject' named Gertrude which he used Professor Eberhardt as a 'Source' on. It says in the file that the subject's IQ was raised from 140 to 184 as best they could determine. After a year of evaluation in Heidelberg, they sent her to Argentina. This was 1969. Gerbert was married in 1969 to a German girl. Siegfried was born in May 1971. As you all know by now, he finished his Doctoral work at Heidelberg when he was only twenty two and three months and they gave him the Physics Prize."

"You don't think Baumgartner knows you broke into his house?"

"For sure he doesn't know it was me. The place was not well protected. It is in a nice section of town which is heavily patrolled by the police. I don't think he knows anything about this. We were careful."

Guenther adds.

"Let us hope he does not know we are so interested in him. He will be dragging all manner of red herrings across our path if he does."

John asks.

"What makes you say that Guenther."

"The guy is a war criminal. We should have finished him off at Nuremberg. He got a pass because he was a past master at getting people to talk by injecting chemicals into them. We had a field day with a number of Stalin's spies we captured using the drugs he showed us how to use. We are practically certain that he and his staff killed a few hundred Dachau prisoners at their clinic in Herbertshausen doing mind control experiments on them. We have reason to believe, actually we know, that Baumgartner was very high up in the SS. I will tell you a little story out of school here. At the end of the war, we found some very high quality tape recorders in the Herbertshausen installation where Baumgartner was working. We found voice recordings and what we believe to be electroencephalograms on tape. We had nothing of this quality. The voice recordings were made by some of the Nazi higher ups including Hitler, Himmler and Goering. Baumgartner was apparently trying to brain wash some of his 'patients' from Dachau. They figured that if they could get the prisoners to start spouting the Nazi party line they had indeed achieved some level of mind control. This stuff was so incriminating that it got buried deep so that no one could find out what a son of a bitch Baumgartner was. I am going to revisit this material."

"This was an SS operation?"

"Absolutely. That nutcase Himmler was into any and all crackpot schemes that had anything to do with ESP, clairvoyance, fortune telling, mind control – you name it. Baumgartner started experimenting with rats in the early thirties and claimed to have been able to 'teach' them to read directional arrows. Himmler picked up on this and set him up in a lab north of Munich to see if he could transfer intelligence to people. Wilhelm Bachmeier was SS. He knew Eberhardt and Baumgartner knew Eberhardt. You might view Baumgartner as a mini-Mengele. That reminds me. Mengele got out of Germany one step ahead of the hangman's noose and fled to Buenos Aires. The whole damned crowd is over there.

I'm sorry for the digression. The problem at hand is that Siegfried Bachmeier is as smart as anyone in the Heidelberg Physics Department, maybe smarter. I heard from a friend at Princeton that the Heidelberg Physics faculty is talking about Siegfried like he is the second coming of Eberhardt or Heisenberg. Whether he was born that way or, God forbid, Eberhardt was able to make him that way isn't so important at the moment.

We have to assume that he is in Argentina and that he will be up to no good. You all saw how much trouble that combination of Rashid's money and Eberhardt's brain has caused already. We don't know who has Rashid's money but now it looks like young Siegfried might have Eberhardt's intelligence. We don't know where Eberhardt is and we don't know if he has created more than one Siegfried either."

"Guenther, we know that Rashid sold off SASC in pieces for relatively short money. We think he sold the mining operation and the remaining ore ship to the Pakis. It is my understanding that now that the Pakis own the ship it is off our target list. That still leaves much of his wealth unaccounted for. (*There is a moment of silence then he resumes.*) Linda just handed me the DNA report. There is something like a ninety nine percent probability that Wilhelm had blond hair."

"Are we going to do anything about Siegfried?"

"I talked with Harold about that very subject.

(Harold Whitworth is the Secretary of the National Security Agency who may be retiring soon. The 'search for the guilty' over the nuking of New York is in full swing and the head of the NSA is having unpleasant dealings with the Congress almost on a daily basis. He doesn't need the money or the power associated with running the NSA or the aggravation from Congress. He has been in this job for eight years under three administrations. Last week he reminded two senators on the Armed Forces Committee that they were the very two people who caused SOSUS to be shut down last year. Apparently he said "If you want to find some candidates for the guilty, look in the mirror." The last time someone ripped into a senator like that was when Howard Hughes zapped Senator Brewster. The smart money is betting he will pack it in before Christmas.)

He says that the main man does not want to give the Argentines anything else to bitch about at the moment."

Henry has been taking this all in.

"Fred did quite a bit of nosing around Baumgartner's computer. I remember him mentioning he found several references to "Gertrude". Why don't we get him in here and let him tell us what else he found."

John punches another phone and asks Fred to join them which he does shortly.

"Fred, what did you find out about these "Gertrudes" in Baumgartner's computer?"

"I found four mentions of a Gertrude. It was kind of strange. They were only identified by someplace in Germany."

"Like where?"

"Give me five."

Fred goes off to consult with "Charlie". When he comes back in there is a large map of Germany on the table.

"And?"

"Greifswald, Heidelberg, Lubeck and Rostock."

Henry interjects.

"Guenther, weren't you talking about Lubeck and Rostock last year as having something to do with Schroeder and Eberhardt?"

"Yes. We were able to place Runkel, Schroeder and Eberhardt in Rostock on one occasion in January 1945."

"Do you think these could be code words for people?"

"It is conceivable but they could just be where these "Gertrudes" came from. You raise an interesting point Hank. Himmler had a whole village south of Rostock where he was breeding SS troops with blond hair blue eyed women trying to make the perfect Aryan. This was going on from the late thirties to nearly the end of the war. Nothing ever came of this as far as we can tell."

"You were telling us how Baumgartner was tight with Himmler and trying to do the same thing."

"Yes. How far back do the records you have found in Baumgartner's computer go Fred?"

"About 1967."

"Was there a town name associated with the earliest mention of Gertrude?"

"Heidelberg."

"Schroeder taught at Heidelberg. This is just a hunch but do you have any pictures of Schroeder handy?"

"I have a photograph of him and Runkel in 1943 that was in Runkel's house in Bechtelsville and I have some recent photographs that Henry took of him in Frankfurt. The problem with those is that Henry beat him up pretty good before he took the photographs."

"Henry favors the direct method of interrogation."

"There are probably some photographs that the Frankfurt police took of him after the mishap in Frankfurt. They probably cleaned him up for some of these."

"Do we know where he is buried?"

"Where are you going Guenther?"

"If he wasn't cremated we can probably get some useful DNA from the corpse."

"So you want to have someone rob some grave in Germany to check if this Gertrude who we suspect was Siegfried's mother was mated with Schroeder?"

"Yes."

After some more discussion this task falls into Mitch's lap.

Agents Jack Munson and Lucas Raymond are sweating profusely this exceptionally warm German evening. There is a distinct 'clunk' as Jack's shovel hits something hard. The coffin was only one meter below the surface just below the frost line. The CIA got lucky. Schroeder was buried in a rural cemetery out of sight of any road. The records of who was buried where were in the office of the local tax assessor. This did not present much of a problem for the CIA. They photographed the pertinent page and left as quietly as they got in. They had to crank up the zoom to maximum on a satellite going over the cemetery on a sunny afternoon to nail down the exact location but that was not that difficult.

They hurriedly scrape the dirt off the coffin. It is a very expensive coffin with a copper exterior. It takes a little while to get it open. They extract some skin and bone samples from the corpse, close the thing up and bury it again. As usual, there is a little dirt left over after the hole has been filled back in. Nothing can be done about that. They simply pile it back on and then replace the sod they carefully removed at the beginning of their nighttime gardening exercise. It isn't perfect but it is pretty good.

The samples are in Langley the following evening.

Fred and Henry are in John's office. The three of them are having a conference call with Guenther and Mitch. There is a three nines probability that Fritz Schroeder is Siegfried Bachmeier's father. Guenther is doing the talking.

"I asked a friend of mine at Heidelberg about what he knew about Schroeder and the ladies. The story was that he was reprimanded for fooling around with some of his students twice. My friend told me that he heard, although he does not know for a fact, that Karl Eberhardt interceded on his behalf the second time. I asked him whether he remembered the time frame for either instance. He thought it was late sixties."

"Well, that's about right if he knocked up Siegfried's mother."

"There still looks like there is a discrepancy between when Siegfried was born and the time Fred found in Baumgartner's computer. I asked him if he knew of any association between Schroeder and Baumgartner. He said he didn't know."

"Maybe the date is wrong in Baumgartner's computer. He could conceivably have the wrong dates in there if they were doing everything they could to keep this whole thing quiet."

"I have no way to figure that out Hank. All the data I have was entered into Baumgartner's computer in the past two years. I think he was just digitizing his records."

"Suppose Siegfried is a year older than we think he is. We haven't got a clue about when he was really born.

Wilhelm Bachmeier could have arranged for practically anything to happen. Maybe his son Gerbert was simply a pawn in some game that Bachmeier, Eberhardt and Baumgartner were playing trying to produce a superman. Maybe we could learn something from those old wooden filing cabinets that I was afraid to touch."

"We were lucky to get the DNA samples with so little trouble. Breaking into Baumgartner's files in his house might not be so easy. We will be in big trouble if we get caught doing that stuff."

"Mitch, don't you have any German gangsters you could hire to do that?"

"I will ask Will." *(Willard Mason is the Head of Station for the CIA in Frankfurt.)*

John has been listening to this repartee between the other four. Now he speaks up.

"You better be sure you know these guys. We don't want to end up like the French did in Pakistan."

(The Pakis ended up severing diplomatic relations with the French after they found out that the perpetrators of a bombing in the best section of Karachi that killed several very prominent innocent people but not the terrorist they were targeting, was done by hoodlums paid by the French.)

This caution has about as much effect on Mitch as pouring water on a duck's back.

"Let me worry about that John."

Professor Baumgartner presented a paper on his recent work on a drug that suppresses epileptic attacks this afternoon. He and his grad student driver are walking through the Max Planck Institute for Medicine faculty parking lot when an Opel bolts out of a nearby parking space and smacks into Baumgartner's left leg. The student is so stunned by the occurrence that he doesn't even notice what kind of car it was. All he can tell the police is that the hit-and-run vehicle was black or maybe it was Navy Blue. He thinks it might have been an Opel but maybe it was a Volkswagen.

This event has the predictable result of putting Professor Baumgartner in the emergency room of Heidelberg Hospital six minutes later. Since he will be staying in the hospital with his broken leg until at least Sunday morning, there isn't anyone home at the Professor's residence Friday night. Jack Munson and Lucas Raymond are also accomplished second story men in addition to their talents as gravediggers and hit and run drivers. They gain entry to the Professor's residence and soon have the two wooden file cabinets opened. They photograph nearly two thousand pages. It takes four hours. They leave as stealthily as they entered. They do not notice that the bottom drawer of one of the cabinets has a loose wheel.

Office of the Director

CIA Headquarters

Langley, Virginia

October 18, 1993 Monday 1750

Rupert Thorpe is in Mitch's office.

"Mitch there is more than enough here to hang this son of a bitch. I haven't read every last word but I counted sixty three prisoners from Dachau that that bastard killed with his fucking mind control experiments."

"Was there any stuff there from after the war?"

"There was nothing between 1945 and 1949. Then he must have gotten a new lease on life. He picks up again in early 1950 and it runs to 1955. I talked with Jack Munson today. He said they didn't have time to photograph everything. They were told to get hold of the stuff during the war first."

"They did well to get this much in the time allotted. We probably can blackmail that bastard with this information if we choose to. Thanks for wading through all this stuff so quickly Rupert."

"Thanks Mitch."

He is on the phone with Randy Biggs. They are discussing their joint efforts to find out what they can about Professor Baumgartner's thought transference capabilities. They are also greatly concerned about Siegfried Bachmeier and his possible involvement in any weapons manufacture in Argentina. If in fact they were able to transfer Eberhardt's intelligence and experience to the young Bachmeier, he will certainly know how to build nuclear weapons.

"So the gear has arrived in Heidelberg?"

"Yes Guenther. I am leaving tonight and Fred and I will start installing the equipment Wednesday."

"They are going to let you put it in the same room as the MRI's?"

"Yes. They also are going to have us hook up our machine to both of the MRIs as well as the EEG equipment. When Henry saw the MRI equipment he asked them whether they thought our machine might help there also. They called me the week after he was there and I volunteered that we probably could help there as well."

Messieurs Biggs and Reinhardt have been busy the past three weeks. Fred managed to hack into Professor Baumgartner's home desktop and copy the contents of his hard drive into DCAC's computer shortly after Henry's midnight visit. Analysis of Baumgartner's files showed that he had figured out some way of sort of transmitting the EEG signal from the 'source" to the "subject" after processing it through a custom made gadget that he had

*Philips build. Fred has not been able to find any expla-
nation about this Philips black box in Baumgartner's
files. Randy thinks that he will be able to figure this out.
He does this sort of thing for a living all the time with his
radar work. The machine that Randy has built is simply known as a Cerebrionics CCX-1. He set up a bogus
company by that name with a stated place of business
in Memphis Tennessee not far from St. Jude Research
Hospital. The machine itself was built in Germantown
at the Memphis Targeting facility. They are going to put
it in Baumgartner's lab and eavesdrop on everything in
addition to massaging the EEG signals. They hope to
learn something about how Baumgartner was able to
teach the chimp. They then turn to discussing Siegfried
Bachmeier.*

"You had a chance to read his dissertation?"

"Yes I did Guenther. He is getting close isn't he?"

"Well, yes and no. There aren't so many accelerators
around that can be used to make these new particles he
thinks he found and they are not in the least portable.
As best I can make out, these photolinos, as he called
them, were a result of some secondary scattering and
were not what he was investigating per se. On the other
hand he did manage to make the connection between
production of these particles and producing electrons
from a piezo-electric source. I can not help but believe
that he will eventually figure out that he can make a particle beam weapon with the right piezo-electric source.
Then he will figure out that this is the trick with the fibrils
in the Plodamax."

"Well, he still has to figure out how to decorate the
insides of the fibrils with Selenium."

"Did you see the September issue of the Journal?"

"No."

"There is an article in there about inserting Silicon and Germanium atoms into the carbon lattice of a nanotube. They claim that they can make nanotubes as big as four hundred nanometers in diameter and they are straight as a string."

"Ouch!"

"Ouch indeed. So you see where I am going with this. You remember that we didn't have any luck until we figured that out. Now it looks like the cat is out of the bag.

Good luck this week. I hope it goes well."

"Thanks."

Professor Emeritus Wilfried Baumgartner's Laboratory
Heidelberg, Germany
October 27, 1993 Wednesday

Henry and Christina have just introduced Randy Biggs as Herr Doctor Doctor Engineer Randolph Barton to Professor Baumgartner. Fred, the DCAC computer maven is posing as Fred Mackintosh, a Cerebrionics technician who is there to assist Randy with the installation. There is a small crowd of curiosity seekers from the other parts of the building here as well. The Cerebrionics CCX-1 is a blue box about four feet high and three feet square. It has a built in desk top computer with a keyboard that folds out from the side of the machine. In addition to the flat screen computer monitor there are two dual trace oscilloscopes along with their associated controls. There is another two foot cube sitting on top of the CCX-1. This is the power supply. It will take the 220 volt three phase 50 hertz current from the lab jack, rectify it and then invert it to 115 VAC single phase 60 hertz current that things made in the US run on.

Randy apologizes for this but says it was much quicker and less expensive than manufacturing the CCX to run on 50 cycle current. He does not explain that there are some exceedingly clever electronics in both of these boxes that have nothing to do with processing EEG or MRI outputs. It takes a while to tie the Cerebrionics equipment into all the other equipment. Everything they can check out up to this point does. One of the grad students asks whether he could see the wave form from the inverter. Fred hits a few keys on the CCX keyboard and the voltage output waveform is up on the screen. It is power line quality and provokes several 'thumbs up' from the spectators.

They round up a volunteer to act as the source to generate the EEG. The lab is equipped with some very advanced EEG equipment. The source has a helmet-like affair that more or less resembles an old-time football helmet. The subject 'helmet' is much larger, nearly eighteen inches in diameter. They will not be using a subject today but the Professor has Manfred Bauer explain how they think it works. Bauer goes on to say that Professor Karl Eberhardt designed it twenty five years ago.

They get on with it. The student puts the source helmet on and fastens the chin strap. The cable from the helmet is plugged into the CCX-1 and they are ready to go. At first the screen is blank provoking several comments about the contents of the grad student's head. Fred types a little on the CCX keyboard and fiddles with some of the controls on the scopes. The EEG appears on the computer screen and one of the scopes. Fred types some more and the carrier wave is substantially subtracted out leaving only the information part of the signal. Randy asks the student to say yes and no twice. Fred superimposes the two traces. They are very close and the signal associated with each word is definitely different and recognizable. Everyone is impressed. But soon there are comments about the grad student's limited vocabulary. It is very funny, especially with the German syntax. Finally, Professor Baumgartner, whose left leg is in a cast, good naturedly admonishes the hecklers that they are delaying everyone from going to lunch. Randy explains that they have to send these traces to Memphis via the net and that they have a computer there which can clean them up much better. Professor Baumgartner will have his results back within two hours Monday to Friday 0700 to 1900 Central Standard Time. To protect the privacy of the patient, Baumgartner should identify the source of the image any way he wants. Cerebrionics does not want to know anything about anyone who Baumgartner is running EEGs on. Randy does not tell him that inside the blue box there are also highly sensitive electronics which will detect and record every word spoken within earshot and every keystroke on every keyboard in this room and the adjacent one – nor that Fred has Baumgartner's computer at home completely hacked so they will know who is involved in the show as soon as the data is transmitted to that computer – nor that there are also some other electronics which can do some rather sinister things to anyone whose head is in the helmet of either the source or the subject with the EEG equipment – nor that these electronics can also cause the MRI's to do some nasty things as well – nor that the CCX-1 can measure cerebral electrical activity one order of magnitude weaker than what they will show to Baumgartner. It is capable of resolving the very fine structure of the brain waves which don't even show up on any electroencephalograms anywhere else. This very fine scale information will find its way into the computers at Los Alamos and Memphis Targeting but not into the computers in Heidelberg.

It is nearly 1300 by the time they go to lunch at an excellent restaurant not far away. They have a leisurely meal including several bottles of Riesling. Randy buys. Professor Baumgartner thanks him for lunch and says that is enough for him for today. Randy says we will be back tomorrow and try to finish up. They shake hands and one of the grad students drives the Professor home.

It would have been a little awkward to have both Randy and Fred stay with Henry and Christina at their apartment – it only has two king sized beds so Randy and Fred ended up staying in the Crown Plaza.

Tuesday morning they had breakfast together at the Crown Plaza. Randy and Fred had plenty of time to check out the various electronics in the Professor's lab while finishing up with the Cerebrionics installation. They notice that the Professor has a Philips disc burning apparatus. It was one of the first on the market and fetched over $50,000 when it first appeared. They remark about this to one of the grad students who says Professor Baumgartner got this free from Philips. The grad student goes on to add that it is only used when Baumgartner is supervising the experiment being done that particular day. He is the only one who has access to the machine. They finished about 1130, just about the same time that Henry and Christina completed the commercial agreement with the University.

Rancho de Mil Robles

San Pablo de Arno, Argentina

October 27, 1993 Wednesday early afternoon

Siegfried studied the contents of two of the floppy disks Basima gave him. He is trying to relate Karl Eberhardt's explanation of how the fibrils in the Plodamax work to his Doctoral Dissertation. He theorized the existence and then experimentally produced what is believed to be a new particle which he named the 'photolino'. He was able to produce these in the CERN particle accelerator by bombarding several elements, most notably Selenium, Tellurium and Polonium with relativistic protons. The new particles were apparently the result of some secondary scattering which previous investigators had simply missed. There was some indication that the photolinos were ejected from the targets in a process very similar to the way that electrons are ejected from a piezo-electric crystal when it is compressed. He is wondering whether it might be electrons ejected from the part of the fibril which first experiences the detonation wave that are streaming down the fiber and igniting the explosive at the other end. Karl thought the fibrils were working as 'light pipes' but Siegfried is not convinced. He wants to talk to Aldrich Kessler. He knows more about the fibrils than anyone else he is likely to be able to talk to. Oskar and Basima say that they can try to have Kessler come to Argentina.

That was last week. Kessler arrived at Ezeiza this morning. Basima and Oskar met him and took him directly to Rancho de Mil Robles. Introductions were made and it is now lunch time. Siegfried escorts them out to the patio and the ranch chef brings the first course shortly.

"Thank you for coming Professor Kessler."

"I have heard good things about you Siegfried. Congratulations on winning the Physics Prize. I read your excellent dissertation. I am only a humble physical chemist but you have some very interesting insights in your work."

"Thank you."

They have a quiet meal. The Professor tells them he has a place in Krugersdorp less than forty kilometers from the Johannesburg airport. He tells Oskar that Abbo Fassbinder sends his regards and congratulations on a successful mission. It turns out that he got a good night's sleep in the First Class seat Basima bought him so he is in self-declared 'pretty good shape'. He manages to more than hold his own with the amount of meat and wine consumed compared to Oskar and Siegfried. After lunch they adjourn to the Wilhelm's study. Oskar starts.

"Aldrich, we have reason to believe that the Americans killed Rashid in August."

"What a shame. He was a very smart young man."

"We think they also killed Wilhelm Bachmeier, the head of our organization here in Argentina. He was Siegfried's grandfather. Now I head up our organization here. I presume that Basima informed you that Professor Eberhardt died in late June."

"That is most unfortunate. He was a true genius."

"Before he died, he gave Prince Rashid several floppy disks. One of these is concerned almost entirely with Plodamax. He specifically requested that we try to get you to continue to help us learn how to make the fibrils."

Basima picks up.

"We no longer have access to the facility you had in Saudi Arabia nor to FPI. The Americans seized Filamentary Particles Incorporated the day after New York was bombed. I only have a few grams of this material which you can use as a reference. (*She does not mention that she has nearly two kilograms of the fibrils in a safe deposit box in Banco de Boston.*) We are prepared to build you a new facility here if you are willing to continue this work."

"This will be very difficult without the fibrils. We will have to learn how to make them before we can do anything else. This may take years."

"We are working on that already Professor Kessler and Siegfried have some ideas that you may find interesting."

Professor Kessler is not quite as ardent a Nazi as either Eberhardt or Schroeder. He is also not as well off as he might have been if he had not gotten mixed up with this crowd. When he had to flee Germany a few months ago, he couldn't very well leave a forwarding address so his pension from the University is no longer getting to his checking account. Rashid paid him very well but that money is probably only going to last another six or seven years. This is going take time. He will have to live in Argentina.

"How much does an apartment in a nice part of Buenos Aires cost?"

"Apartments in Recoleta are very expensive. However one can find perfectly nice places to live north of the city for no more than seven or eight hundred dollars a month."

"You said dollars?"

"Yes, most rents in the better properties are collected in dollars. The Argentine currency is somewhat unstable."

"Well, I am seventy three. I hope to take a few years vacation before I reach the end of my years. I could give you two more years for ten thousand a month plus a bonus if I can produce a material with half the detonation velocity of Plodamax."

"Okay, that is perfectly reasonable."

They go over what the Professor will need. This is going to take a while if he can do it at all. He was working with FPI fibrils but they don't have any of those. They really have to start from the ground up. Aldrich says that it is most desirable to do this work in relative isolation because it can get noisy. Oskar suggests that he might be better off at Rancho Don Martinez. They have some infrastructure there and it is relatively isolated. They show Aldrich some photographs of the ranch and where it is on a large map of Argentina. They will provide him with a cook and a housekeeper. He will have negligible expenses. That clinches it.

It turns out that Kessler has a false South African passport. It was obviously good enough to get through Immigration at Ezeiza but Oskar thinks that it will be better to produce an Argentine identity for Aldrich. They take him to Zarate to Rudy Kleist's photography studio. Rudy says he will have a passport and driver's license for Aldrich by tomorrow afternoon. Oskar compliments Rudy for the great job he did helping Wilhelm produce the movie back in May. Oskar takes Basima home to San Isidro and then stops by the Belen yard to talk with Raphael a while and tell him of the decision to do the fibril research in Pelicura. They call Benno Weber who is now the manager at CCM Bahia Blanca and tell him to check that the ranch has been cleaned up. They don't want Kessler noticing that there are signs of damage there. Benno had already sold the damaged machine tools in the bunker to a large scrap dealer in Bahia

Blanca and as far as he knows, they are on their way to Korea or India or someplace to get recycled into steel plate. Oskar is very glad about that turn of events and thanks Benno. He says he thinks they will drive down there Friday. Benno suggests that they give him until Monday and they agree.

Siegfried drove Professor Kessler back to Rancho de Mil Robles and they had supper together. They talk a little about the fibrils.

"What do you think about the idea that the transmission of the ignition signal down the fibers might be electrical in nature as opposed to optical?"

"Well, it is an interesting idea Siegfried. Some people are getting a piezo-electric effect out of small Selenium structures. It is conceivable. You know that we found Selenium in the fibrils?"

"Yes, Karl mentioned that several times in his notes."

Aldrich cannot manage to suppress a yawn at this point. The long flight and time change is catching up to him. This discussion can wait for another day.

Rancho Don Martinez
Pelicura, Argentina
November 18, 1993 Thursday

Professor Kessler has settled in here. Oskar and Siegfried took him to see the place the first of the month. Benno Weber did a good job of cleaning up the evidence of the raid. The entire interior of the bunker had been covered with a mildew resistant glossy white paint. Benno had all new lighting installed. There were a few chips in the concrete but the place looked almost inviting.

Kessler wanted at least one technician preferably two, more or less as a safety precaution so if one person got hurt the other could seek aid. Oskar agreed to this immediately. They stayed in Villa del Mar at the Hotel Tamarisces for two days and returned to Rancho de Mil Robles Wednesday the third. Equipping the laboratory in Pelicura was moving along at a good pace. They managed to find a used electron microscope and a used mass spectrograph in Buenos Aires. The Copper-Beryllium bronze non-sparking tools are on order from the United States. Most of the mixing equipment was available locally. Kessler wanted some of the mixing equipment copper plated as a safety precaution. This has turned out to be a bit of a problem because it changes the clearances between some of the parts. They have a shop in Buenos Aires dealing with this but the equipment will not be ready until after Christmas.

Oskar, Basima and Siegfried flew down to Bahia Blanca this morning. They showed up at Rancho Don Martinez just before noon followed by a truck from a piano dealer in Bahia Blanca.

Today is Aldrich's seventy-fourth birthday. He is most appreciative of the full size upright they present him with. This is promptly installed in the living room of the ranch house. They eat outside while the piano tuner does his thing. After lunch Aldrich apologizes for being a little rusty but manages to play Für Elise without missing a note. Then Kessler reviews where they are. They have located a supplier in Argentina and another in Brazil that produce RDX. They are making very little progress on the fibrils themselves. They can not find anyone in South America making anything even vaguely resembling what they are looking for. They did locate a Japanese manufacturer that makes very fine fibers from quartz. Kessler has spoken to these people. They only do quartz. That won't work according to Kessler. He thinks that the fibrils in the Plodamax have a significant fraction of a very low melting temperature glass containing some Selenium and Iodine. Basima is the one who was most closely associated with FPI.

"Basima, Rashid told me that you visited FPI."

"Yes Aldrich, I visited them twice."

"Did they show you their manufacturing facility?"

"I was on the Board of Directors. We had a tour of their facilities but I didn't know what I was looking at and nobody asked many questions."

"Did they have a 'clean room'?"

"Yes, but we didn't go in there. Our guide did mention that the clean room had an Argon atmosphere but that is all I know."

"That is very interesting. It is another straw in the wind that they are using some sort of process which requires an oxygen free environment. Do you think there is anyone there who could tell us what they are doing?"

"I had some contact with the head of manufacturing. Rashid made him President of FPI for his last year on the job as a 'thank you' for helping us with a problem we had there. He is retired."

"Do you have any way of contacting him?"

"You must remember Aldrich that the US government seized FPI the day after New York was bombed. It is likely that someone at FPI has figured out why. I don't think we can talk to them."

Siegfried interjects.

"I think there is an intermediate step in the manufacture of the fibrils after they leave FPI and before they reach Granite State Explosives."

Basima does a double take. How does he know that? Rashid told me that Karl thought that was the case but Rashid never met Siegfried so how did Siegfried find this out? How has he even heard of GSE? He must have gotten that from Karl.

"That is certainly a possibility Siegfried. Karl expressed that thought several times to me."

This is the second time that Aldrich has heard of GSE. Werner said something about them when they were working in the Saudi desert. He quickly puts two and two together. GSE is the manufacturer of the Plodamax.

"If we can't get close to FPI, could we possibly obtain some of these fibrils from GSE?"

Basima relates the tale of how Rashid was able to steal some Plodamax from GSE in early 1991. That was finished product not fibrils. She says that this material is gone. The Paki nuclear folks probably have the last of it. She doesn't know how much that might be.

"The explosive you made was good enough for Karl to make bombs both for us and the Pakis Aldrich."

"I only figured out how to mix the fibrils with the Hexogen Basima. The material I was able to make had less than half the detonation wave velocity of the Plodamax. Now we have to find out how to make the fibrils you were providing from FPI. If only we knew a little about their manufacturing process. Was the whole thing done in the Argon atmosphere clean room?"

"No. I am sorry if I gave you that impression. Most of the equipment was in a much larger clean room. They had some equipment where they were doing some sort of epitaxial growth in vacuum furnaces. I presume they were talking about the fibrils but they didn't spell it out in that many words. These were in the main part of the manufacturing area. There was a lot of discussion about the similarity of what they did with semiconductor circuit manufacture."

"That is most interesting. It would appear that I have been chasing up the wrong tree. I did some epitaxial growth work on Silicon some years ago. Nobody knew how to make anything as small as the fibrils in Plodamax then. I will read up on that."

Oskar has been quietly listening, now he says something.

"Basima, didn't you mention there was another customer using this material?"

"There were several customers Oskar. The largest user was an outfit someplace around Memphis Tennessee named Advanced Opti-Maser Transmission (AOMT). I was told that they were working on high speed data transmission. That is all I know."

"Possibly we could buy some of these fibrils from them."

Siegfried has something to add to this.

"I heard of them when I was doing my research at CERN. They are leaders in this field of data transmission.

I am going back to Heidelberg in December to collect my diploma. The graduation ceremony is just before Christmas. While I am there I will see what I can find out about AOMT and fibril growth using semiconductor technology."

John, Henry and Fred are on a conference call with Guenther and Randy. They are going over what they have found so far. The CCX-1 has been in Baumgartner's lab for a little over a month. Professor Emeritus Baumgartner only shows up two or three days a week and that is the only time they try thought transference on human beings. So far, the human subjects appear to be mostly epileptics. Fred has had 'Charlie' looking at this a bit and he has found that the University has a sizable grant from the German government to continue trying to cure epilepsy. Baumgartner's lab receives the lion's share of these funds. All the rest of the EEG work is spent on chimps. When they have human subjects Baumgartner occasionally unlocks the interface box types something into it and relocks it. They record what he types but it is some sort of code which they have not figured out. The images from the Philips MRI are all recorded in two computers in the University lab and most of those find their way into Baumgartner's desktop as well. The typist often hit '5' when he or she meant to type '4' and so would have to backspace and fix it up. It didn't take Fred very long to notice that the same thing happened with regularity on Baumgartner's home desktop machine. Baumgartner invariably printed the Excel® file he generated on his home machine and then immediately erased the file. He then took this printout and typed the last line into the black box the next day. Why he didn't simply transmit the code from his home to the lab is a bit of a mystery. After analyzing seven such instances they were able to reason out that the keyboard associated with the black box was not tied into the lab computer network. Apparently they are the only ones besides Baumgartner who know what he typed in there. So far, Baumgartner is the only one who knows what the code he types into the black box means.

Fred has had 'Charlie' examine everything in Baumgartner's home computer and there are no references to Karl Eberhardt or Siegfried Bachmeier. Henry says he is planning on being in Heidelberg from the middle of December until the first week in January. It would not be a problem for him to talk with the grad student who told him about the several instances when Eberhardt and Bachmeier were supposedly getting simultaneous EEGs. If they can get the dates they might be able to learn something. Randy and Guenther are not enthusiastic about doing that – it might arouse suspicion. After some discussion Henry convinces them that if he and Christina show up there as more or less just making a courtesy call to check up on the CCX-1 it will be okay.

Captain Ridwan has completed selling off all the maritime assets of SASC. She has spoken with him once or twice a month since September. The SASC internal phone system is still intact and she has been able to access it through the TASA office in Buenos Aires. This morning, her new phone line has finally been installed. She is now able to access the SASC system from a secure phone in her home. She has the option of using the voice altering equipment from her home so that she can sound like Rashid did to the party she calls. She has just finished speaking to the Captain. She spoke with and without the voice altering equipment and he said she definitely sounds like Rashid did when she uses the voice altering equipment. The Captain goes on to relate some very bad news.

"Rafiq *(Rashid's half brother and nominally co-owner of Rashid's business empire)* was killed in an automobile accident in Switzerland two days ago. I understand that he went off some road around St. Moritz and plunged two hundred meters down the side of the mountain."

This is devastating news. This whole fragile business alliance that Rashid cobbled together is going to blow up. Rashid said that Rafiq is the only half sibling that he had any confidence or trust in. Rafiq has a younger brother who will inherit and this will be trouble for sure. He is only twenty and he is a first class brat who Rashid openly disliked. The Captain seems to appreciate this but he has no suggestions. He tries to be helpful and tells her that the shipyard in Durban is doing nicely but they both know that Rashid's share of the Saudi oil income is more than likely gone. All this grief has been caused by the Americans, the Jews and the French. The Jews killed her father using French and American warplanes. Rashid believed that the Jews or the Americans killed Ahmed using American missiles and possibly the French put a bomb on his father's plane. The Americans drove her and Rashid into hiding and had essentially destroyed SASC. That is the reason he had to appear to give up his business empire. Then the Americans killed Rashid four months ago and now this happens. She resolves to take up the struggle, but how. She has money but she does not have power....

"Basima are you still there?"

She must have been twenty seconds thinking about this terrible news.

"I am sorry Abdul. I was just thinking that this is a disaster."

There is another ten second delay before she continues.

"Did you find Albert Debbinck?"

"Yes Basima. It turns out that he is a mining engineer. He is retired but retains control of his company he built. I met him in a small town about two hundred kilometers north of here. Apparently he is an important man in the AWB (Afrikaner Weerstandsbeweging) which I think you know is a Nazi-like organization here in South Africa. He knew Wilhelm Bachmeier. He was most distressed to hear that he was dead."

"What does he look like?"

"Funny you should ask. That was the first thing that struck me. He is a huge man two meters tall (6'7") and maybe one hundred forty kilo."

Basima is remembering what Oskar told her. He said that Siegfried described this guy who he had never seen as a 'big Dutchman who went to Heidelberg'.

"How did you manage to talk to him?"

"Rasul Bishara goes with me practically everywhere. Most of the people I talk to speak English so I talk to him and he talks to them. I am learning a little English but it is slow going. There was a diploma on his wall. He had a geology degree from Heidelberg."

"Did he say what his company mined?"

"He has two mining properties. He mines Uranium on one and Copper in the other. He said that the Copper ore was high in Selenium and gold content."

Henry and Christina's Apartment
Kirchheim district Heidelberg, Germany
December 19, 1993 Sunday

Henry left Boston last night and arrived in Frankfurt at 0800. When he got to the apartment Christina opened the door while he was getting his key ring out of his left pants pocket. They spent the next two hours catching up on their romance. They sat down for a relatively early supper at a nearby restaurant at 1800. She gives him the good news.

"I will accompany you back to the US in the New Year. I gave my employers notice a month ago."

"That is the best Christmas present I could get. Won't you have to marry me to do that?"

"No, I already have a permanent visa. I can come and go as I please."

Henry insists on having a Trockenbeerenauslese for dessert to celebrate this news. It has been a long day for him and he starts to close his eyes before the bottle is empty. Christina drives them home.

They arrived at Professor Baumgartner's office right on time. After some idle chit chat they get a tour of the lab again. The Professor is very happy with the results so far from the CCX-1. He wants to know how much another one would cost. He would like to buy the equipment that Cerebrionics has that processes the raw data and sends him back the excellent quality movies. Henry says that Cerebrionics has a very large computer that massages the data with a great deal of proprietary software. There is no plan to sell this. The Prof also wants to know several technical details about the machine that Henry says they will have to get back to him about. Christina works the conversation around to the 'nice young man' who they saw the first day when they met Professor Schmidt and Enos.

"That really is quite remarkable what you were able to teach Enos."

"Thank you Fraulein Grunwald, you are most kind. Manfred did most of the work, he was my best student. He finished his dissertation last month and has accepted a position at Merck in Darmstadt."

"How is Enos doing?"

"He is doing fine. His vocabulary is up to 227 words now."

Henry says they will get back to him shortly on his questions. They chat a little longer. Christina says "Frohe Weihnachten" *and the Professor says* "Frohe Weihnachten Fraulein Grunwald and Merry Christmas Mister Hartwell."

They shake hands and leave. It is 1030. They want to go to Darmstadt and see if they can chat with Manfred Bauer again but they will have to clear that with John and Guenther. It is too early to call the US so they drive to Darmstadt anyhow and eat lunch there. They call John at 1300 local time. It is 7am EST in Woburn. John says don't do a thing. Fred thinks he has found the dates that both Eberhardt and Bachmeier were there in Baumgartner's lab together. The electronics in the CCX-1 have detected signals which are emitted by hard drives. They have reason to believe that there is a device to burn disks inside Baumgartner's black box. They know the thing has a lock on it and only Baumgartner has a key. Fred is speculating that Baumgartner may have copies on hard disk of the suspected transmissions from Eberhardt to Bachmeier.

"Hello Siegfried. I am so glad that you came back for your graduation."

"Thank you Professor. I am looking forward to doing a little skiing after graduation."

"With Heidi?"

"Yes."

"She won't be finished here for at least another year."

"I think we can stand that. Prof, I want to talk to you about me and Karl. Could we go into your office?"

They do just that and Baumgartner shuts the door.

"The first thing you need to know is that Karl is dead. He had a heart attack. He left me a letter telling me about the thought transference project. He must have written the letter after our last session which was last June I think."

"Yes, that is correct."

"Did you know he wrote this letter?"

"No."

"He told me that you and he were able to increase my mother's intelligence. I have been getting flashbacks since you started these sessions with Karl. I am wondering how much my accomplishments here were due to what my mother gave me or what you and Karl gave me."

"I do not know the answer to that question Siegfried. We have no evidence that we made you more intelligent than the day you were born. We knew you were a genius when you were two years old. *(The exact same words Karl wrote in his letter.)* We do know that we were able to successfully transfer a great deal of information to you about nuclear fission and quantum mechanics. We did not contribute to your discovery of the photolino. You did that yourself. I think that what we were able to download from Karl to you about quantum mechanics may have helped you make your discovery a little faster than otherwise but you did this by yourself."

"What about the flashbacks"

"It is not uncommon."

"So presumably, somewhere in some crevices in my mind I may already have Karl's entire life history already stored away."

"That is conceivable."

"Do you think that hypnosis might enable me to access this information?"

Baumgartner does not want Siegfried to access all the information that he may have received from Karl's brain. Karl knew lots of things that they did not want Siegfried to know. He had to administer psychoactive drugs to both of them when they having these mutual sessions to enhance the firing rate of the synapses. This was not a well controlled or understood thing to do. They didn't do it until they had determined by experiments with others that nothing disabling happened to the subject or the source. That is why the first session occurred eight months after Siegfried matriculated at Heidelberg.

"I don't know Siegfried. We don't do that here."

(We do that with psychoactive drugs but I am not telling him that.)

"Karl suggested that I might be a source for you."

"I think we should wait on that Siegfried."

(That's all I need. The stuff Karl knew about me in more 'subjects'.)

Siegfried detects that Baumgartner has a certain lack of enthusiasm about this entire matter and decides that he can put this off for a while anyhow. They go back into the lab. Siegfried notices the CCX-1.

"This wasn't here the last time I was here was it Prof?"

"You are very observant Siegfried. That is an experimental gadget that enables us to make movies of the electrical signals in the brain of the source. We are evaluating it."

"How does it work?"

"They say it subtracts out the EEG carrier wave leaving only the information containing portion of the signal."

"That doesn't sound so difficult."

"It is not so easy because the carrier wave is not constant. Apparently they have some logic which enables it to deal with this."

"Who makes it?"

"Cerebrionics. It is a medium sized American company in Tennessee. I think they are based in Memphis."

Siegfried has a flashback. Where have I heard that name before?

"It must have an enormous data handling capacity."

"All I know is that is more than sufficient to handle the data from the MRI."

"I was talking with some friends about high data handling capacity recently. I am going to call a friend at CERN about that subject later today. I seem to remember that an American company makes this equipment. I think they are somewhere around Memphis also. How long have you had this thing?"

"They put it in at the end of October. I think they were here the 27th and the 28th.

"I wasn't feeling well the 27th but I was there the 28th when they got it running."

"That wasn't the first time they were here was it?"

"No. Their sales manager and some 'sales trainee' were here a month before that. Professor Schmidt and I had already agreed that we were going to try this thing so I didn't come in that day. Your friend Manfred told me that the 'sales trainee' was exceptionally good looking. I must confess that she is a beautiful woman. If you had been here two hours ago you could have made that judgment for yourself. She and the sales manager were here earlier this morning to see how we liked the machine. On their first appearance here in later September your friend Manfred showed them around and I hear that Enos put on quite a show. Manfred said the sales manager noticed your picture in the Alumni Magazine so he told the guy how smart you were. He is your biggest fan. He has asked me several times why you didn't stay here and teach."

Siegfried does not want to get into that discussion.

"You are going to let me buy your lunch today aren't you Prof?"

"Yes. Thank you in advance. Any excuse will do to escape these Monday Seminars."

"Let's go."

Gato Negro Tango
Avenida Corrientos
Buenos Aires, Argentina
December 31, 1993 Friday late evening

The waiter has just finished removing the dessert dishes. Oskar is wearing a black tuxedo and Basima is wearing a white silk dress with a slit cut to her thigh. It is New Year's Eve and Oskar asked her to celebrate with him at the premier supper dance club in town. There is a mixed crowd. The women are very well dressed and very good looking. It looks like they are anywhere between the late teens and the early forties and the men are ten to twenty years older. You can practically smell the money. Oskar points out that the two best tango dancers in the city are there. He asks her to dance as soon as the first strains from the bandoneón waft across the room. Oskar says they have to get their dancing in early because the best dancers will be on the floor later and the people watching don't like to see clumsiness on the dance floor – especially tonight. They are a handsome couple. He is not clumsy but of course he is not in the same league as the professionals. She follows effortlessly. They are very close sometimes and he can feel her breasts against him. A couple near them are very good dancers and they watch as they perform several dips. They try a few of those. Oskar is getting somewhat aroused being this close. She has nice legs as well as breasts and a pretty face. It has been a while. One can not keep such feelings from one's dance partner. She doesn't seem to mind. They only stay long enough to toast in the New Year. When they get back to her home she invites him in for a nightcap. This soon leads to them going upstairs.

It is nearly 1230 New Year's Day when they awake.

"Good morning Basima. You look beautiful in the morning too."

"Thank you Oskar. I thoroughly enjoyed last evening. I hope we can do this again but I think it is not morning."

The clock is on her side of the bed. When she gets up to go take her shower he notices that it is early afternoon.

"I am a little late. I am supposed to be at a party out at Rancho de Mil Robles which I think starts in half and hour. Most of our people at CCM Belen will be there. I cannot show up in this tuxedo I have with me. I have to stop in Zarate."

"Can I come?"

(This gets Oskar to thinking. That is a loaded question. If I show up two hours late with a beautiful woman on my arm everyone will be quite certain that we spent the night together. Do I care? They are going to think that anyhow when I show up late even if I am alone. I am sure that blabbermouth sister of mine has already told everyone she knows that Basima and I have had several lunches at her husband's restaurant.)

"I don't see why not."

They arrive at Rancho de Mil Robles at 1550. She has a blouse and jeans on and he has a CABJ sweatshirt and jeans on. Most of the men who work at CCM Belen and their families are there. There must be at least two hundred people at this party. Shortly after they arrive there are numerous conversations going on about who the Captain's woman is. Siegfried brings them a couple of mugs of Becks.

"I called Zarate about half an hour ago. I was beginning to worry about you Captain."

"We must have left a little before you called."

Oops, if there was any doubt there isn't now.

"Well, I am very glad to see you both."

Raphael comes over with his beautiful wife Teresa and introduces Teresa to Basima. Teresa has heard about the stunning woman from Saudi Arabia. She is relieved to see the woman is with Oskar. She and Basima hit it off immediately.

It is a beautiful summer day. Oskar introduces Basima to his friend Hermann Schleifenbaum and his wife Roberta as well as three of the yard foremen. It is a little difficult for her. They all have to try to remember one new name but she is introduced to more than forty people – it is something of a blur. Everyone knows Oskar. The afternoon passes quickly. There are games for the children and plenty to eat and drink. Around 1900 people start heading home. It looks like most of the driving home will be done by the wives. Oskar and Basima say their goodbyes and go back to Zarate.

The remaining guests spend a fair amount of time talking about 'the Captain's woman'. Siegfried notes that she was educated in Europe and the United States has a Doctorate in Psychology and speaks five languages that he knows of. The consensus is that the Captain will have his hands full.

Oskar, Basima and Siegfried are sitting around a table on Oskar's patio. They are discussing Siegfried's trip to Heidelberg.

"So you think there may be some connection between AOMT and the Cerebrionics outfit that had this machine in Professor Baumgartner's Lab?"

"I am not sure, Oskar. When I talked to my friend at CERN, he said he remembered something about MRI's in some of the literature from one of the vendors who was bidding for this particular high speed data transmission project that he worked on. He did not remember if it was AOMT. He checked his records and it looked like they asked AOMT to bid but then they declined. He thinks that the US government stopped AOMT from bidding. We were talking about the problem with making small hollow fibrils. He mentioned that there was an article in the September issue of the American Physics Journal which might be of some interest to me. I brought a copy of the article back with me and I am going to talk about this with Aldrich.

At your suggestion Basima I got hold of that computer guy that SASC has in Frankfurt. He found out that AOMT was on the DARPA *(Defense Advanced Research Project Administration)* list. They must be doing some work on secret military projects. This computer guy also thinks that the US government told them not to bid.

"What about Baumgartner and using you as a source?"

"Baumgartner was not in the least receptive to using me as a source. He did not think hypnosis would be of any use in trying to summon up my subconscious either."

"Did he have anything to say about the Cerebrionics machine?"

"No. All he knew was that it was very fast because it was taking the EEG data, computing a carrier frequency, subtracting the carrier frequency and procucing a fuzzy trace of the information part of the brain wave in real time. He said that he had to send this data to Memphis and that it came back with a very good trace in one to two hours."

"I remember that you said that he gave you a sedative when he was running your EEGs."

"Yes Basima."

"I have done a little research of my own. You may not know that Heidelberg is preeminent in Psychopharmacology. The head of the Biology Department is a specialist in this and he is Baumgartner's protégé. It would not surprise me if they used psychoactive drugs when you were having these sessions with Karl. It seems a bit strange that he didn't want to try hypnosis or something."

"I am wondering about that myself."

Basima's residence
San Isidro, Argentina
January 11, 1994 Tuesday

She is on the telephone with Salil. She is using the voice altering equipment that Rashid gave her. Salil hears the same voice he has heard for the past five years. It is the voice of his Saudi benefactor who he only knows as Ali. Prince Ahmed used equipment like this and then Prince Rashid did the same. She has kept in touch with the Palestinians on a monthly basis and has also managed to find a way of sending them money. But that is not what Salil wants today.

"Ali, we hope you can spare us another two stingers."

"Salil, the last one I sent you was misused. You will remember that the Israeli press said that there was some sort of two stage rocket used in your last attack on the airliner. We do not send you weapons so that you can turn them over to the Iranians to examine."

Salil knew this moment was going to come some-time. He tries to put the best face on it.

"We were simply unable to get close enough to the airport to use the stinger. We had to have more range. No one is sorrier than I am that the thing didn't work. We lost thirty seven people in the vicious Jewish counterattack."

"You got off lightly compared to the Iranians. *(She is referring to the three thermonuclear weapons that Israel dropped on the Iranians in reprisal for bombing Haifa and Tel Aviv.)* I think it is not wise to attack Israel again at this point."

"I was thinking about attacking the US. We have a loose alliance with some others who also feel that the

US must be punished for all the help they g ve the Jews in addition to their slaughtering our Holy Warriors other places. We think that setting off another bomb on the anniversary of the bombing of New York would send a message to the US that they can not relentlessly attack us without some retribution."

"These people have nuclear weapons?"

"No, we were going to use a conventional explosive the same way we did in Philadelphia. That was a very successful attack."

Basima thinks she saw something on the disks Eberhardt left about the attack in Philadelphia. She will have Oskar and Siegfried look at this more closely.

"How do you expect to get a boat into the US Salil?"

"We were hoping you could help us with that. We will provide a crew to execute the mission."

Basima is aware of the fact that the Palestinians made a major contribution to Ahmed's efforts to disrupt stinger manufacture and to Rashid's effort to bomb the nuclear powered American aircraft carrier.

"Let me think about that Salil. It may be possible. You should have mentioned this earlier. May 26th is only four months away. I will call you soon."

Her thoughts turn to Captain Ridwan and Rasul Bishara. They have been to the US several times and were highly instrumental in the successful attack in Philadelphia. Rashid said that Werner's uncle was the head of some Nazi association in US and that they enabled the attack in Philadelphia. Rashid said that Karl Eberhardt and Siegfried Runkel were very old acquaintances. She needs to talk with Oskar before doing anything else about this suggestion from the Palestinians. She finds him in Belen. The conversation is in German."

"Guten Morgen Oskar."

"Guten Morgen mein Schatz."

He has taken to calling her darling when they are talking in private.

"I had a phone call from the people who helped us bomb the aircraft carrier in Philadelphia this morning. They are suggesting that they could bomb New York on the first anniversary of our attack. I know Rashid and Werner were working closely with Werner's uncle in the US. Do you have any knowledge about this man?"

"Wilhelm killed him and his sons a year and a half ago."

"I thought he was a Nazi too, why?"

"Wilhelm didn't want to talk about it much but he did say that Siegfried Runkel probably had a mental breakdown after his youngest son was killed on the aircraft carrier. You know he and his two sons escaped the US to Buenos Aires the day of the bombing in Philadelphia. He was despondent. Wilhelm had him in an apartment in Zarate but he kept getting drunk at the local steak house and would start rambling on about Nazi secret weapons. Wilhelm was afraid he would say something that would draw attention to our efforts here – especially since we had kept the presence of U-1241 secret for so long."

"How big was this organization in the US that he headed?"

"I don't know."

"Rashid said that some of his organization was in New Hampshire where GSE is located. I gathered that Rashid had an acquaintance from his school that stole the Plodamax from GSE."

"I don't know."

"It is my understanding that Werner Runkel's father controls a large demolition company in Germany. Rashid told me he was very helpful in their efforts to bomb the aircraft carrier."

"I never met the man Basima. My father said he did visit Argentina around the time of the war with Britain. I was in the Navy."

"Do you think that Wilhelm might have left any notes about any connections he had in the US?"

"I don't know but I will look."

There is no doubt that the Americans have greatly disrupted their efforts. There is no single source of the history of their efforts. Eberhardt seemed to know what everyone was doing – at least in general. Perhaps there is something in his notes. She decides to look more carefully. Eberhardt had different kinds of information on the different floppies she had. There was one that seemed to deal with personnel. Unfortunately it was full of pseudonyms phony addresses etc. She goes back and reads what Rashid left her. There in his notes she finds reference to some software on disk 4. She installs that software and follows the instructions. When she processes the personnel disk file with this software a decoded file emerges. It is a treasure trove. It is in German but she is fluent. There are names and phone numbers in the US, Germany, Pakistan, South Africa, Argentina and Brazil. It is nearly 1700 when she calls Oskar back and suggests that he might want to look at this material.

He comes to San Isidro and they go for an early dinner at La Cabaña. They have frequented the restaurant often enough so that the grill master selects a small filet for Basima without having to be asked. Oskar can still down most of a kilo T-bone. After dinner they return to Basima's and she goes over what she has found from Karl's records. Something in Karl's notes rings a bell with Oskar.

"You see this reference to Gertrude? There is no corresponding pseudonym. Gertrude was Siegfried's mother. Gertrude must be the woman that Baumgartner and Eberhardt electroencephalographica ly educated."

"So you think Wilhelm could have been both Siegfried's father and grand father?"

"This is deliberately confusing. You can read it two ways."

They dwell on this a little longer and then move on. There is a section about the Nazi movement in the northeastern part of the US. Siegfried Runkel is mentioned prominently. They see that there is a chapter based in Manchester, New Hampshire and that this chapter made major contributions to the bombing of the LNG tanks in Boston. Oskar admits that he never heard very much about that. There is a reference to an Armin Wurtzberg as one of Siegfried Runkel's lieutenants. There is a telephone number which they trace to Manchester, New Hampshire. They talk about how to go about contacting this man. Basima is fluent in English. She will do it. If this man is amenable he might be of help in mounting this terror attack in May.

There is also a section about the Nazi's in Brazil. They find prominent mention of Hans Obermeyer. Oskar notes that Obermeyer has a boat building business in Porto Alegre and that he built Gerbert's boat. He is the son of Wolf Obermeyer, the SS commander in charge of all prisoners in Russia. The elder Obermeyer managed to escape through Switzerland to Brazil in early 1945. They find mention of another Gertrude that Hans married. Now they are beginning to wonder what Karl was talking about. Is Gertrude some kind of code word?

Oskar's mention of boat building reminds her that the Palestinians want to launch a boat attack on the US. They bat this around a while. Oskar is definitely against such an effort. She agrees.

There is a four way conference call going on. John, Henry and Fred are in John's office. They are connected to Guenther, Randy and Mitch. Mitch is talking.

"We tracked the thing to the ranch in Pelicura easily enough. We even have photographs of the TASA truck that carried the gadget from Ezeiza to Pelicura next to the north side of the ranch house."

Guenther comments.

"That is where the bunker is. I imagine you are going to tell us you have lost the signal."

"Not entirely. We are still getting a signal when the satellite is north of the ranch house but not when it is south of the ranch house."

Henry has something to add here.

"If you remember the pictures they took during the raid, there was this big stack of lead between the control room and the room with the machine tools. Maybe the lead is blocking the signal."

Randy gets into it.

"That does not make a great deal of difference. The instrument we built records the spectra it sees and sends a burst transmission to the satellite when it is interrogated. The instrument gathers information very rapidly so the burst transmission only results in about a thirty to one time compression. We were planning on the satellite being in range for an average of thirty eight seconds. We would have been able to transmit about eleven hundred seconds worth of results. Now it sounds like we are down to half of that. Even so, we have a satellite in the vicinity about every ninety minutes so we can get roughly nine minutes worth of data on every pass. We presume that the instrument will not be operated around the clock. There is some time involved in sample preparation etc. We think they will generate no more than five hours a day worth of results. That is three hundred minutes. We can gather about half that. It should be enough to figure out what they are analyzing. If it isn't we might consider placing a relay station nearby. We could pick up a very weak signal if we were within fifty meters or so I think. There would be no problem sending it skyward from the relay station."

John can see it coming but he asks anyhow.

"How big is something like that going to be?"

"We could probably get by with something a foot and one half long by six inches in diameter which would include a battery and a solar cell."

"How to you get it there?"

Randy proceeds to quote from Tom Lehrer's song. "Once the rockets go up who cares where they come down, that's not my department says Werner Von Braun."

"So you want Henry to put it there?"

"Henry understands the gravity of the situation. What say you Hank?"

"I think a lot of people in the neighborhood know what George and I look like. This operation might have a better chance of going undiscovered if we sent someone else. What about sending some sort of probe like we did at Belen?"

They knock this around a little. Henry is the best man for the job – he has been there twice. Henry is thinking that his new roommate might not be overjoyed at him going on this adventure but she knows what kind of work he does and this goes with the territory. John is wondering whether his new roommate speaks Spanish. No one would expect a man and woman team.

"Okay. I presume that you can have the device and a vehicle waiting for us in Santiago. It is a two day drive to Pelicura. This time of the year we might do better, there won't be any snow."

A little bit later John and Henry are playing backgammon at lunchtime.

"Does Christina speak Spanish?"

"I think she knows a little probably not much more than me. Are you thinking what I think you are thinking?"

"Yes, if it were okay with her."

"She might. We can talk about it tonight. Better yet, why don't you come down and have a drink with us this afternoon and you can ask her."

"On second thought Henry, maybe this is not such a good idea. The bad guys don't know anything about you and Christina. I sure as Hell don't want a repeat of that Babs thing, you know that."

"Me neither. Come on down and have a drink. We can talk about it."

Henry does have the foresight to give Christina a 'heads up' that John is coming by for a drink.

Rancho Don Martinez
Pelicura, Argentina
March 1, 1994 Tuesday 0800

The Wardnor spectrometer arrived last week – more than a month late. Benno Weber came out to the ranch three times and helped Prof. Kessler get the thing up and running. Kessler used his new toy all weekend and is very excited with the first results. The machine can resolve elemental composition differences on a very small scale. For the first time he has been able to quantitatively determine the elemental composition of the Plodamax in the immediate vicinity of the fibrils. It seems that there are very small quantities of Germanium and Silicon present in the sample Basima gave him. These almost certainly are in the fibrils as opposed to in the C-4. He has designed an experiment to make that distinction. Unfortunately there is a lot of noise in the data and the analysis technique in and of itself alters the material. He will have to examine several thousand fibrils to quantitatively establish the amount of Germanium and Selenium that is in the C-4 next to the hollow fibril as opposed to inside the fibril wall. He already knows that there is more Selenium in the Plodamax fibrils than the fibrils from FPI but there also seems to be Selenium in the C-4 that is in the Plodamax.

Benno met Siegfried at the Bahia Blanca airport. They arrived at the ranch late morning.

"Good morning Siegfried. I'm glad you came so soon after we got this thing running. I already have a problem which I think you will know how to solve better than I do."

Aldrich goes on to explain the problem as he sees it in the light of the brand new results. Siegfried keeps

thinking about his theory that the generation of the pho-
tolinos is similar to piezo-electric generation of elec-
trons. He knows that it is possible to generate electrons
by rapidly crushing Selenium. Now it appears that the
FPI fibrils do not have nearly as much Selenium as the
fibrils in the Plodamax. He has studied Kessler's and
Schroeder's results. It is beginning to look like some
Selenium was put into the Plodamax in the C-4 phase
simply to confuse anyone trying to duplicate the material.

"Aldrich, I think that it might not be necessary to do a large number of micro-analyses. As I understand it you can separate the C-4 from the fibrils in the Plodamax."

"Yes. I have done that and I find that there is some Selenium in both fractions. The problem s that I don't know if any of the Selenium in the C-4 fraction is material that was extracted from the inside or the outside of the fibrils."

"Do you know of any manufacturer of C-4 or Hexogen that puts Selenium into it?"

"Not that I know of Siegfried."

Siegfried has another flashback.

"Did you ever hear of Fritz Schroeder?"

Kessler wonders how Siegfried could possibly know Schroeder.

"Yes but he was assassinated three years ago. How do know of him Siegfried?"

"I don't know but his name popped into my head. It is somehow associated with Arsenic. You saw that there was a fairly sizable Arsenic peak in the Plodamax."

"Yes, I did. I saw Fritz's notes. He also noticed that there was arsenic in the Plodamax."

"Arsenic is a decay product of Se^{75}. Do you know how old this sample you are working with is?"

"I am not sure Siegfried."

They talk about this a little while and then out of the blue Siegfried says.

"Did you ever hear of a Siegfried Runkel?"

This takes Aldrich by complete surprise. He knows that the Runkels have a large demolition company and that they supplied some of the Hexogen that he worked with in Saudi Arabia – but how does Siegfried know this? It is inconceivable that he ever met either one of these people.

"I have a passing acquaintance with Heinz Runkel. He owns the largest demolition company in Germany. How do you know that name?"

"I don't know Aldrich, I just do."

"I noticed there was a small Iodine peak as well. Do you have the manual for the machine handy?"

Aldrich goes to the file cabinet and produces the manual. Siegfried quickly finds the table of isotopes. There is an isotope of Tellurium which is very close in atomic mass to Iodine but the instrument can easily resolve this slight difference. That is definitely Iodine in the sample.

"Siegfried, I saw mention of Iodine in Fritz's notes. He was speculating that the fibrils had some sort of low temperature melting glass in them."

They go around about the distribution of the Selenium some more but it is an academic discussion until they know how to make the hollow fibrils. Finally, Aldrich makes a suggestion.

"There might be something in the patent literature. We could search for any and all FPI patents and see if anything useful is there."

Oskar Siegfried and Basima are talking about the negative results of the patent search.

"How old is this FPI company Basima?"

"I think it is about twenty years old."

"Do you know if they always had the same name?"

"That is an interesting question Oskar. I don't know the answer but I do know that I heard a lot of talk about some senior scientist who passed away unexpectedly just before my first visit there. I remember his name distinctly. It was Winfred Wyatt Wilson. It sounded like he had been there since day one. We could try a search by author and see what shows up."

The telephone system in Zarate does not support internet connections very well. They call the TASA office and ask Hector to do the search. An hour later he has some positive results. He is on the speaker phone.

"There are a number of patents by this man. They have to do with some sort of carbon nanotube manufacturing – I don't know what I am looking at but I can fax these patents to you right now."

While he has his secretary send this material he continues.

"His address at the time these patents were applied for was in North Reading, Massachusetts if that is any use to you."

"That is useful Hector. North Reading is less than thirty kilometers from the FPI plant in Peabody. Now that you are saying it I remember pictures on the conference room wall of Doctor Wilson standing in front of FPI's previous headquarters which was in Woburn."

Siegfried scans the patents and sees immediately that this is what they are looking for. He has some knowledge of the semiconductor industry. Apparently FPI was cutting circular grooves in Silicon wafers and then growing cylinders of Selenium out of them.

"There is some tricky chemistry involved. He will have to talk to Aldrich about this. The patents are all fifteen to twenty years old. The equipment they say they used in these patents is all obsolete. We should not have too much difficulty finding suitable used equipment. This stuff is so old that we will probably have to look in Asia."

Now Siegfried is remembering that there was a small amount of Arsenic in the Plodamax sample that Aldrich examined. There was no Arsenic in the FPI fibrils and no Arsenic in the Plodamax that Aldrich made with the FPI fibrils and the German hexogen. He remembers Aldrich said that sometimes different isotopes of some elements had different crystal growing 'habits'. He is wondering whether there was any Selenium[75] in the Plodamax and whether it was needed to grow the Selenium tubes. He just said it! Selenium tubes! Yes, that is how they are doing it. They are growing Selenium tubes up off the surface of some substrate, probably Silicon and then they are coating them with a low temperature melting glass.

END OF PART I

John and Henry are listening to Randy Biggs.

"This is the damnedest thing. They got the machine up last Saturday as we discussed Tuesday. They used it about five hours a day Saturday, Sunday and Monday and now they haven't used it since."

"Maybe it broke down."

"I don't think so. It took a little while to piece together and analyze the transmissions. Now we know that they looked at some Plodamax that was made at Granite State Explosives. They also looked at some FPI fibrils. The same kind we use in the Plodamax. They also looked at something that had FPI fibrils and we think Hexogen made in Germany. I think they found out what they needed to know. This instrument is way ahead of anything else available. It is like you are looking for something in a dark room and suddenly a light comes on.

Yesterday I found out that someone was searching the patent files of W.W. Wilson. He is the guy who invented the process that FPI has to make the fibrils. If Siegfried is as smart as he appears to be he will figure this out in short order. I talked with Guenther last night. He says it will be difficult to stop them from acquiring the wherewithal to make the fibrils. The equipment Wilson used is obsolete by today's standards but you can still find it in used equipment houses."

"When did Wilson invent this stuff?"

"Late seventies."

"So there is no need for Henry to make another trip to Argentina."

"Yes, it appears to be no longer necessary to worry about getting one hundred percent of the information from the Wardnor machine. We have to go about this differently. It will take them some time to figure out the rest of the process."

Micro Electrónica Avanzada
Avenida Eva Peron 125
San Rafael, Buenos Aires Argentina
May 23, 1994 Monday

Hector and Siegfried are giving Aldrich Basima and Oskar a tour of the newly constructed MEA manufacturing facility where they hope to produce selenium microtubes. It is located in an industrial park less than ten kilometers from Ezeiza. The infrastructure of technicians and vendors they need to produce the sub-micron sized Selenium tubes was not to be found around Bahia Blanca. Furthermore, Siegfried did not want to make the commute from Rancho de Mil Robles to Pelicura every week or so. They managed to obtain all the photolithography equipment they needed on the used market in Korea. They also purchased two used eight meter by twelve meter clean rooms in Sao Paulo. These have been tied together to form one eight meter by twenty four meter room. Hector Alvarez did an excellent job of keeping the construction on schedule. Siegfried obtained a license to handle Se[75] as well as making arrangements to purchase their modest needs from the government isotope production facility nearby. They have all donned 'bunny' suits and just entered the clean room through the only air lock.

"This equipment looks new Siegfried."

"It was refurbished by the dealer we bought it from Oskar. It is approximately ten years old and totally obsolete as far as the circuit manufacturers are concerned but it will be quite suitable for our purposes."

They walk down the length of the clean room. Following the photolithography equipment there is a

Perkin-Elmer sputtering machine which Siegfried has chosen for building up the Selenium tubes. From there the material will go through several other vapor deposition steps to build up a layer of low temperature melting glass around the Selenium.

"We hope to be able to produce approximately one hundred grams of fibrils per day once we get everything working properly."

They turn around and walk back the length of the room and exit through the air lock they came in by. Once into the conference room Hector continues.

"We have provisions to operate the clean room in an Argon atmosphere if we so desire. You probably noticed that we have to pass the product from one stage to the next by hand. Automating these transfers through appropriate automated transfer locks was going to take two months longer to build and might have attracted some attention to us. In principle we are just trying to make micro Selenium rectifiers. It is a convenient cover story and readily explains all the equipment we ordered. We have already lined up a source of Se^{75} which we can use as seed material – again, using the same cover story."

It is nearly noon and Aldrich is catching a 1300 flight back to Bahia Blanca. They drive him to the airport and then proceed to La Ostra Sonriendo for lunch. After lunch Hector heads for the TASA office while Siegfried, Oskar and Basima go to her home. Siegfried has spent most of the past two months getting the fibril facility up. Now he is ready to address his concerns about Baumgartner. He is anxious to talk about thought transference.

"Basima, you said you had a passing acquaintance with hypnosis."

"A little."

"It continues to bother me about the way Baumgartner was not in the least interested in using hypnosis to see if we could find out exactly which of Karl's thoughts have been transferred to me."

"I have been thinking about that also Siegfried. If in fact all of Karl's thoughts and experiences have been transferred to you, you may subconscious y know many things about everyone who Karl knew. Conceivably you know things about Baumgartner that he coes not want you to know. You know from Karl's letter to you that Baumgartner was party to the killing of several hundred prisoners during the 1930's and 1940's. These killings were clearly war crimes which could have resulted in Baumgartner's trial and execution. Instead, he continued on at Heidelberg like nothing had ever happened."

"Do you think you could hypnotize me and see what I may know about this?"

"I can try Siegfried. I have given the matter some thought since you first broached the subject and talked to one of my former professors who is retired. She said that Dr. Braid's technique is as good as any. This is very simple and we will soon know if you are susceptible to hypnosis – at least with my clumsy efforts. If you are not then, and if you are intensely interested, we would have to get some outside party who may have other techniques that I don't know. I am sure you will want to have Oskar present in any event."

"Of course."

"When would you like to try?"

"Now, if that is okay with you."

They go inside to her living room. She draws the curtains so that the room is fairly dark. She has Siegfried lay on one of the couches and Oskar brings her a dining room chair to sit on next to the couch. Basima returns from her den with a highly polished six sided pencil and a small reading lamp. Oskar plugs the lamp into a nearby outlet and places it on the end table behind Siegfried's head. She proceeds to twist the pencil back and forth with the reflection off the sides hitting Siegfried in the eyes. She slowly works the pencil back toward his forehead until Siegfried barely can see the pencil. His eyes flutter and then they close.

"Can you hear me Siegfried?"

"Yes Basima."

"Do you remember how you got here?"

"No."

"Do you remember Professor Baumgartner?"

"Yes."

"Do you remember any occasion when Professor Baumgartner and Doctor Eberhardt were together in Heidelberg?"

"Yes."

"What do you remember?"

There ensues what might be described as a large data dump. It is somewhat disjoint but the gist of it is he sees himself as Karl Eberhardt. He and Wilfried (Baumgartner) both have full heads of dark brown hair. They are at a concert. They have two blondes accompanying them. The blondes are half their age but they seem very intent on being very friendly. They leave the concert early and go to Baumgartner's apartment. He gives the girls a little more of the drug he administers before he does the experiments in his lab and then they have a sex orgy until early morning. He and his chauffer drive the girls back to their apartments and then go to his apartment. The next day he goes to Wilfried's laboratory. The girls are there.

"What were the girls' names?"

"All the female subjects were called Gertrude. After he gave us each a shot of something I remember Wilfried was making fun of me. He said the only women I could inseminate with my knowledge were the ones I inseminated the old fashioned way. Then I fell asleep."

She probes around this area for a while. It seems that the psychoactive drug that Baumgartner has zeroed in on as being most effective in aiding thought transference is also a powerful aphrodisiac for women. As the 'conversation' continues Siegfried starts talking more and more in the first person as if he is Karl Eberhardt.

"Wilfried you must find something else. You killed your mistress with the same dose that you are using on your subjects in the EEG experiments. I had to talk to people I do not wish to talk to, to get you out of that mess."

Then his voice changes. He sounds much older.

"You did a good job on that movie Wilhelm. I am sure that Leni will not be offended."

Oskar quietly whispers in Basima's ear

"Those are the exact words Karl used at the send off party for U-1241."

Suddenly he sits up and is awake, perhaps returned to the present would be more descriptive.

"What happened?"

"You were talking in the first person as Karl. You were talking about you and Wilfried having sex with some of the subjects."

"What subjects?"

"The ones Professor Baumgartner is doing his experiments on."

"Do you know the time frame?"

"No."

"You became quite agitated about having to use your influence to get Wilfried out of some mess he created by over dosing his mistress. Then you changed the subject and sounded much older. You were saying something to Wilhelm about some kind of send off party for U-1241 and then you woke up."

"Do you think you could do this again now?"

"I think that is enough for today Siegfried. You were under hypnosis for nearly two hours. It can be very tiring. I also think that we should hold the next session at your ranch."

122

It is one year to the day since New York was bombed. The final tally stands at 328,765 dead. Property damage is estimated at three hundred billion dollars. After months of arguing it was decided to simply level everything south of Wall Street and cover it over with a few feet of dirt. This has been accomplished and a park commemorating the disaster is nearly completely planted and landscaped. The population of New York City has declined to under seven million for the first time since the Great Depression. Commerce came to a complete halt for nearly four months. There was simply no way to get in and out of Manhattan except by surface transport. Many large corporations have fled to New Jersey or abandoned the Greater Metropolitan Area entirely.

The US Army Corps of Engineers was put in charge of restoring the subway system. One month after the event the IRT tunnel on the Manhattan side was plugged. First they dumped several thousand cubic yards of crushed stone into the wound. This formed a relatively stable surface to pour concrete against. Then they pumped some three thousand cubic yards of concrete down a Tremie pipe extending from the surface on the Manhattan side to the wound. This filled the part of the tunnel beneath the East River adjacent to the crushed stone to a depth of twenty feet or so. Once communication with the harbor seawater was severed the pump-out process proceeded. It was deemed highly unsafe to even try using the high voltage transmission lines in the tunnels under Manhattan to power the multi-thousand horsepower *centrifugal pumps. The Corps brought in three trailer mounted ten megawatt gas turbine powered four thousand volt generators. These were hitched directly to the pump motors. The water level was down to nuisance level in the tunnels one week later. Something of the order of six billion gallons were pumped from the subway tunnels back into New York harbor. Various environmental groups vigorously protested polluting the harbor with this water but they couldn't find a judge who would issue a restraining order to stop it. Most of the seawater was just plain New York Harbor water. It was estimated that only a few million gallons were initially heavily contaminated with the Sodium^{24} isotope. This isotope is relatively short lived such that in the two months that elapsed before the tunnel was plugged this radiation was gone. Very little Co^{60} got into the subway tunnels. Almost all of that radiation was pumped out with the water. The radiation level fell to roughly eight times normal US background levels. This was not commendable but was deemed acceptable for brief exposure during the average subway ride. Approximately one sixth of the subway system rolling stock was caught in the flood. Several thousand victims' mortal remains were painstakingly identified and returned to next of kin. The contaminated subway cars were simply loaded onto barges and dumped one hundred miles offshore provoking more howls of protest from the environmental lobby. It was a Herculean task and the Corps of Engineers got that part of it done in four months. Accident investigators determined that the damage to the subway system could have been accomplished with conventional explosives placed so that they breeched any of the tunnels under the water surrounding Manhattan Island. The Corps installed some enormous knife gate valves on the Manhattan side of the subway tunnels coming from Brooklyn, Jersey, the Bronx and Queens to greatly mitigate the effects of any* *similar attack in the future. Almost all the wire in the tunnels had to be replaced. The rails survived submersion surprisingly well. On Christmas Day Mayor Robinson rode the first train to Times Square.*

John and Henry are playing backgammon when Linda walks into John's office and turns the television on. It looks like they are watching the view from a traffic helicopter but it is not traffic. There is a black speedboat racing north. They watch in rapt fascination as the boat goes under the Verrazano Narrows Bridge. The helicopter reporter is saying it must be doing nearly eighty miles an hour. About three quarters of a mile north of the bridge, the boat vanishes in a tremendous explosion. Shortly thereafter the picture shakes violently as the shock wave slams into the helicopter. Then the picture vanishes. Soon, the local station returns to its newscast.

"Incredible. It is our understanding that an Army Apache helicopter just destroyed that speedboat you saw with a Hellfire missile. We believe that our sister station's traffic reporter Brian Smith and his helicopter were knocked out of the sky by the blast. Ever since the bombing of New York there has been constant patrolling of the harbor by helicopters. I can not imagine what the person driving the boat was thinking."

Henry and John are shaking their heads.

"Do you think that was another of these V-1500s?"

"I am more inclined to think it was a copycat terrorist bunch. Those guys that succeeded last year would certainly not be doing this in the middle of the day. This is the same sort of nonsense that goes on in Karachi. This has all the hallmarks of some suicide bombers."

They knock this around briefly. Now it seems like every station has gotten hold of this bit of video and the talking heads are all talking. It does not escape notice that this is the first anniversary of the bombing. The talking heads are speculating about who in the Middle East may be responsible. There have been several instances in the past few months where numerous jihadists have been killed by US forces and the Israelis killed thirty seven Palestinians in the Gaza Strip a few months ago. Then speculation turns to the Iranians who are still claiming that the Israelis used American thermonuclear weapons in an unprovoked attack that killed half a million of their people. They turn it off. Henry comments.

"They will probably give more air time to the reporter's unfortunate demise than to the terrorist act itself. When you get right down to it, the only people who were really concerned about the bombing of New York were the New Yorkers. That is the same thing that happened over there in Iran. No one cared except the Iranians."

Rancho de Mil Robles

San Pablo de Arno, Argentina

May 26, 1994 Thursday

After Basima found out that this 'party' Siegfried referred to took place only one year ago and that Oskar actually attended this party, she thought that it might be useful to hold the next hypnosis session in the exact environment where the party took place. The familiar surroundings might help Siegfried 'remember' things more clearly. Oskar decided to bring his father's Kapitän Zur See uniform. They came to the ranch yesterday and Oskar showed her the film Wilhelm had prepared. As far as he knows, Siegfried doesn't know anything about this party. Whatever he does know must have been put into his brain by the thought transference sessions he had with Karl. They discuss whether there would be any purpose in trying to show Siegfried the movie when he is under hypnosis. Basima thinks there is a good chance he might wake up if they did that.

"We might be able to not wake him Basima if there was no sound. I remember Karl whispering something in Wilhelm's ear during the movie. We might find out that Siegfried notices the same thing."

Oskar goes on to explain that Wilhelm had the original film on video tape. She watches "Triumph des Willens" in its entirety in the hope that she will learn something of the ambience of Nazi Germany when Eberhardt was a young man. They set up the ranch house dining room with the two tables arranged the same way as they were at the send-off party complete with tablecloths and place settings.

The hypnosis session starts in the den. Basima is able to get Siegfried to stand up and walk into the dining room. He walks to the chair where Karl sat without any further prompting. Oskar has his father's uniform on when he sits down one seat away on Siegfried's left. Siegfried starts talking about what a great job Wilhelm's people have done preparing the boat. After a while, they draw the heavy curtains and darken the room. They roll the film Wilhelm prepared. When the film is showing a Hitler Youth battalion, Siegfried whispers to his left.

"You didn't have any grey hair then Wilhelm."

As the film ends, he stands up and is softly singing "Deutschland Über Alles".

Oskar also stands. When Siegfried stops singing he picks up his wine glass. Oskar does the same. They toast the success of the mission then Siegfried sits down. He sits silently for a minute then he excuses himself to go to the bathroom. After he returns to the den and sits down in the chair he was in not so long ago.

"It has been a long time Wilhelm."

There is a pause when Wilhelm must have been speaking.

"Your people did well. I think there is a good chance we will succeed."

He closes his eyes. After a few minutes Basima speaks softly.

"Ziggy, it is time to wake up."

He wakes up. They talk about the session. He says that he thinks he was singing for a while. He thinks he saw his grandfather when he was very young. Then he suddenly exclaims.

"My grandfather had blond hair. My father had dark hair. Why do I have blond hair? I thought that blond hair was a recessive gene."

Nobody has any answers to that question.

This is the end of the fifth hypnosis session for Siegfried. Unlike the first session when he snapped awake suddenly at the end, for the past four he has just stopped talking and apparently gone to sleep. Sometimes he hummed a few bars of the Horst Wessel song while he appeared to be sleeping. Perhaps thirty to forty minutes later, he had a facial tic and awakened shortly thereafter. He has had the same bad dream before he awakened twice.

After the first session, Basima purchased a tape recorder. Siegfried doesn't seem to have any memory of the sessions and he does not want to hear the recordings or be told what he said. When under hypnosis he continues to talk as Karl Eberhardt in the first person. As best they can piece together, Siegfried 'remembers' most of Karl Eberhardt's life from the time he was a teenager in the 1920's up until his last session in Baumgartner's lab in the summer of 1993. They find out that the Siegfried's friend Heidi has been 'electroencephalographically educated' (EEE) much as his mother was. Apparently Baumgartner and Eberhardt were still trying to produce 'supermen' along the lines laid out by Heinrich Himmler sixty years ago. They were expecting to breed Siegfried and Heidi to produce an even more impressive specimen than Siegfried is already. They can sense from what Siegfried is saying that Eberhardt had some conflicts with Baumgartner.

Basima is very interested in this recurring dream. Siegfried dreams that he was working on his dissertation at CERN when he was drugged. But that is all he remembers. There is no apparent basis in fact for this dream since all the sessions where he was drugged were in Heidelberg.

Twice Siegfried has been angry with Professor Baumgartner after the session and twice he has expressed appreciation for the EEE. He doesn't say anything while under hypnosis but when he has awakened angry with Baumgartner he has also complained about headaches. He also thinks that Baumgartner recorded both his and Karl's brainwaves during their mutual sessions and he wants these recordings. He wants to find out exactly what Baumgartner is doing. Basima reminds him of the large list of people that Eberhardt left on the encoded floppy. She has printed a copy of this list. It is separated by country. There are many names in Germany along with their estimated birthdays as best Karl knew when he made the list. Amongst these names are Schroeder, Fassbinder, Kessler and Runkel. Basima has heard some of these names from Siegfried's voice during the hypnosis sessions. She wants Siegfried to listen to his third session but he again does not want to do that. He says he thinks he is in some kind of feedback loop within himself during these sessions almost like he has done this before. He is afraid replaying these sessions will further exacerbate this feedback problem. When they decide there is no more to be learned from these sessions and there will be no more sessions he will then be glad to listen to the recordings.

This is not all exactly clear to Basima or Oskar but they acquiesce. Siegfried will need some help to get these supposed recordings from Baumgartner. Kessler also taught at Heidelberg. He is the one most likely to know how to get at Baumgartner but he is not going back to Germany. The only one they know anything at all about is Heinz Runkel. Basima explains how Werner Runkel was part of their organization that successfully mounted two attacks on the United States. He was either killed or captured by the Americans a year ago. It is prudent to assume he was captured and has told the Americans everything he knows. Heinz Runkel was informed of his son's presumed capture last year. He might know someone who could help with Baumgartner. Basima calls Heinz Runkel.

"Hello, Herr Runkel, this is Basima Karim calling."

Kurt Runkel answers the phone. Although he has never met Basima he knows that she is closely associated with Prince Rashid and that his father was receiving a handsome consulting fee from the Prince supposedly for his expertise in the field of explosives. These payments have continued uninterrupted for the past two years.

"Hello Fraulein Karim. You must be looking for my father. I regret to inform you that he passed away two weeks ago. I am Kurt Runkel. Have you heard anything more about my brother?"

"I am sorry about your father. We have not heard anything more about Werner. We were hoping he might help us with a certain problem we have."

"Perhaps I can help you."

"Do you know anyone at Heidelberg University?"

"No, but my uncle Ernst Beckenbauer might. He went there. He is an inspector in the Frankfurt Police."

This is a huge coincidence. During the second session, Siegfried, speaking in the first person as Karl Eberhardt, repeatedly mentioned a Freddie Beckenbauer. She is trying to remember the details but will have to refer to the recording of the session.

"I have heard that name before. One moment please."

She goes to her desk and picks up the list of names that Karl left. She finds a Wilfried Beckenbauer with the annotation '9/84 deceased'.

"Was your uncle's father named Wilfried?"

"I am not sure. Let me ask my mother."

He returns shortly.

"Yes, she says his name was Wilfried Friedrich Beckenbauer."

This is very interesting.

"Could you ask your mother whether he had a nickname?"

"She said that everyone called him Freddie."

"Did you ever meet Karl Eberhardt?"

"Oh, yes several times. He visited my uncle's home for a family get together around Christmas."

"You are related to Karl Eberhardt?"

"No, he is not a blood relation. I am distantly related by marriage. I think he was my grand uncle's brother in law. I do know that he was close to my grand uncle. They used to talk about the war and their youths in the 1930's."

She needs to find out more about the relationship between Eberhardt and Beckenbauer. Perhaps this will lead to some way to get at Baumgartner. Siegfried is adamant that Baumgartner has recordings of his and Eberhardt's brain waves somewhere.

"Thank you Kurt. We would like to pursue this matter further. As you know your father had a consulting arrangement with us. We would like to continue this with you. Your uncle has helped us in the past. He may be able to help us again. Would you be so good as to ask him if he knows Professor Baumgartner?"

"I know he does. Baumgartner's name came up fairly often in these discussions at my uncle's home. My uncle does not have any children. Although no one ever came right out and said it, I got the impression that Eberhardt and my grand uncle thought that Baumgartner was somehow responsible for my aunt not hav ng children. Let me ask my mother. This might take a while. Do you want to have me call you back?"

Basima is not about to give out any phone numbers in Argentina. She has had this phone call patched through the SASC office in Frankfurt. She gives Kurt this phone number but says she will call back in half an hour if that is okay with him.

Later that afternoon

Basima called Kurt Runkel back about 1800 local time. It is 2200 in Germany.

"My mother has nothing good to say about Wilfried Baumgartner. It seems that he did some kind of experiment on her sister which they believe made her sterile. She knows that they were big into drugs to cure epilepsy at Heidelberg. There was a scandal over some of these because they caused sterility in several people they were administered to. She admitted that the drug did stop the frequent grand mal seizures her sister suffered."

"Did she say when this was going on?"

Kurt must have put his hand over the phone but Basima still easily hears him shout.

"Mutter wann war das?"

"She says it was late sixties."

"Thank you and please thank your mother for me."

Grundenberg Friedhof
Peterstal, Germany
June 7, 1994 Tuesday afternoon

The grieving relatives of Gerwald Eiffel have listened to the words of their pastor. Herr Eiffel's grave is a mere five meters from Herr Schroeder's grave. The Eiffels and the Schroeders are related by marriage. Ferdinand Eiffel has been standing next to or on Fritz Schroeder's grave listening to the homily. He notices the ground here is slightly higher than the surroundings. This strikes him as somewhat unusual. Fritz was buried here three years ago. That is plenty of time for the dirt to have settled. The grass he is standing on is higher not lower than the surroundings. Then he is remembering that he buried his uncle in a copper casket. Could it possibly be that someone dug him up and stole the copper? He says something to his brother next to him. They agree that the land is higher over Fritz's grave. Shortly after the ceremony they contact the police chief and he agrees that they should take a look at this. Late that afternoon, they dig Fritz up again. It is immediately obvious that the casket was tampered with and when they open it they see that Fritz has a few more holes in him. The police chief opines that someone took samples of Fritz for DNA identification purposes.

Wilfried is looking through the Rhein Neckar Zeitung. There in the section of local news from the surrounding villages he sees that someone tampered with Fritz Schroeder's grave. The police chief of Peterstal says it looks to him like someone wanted some DNA samples from Professor Schroeder. He starts thinking back to that night twenty four years ago before 'Gertrude Heidelberg' left for Argentina. He and Karl arranged for Fritz Schroeder to inseminate her the old fashioned way at the time of her optimum fertility. She was hustled off to Argentina and was in bed with Gerbert Bachmeier two days later. Wilhelm found a beautiful woman a few years after he arrived in Argentina. She was quite the looker but more or less an airhead. Not surprisingly Gerbert wasn't the sharpest knife in the draw so Wilhelm didn't think he would be of any use in developing supermen. They chemically sterilized him a few months before his new bride was to arrive from Germany. Wilhelm checked this by getting a sperm count from some semen in the hooker he provided for his son on his birthday.

Wilhelm is dead probably at the hands of the Americans. Presumably Gerbert is alive and in the hands of the Americans. If they are the ones who disturbed Fritz's casket, they will find out that Gerbert is not Wilhelm's son. If they have any DNA samples from Siegfried they will find out that he is Fritz's son. This is big trouble. He goes down into his cellar and opens the safe where he keeps the records of the 'Gertrudes'. All is in order. He resets the auto-destruct mechanism and closes the safe. If someone attempts to tamper with this safe, the three hundred grams of gunpowder inside will be ignited and promptly incinerate the paper inside the safe. He goes back upstairs and checks his filing cabinets. The wooden cabinet where he kept his notes from the wartime research is a bit sticky opening. He manages to get the bottom drawer out and sees that a wheel has come loose. This happens from time to time.

He doesn't think much about that. He screws it back on and closes the cabinet. Then he notices that the mechanical counter that indicates how many times the file cabinet has been opened is showing 709. That is odd. He could have sworn that the last time he opened it was showing 707. He remembers it was the same as the airplane. He opens it again and starts looking through the papers. He notices that the papers in many of the folders are not carefully aligned. He has always been quite meticulous about this. Someone has been in this cabinet in the past year.

He has a rush of terrifying thoughts. There is ample evidence of his war crimes in this file cabinet. If this is the work of the Americans someone will knock on his door soon and he will spend the rest of life in prison. Suppose Siegfried is the one behind the grave robbing and the disturbance of his papers. Presumably he has photographs of the contents of this file cabinet. He will have found out how many people we killed or disabled with migraines during the research. He is already showing some epileptic symptoms. He will figure out how that happened. It is good that Karl is dead, if he found out that the experiments hurt Siegfried he would surely kill me. I wonder if he transferred the knowledge about Siegfried's lineage to Siegfried. Why is Siegfried so interested in knowing what ever he can find out that he wanted me to hypnotize him? That girl, Karl knew all about Heidi. It is readily conceivable that Siegfried knows that she is to be bred to him to produce supermen – she might know this as well. We know she learned a great deal about what was in Karl's mind during their sessions. Depending how well Karl was able to focus on what we were trying to do to increase her intelligence she may or may not know much about what Karl knew about me. On the other hand, I have every reason to believe that he tried to teach Siegfried everything he knew and probably everything he ever experienced. Karl would often repeat the words of Von Moltke, "Fools learn by their own experience, I learn by the experiences of fools." I wonder if this new machine I have can produce movies from the recordings I have of the sessions with Karl and Siegfried and Karl and Heidi and I can figure out what they were thinking....

DCAC Office
Woburn, Massachusetts
June 24, 1994 Friday

Henry and Fred are in John's office. They are having a conference call with Mitch and Guenther. They received a huge gift of information from Baumgartner. He took the recordings he made with Eberhardt and Siegfried and Eberhardt and Heidi and fed them into the CCX-1. He needed some advice from Randy about how exactly to go about this which Randy was glad to give him. Copies of these recordings now reside in computers in Germantown Tennessee and Los Alamos New Mexico. Randy sent back some not so well massaged 'movies' of these recordings so that Baumgartner didn't have the best picture of what he had. On the other hand, Baumgartner did not send the traces from the source but rather the traces after these traces were massaged by the black box that Philips built. These are qualitatively similar to the traces that have been fed to the CCX-1 but there are some differences. Guenther has had some very high powered statistics people looking very hard at these 'movies'. They have discovered that the 'carrier' frequency goes through a fixed sequence during the sessions involving Karl Eberhardt as the 'source' and Siegfried Bachmeier as the 'subject' and another different fixed sequence when it is Eberhardt and Heidi. One of the statisticians is an accomplished piano player with 'perfect pitch'. He can listen to a concert and go home and play it on his piano. Somehow he discerns that the variation in the carrier frequency is the same as the notes in the first few bars of the Horst Wessel song when Siegfried is the subject. Having been duly alerted as to what to look for, they find that the carrier frequency sequence with Heidi is the same as the first few bars of Kling, Glöckchen (Ring, Little Bell).

They figured out the dates the recordings were made. Most of these recordings show an exceptionally high total synapse firing rate. They know that the 'source' has extraordinary intelligence. They determine that all these recordings on disc were made in the 1988 to 1993 time frame. The last one is approximately one year ago. There have not been any since. Siegfried was only at Heidelberg for three years and left near the end of last August. He came back once in December. They know he has a girlfriend there. They discover that Heidi Freud has been at Heidelberg since 1987 when she entered as an undergraduate. Randy and Fred both remember her from their trip to Heidelberg. She was smart as a whip and very good looking. Randy notes that she would give his secretary Rhonda a run for her money in that department.

Guenther had a colleague at Los Alamos who was a junior level nuclear physicist working in Cologne the last two years of the war. Gregor Boehm was snapped up by the Americans and brought to the US in late 1945. He was sent to Los Alamos where he worked for five years. Then he was sent to Princeton to finish his Doctoral work. He then worked at Los Alamos until he retired in 1984. His native language is German. Guenther explained enough of the present situation to him so that when he had an EEG he was able to think the kinds of thoughts and use the kind of words which they think Karl Eberhardt might have used in Baumgartner's EEE process. He spoke the words before he thought the words so they have the sound recordings as well as the EEGs. Guenther and Randy have been having their computers chew on this a while. They have identified the brain electrical activity associated with nearly five hundred German words that are closely related to nuclear physics. It was a prodigious task which could only be done by people who knew what they were doing and had vast computational power at their disposal.

They have also identified the brain wave patterns associated with the pronunciation of 'Siegfried' and 'Heidi'. Baumgartner's old files showed that he consistently used various psychoactive drugs on the subjects to enhance the total synapse firing rate and thus speed up the information transfer. They have every reason to believe that he did that during the sessions with Siegfried and Heidi.

They obtained some 'receptor helmets' like the ones they saw in Baumgartner's lab from a medical instrument manufacturer in Germany. They tried to transfer information from a 'source's' EEG to a 'subject' with no success. Then, Randy made a 'transmitter helmet' which was a mirror of the 'receptor helmet'. They have not had any luck with this either as far as they can tell. Baumgartner must have some other equipment they don't know about which he uses to implant information into the 'subject's' mind. They are also not using any drugs on the subjects.

At this point this is what they know. There were five joint sessions where Karl's brain wave patterns indicate that he was thinking about Siegfried Bachmeier and seven going back to 1987 where he was thinking about Heidi Freud. It is pretty clear that Eberhardt, Baumgartner and Wilhelm Bachmeier are intending to use Siegfried and Heidi as a 'breeding pair'. Fred notes that this should not be a hardship for Siegfried. There is some mention of Hans Obermeyer which reminds everyone that this same sort of thing might have been going on in Brazil as well as Argentina. The good news *is that Karl Eberhardt has not been in Baumgartner's lab since the end of May last year. That's the bad news too. Nobody has a clue where Eberhardt is.*

Henry prefers the direct approach.

"Why don't we just kidnap Heidi so Siegfried and Heidi don't do any breeding?"

This is not a totally bizarre suggestion. They knock it around a while. It would probably be easier to just chemically sterilize her. They aren't going to do anything like that without further discussion but Mitch agrees to have some of his folks in Germany at least gin up a plausible plan – something like a war game.

Baumgartner's Laboratory

Heidelberg University

June 27, 1994 Monday 0930

Siegfried, Manfred, Heidi and the locksmith are in the lab. The locksmith has a core extraction key for the series of locks in the doors of the Primate Research Center. He just pulled the core on Baumgartner's lab door, put in one of his own and opened the door. Since Heidi and Manfred were regular frequenters to this lab, nobody paid any attention.

It didn't take the locksmith more than a minute to get into the cabinet with the Philips recorder. The discs were labeled. It was easy. They put the discs that involved Siegfried and Heidi into Manfred's attaché case. Siegfried was looking at the CCX-1.

"Does anyone know anything about this contraption?"

Manny answers.

"They make these things in Memphis Tennessee."

"It is probably just a coincidence but there is another outfit in Memphis that makes very specialized very high speed data gathering systems. I think they build things for the US military or people who do research for the US military."

Then Heidi comments.

"I don't know Ziggy but the Prof was on the phone with the Cerebrionics people a couple of weeks ago asking them something about data display. It had something to do with Enos but I don't know exactly what. I think he had some discs of Enos' brain waves and wanted to know if he could generate 'movies' from the discs."

"Well, did he?"

"I don't know."

"Do the Cerebrionics people have any more of these machines anywhere else?"

Manfred answers this one.

"I chatted with the Sales Rep and his assistant about that when they were here the first time. They said this was the first one. They hoped to get one installed in at least one more university probably in the United States. The Prof wanted to buy a machine like the one Cerebrionics uses to enhance the raw data. They said that was a proprietary machine with very proprietary software and there was no plan to sell any of these. I might point out that when the 'movies' come back they appear to be in slow motion. Apparently, there is so much information coming from the brain of the source that one has to stretch the time axis by a factor of twenty five or so before just a blur appears on the screen."

For some reason or other Siegfried wants to look inside the CCX-1. This doesn't tax the locksmith's abilities much and he manages to get the thing open in about a minute. There isn't anything to see in there besides a bunch of circuitry. They close it up.

Manny says.

"Ziggy, what are you going to do about the transmitter?"

"What transmitter?"

"The gadget they put the subject's head in."

"I never saw this."

"That is very interesting. We use it all the time it isn't a secret. Baumgartner must have sedated you before your sessions with Eberhardt. I was never allowed in the lab during these sessions but I know we used to knock Enos out to keep him still during his sessions. I also know which drugs we used, mostly."

"Why did you add mostly, Manny?"

"The Prof was somewhat less than open about that aspect of the work. I think he might have had some stuff around that I didn't know about. We always used drugs whenever we were teaching Enos or treating any of the epileptics. I can only guess that only Baumgartner and Eberhardt were in the lab when they apparently conducted these sessions with either of you. I am sure they doped you up to some degree. The other thing which may be quite important is the sound track fed to the subject. When we were working with Enos, we usually played a constant note into both ears. I think it was middle C. Since I was not there when either of you were the subjects, I don't know what the Prof did in your cases"."

"How did he do that?"

"We put some earphones which were fed the music through two meters of plastic tubing so that there were no electrical disturbances from the earphones."

"Where is this stuff?"

"It is in the back room in a locked cabinet. I am sure Herr Doberman *(the locksmith)* will have no problem getting the cabinet open but the transmitter is kind of big. We will not be able to take it without raising quite a few eyebrows."

They go to the back room and sure enough, it is too big to leave with.

"Who made this thing?"

"I think some specialty medical instrument people did. I think Philips made the interface box. The guy who I think built the interface box has been here a few times fussing with it."

They close everything up and are just getting ready to leave when Professor Baumgartner enters the laboratory. This is not complete happenstance. When they opened the cabinet with the disks, an alarm went off in Baumgartner's study. His home is not far from the school and it doesn't take long for him to get to his lab.

"Good morning Siegfried and Heidi and Manny."

He does not know the locksmith but he can guess what is going on here.

"I would like a moment alone with you Siegfried."

The professor is usually not this abrupt. Siegfried has a few questions of his own. If the Prof wants to discuss this privately, it will be okay with him. They go into the Prof's office and shut the door.

"I see that you broke into my lab and the cabinet where your disks are kept. You could have just asked for them Siegfried."

The Prof is plenty angry but he is also plenty scared. Someone, hopefully not Siegfried et al, was in his files at home, now this. He can not have Siegfried as an enemy. He knows too much.

"I found out that you must have drugged me before every session. This morning is the first time that I saw the transmitter helmet."

"It was necessary to sedate the subject to achieve optimum results."

Siegfried is angry and this sounds like bullshit.

"I am talking about psychoactive drugs not sedatives."

"Yes, we did use some psychoactive drugs occasionally."

"I have had a number of headaches."

"That is an unfortunate side effect that we have had less than complete success in eliminating. I did the best I could to keep that from happening in your case.

You must know that you are Karl's and my hope for the future."

Siegfried has never heard it said this directly but now he sees. It looks like they did the best they could but they haven't got this thing worked out completely.

"I still get headaches."

"I can do something about this but I do not recommend this. The drug that will eliminate the headaches is somewhat addictive. Professor Schmidt has a few people working on a non-addictive alternate but they haven't got there yet.

Siegfried, what is done is done. I am sorry for these side effects but I have no one hundred percent safe cure for them at the moment. I also have some other problems. I think that the Israelis or possibly the Americans are trying to kill me. Some things that went on long ago are not accepted as legitimate research.

Out of the blue, he says Did Karl or your grandfather ever talk to you about this?"

Siegfried has some kind of subconscious inkling that there were numerous casualties involved in this EEE business especially before and during the War.

"No."

"Did you know that we did some research in Argentina long ago?"

"No."

"I never went there but I have some of the old reports."

"Why are you bringing this up Prof?"

"I am thinking that Argentina might be safer than Germany for me."

Siegfried processes this bit of information for a while. Manny says the Prof has a few tricks up his sleeve that he doesn't know about. He might have quite a few that no one knows about. I would be in a better position to find out all about this if the Prof were in Argentina rather than here in Heidelberg.

"Do you know anyone over there?"

"I met you grandfather twice long ago, and of course, I knew Karl quite well. Professor Hartmann has been to Brazil."

Why didn't he just say no?

"If you are serious about leaving Germany I can put you up for a while."

The Prof seizes on this somewhat tepid offer.

"Thank you. When are you going back?"

"Tomorrow night."

"I will tell Emil *(Professor Schmidt)* that I am going to Argentina for an extended period. He will understand."

They rejoin the others and tell Manny and Heidi that the Prof has agreed to come to Argentina and help them.

What they don't know is that the CCX-1 has recorded everything said in the lab (but not the conversation that took place in the Prof's office) and also noted that they opened the cabinets of both the CCX-1 and the Philips disc recorder. This information is already in the Memphis Targeting and Los Alamos computers.

Siegfried and Heidi are having lunch with Basima and Oskar. They have Prof Baumgartner in the Crown Plaza downtown. He will be joining them for dinner this evening. Siegfried must have filled Heidi in about Oskar's woman on the long flight back to Argentina. Basima apparently knows that Heidi has been electro-encephalographically educated and is extraordinarily intelligent. They are both very pretty and they hit if off well enough on this first meeting. The four of them are talking about the discs that they 'retrieved' from Baumgartner's lab.

Oskar knows a Doctor Antonio Renquist who is Chief at the Hospital Alemán. He has been in touch with him recently and arranged for a time when the hospital's EEG equipment is not being employed to produce paper traces of some of what is on the discs. Siegfried has figured out that they have images of the output of the Philips box as well as the input to the Philips box. He is more interested in what the output from the Philips box looks like. He also tells them that Baumgartner has another 'helmet' which he uses to transmit the brain waves of the 'source' into the brain of the 'subject'. They will attempt to purchase 'receptor' and 'transmitter' helmets from Germany. They also think that they can obtain another box from Philips. Now that Baumgartner is in Argentina they think there will be no problem duplicating his equipment in Heidelberg.

That evening they dine at La Ostra Sonriendo. Heidi has been to Spain a few times and does surprisingly well reading the menu. The Prof has also been to Spain several times and has no problem with the menu. Basima helps them out describing some of the items which are local to the Rio de la Plata.

Office of the Director
CIA Headquarters
Langley, Virginia
July 5, 1994 Tuesday morning

Mitch is on the phone with Arthur Mollendeck in Frankfurt. Mollendeck is the new Head of Station in Germany.

"What do you mean gone?"

"As best we can find out, Siegfried came to Germany sometime the week before. He and his girlfriend, this Freud woman, left here on the Thursday night flight to Buenos Aires."

"You are sure?"

"Yes, our guy at Lufthansa has access to the passenger lists. He took a peek at the lists for the Frankfurt-Buenos Aires flights and found Siegfried and Heidi on the Thursday night flight."

"Shit."

"That's not all. Baumgartner went with them. We have no way of knowing for sure but we think that Baumgartner figured out that someone had been in his files. Thursday night Baumgartner's house was substantially destroyed by fire. They must think that this was arson. No doubt someone found out he left the country earlier in the evening and put two and two together. They have the whole place cordoned off. We can't get anywhere near it. There are police everywhere."

Later it will be discovered that it was indeed arson. All the files and Baumgartner's computer were destroyed. Apparently he disconnected his computer from the web Tuesday evening. They suspect that he has what he wanted to take to Argentina on discs.

Mitch calls Guenther to tell him the news.

"Too bad he was on the plane instead of in his bed. He made some sort of a deal with Siegfried. We couldn't overhear it because they were in his office. We know they took all the recordings of the sessions Eberhardt participated in. We also found out that they are playing middle C into the chimp's ears when they are using him as a subject. This reinforces what we found by analyzing the data two weeks ago. Somehow, these notes aid in the transfer on information to the subject."

"So now they are going to be able to figure out what we know?"

"Of course. Baumgartner set this whole thing up. The folks in Argentina are going to know more about this than we do. On the other hand, they do not have the high resolution signals. Mitch do you have any connections in South Africa?"

"We have a small presence why do you ask?"

"We think we have deciphered a mention of a Maarten Debbinck in one of Karl Eberhardt's sessions with Siegfried Bachmeier. Debbinck was a Nazi Collaborator who caused the deaths of several thousand of his fellow Dutchmen. He disappeared near the end of the War. He probably went to South Africa. You know a lot of the Nazis went there. They have this AWB outfit down there complete with the racial purity and other stuff that makes these Nazis right at home."

"I am vaguely familiar with that Guenther."

"The South Africans have a sizable production of yellow cake and we believe that at one point in the seventies they had a few nuclear weapons. We think they were working with the Israelis at the time. We know that the Israelis have nuclear and thermonuclear weapons.

Mitch, do you think you could find out if Debbinck is still alive? He is in his early seventies."

"Can you give me anything besides South Africa Guenther?"

"Yes, he went to Heidelberg in the late thirties and has a degree in Geology. As you know, they do a lot of mining in South Africa. You might start there."

Basima, Oskar and Siegfried are in her study. They think they have found something for Baumgartner to do, until they figure out what to do with him. He is, after all, a world renowned expert in the treatment of epilepsy. Oskar managed to get him a job as a consultant at Aleman Hospital. He doesn't really trust this guy but recognizes that he may be useful sometime in the future. In the meantime, they want to find out what they can from Siegfried's previous sessions without involving Baumgartner. Basima says it is time for Siegfried to listen to portions of two of his sessions while hypnotized. He is not anxious to do this but she feels he will see the merit of her request after he listens. He hears himself speaking in the first person as if he is indeed Karl Eberhardt for the first time.

"**Damn it Wilfried.** I told you to get a surrogate. Child birth is a dangerous business. We invested five years in that woman and now we have nothing to show for it. At least she produced a son. We can find out if her intelligence was transmitted to him in a few years."

This goes on a while. They only hear 'Karl's' half of the conversation. He is very angry about the death of Siegfried's mother.

Basima removes that tape and puts another into the recorder. She fast forwards it about one third of the way. In this next portion, apparently Siegfried is acting out something that happened in the past three years. Karl is telling Wilfried that he is not going to make the same mistake twice.

"This girl we have been investing our time in. We will get Siegfried to impregnate her and then we are going to take the embryo and put it in some less valuable woman. With any luck we can produce six or seven children a year. Bruno Hartmann knows how to do this. I don't want anything going wrong this time."

Professor Hartmann is way up in the Heidelberg University Hospital hierarchy. He is a world class practitioner of embryo transplanting.

"Do you know what period I am reenacting as Karl, Basima?"

"I think it is after you matriculated at Heidelberg."

"So he is talking about Heidi?"

"We think so."

"Why didn't you say something earlier?"

"You have been quite adamant about not wanting to listen to them. As long as your woman was in Germany and you were here it wasn't so important that you hear this. The other thing is that one of the participants in that conversation is here now. We wanted to go over this with you before we even think about involving Baumgartner."

They sit quietly for a few minutes. Siegfried speaks first.

"I sort of had a feeling that this was going on. I almost think that Karl told me that in one of our sessions in Baumgartner's lab. I need to talk to Heidi about this. I do love her and I think she loves me. If this procedure is not painful to her it might not be such a bad idea. It might even be lower risk than her carrying the embryo to term. We would raise the children. After all, they will be our children. Can you help me with this Basima?"

"Unfortunately, I never could have children Ziggy. I can not really relate well from a woman's standpoint to everything associated with producing a child."

Reina Beatrix Hotel

Arikok National Park

Aruba, Netherland Antilles

July 8, 1994 Friday

The Secretary of State of the United States and the Argentine Minister of Foreign Relations signed an agreement today greatly relaxing tensions between the two nations. Starting Monday neither country will require the other's citizens to obtain a visa in order to visit the other country. The United States will lift the ban on American companies furnishing spare parts to Argentina and Argentina will stop harassing American owned businesses in Argentina.

There was a press conference after the signing. A lot of provocative questions were asked by both US and Argentine journalists. Mostly the questions concerned who was going to lose or gain the most jobs because of this partial reconciliation. For sure, a number of American ex-patriots lost out because their well paying jobs were taken by locals when the harassment drove them out of Argentina.

Hotel Moreno

San Carlos de Bariloche, Argentina

July 12, 1994 Tuesday evening

Siegfried and Heidi flew to this famous ski resort area yesterday afternoon. There is nearly a meter of snow on the slopes. They spent the whole day skiing. It is far enough away from BA so that they feel alone together. After a fine meal they retire to their room. Siegfried does not have any idea about what her reaction might be but he tries to sneak up on the subject by talking about their sessions with Karl Eberhardt.

"How many sessions did you have with Karl? Do you know how he and Professor Baumgartner chose you from all the pretty girls in Heidelberg?"

"I don't know for sure Ziggy but my parents both have Doctor's degrees from Heidelberg so I guess they thought I had some native intelligence."

"You know that they electroencephalographically educated you and me both?"

"Oh, yes."

"When you were having your sessions with Karl did he convey any information about me to you?"

"Yes. During the last two sessions we had, I think he was saying that you would be a good choice for a mate."

"Was that before or after we met?"

"I think the first time was a week or two before we first met. I think he and Professor Baumgartner were both trying to put us together."

"Do you know that they view us as a 'breeding pair'?"

"I don't know. I could believe Baumgartner would do something like that. He certainly was rumored to do some breeding with some of his students long before our time."

"I guess I just need to blurt this out. They did view us as a 'breeding pair'. Karl had some pretty strong opinions about that. You may not know that my mother was subjected to the EEE process much as you were. She died giving birth to me. Karl was furious with Wilfried for allowing this to happen. He was saying how they should have done an embryo transplant and put my egg in some 'less valuable woman'. How do you feel about that?"

"How do you feel about that?"

"Well, from the standpoint of your health, it is probably safer for you to let someone else carry our egg. I certainly don't want you dying in childbirth."

"I need to think about that a while Siegfried. I want to have your children."

Then she playfully adds.

"We could still start them off the old fashioned way, couldn't we?"

Rancho Don Martinez

Pelicura, Argentina

September 5, 1994 Monday 0900

There have been the usual numerous startup problems at MEA. The forty percent contingency allowance that they planned on ended up over one hundred percent by the time they had the thing working. Basima seems to have an endless supply of funds. She funds MEA by buying stock in MEA with electronic transfers from an account in Liechtenstein. Finally, last week they succeeded in making a little more than one hundred grams of glass coated Selenium tubes about half a micron in diameter by three microns long. These were immediately sent to Pelicura. Professor Kessler managed to incorporate these into some cyclonite with four percent by weight paraffin wax binder. Siegfried flew down to Bahia Blanca yesterday and is staying at Hotel Tamarisces. He and Aldrich had breakfast together and then drove to the ranch. Aldrich's technicians have everything ready. At 0900 sharp they fire the test specimen which is two millimeters in diameter by one hundred millimeters long. The shock wave travels the length of the specimen in 7.35 microseconds. They calculate a detonation wave velocity of 13610 (+/- 200) meters per second, not quite sixty percent higher than hexogen alone. This is an enormously disappointing result. The detonation velocity of Plodamax is more than seven times this. They run a control test with the Hexogen alone. They measure 8600 meters per second. The Hexogen is within spec. Aldrich was definitely doing better with the fibrils from FPI when he was working in the Saudi desert. There is either something wrong with the fibrils they can make or something wrong with the way the fibrils are mixed with the explosive. They talk about this a while.

"Aldrich, does anything strike you about what might be different between the results here and the results you got in Saudi Arabia?"

"Aside from the fact that I had fibrils from FPI and Hexogen from Germany?"

"Yes."

"It must be the fibrils. We just tested the Hexogen and it is okay. I must point out Siegfried that we never achieved the detonation velocity of Plodamax. The best I could do was about half, even with the FPI fibrils. The other thing was that the fibrils from FPI were typically five to six microns long. This is roughly twice that of the first ones produced at MEA. When I analyzed the Plodamax and separated the fibrils they were an average of three microns long. I know that there was some degradation of the fibrils caused by the separation step. I used the same procedure on some of the material you just sent me last week. The fibrils I recovered were less than two microns long."

"I was going over some notes that Karl left me. He mentions some work done at Peenemunde in the early forties trying to produce super high detonation velocities. They had the best results using quartz dust which is why Karl thought it was some kind of optical phenomenon that was going on in the fibrils. There was a school of thought that the phenomenon was electrical in nature so they tried using Iron filings in Hexogen and aligning them with a magnetic field. They could get them lined up pretty well but nothing happened to the detonation velocity. I wonder whether if we had a super strong magnetic field we could cause our fibrils to line up."

"That sounds quite difficult Siegfried, I think Selenium is diamagnetic. It might be easier to see if you could add a little Iron when you are building the fibrils so the magnetic field had something to get hold of."

"Do you have anymore test specimens Aldrich?"

"Yes, I have two more. I always make three if I can."

"Did you notice that there was a faint greenish cast in the light from the detonation?"

"Maybe."

"It reminded me of something I saw, well, I didn't really see it, some instruments I had saw it, when I was a CERN."

"What was that Siegfried?"

"The instruments indicated that most of these photolinos had an apparent wavelength in the green."

"I have a spectrum analyzer."

Aldrich tells his technicians to set up another test with the spectrum analyzer monitoring the test specimen. Hagen Bauer, his chief technician wonders whether the instrument can survive being close to the explosive. They agree that the instrument can not be in line of sight with the explosive. They will set up some mirrors.

An hour later they run another test. They observe 13500 meters per second detonation velocity. The instrument shows a very weak pulse at 500 nanometers (on the yellowish side of green). This gets them both to thinking.

"I wonder whether the light is the same coming off the side of the test specimen as along the axis."

"That may not be so easy to experimentally determine Siegfried. We won't be able to attempt that today we have exhausted our mirror supply."

They used first surface gold mirrors. The one in line of sight of the detonation was shattered. They call Hector at MEA and ask him to find some more mirrors in

BA and fly them down to Bahia Blanca ASAP. Then, they call Oskar to tell him the results.

"Good morning."

"Good morning Siegfried. How are things going at the ranch?"

"They are not going so well. We only obtained a modest increase in detonation velocity compared to the Hexogen control. We have been talking about some work done at Peenemunde that Karl referred to. This leads us to believe that there might be some merit in lining up the fibrils in the Hexogen. I am wondering whether we could do this with the Selenium tubes if we had a very strong magnetic field, possibly like the MRI."

"What do you think Aldrich?"

"I think we haven't got the fibrils quite right yet. We were talking about possibly doping the Selenium with Iron to give it at least some ferromagnetic properties. Siegfried is thinking about a very strong magnetic field like in an MRI machine."

"I don't think we want to be seen buying an MRI machine Siegfried. We are beginning to think that the way the Americans figured out that we were doing what we were doing at the ranch last year was from their observation of the TASA trucks going back and forth between the two shipyards and to the ranch."

"Aldrich, didn't you order that fancy spectrometer through TASA?"

"No, we used MEA to place that order but we had it delivered to the TASA warehouse."

"I hope that does not come back to bite us."

Oskar is beginning to think like Wilhelm. He is getting more and more suspicious about anything and everything.

DCAC Office

Woburn, Massachusetts

September 12, 1994 Monday

John is on the phone with Guenther. Guenther is doing the talking.

"It seems that Kessler used the Wardnor last week for the first time in several months."

"Yes, Fred told me about that."

"We were afraid to put any extra equipment in the Wardnor cabinet that looked different from the equipment inside the Wardnor at CERN. We presumed that Siegfried knows what the inside of the cabinet in the CERN machine looks like. We do know that the material examined had small amounts of Selenium, Sulfur and Iodine in something with the atomic makeup of the cyclonite molecule. More worrisome is the fact that the Selenium detected in the samples Kessler looked at, had in addition to the most prevalent isotopes a tiny fraction of Se^{75}. Se^{75} is a man-made isotope that is not found in Selenium ore."

"And?"

"They have probably figured out that you have to have some Se^{75} to start the tube growth."

"Is that what they are doing at FPI?"

"You can do it that way."

"Do you think Basima might have learned that when she visited there?"

"I don't know."

"Where are you going with this Guenther?"

"I was thinking that maybe Henry might go there and see what he can see."

"That is not a good idea Guenther. Siegfried's girlfriend knows what Henry looks like. She was in Baumgartner's lab when Henry and Christina visited there the second time."

"Hmmm. I really think we need Henry. I will get Mitch to find a couple of his guys who he trusts to actually get close to their operation. Henry can stay in the background and kind of supervise the show."

"Didn't they send the same guys back to Argentina after the Arikok agreement?"

"Those guys will not be involved in this operation. Mitch says they think they know who is screwing around there but they are giving him some more rope to hang himself. They are probably going to kill him before the end of the year."

John is thinking. Maybe that's why Guenther wants Henry as opposed to someone else.

Hospital Aleman

Buenos Aires, Argentina

November 11, 1994 Friday

Professor Bruno Hartmann has just finished transplanting the fourth embryo from Heidi's uterus to that of a paid surrogate. The surrogates have been provided by Hans Obermeyer in Brazil. They are all staying in a private resort hotel on the Rio Plata. They are being fed a diet that provides everything pregnant women need. There is a gym at the hotel and they are all working out with individual trainers three hours a day. The four women provided are all doing this for the first time. Obermeyer and his father before him have been doing this sort of thing in Brazil for a long time. Hartmann visited Brazil only once to give them some advice. That was twenty five years ago. There are a number of people alive and well in the German community in Porto Alegre who were produced this way.

By contrast, this is his fourth visit to Argentina since August. He seized the opportunity to work with hyper-intelligent breeding stock like Heidi and Siegfried. That is why Professor Hartmann is here and is personally supervising all aspects of this experiment. He insisted that the surrogates be women who had never borne children and they were all thoroughly examined to be sure they had no diseases that might adversely affect the children.

He gave Heidi a little bit of sedative to moderate the slight discomfort the procedure sometimes induces. She is now fully awake again. Siegfried and Heidi stayed at the Intercontinental last night so that they wouldn't have to contend with the long drive in from Rancho de Mil

Robles this morning. They have a private room in the outpatient section of the hospital and he is talking to Heidi and Siegfried.

"You did well again Heidi. Now we will wait and see what happens. Your other three children are progressing normally. I visited them Tuesday and Wednesday. If these four turn out okay we might want to try for more. I have two embryos in the hospital freezer. They are sort of an insurance policy although I much prefer to use non-frozen ones."

"When will you come back Prof?"

"I expect the first child to be born in April. The doctors here in the hospital are perfectly capable of determining whether the child is healthy. There will be a few signs of high intelligence by the fourth month. I will come back here in September next year."

"Thanks Prof. Do you think we might go ahead and make one of our own?"

"You already have four of your own in the works. You will have the luxury of finding out what you have created without any discomfort or risk to Heidi. That is the purpose of this exercise. Why don't you wait until I come back here?"

Hotel Marquesa Romario
Avenida 9ᵗʰ de Julio
Buenos Aires, Argentina
November 18, 1994 Friday 2045

Henry is traveling alone. He flew to Montevideo, Uruguay and then took the ferry to Buenos Aires. He is made up to appear to be in his seventies and he walks with a pronounced stoop. He is a retired engineer who has come to visit some friends. Last week agents Sam Driscoll and Ramon Maguez arrived at the same hotel. Everyone has false papers. The CIA folks are posing as construction machinery salesmen. The Argentines have announced that they will start a multi-billion dollar highway construction project next year. Cyclops Machinery hopes to get a piece of this or so they telling people. The hotel has a rather nice restaurant and that is where they eat. They are now in Driscoll's two room suite. As soon as they close the door, Henry starts.

"What do you know?"

"We found out that this Micro Electrónica Avanzada outfit not far from Ezeiza is the one buying a lot of Se^{75} from the government isotope production lab. We also found out that there is a lot of cell phone interference around this MEA place."

"What has that got to do with the price of tea in China?"

"We think the cell phone interference is coming from MEA."

Henry is not completely ignorant of this subject but is to pretend that he is. Guenther has had Los Alamos duplicate the experiments that they think are going on in Pelicura. They too observed the faint green flashes. Guenther says they have a long way to go but that Siegfried et al have taken the first step toward producing a weapon. Apparently the Wardnor did have an ability to detect emissions in the cell phone frequency range built into it. There were several instances of emissions in this frequency range detected. This is too much of a coincidence to have been caused by anything else than their testing the samples they are making. Guenther put two and two together and has gone so far as to have the CIA establish this branch office of Cyclops Machinery in an office building less than two hundred meters from MEA. All of this is being kept very secret. No one in Argentina knows anything about any of this. The only person in the CIA who knows what is going on here is Mitch Rogerston.

Cyclops Machinery SA
Suite 6A
187 Avenida San Martin
San Rafael, Buenos Aires, Argentina
November 19, 1994 Saturday 1000

Henry and the two agents are having coffee with the two technicians. The technicians report that they are recording at least one episode of cell phone interference every day now. The MEA building is visible out the rear windows of the Cyclops Machinery suite. There are several cubic feet of sophisticated electronics monitoring the emissions from MEA. There is also a very sophisticated transmitter which can send a well collimated high frequency signal to the northwest. MEA has a cover story that they are working on improved weld inspection techniques.

Micro Electrónica Avandaza
San Rafael, Argentina
November 21, 1994 Monday 0900

Siegfried, Aldrich, Oskar and Basima (the MEA Board of Directors) are in the meeting room next to Hector's office. MEA is making excellent progress. Now that Aldrich and Siegfried have figured out how to align the hollow fibrils they have been able to make much smaller test specimens. These are comparatively not very noisy when they are detonated so they are using these for quality control purposes right in MEA. This definitely beats sending the fibrils to Pelicura and doing the quality control testing there. Siegfried and Aldrich are well aware that this is causing local cell phone interference but they don't think that is a serious problem. Oskar wants them to install electromagnetic shielding around the laboratory where they are doing the quality control tests. Suddenly Siegfried has one of his increasingly frequent flashbacks.

"That is exactly what I told Wilfried to do in 1943. It didn't work then and it probably won't work now."

Basima notes this and moves the discussion along before anyone can say anything.

"Ziggy that was in the notes wasn't it?"

The mention of his name snaps Siegfried out of this almost trancelike state. This is the desired effect. Basima spent some time learning how to snap him out these trances. Neither she nor Oskar wants this thing known. They have not told Hector anything about this. That is why he is not in the plant this morning. They had to tell Aldrich some of the story because they are certain that Siegfried does this in Pelicura when he is alone with Aldrich.

Suddenly a light bulb goes on in Siegfried's head.

"Of course, Wilfried knew that his instruments could not detect the source's transmissions because of the very high frequency. They didn't have anything that operated in the gigahertz range where cell phones do today. Somehow we are producing a signal that effectively interrupts cell phone communication for a brief period. It doesn't surprise me that these test specimens are producing emissions in the cell phone frequency range. I have a friend who knows all about this sort of thing. I need to talk to him about this."

Ludwig Bieber's Office
Heilbronn University MHD Research Station
Neiderhofen, Germany
November 24, 1994 Thursday morning

Ludwig is five years older than Siegfried. Of course, all of Siegfried's contemporaries are five years older because Siegfried is a prodigy. Ludwig is no slouch. He earned his Doctorate in Electrical Engineering from Heidelberg two years ago. Heilbronn snapped him up with the promise to make him the head of their MHD research effort which has received an enormous grant from the federal government. Ludwig is two inches taller than Siegfried and a muscular ninety kilos. They embrace as Siegfried enters his office.

"Pretty fancy digs here Wig."

"They have to give me something. Siemens offered me twenty percent more than the school did but I didn't want to work in München. It is quite pleasant here."

"Not far from Gabby either."

"That too."

"I was wondering whether I could pick your brain about something I have been working on."

"You probably know more than I do Zig but I will try."

Siegfried outlines his effort to make 'light pipes'. He purports to be trying to make a new kind of light bulb. He thinks that the faint green light that he has sometimes observed is a phenomenon somehow related to photolinos. They talk for most of the morning. Siegfried takes his friend to lunch at a local Gasthaus. They talk a little about Argentina. Ludwig has never been there. Siegfried offers to fly Wig and his girlfriend over to visit him. He will put them up at his place for a few days but they probably will want to stay in Buenos Aires most of the time. He will provide hotel accommodations for them. Wig says that sounds like a good deal.

"What kind of time frame are you thinking Zig?

"Well, if you came over for Christmas you probably would not interfere much with your work. It is pretty slow around here then isn't it? It will be summer when you get there. Even so, depending on the local weather in the South, you might be able to get some skiing in. I wouldn't pack skis because there usually isn't any decent snow cover down South by the end of December. You can rent them down there if there is any skiing."

When they get back to Wig's office he calls Gabriele. She wants to go. They work out their schedules.

"You're on. We will travel the twenty first and return the fourteenth of January."

She is reading a synopsis of local news in Clarin while he is reading the sports section of Argentinisches Tageblatt.

There is the usual collection of accidents reported in Clarin.

Almagro

A two vehicle collision at 0100 Wednesday morning resulted in the deaths of Sr. and Sra. Ricardo Lopez. The driver of the other car Sr. Gabino Munoz was found to have a blood alcohol content of 0.17%. He is being held at the Almagro police headquarters.

...

...

Recoleta

Hubert Wallace a trade attaché of the American Embassy was found dead with a single bullet in his forehead. His wallet was missing. The police suspect that this was simply a robbery gone bad.

...

...

San Isidro

A boater at the San Isidro Marina did not return from a Tuesday cruise. There was an uncorroborated report that this man had been drinking heavily and brandishing a pistol before leaving the dock Tuesday afternoon.

"Oskar, look at this."

He does. That is the organization's spy in the American embassy. He never ceases to be amazed at how good a memory she has. He thinks that he probably only mentioned Wallace once a few months ago.

DCAC Office
Woburn, Massachusetts
December 1, 1994 Thursday late morning

Guenther, Henry and Randy are in John's office on the speaker phone with Mitch Rogerston in Langley and General Louis Rocker, head of DARPA, in Arlington.

"Louis, we need to get that satellite up sooner rather than later. Siegfried was in Germany last week. We think he went to see Ludwig Bieber. I hope he is not mixed up in this. He is one of world's foremost experts on magneto hydrodynamic power generation. I think that Siegfried has figured out that he can probably generate a pretty impressive lightning bolt if he does things right. I might also add that one can produce a staggering amount of power for short times with some MHD generators. You are familiar with the Rogers Project. We think he might be able to weaponize what he is doing in two years or less."

"What do you think Randy?"

"I think Guenther has it about right. The young man is moving awfully fast."

"Do you think that we could get any help from the Argentines?"

"Louis, surely you jest."

"Well, I'm in a pretty good mood this week, the Redskins won big Monday night."

"We want to put a Rogers Project weapon in space as soon as we can."

"They have this fibril production facility fairly close to the Buenos Aires airport. We could launch the thing into polar orbit from Vandenberg. On the first pass we think we could zap their facility for maybe two or three seconds. That is about as long as we can run it before it gets too hot. This is likely to damage every bit of wire in their shop. Some of the stuff you need to make the fibrils has a rather low tolerance for any kind of abuse. It would set them back a few months. If we really got lucky we might kill some people who were useful to them. We think we could then ditch the satellite in the South Atlantic. It will not overfly anyone who can see it. No one will have a clue."

Guenther Reinhardt's Office

Los Alamos National Laboratory

Los Alamos, New Mexico

December 6, 1994 Tuesday 0830MST

There has been considerable back and forth between Guenther, DARPA, NSA and the President since the first of the month. President Simmons was the commander of a B-52 Wing during the Vietnamese War. He does not want to be a party to causing more innocent civilian casualties in Argentina. The operable word here is innocent. He couldn't care less about the casualties inflicted in any of the places that were raided or the treatment of the people captured at Rancho Don Martinez. Nevertheless, they are busy trying to put relations with Argentina back together again. He wants assurances that this adventure with the Rogers Project will not be a public relations disaster like the raid on Rancho de Mil Robles. He is vaguely familiar with the Rogers Project. Mostly he knows that it is named after Buck Rogers a science fiction comic book hero in the first half of the century. Guenther assures Robert Grainger (the new interim appointee Secretary of NSA) that the instrument of destruction is remarkably accurate. It has produced a Gaussian distribution when fired from a satellite at a stationary target in the Goldwater Bombing Range. It has a Circular Probability of Error (CEP) of 1.5 meters when fired at the stationary target from a satellite 180 miles above. The target building roof is roughly a twenty seven meter square. They are aiming at the center of the roof. The satellite will only be 100 miles up. Given the same angular error demonstrated in the tests, the CEP from 100 miles up is expected to be less than one meter. It would take an error of 13.5 meters from the center before the bolt fell outside the building. There is less than one chance in 10000 that the bolt will miss the building. Even if it does, the next closest building is twenty meters away. They have a high frequency transmitter less than 200 meters from the target. The satellite will use this signal to make second order adjustments to the range. This signal will eliminate the errors in the GPS system since the location of the target relative to the transmitter is known within a few millimeters. There is very little likelihood of civilian (other than the people in the target building) casualties. This information has been duly relayed to the President. President Simmons continues to marvel at how accurate weapons have become since the time when he was setting fire to Vietnamese jungles and bombing Haiphong. He has assurances from NSA that there are no around-the-clock operations going on anywhere near the target. He will approve the strike but it must be at night when there are very few people in that light industrial park. Probably Sunday night would be best. And, of course, the fewer people who know about this the better it will be.

Ezeiza Aeropuerto
Buenos Aires, Argentina
December 22, 1994 Thursday 1030

Siegfried, Oskar and their driver are there to meet Ludwig and Gabriele as soon as they get through customs. They all pile into the big Mercedes van and drive out to Rancho de Mil Robles. They get Ludwig and Gabriele settled in the guest wing and then have lunch on the patio along with Heidi and Basima. Gabriele and Heidi know each other from school. It is a pleasant surprise.

In the time between Siegfried's visit to Germany and Ludwig's arrival in Argentina, Basima and Siegfried have gone over Karl's list again rather carefully. They have identified a Wolfgang Bieber who Karl's notes indicated lived in Frankfurt. Basima starts.

"Ludwig, do you prefer Ludwig or Wig?"

"Wig is fine."

"Wig, a friend of ours made note of a Wolfgang Bieber he knew in Frankfurt. Are you any relation?"

"Yes. Wolfgang was my grand uncle. He passed away three years ago."

Ludwig is thinking. Where is this going? The inside of this ranch house is full of Nazi memorabilia, the same as my uncle's place in Frankfurt. He doesn't have long to wait. Siegfried gets right to the point.

"It is our understanding that your grand uncle had a prominent position in Germany during the War."

"Yes, he was involved in weapons research at Peenemunde. I must say that the collection of memorabilia that you have here puts his to shame."

He says the right thing. They certainly do not want an anti Nazi on their team.

"Wig, we would like you to consult for us. This would likely take a few days a month. Would you be interested?"

"I think I could do that as long as I wasn't absent from Niederhofen for more than one week a month."

They exchanged gifts Christmas Eve. Gabriele and Ludwig gave Siegfried and Heidi an impressionist painting from a celebrated Heidelberg artist that they both admired when they were there. Siegfried and Heidi gave Gabriele a gold chain necklace that weighed in at two hundred grams and Ludwig a suede jacket made by a renowned Argentine leather producer. Oskar and Basima celebrated at Oskar's ranch with Raphael and his family. The weather is perfect and the ranch is in a very pretty part of this beautiful country. Siegfried and Heidi entertained their guests out in the hinterlands the next few days.

Ludwig is fascinated with the photographs on the walls of the den. Siegfried tells him that his grandfather bought this ranch and built the ranch house in the late forties. His father was born here. He shows him a picture of his grandfather with Karl Eberhardt. They were lifelong friends. Siegfried points out a picture of Oskar's father with his U-boat. He tells him that Oskar's submarine sank a British warship during the Malvinas War. Ludwig notices that there are no pictures of Siegfried's father. It seems a bit odd that that is the case in the grandfather's home but then he also notices that these are all black and white photographs and fairly old. He sees what appears to be a more recent photograph with a group picture with Karl Eberhardt, Wilhelm Bachmeier, Oskar Brandt and Hermann Schliefenbaum. Wilhelm is wearing a Waffen SS Standartenfürher uniform and Oskar and Hermann are wearing Kriegsmarine Kapitän uniforms. They are obviously having a toast.

Buenos Aires
December 28, 1994 Wednesday

Oskar and Siegfried brought the guests in and got them settled in the Intercontinental before noon. Basima and Heidi are entertaining Gabriele this afternoon.

Aldrich Kessler joins them for lunch at the hotel. Then the four men drive out to MEA. The rest of the afternoon is spent discussing the progress at MEA. It soon becomes apparent to Ludwig that 'light pipes' had little to do with what they are trying to do. Siegfried tells him that they can move charged species through a magnetic field at velocities in excess of 15,000 meters per second. Ludwig knows that this is several times the velocity he can obtain in an MHD generator while retaining a high population of ions. They think they can do much better.

"How are you doing that Zig?"

"We have a special explosive we are trying to make better than it is."

"What is that?"

Siegfried, Oskar and Aldrich have been all around this tree. They have got to give Ludwig enough information so that he can help them.

"Wig, I am going to reveal our most valuable information. Please do not repeat this. We are achieving these high velocities by detonating Hexogen which contains some glass coated Selenium fibrils which we make here. The fibrils either transport electrons or photolinos or light much faster than the detonation velocity in the explosive. We believe that this enables a 'leap frog' effect wherein the explosive at the other end of any fibril is ignited by what ever is traveling down the length of the fibril. What ever it is reaches the end of the fibril away from the detonation at nearly the speed of light.

We believe that after no more than one or two molecular vibrations the explosive at the end of the fibril is detonated. This is how we think we achieve these detonation velocities which are higher than theoretical. We are still trying to do better than we are doing."

"What makes you think that this is producing a stream of charged particles? If you want to produce MHD power you will need a lot of these."

"We have fired test specimens through a Helmholtz Coil and we are getting enormous voltage spikes."

"Have you tried any Cesium addition?"

"Not yet. I see certain similarities with my work at CERN. We can not rule out the possibility that we are seeing a piezo electric phenomenon."

The discussion goes on quite a while. Ludwig thinks there might be something here which could actually be useful for power generation. They return to the hotel in the middle of the rush hour. Siegfried and Heidi are staying at the hotel for the balance of the week. Oskar and Basima are staying at her place in San Isidro. They have supper at La Cabaña. Ludwig and Gabriele are impressed with the amount of beef consumed here in Argentina.

Aldrich, Ludwig and Siegfried visit Pelicura Thursday and Friday. They explain what they are doing there. Ludwig gives them some pointers on how to go about getting more accurate voltage measurements. The equipment will have to come from Germany. Siemens has an office in Buenos Aires. Siegfried has Hector order everything on Ludwig's wish list.

USS Georgia

South Atlantic Ocean

10 kilometers East of San Clemente de Tuyú

Jan 1, 1995 Sunday night

The boat is now equipped with two UA-63 Model 4 drones. They have replaced two of the Model 3's. The outer surface of the submarine's sail has been modified so that it is now fairly stealthy with respect to radar detection. The tubes from which they launch the drones are stealthy as well. These tubes can be extended ten feet above the deck so that the UA-63 drones can be launched while only a few feet of the sail and the top of the tube are above the water. At 0200 Zulu Jan 2, 1995 an unmanned UA-63-4 leaps out of its tube and flies toward San Rafael. At 0305 Zulu, the drone flies over the MEA building at approximately two hundred meters. It deploys its wings for a period of fifteen seconds. It is not stealthy with the wings deployed. It stows its wings and returns eastward. At 0415 Zulu it descends into the Atlantic and sinks in one hundred twenty fathoms.

Vandenberg Air Force Base, California
January 1, 1995 Sunday 1840
PST (January 2, 1994 0240 Zulu)

A modified Minuteman I was launched skyward from pad 3. Twenty five minutes later the first test of a Rogers Project device used in anger occurred over Buenos Aires. The satellite acquired the beacon being beamed up from Cyclops Machinery at 0301.787608 Zulu. A slight adjustment in the course of the satellite was made shortly thereafter. The satellite confirmed the radar image of the MEA building at 0304.576283 Zulu. It determined that it was as close as it was going to get with the range to the beacon of 163003.90 meters. The electronically steered bolt was fired at the building three microseconds later. Passage through the atmosphere attenuated the bolt by roughly thirty two percent. The remaining sixty eight percent slammed into the MEA roof. This resulted in an enormous current surge through every wire in the building. These effects preferentially spread through every good conductor in the vicinity until the current was reduced below the value needed to vaporize the wires. Essentially every wire in MEA was vaporized. Two minutes later, five hundred miles to the southeast the satellite retro rocket was fired. The machine largely burned up reentering the atmosphere. What was left fell unnoticed into the South Atlantic about two hundred miles east of the Falkland Islands.

The bolt fired at the MEA factory in San Rafael had at least one unintended consequence. There was a voltage spike which tripped many safeties, some as far as one kilometer away from the target. Several small fires were started in the target building when some of the wire insulation caught fire. These quickly died out when the sprinkler system came on.

MEA
135 Avenida Eva Peron
San Rafael, Argentina
January 2, 1995 Monday 0800

News of a problem in the San Rafael Industrial park is all over the Buenos Aires news media this morning. There are reports of a bolt of lightning, straight as a string, around midnight. When the four men show up at MEA they find a real mess. It is wet inside. The place reeks of the smell of burnt insulation. After a while they discover that there are fifty centimeter diameter holes in the roof of the building and the roof of the clean room. Apparently what ever made those holes destroyed the wiring in the building. Ludwig comments.

"I did some work where we were using exploding bridge wires. Some of these wires look like they were hit with enough current to make them explode."

The clean room has essentially been destroyed. The last word that one would use to describe its present state is 'clean'. Some of the glass observation ports in some of the machines that operated under high vacuum were broken. This allowed the air and probably some smoke into these machines. The holes in the roof and the clean room look like they might have been caused by a meteorite which is what the media is speculating. That doesn't look like a reasonable explanation of what happened to the wiring. It will take some time to replace the damaged equipment. In fact, it probably will be easier to start over again than to try to repair the installation. Siegfried is already wondering whether this was a man made phenomenon.

Cyclops Machinery SA
Suite 6A
187 Avenida San Martin
San Rafael, Argentina
January 2, 1995 Monday 0800

Sam Driscoll and Ramon Maguez show up around quarter to eight. Most of the excitement is concentrated on the next street which happens to be where MEA is located. There are two San Rafael fire trucks and three Electricidad de Buenos Aires vehicles on Avenida Eva Peron. It looks like the fire trucks are getting ready to go home. They are pleasantly surprised when they get to their office. Apparently Avenida San Martin was on a different transformer than Avenida Eva Peron. They have power. Of course, they are just as clueless as everyone else about what happened. Knowledge of the recent happenings in San Rafael is confined to a few people far away both in distance and pay grade.

DCAC Office

Woburn Massachusetts

January 2, 1995 Monday 1000

It is morning coffee break and John and Henry are playing their first backgammon game of the New Year. John is just about to move when the phone rings. He sees the caller ID and hits the speaker phone.

"Hello Guenther."

"It worked perfectly."

There is a bounce in Guenther's voice this morning. He sounds twenty years younger and happy for a change.

"We zapped those clowns last night. We zapped them good. I will send some pictures to Fred's computer."

"The aiming was so precise that we only put about a one and one half foot diameter hole in the roof. That is very fancy shooting from a platform moving more than four miles per second one hundred miles away."

"Congratulations Guenther."

"We have some infrared pictures around two am there that suggest that there may have been a little fire in the building. We have a few pictures since it was daylight there. It is a mob scene with police, fire trucks and utility trucks all over the place. I haven't had this much fun in years."

Then he reverts back to his usual pessimistic self.

"The downside to this is that they may well rebuild somewhere that we don't know about. If they are a tenth as smart as we know they are they will do just that. There is more bad news. That Bieber guy I was talking to you about last month left Frankfurt for Argentina the twenty first of December. We have been watching him rather closely since Siegfried went to visit him. After we saw him check in for the flight to Buenos Aires we were able to get someone out to the airport before the Lufthansa flight from Frankfurt landed. They saw Siegfried and two other guys we don't know meet Bieber and some woman with him at the airport. This is very bad. Ludwig Bieber is very knowledgeable about things electrical in general and MHD in particular. We are pretty sure that his grand uncle was working on nuclear weapons development during the War. We do not want him teaming up with Siegfried."

"Are you saying what I think I'm hearing?"

"I'm not sure yet."

Basima's Residence
San Isidro, Argentina
January 2, 1995 Monday late afternoon

Aldrich, Hector, Ludwig, Siegfried and Oskar are trying to figure out what happened at MEA. There is compelling evidence that this was something akin to a lightning strike. In addition to destroying the processing equipment, the strike overwhelmed the surge protectors that their PC's were plugged into. They have lost all their electronics and their production history records. Hector had the wiring diagrams for the building and the equipment at the TASA office. He brought these to Basima's. With the diagrams in hand, Ludwig has ginned up a quick and dirty EXCEL® program which enables him to estimate how fast any particular wires might have been vaporized. It doesn't take long to figure out that something of the order, initially at least, of a one hundred thousand ampere current surge occurred. Hector had some connections in the utility company. He found out that the nearby step-down transformer failed on the high voltage side. As best they can figure there must have been a voltage spike on the low voltage side that when stepped up broke down the insulation in the high voltage windings.

"Zig, you were saying that you were able to move ions at several times the velocities achievable in a flowing combustion system. Did you ever try to use these to produce MHD power?"

"No."

"The reason I ask is that if this lightning strike or whatever it was had to come any distance at all, there would have to have been an enormous potential difference.

We can generate twenty or thirty thousand volt potentials with combustion system velocities but if you could do this at much higher velocities you could conceivably do a lot better."

This remark immediately rings the same bell with Siegfried and Aldrich. If they had the real Plodamax, they might be able to generate some monster voltages. They both start to speak at once. Siegfried is first.

"How much higher?"

"Maybe one hundred to two hundred thousand meters per second."

Aldrich comments.

"I have seen such velocities. The Americans have a proprietary explosive which has detonation velocities in this range."

Oskar comments.

"We are practically certain that the Americans found out some things in the past two years from their spy satellites. Most of the ones which overfly Argentina are in polar orbit and they are launched from Vandenberg in California."

. The Americans do not announce when they launch any of their military satellites. They have no way to establish if a satellite had anything at all to do with the mess in San Rafael. If the thing has been up there a while, a month, a year, who knows, they won't figure it out. Oskar continues.

"Possibly it was not a satellite. We have reason to believe that the Americans found three of our locations using information they gained from their spy satellites. Then they raided these locations with some kind of aerial assault vehicles which we believe they launched from a submarine. We have reason to believe that these vehicles are stealthy. They could have been a hundred meters above MEA and no one would know. MEA is right next to Ezeiza. If it was anything not in space they might have seen it."

Hector knows the right buttons to push to find this out. Five minutes later he returns with the news that there was a very brief, ca 10-15 seconds, blip on the airport short range radar at shortly before 0205.

Oskar is remembering what he found out about the raid on Rancho de Mil Robles. He mentions that there were some strange blips reported from the Rosario airport radar that night. This results in rapid agreement that the Americans must have pulled this stunt off with one of these aerial assault vehicles. No one wants to think that they can do this sort of thing from a satellite. Oskar has copies of all the information gathered from the examination of the two UA-63s abandoned at Rancho de Mil Robles in the files at CCM Belen. He calls CCM Belen and tells them to bring that information to Basima's.

Ludwig has been taking this all in. There were a few articles in the German press about the Americans raiding some places in Argentina a while back. He has learned in his brief time here that Oskar was a submarine captain in the Argentine Navy. There was a picture of Oskar's father in the den of Zig's ranch house and it looked like he was the captain of that U-boat in the picture. He has heard rumors that a WWII U-boat was involved in the bombings of New York and Israel. He is beginning to wonder whether these are the guys who were responsible for the bombings. Then he remembers seeing the picture with Zig's grandfather, Karl Eberhardt, Oskar and Oskar's friend that was at the ranch the other evening. Oskar looked about the same as he does now. It must have been quite recent. Then he remembers what high esteem his grand uncle had for Eberhardt.

He notices that Basima is watching him closely. Does she know what I am thinking?

Two inspectors from the National Atomic Energy Commission (NAEC) showed up here half an hour ago. They have already found some evidence that some Se^{75} is out of its containment vessels. They are practically fawning in front of Doctor Siegfried Bachmeier. They suggest in the most deferential way that the NAEC is proud that the best nuclear physicist in the world has returned to his homeland instead of staying in Germany and teaching at Heidelberg but we can not permit any further activities having anything to do with radioactive anything in San Rafael again.

This gets a rise out of Siegfried (What nonsense, those people are seven kilometers from here in just as heavily a populated area.) but before he can say a word Oskar answers.

"They are right Siegfried. There are too many people around here. We probably should be doing this someplace else much further away from Buenos Aires. I don't think that Señors Martin or Perez want the fact that a little Se^{75} from the sputtering machine got loose widely known anymore than we do. We will get it cleaned up.

He turns to the two inspectors.

Is that okay with you?"

The fact that he had a heads-up yesterday evening from one of their contacts in the NAEC that these two would show up this morning enabled him to organize a $20000 payoff which he handed them in a sealed envelope labeled "Preliminary Accident Report of Damage *from Meteorite". This is a pretty good deal for these two. The tiny amount of Se^{75} that got loose isn't much of a radiation hazard and has largely been appropriately contained and they will be able to report this as having been done at their direction and under their close scrutiny. Their bosses will be happy, Oskar will be happy, and they each have one hundred one hundred dollar bills in their pockets that the tax collector knows nothing about.*

There wasn't going to be much use scrapping about this anyhow. The NAEC has all the high cards, from supplying the isotopes to having their inspectors say grace over what happens anyplace using them. This is the lowest cost solution to the problem. After they are gone Oskar tells Siegfried what happened. Siegfried thinks about this for a brief time and says to himself.

"I guess that comes under the category of gaining wisdom."

The Directors of MEA and Hector Alvarez are meeting in the living room. They have already decided that they will move their operation to a property far west of Buenos Aires. Oskar didn't know that this property existed until he looked through Wilhelm's records after the disaster at the Lake House. The first references to it appear in the late fifties. There is no reference as to how Wilhelm obtained this property. He knows that Wilhelm was using it as an adjunct to Rancho de Mil Robles. There are presently nearly four thousand cattle on the property. Apparently the property was the scene of silver mining a century ago. There is an extensive network of tunnels under the property. This may be why Wilhelm bought it. They are hoping that they can rebuild the factory in these tunnels. The Americans will not be able to see what is going on from their spy satellites. Oskar thinks that they may as well take the operation in Pelicura and put it out there when they are ready. There is no reason to keep that operation there. The Americans struck there once already.

In addition, they are going to buy another piece of property in Rojas, a town south of Pergamino, and tell the NAEC that that is where the new factory will be located. They expect that the Americans will find out about this location. They will put up something that will pass for a replacement of the factory in San Rafael there. They have pretty well convinced themselves that the Americans had something to do with the mishap in San Rafael Sunday night. Oskar is speaking.

"There was an unidentified radar contact off Punta Francesca Sunday night. What ever it was only appeared for about one and one half minutes."

"When?"

"Around 2300 Sunday night."

"How far is that from San Rafael?"

Oskar goes to Basima's book case and brings back a road atlas. He puts his pinky on Punta Francesca and he can just stretch enough for his thumb to be on San Rafael. This is a handy body dimension to know. Oskar's span is twenty four centimeters. He looks at the scale on the map. It is five kilometers per centimeter.

"It's about 120 kilometers. When they raided Rancho de Mil Robles we think that they flew about three times that far each way. It is well within the range of their aerial assault vehicle."

"There were no further radar contacts?"

"We didn't hear of any. It makes me think that they sent an unmanned drone from the submarine to San Rafael and then they dumped it into the sea when it returned. The sub had plenty of time to get far away from where the drone was launched. I suspect the drone is on the bottom in a few hundred meters of water."

Discussion returns to what they must do to keep the location of the factory hidden from the American spy satellites. The first thing Oskar insists on is concealing transport to and from Rancho de la Veta Madre (Mother Lode Ranch). He thinks that the identification that all trucks over seven tons must have on their roofs and sides will make it impossible to bring any kind of heavy equipment to the ranch during daylight hours. He is convinced that that is how the Americans found Rancho Don Martinez.

Hector has looked into this matter somewhat further and found that trucks carrying livestock are exempt from this rule. They have a large map of Córdoba Province spread out on the coffee table. Hector points to Villa Maria.

"We could set up a warehouse operation for TASA there. It is only two hours away from Córdoba. It would be a reasonable place to have a warehouse if we were doing a lot of business between Buenos Aires and Córdoba because that sort of space is very expensive in Córdoba. It is also less than three hours to Veta Madre. We could transfer the material from a TASA truck to a cattle truck and bring it to the ranch that way."

MEA
San Rafael, Argentina
February 21, 1995 Tuesday

The mess that Guenther, Randy et al created seven weeks ago has been cleaned up. The presence of a little bit of Se^{75} never got out into the open press. On the other hand, the head of the facility which furnished the Se^{75}, one Señor Franco Montana, put his hand out for another twenty thousand US. At Basima's suggestion, Oskar had Rudy Kleist film this transaction, unbeknownst to Señor Montana of course. Basima further suggested that he might consider running for elected office. He would be in a much stronger position to deal with these people. His reputation as an Argentine military hero would make him a shoo-in for elected office. His Nazi organization has had reasonably good relations with the Peronistas and their surviving party the Justicialistas for decades. They have some good luck. One of the senators from Buenos Aires was killed in a small plane crash three weeks ago. Oskar managed to pull a few strings and get himself appointed to fill out the rest of this man's term. The first thing he did was launch an investigation of the NAEC facility where the isotopes were made for possible corrupt practices. A copy of Rudy's film showed up in Señor Montana's in box. This prompted the return of the twenty thousand US and assurances that nothing like this would happen again. Oskar was of a mind to let another copy of this film out to the press but Basima said Señor Montana would possibly be of some use in the future if he stayed where he was.

The building has been reworked entirely and is being used as an MEA office in the Buenos Aires vicinity.

The construction of the dummy plant in Rojas is coming along nicely and the construction of the real replacement plant is just getting started. They found the necessary used equipment in the Far East. They ordered two sets of essentially equivalent machinery but they bought one set in Japan while Hans Obermeyer bought the other set from Korea and had it delivered to Porto Alegre, Brazil. Oskar and Siegfried are discussing this as well as other matters.

"Hans has been a big help to us. I wonder why."

"I think he found out that Professor Hartmann came to Argentina. I think he thinks we are the ones who managed to arrange that. I think he is hoping that we can arrange for Hartmann to visit Brazil. My own feeling is that we should not do that. Let him speculate about what is going on here."

"Oskar, I think it is time to get Baumgartner involved in this. We have duplicates of all the equipment in Heidelberg except the CCX machine."

"Let's wait a little bit longer on that Ziggy. You know, that Basima and I have gone over the recordings of your hypnosis sessions very carefully. When you are speaking as Karl Eberhardt, you convey the impression that you can not trust Baumgartner. I think that it will turn out that we are going to need him primarily for his expertise in which drugs to use."

They noodle this for a while. Siegfried calls Rancho de Mil Robles. Heidi says that she thinks he should talk with Manny a bit about this. He just catches Manfred while he is putting on his overcoat preparatory to heading for the parking lot. It is thirty degrees Celsius in San Rafael and minus three in Darmstadt.

"Yes Ziggy, like I said before, he was quite secretive about what drugs he was using. Have you asked him?"

"We have some difficulty figuring out how much we trust him Manny. I would feel a whole lot better if you were able to find this stuff out for me."

"I did get a call from Professor Schmidt last week. He wanted to know if I would be interested in doing any post doctoral work. I gathered that you and I probably know more about what Baumgartner was doing than anyone in the department. He wants to put me in charge of the whole primate research effort with the MRI's. The problem with that is that he is muttering numbers like half of what I am making here at Merck. I talked with my boss and he is not too keen on me spending much time in Heidelberg."

"Manny, it would be most useful if we had verification that whatever Baumgartner tells us is true."

"That bad huh?"

"We just don't know. Try talking Schmidt into some kind of one or two day a week deal. I would more than match whatever Schmidt offers to make sure you come out whole. Give your boss some bullshit about feeling some kind of moral obligation to help the school out just temporarily."

"You don't need to do that Ziggy."

"I will do it. Don't worry about it. My grandfather left me a ton of money. Ask Wig if you don't believe me."

"Well, he did say that you and Heidi treated them like royalty when they visited you. Angelika was looking at Gabby's necklace pretty carefully when we had dinner with them last Saturday. I can already see a few thousand marks disappearing out of my checking account when her birthday comes around."

Rancho de la Veta Madre
Provincia Córdoba, Argentina
February 28, 1995 Tuesday 0845

Benno Weber is on the phone to Oskar at CCM Belen. This in and of itself is a significant accomplishment. They were very concerned about the security of their communications to and from this facility. They have gone so far as to string thirty one kilometers of coaxial cable from the ranch house to a bar. One of the people in Oskar's organization owns that bar. Equally important is the fact that the bar is on the main drag between Rosario and Mendoza. The now-privatized Argentine phone company has installed fiber optic lines linking Buenos Aires to Córdoba via Rosario and Villa Maria and on through Villa Maria to Mendoza. The bar is more or less a branch office for a well known bookmaker in Córdoba who is also in Oskar's organization. No one is questioning why they got one of the first land line connections to the fiber optic network which is mostly being used to support the burgeoning number of cell phones. The other good thing about this phone line is that the NSA will not be picking up phone conversations on fiber optic land lines. They are not sure that any cell phone communication is secure from NSA eavesdropping. In the highly unlikely event that anyone even finds out that scrambled communication is being conducted on this phone, the fact that this is nominally a bookmaker's telephone should allay any suspicions that this is not perfectly normal. Rancho de la Veta Madre is now tied into Oskar's high security phone system.

There were no utilities within thirty kilometers. There is a network of tunnels left by the silver miners so they are going to start with a roof overhead so to speak. Benno is in charge of construction and CCM personnel from Belen and Bahia Blanca are moving along smartly. Benno was chosen because he is an electrical engineer who knows something about handling power. The first thing they had to do was set up their own electrical service. Everything was being done underground so there wasn't going be any combustion powered equipment in use in the tunnels. It had to be electrical equipment. They have installed two 200 kilowatt Volvo Marine generators. The fibrils plant will use about eighty kilowatts when all the equipment is up. The construction equipment was quite capable of absorbing more than 400 kilowatts but they will schedule the construction equipment operations so as to not exceed 300 kilowatts at any time.

Prior to starting the fibrils facility Benno will install a one hundred kilowatt non-interruptible power supply which will keep the fibril operation running for ten minutes if a generator goes down. They had some problems in San Rafael due to unreliable electric power. Even a flicker often shut them down and screwed up the fibril growing step in the sputtering machine. They would have to start over again and lose a day's production. They haven't got a clue about how to make the process continuous so they are slugging along with a labor intensive batch process. They will get the other generator fired up and on line in less time than that.

Luke Mayer knocks on the door and quickly enters the ranch house study which is now Benno Weber's office.

"Herr Weber, you need to come see this."

"See what Luke? I am on the phone with Oskar."

"I am sure Kapitän Brandt will be interested in this also."

With a sales pitch like this, Benno says he will call back. They walk off to the mine.

At the other end of the barn with the generators there is a Thyssen mineshaft elevator. It is ancient but it definitely post dates the time when silver was being extracted here. It goes down to the lowest level which is sixty meters below the surface. It had a small diesel engine last week but now it has a twenty kilowatt electric motor. The elevator cables had some signs of corrosion so they were replaced. The rails were given a new coating of grease and the thing is now in use. Luke leads the way into the elevator. He gives Benno a head lamp. They close the gate and descend to the first level which is fifteen meters below the surface. Two other men are waiting at the elevator and they greet Benno. The four of them go off into the north tunnel. There is light only in the immediate vicinity of the shaft. Twenty meters into the tunnel all the headlamps are on. They walk about sixty meters. There is a brick wall blocking the tunnel. There is a steel door mounted in this wall. It is obviously a watertight door from a ship. Luke cranks the wheel and the dogs retract. He pulls the heavy door open with some effort. There are a few squeaks of protest from the hinges. One of his assistants puts some more penetrating oil on the hinges while Luke and Benno go into a huge room on the other side. There looks to be something resembling an old college chemistry lab in most of it – complete with soapstone benches and sinks. There is a roughly four meter square fenced off area near the door on the right hand side that looks like a museum display. There is an island in the middle and what appears to be a salt lake around it. It almost looks like a combination terrarium/aquarium but it is dry as a bone.

"When will we have some light in this place Luke?"

"If you put it at the top of my list, it will have temporary light and air in here by lunchtime."

"It is on the top of your list."

*Benno leaves and one of the others escorts him
back to the elevator. Five minutes later he is talking to
Oskar again.*

"Thank you Benno. That is very interesting. Do you
have a camera?"

"Yes."

"Please take as many photographs as you can."

*No sooner are these words out of his mouth then he
thinks better of this.*

"No. Please close the place up. I don't want your
men disturbing anything. I will get Rudy Kleist to come
and take the photographs."

*Benno trots over to the mine shaft and takes the
elevator down to the first level. Luke and his assistants
are stringing electrical cable off to the mysterious room.*

"Luke, bring the electricity and the ventilation only
as far as the door. I want to leave the room undisturbed.
Oskar wants to see this for himself."

*Ten minutes later, Basima and Siegfried know about
this. Basima says that she remembers something about
some work going on in a mine on one of Karl's floppy
discs. They will meet at her place. Siegfried remembers the conversation he had with Prof Baumgartner
just before Baumgartner elected to leave Germany and
move to Argentina. While Baumgartner had never been
to Argentina he said that he received numerous reports
of the work they were doing here. He did not know the
location of the research facility but he said that he had
had radio contact with them for many years starting in
the late thirties. Siegfried wants Baumgartner to come
with them. Since his arrival in Argentina, Baumgartner*

has impressed the hospital staff. He now has an office in Hospital Aleman where he is consulting on the treatment of epileptic disorders. Siegfried calls and says they have something he needs to see. Please pack enough for a few days and come to Basima's place.

By 1045 they are all in Basima's den. She has located the part of the floppy disc she thinks is of interest. Karl was saying that there was a radioactive spring water source found near Tunis that Baumgartner thought was showing promise as an aid in his thought transference work. Since the loss of North Africa they have not been able to obtain any. They located another source in central Argentina. Baumgartner is listening carefully and now comments.

"That is a long time ago. I remember that Himmler went to Argentina once and Karl went several times."

Siegfried says he does not remember anything about this from his EEE sessions with Karl. They call Aldrich in Pelicura and ask him to meet them this evening for dinner in Rio Cuarto. They think they will need his expertise in chemistry at the new facility. They call Rudy and tell him to bring his equipment. They will meet him in San Antonio and he can go the rest of the way in Oskar's van. This may take a couple of days. Bring enough to wear. They have lunch and set forth to Rio Cuarto. They have guaranteed reservations at Hotel San Martin. It is 2135 when they finally arrive. There is still plenty of time for supper at a nearby steak house.

Rancho de la Veta Madre

Provincia de Córdoba, Argentina

March 1, 1995 Wednesday 0830

The visitors just walked into Benno's 'office'. He is talking with Luke Mayer. There aren't enough chairs for everyone so they adjourn to the dining room. Benno introduces Luke who then says a few words about mine safety procedures. Everyone gets a helmet with a head lamp and a pair of gloves then it is off to the mine. Rudy has so much camera equipment that they get someone to help him carry it all. The mine elevator is big enough to carry them all down at once.

"We think this elevator was installed in 1938. Hector called Thyssen with the serial numbers. They said it was built in 1937."

They walk along tunnel C to the door. After Luke opens it, Rudy takes several pictures before stepping into the room. They are all in the room when Siegfried says.

"I dreamt about this place last night."

Basima immediately comments.

"Ziggy, that was probably because of all the talk about the mine on the long drive from San Isidro."

This snaps him out of his trancelike state, but not before Baumgartner notices this exchange.

"Perhaps that is all it was Basima."

There is a fair sized chemistry lab filling most of this room. On the right near the door there is something that looks like a terrarium. There is what looks like an overgrown saw horse straddling it. The saw horse beam has a grooved wheel running in it. There is a block and tackle attached to the axis of this wheel with something resembling a bosun's chair attached to it. This is all wood and manila rope construction – no metal. There is a large white block of what appears to be honeycomb coral in the middle of the terrarium and the surrounding lower area looks like a dry salt lake. Siegfried immediately heads for it. He reaches down and sticks his finger in some slightly bluish powder in this lower area. He tastes it. Aldrich looks on in horror.

"Siegfried, you know better than to do that."

"It is the same Rochelle salt that we have been using all along Aldrich."

Aldrich and Oskar are just shaking their heads. The young man is a genius but he surely likes living dangerously. Aldrich is wondering how a nuclear Physicist knows anything at all about Rochelle salt. Then he remembers from Siegfried's dissertation that he did some experiments with this material. It is a piezo-electric salt.

Basima makes a mental note to find out how Siegfried knows so much about this place.

Something catches Aldrich's eye. There is a Zeiss microscope on a nearby bench. He walks over to it to take a closer look. He does a double take. Taped to the shelf behind the microscope are instructions for using an oil immersion lens. There are also samples of something that looks like an extraordinarily fine honeycomb coral nearby. What is going on here? You don't need oil immersion optics to look at coral. He points this out to Oskar. Oskar agrees that it doesn't look like any coral he has ever seen. They go back and look at the terrarium more carefully. It is pieced together with perhaps twenty carefully polished sections of 'coral'. They notice that there are infrared and ultraviolet lights mounted in the roof above the terrarium. Oskar asks Benno to shut off the lights. Now they notice occasional flashes coming from the 'coral'. They appear to be yellowish green or white. Baumgartner starts.

"This is exactly as they described it. I think that we need to not get close to that for any period of time."

A few of the construction crew have gathered near the door. Oskar turns to Benno.

"Benno, shoo off those guys hanging around by the door. I'm not sure we want everyone to know all about this place."

Benno has Luke shoo them off but he says that they can't shut the door because they haven't any air supply in the room.

Rudy is taking innumerable flash photographs. They slowly work their way around the big lab being careful not to touch anything. When they reach the wall opposite the door they entered through they find another three eight dog water tight steel doors. Luke opens the one on the left. It leads to a short corridor. There is another similar door at the end of this corridor. He opens this and they find that there is a room full of ancient radio equipment. Everything is vacuum tubes. Aldrich and Wilfried seem to have some familiarity with this vintage equipment. Oskar is remembering back to his youth. His parents had a Grundig table model that had tubes in it. His father never let him know of the existence of the U-boat until his fifteenth birthday. The boat had equipment something like this although not as much.

Basima comments that the air is beginning to feel a little close. Benno suggests they leave long enough for Luke to get some temporary ventilation into the room.

All this time that the others have been investigating the lab and the radio room, Siegfried was alone in the large room. Oskar goes over to collect him on their way out. Siegfried is in the bosun's chair slowly swinging over the island in the terrarium. Oskar asks Benno to give him a hand. They pull Siegfried back over the lab floor and lower the chair. He is somewhat unsteady on his feet so they help him out of the lab back to the elevator. Luke closes the door behind them. Baumgartner reiterates his warning to not spend much time near this thing.

Benno leaves instructions that no one else is to be allowed past the first door except the two men who came in with them originally. These two will be more than adequate to rig up some temporary ventilation. They go back to the surface and have coffee and pastry in the dining room. Siegfried snaps out of his apparent daze when he drinks his coffee. He and Aldrich are soon involved in a lively discussion about the miniature honeycomb coral and the Rochelle salt. Siegfried is already talking about putting the Rochelle salt into the honeycomb and making some kind of multistage piezo-electric device. He is wondering whether this 'coral' is even man made. Possibly this stuff might be useful as templates for fibrils.

There is a phone installed at each elevator stop in the mine. Benno calls level 1 at 1045. The phone on level 1 rings loudly and a light flashes. Thirty seconds later Luke is on the line.

"We are ready Benno."

"Do you have some means to lock the door?"

"Yes, I thought you would want to do that."

"Do we have any power in the room yet?"

"I have a thirty amp extension cord as far as the back wall. I am sure you noticed that we had ventilation ducting in the tunnel from the main shaft to the wall. We have tapped into this and now have cloth ducting extending to the wall at the other end of the lab. We are bringing air from the surface through the cloth duct to the far end

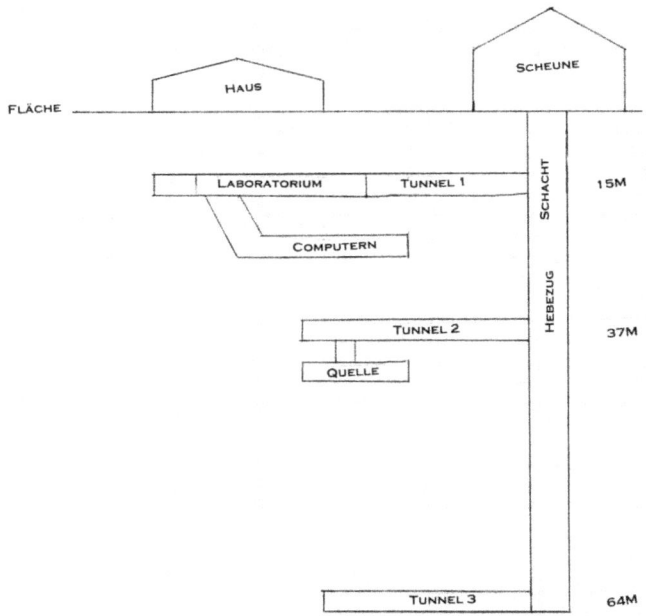

RANCHO DE LA VETA MADRE

of the lab space. I have two fans set up so that we can blow air through those two doors we haven't opened yet."

The visitors are back in the lab in ten minutes. Siegfried wants to stay by the terrarium. They leave one of Luke's workers with him just in case there is a repetition of the earlier incident. They proceed to the other end of the lab and open the center door. It leads to a similar short corridor with a similar door at the other end. This door opens into a library. There are possibly as many as one thousand books on the shelves. Aldrich wants Siegfried and Wilfried to take a look at a few of these. Oskar goes back to the other end of the lab to collect Siegfried. He is smiling and his eyes are closed.

"Ziggy, we need you to take a look at this library we found."

This snaps him out of his trance-like state. Aldrich, Siegfried and Baumgartner look at a few of the books. They are all German copyrighted ranging from the early 1900s to the late 1950s. A large number seem to have information about piezo-electrics. Siegfried finds some course notes on quantum mechanics written by Karl Eberhardt. There is a note written on the first page.

Dear August,

Chapter VII should prove useful in your work here.

Keep up the good work. I feel that you are getting close.

My best regards.

Karl 1958

"Yes, I remember this."
Before he can say anything else, Basima says.

"Ziggy, don't you have a copy of this?"

He returns from wherever he was.

"Yes, I believe you are correct, Basima."

Basima notices that Baumgartner seems to recognize what is going on here but says nothing. She signals for Oskar to join her in the large lab for a moment out of earshot of the others.

"Oskar, these flashbacks are getting more and more frequent. He is also complaining about headaches more often. I am sure that Baumgartner has already recognized these flashbacks"

"Yes, I know."

The three men continue skimming book titles. Possibly fifty of them appear to deal with crystal growth phenomena. There is a collection of books which deal with many natural tube forming phenomena ranging from plant stems to coral. There are three four drawer filing cabinets against the far wall. There are thousands of sheets of paper in each one. Basima and Oskar look at a few of these in the left-most cabinet. They appear to be in chronological order starting in April of 1937. There are many papers written on SS letterhead. They find a letter of commendation to A. Stauffer signed by Heinrich Himmler. Oskar reads the letter. Himmler made the commendation as a result of Karl Eberhardt's glowing report of what they were doing in Veta Madre. The letter is dated 7 Jan 1940. Eberhardt was here sometime before that. She looks in the cabinet on the right. The last sheet is dated May 3, 1960.

"Oskar, what do you want to do with this material?"

"It will be safe enough here. Possibly I should have Rudy photograph all of it."

"This last sheet is signed A. Stauffer. It would appear that he was working here from sometime well before

1940 up through 1960. Maybe Wilfried knows something about this."

They look at perhaps fifty sheets in the three cabinets. Several names recur often. It will obviously take some time to figure all this out. They don't find any dates later than May 3, 1960. They put everything back where they found it and rejoin the rest of the group who are waiting in front of the third door.

The third door opens onto a stairway landing. The stairs descend about five meters to a corridor which leads back under the lab. Luke dons an air pack which he brought along. He disappears into the corridor at the foot of the stairs. When he reaches the end of the corridor he finds several pipes running from floor to ceiling with valves one and one half meters off the floor. There are also several electrical conduits running from floor to ceiling. Three of these run through switch boxes. He paces off the distance back to the staircase. When he reenters the lab he paces off the distance to the terrarium.

"I think those pipes I saw down there are beneath this area. I will verify this later. Is there anything else you want to see Benno?"

"Thank you Luke."

The tour is over. They take the autographed book and go back to the ranch house. Oskar wants to digest all this someplace else.

"Thank you Benno. I would like Rudy to document the work you have done here. He will stay the afternoon to take pictures. Prof, will you please also stay and see what you can see? We would you like to join us for an early supper. You could bring Rudy and the Prof back too."

What's Benno going to say to the boss? Of course he will be delighted to have dinner with him and bring

Kleist and Baumgartner back. Oskar has deftly removed them from the van ride back to Rio Cuarto. Baumgartner apparently has already noticed that Siegfried is having flashbacks. Of course, he might know it happened as a result of the EEE sessions he put Siegfried through.

The ranch is connected to a secondary road which is the southern boundary of the ranch by eleven kilometers of winding dirt road. As soon as Oskar turns the ignition key they start trying to pry out of Siegfried anything he can remember about the circumstances when he was here before.

The ranch has a small herd of semi-domesticated horses which serve the needs of the six gauchos who keep track of the few thousand cattle being raised on the ranch. There is a large fenced in area behind one of the barns some two hundred meters from the ranch house. There are about twenty horses at least one hundred meters away from the dirt road but there is a solitary gaucho on a brown horse practically leaning against the fence next to the road. He is staring at the van as it approaches. Siegfried wants to take a closer look at the horse. They stop perhaps two hundred fifty meters from the house. He walks over to the fence and starts talking. Oskar and Basima are following close enough to hear him.

"I rode your great great great grandfather. He was too handsome to be used to drag timber around. Wilhelm had oxen to do that most of the time."

Siegfried is speaking German to the horse. The gaucho is looking at the Siegfried like he has a few screws loose. Basima perceives that Siegfried is 'Karl' again. Siegfried turns and walks right past Basima and Oskar toward the van. It doesn't seem like he has seen them. She speaks to the gaucho in Spanish. He is the most senior gaucho. His father before him was a gaucho on this ranch. He has lived here all his life and been working as a gaucho for forty two years since he was eleven years old. He says that he saw them go to the barn where the mineshaft is and they were there a long time. If they went down into the mine, it is no wonder that the señor is acting strangely. Basima coaxes him to explain what he is talking about. It turns out that he has never been in the mine but he has seen episodes like just occurred by people who were here many years ago. He goes on to explain that there were fifteen or twenty Germans here when he first started working. He was not allowed anywhere near the barn they were just in. Sometimes one of them would act strangely like the young man who was talking to the horse just now.

Siegfried walks right past the van. Oskar decides to not let Siegfried get too far away and leaves to follow him. Basima continues her chat with the gaucho.

"If you never went into the mine, how do you know that these people who acted strangely did?"

He points toward the barn where the elevator is.

"My father helped install the hoist in that barn before I was born. Sometimes on a hot summer day they would leave the doors open. He could see in there and see people going down into the mine with the hoist."

"And when they came up they acted strangely?"

"Sometimes."

"What did they do down there?"

"I don't know. I don't think there is any silver left down there. I never saw them bring any dirt out. My father told me that they did bring a great deal of dirt out long ago when he helped put the hoist in. This was all carted away to an area north of the barn."

He points down the road.

"I see that your friends are looking at that tree. It is the largest one on the ranch."

She turns to look. Oskar and Siegfried are standing in front of an enormous live oak draped with Spanish moss. Oskar notices the gaucho pointing at them. He coaxes Siegfried away from the tree and heads back toward the van.

"Thank you very much señor. I see that my friends are returning to the van. We must talk again sometime."

When she gets back to the van she finds Siegfried talking to Oskar.

"That tree is even bigger than it was the last time. For some reason the horse was spooked of that tree. I have never seen anything like it. Maybe there was a mountain lion or something lurking there that the horse was afraid of."

Nobody says anything. They are hoping he will give them some clue about when 'he' was here before. Siegfried folds his seat back as far as it will go and is asleep in a few moments. An hour and ten minutes later, barely two kilometers from the hotel, he awakens with a slight tic on his right side.

The other men show up promptly at 1800 and they eat in the hotel restaurant. After the meal Basima, Oskar and Siegfried adjourn to Oskar's suite. Basima has organized a bottle of Carlos I and several bottles of Villavicencio sparkling water. Oskar and Siegfried are enjoying the brandy. Basima has gone to the bedroom to watch television. Oskar is telling him.

"Siegfried, we tried to pry the time frame when 'Karl' was here out of you without much luck. It is clear that he came here sometime prior to January 1940. We just do not know when. Aldrich and Wilfried said that all the radio equipment was made in the late thirties and early forties. Basima and I found what appear to be lab records which extend from April 1939 until May 1960. Is this of any use to you?"

It happens again.

"August, you should have used Military approved vacuum tubes that Telefunken made. You are just going to end up spending more money when you have to replace everything – not to mention the inconvenience if something fails while you are talking to Herbertshausen."

He pauses briefly and then resumes.

"Wilhelm, you have got to get rid of that stuff. Get some decent tubes."

Oskar is thinking. Well, at least that is something. If he is talking about Herbertshausen it must have been before the end of the war. Wilhelm and my father got here in 1945 so I know that Karl visited again sometime after that. I have not found anything in Wilhelm's records about how he came into possession of this ranch. I am going to look in my father's diary when I get home. There might be something….

Hotel San Martin
Rio Cuarto, Argentina
March 2, 1995 Thursday 0700

Oskar wants to go back to Zarate and look in his father's diary. He and Basima talked about this last night but he is not going to mention this to Siegfried, at least not at the breakfast table. They sit down with Aldrich, Rudy and Wilfried. Aldrich has a car and a driver. He will take the other two back to the ranch today and tomorrow if necessary. Oskar wants all the lab records photographed. He wants Baumgartner to look through the correspondence in the file cabinets and see if he recognizes any of it. He will send a driver to pick Wilfried up and take him home Saturday morning.

They depart Rio Cuarto at 0830 and arrive at Oskar's home in Zarate somewhat after 1500. During the long ride they have plenty of time to go over yesterday's events. Siegfried is fascinated by the news that he got dizzy both times he was near the 'terrarium'.

"People told me that something like that happened at CERN. I was working with some Rochelle salt then too. I wonder if there is any connection."

They go around about this to not much avail. Then Siegfried starts talking about the piezo electric properties of the salt and the micro honeycomb.

"I think we might be able generate a potent electrical pulse if put Rochelle salt in some of that honeycomb coral and we squeezed it fast enough, just the way the Plodamax is supposed to work on the fibrils. Maybe we don't need the Selenium and all that nonsense we are trying to do. I think there was some sort of radiation in the vicinity of the 'terrarium' that affected my balance. I am beginning to think that the Rochelle salt and the photolinos are related somehow. I need to talk to Wig about this. He knows quite a bit about modulating all kinds of radiation. I need to talk to him."

Oskar is still fascinated with the dates they found in the file cabinets. He calls Hector on his cell and asks him to search the newspapers for anything noteworthy that happened in May 1960. When they arrive at Oskar's home he checks his phone and there is a message to call Hector.

"Good afternoon Hector. What did you find out?"

"The most newsworthy event in May that year was the Mossad capturing Adolf Eichmann and spiriting him out of the country. Two days after he supposedly left Argentina, the police found two dead men in a flat not far from Eichmann's house. They were both executed with a single shot in the back of the head. The article suggested that there may have been some connection between Eichmann's kidnapping and these killings."

"Did they identify the men?"

"Yes, I wrote that down. They were identified as Niklas Gruen and August Stauffer."

"Was there anything else?"

"I didn't see anything else Oskar."

"Did they say where these two men lived?"

"Yes. Apparently there was a car with Córdoba Province plates on it in front of the house where these two dead guys were. They lived in Tregano."

"Thank you."

Oskar gets a map of Cördoba Province out and finds Tregano. It is less than fifty kilometers from Rancho de la Veta Madre. He calls Benno.

"Benno, would you go to Tregano and find out what you can about a Niklas Gruen and/or an August Stauffer?"

"Several of our people are renting there. Let me see what I can find out from them. You may not know that there is a radioactive spring there in Tregano.

Siegfried interrupts.

"Benno I am still wondering about that dizzy spell I had near the terrarium. Do you know if there is any radioactivity in the mine?"

"I don't know Siegfried. I will send someone to Córdoba and buy a Geiger counter."

Oskar quickly interjects.

"Let's not do that Benno. We have several scintillation counters in Rojas. We will send you one. Possibly Professor Kessler has one. Is he around?"

"Yes. I think he and Professor Baumgartner are looking at all that paper in the file cabinets."

Eight minutes later Aldrich is on the phone. When they mention Niklas Gruen there is stunned silence on the other end of the line.

"Aldrich, are you still there? Did we lose the connection?"

"I am still here Siegfried. Niklas Gruen worked with me briefly during the war. How do you know that name?"

"The last entry that Oskar and Basima found in the papers in the file cabinets was May 1960. Hector went to the library and looked at the microfiche for Clarin for that month. That was the month that the Jews kidnapped Eichmann. Two days later the police found two men they identified as Niklas Gruen and August Stauffer. They both lived in Tregano which is only fifty kilometers from where you are at this very moment."

"We were looking through the correspondence and Wilfried recognized Stauffer. He told me that this guy was tight with Himmler. What you just told me sounds like the Jews had that all figured out."

Associate Professor Doctor Manfred Bauer's Office
Primate Research Center
Heidelberg University
Heidelberg, Germany
March 8, 1995 Wednesday

Doctor Bauer managed to cut a deal which seems to be acceptable to all sides. He is going to give the University two weeks of his time for each of the next two months. This will be reduced to one week a month for the following two months. This will give him enough time to bring someone else in the School of Medicine up to speed. The University will pay him a full time Associate Professor's salary for these four months. This time will accumulate toward tenure if he decides to return to the school any time in the future. Merck is also paying him his full time salary and getting some kind of tax break for letting him help Heidelberg and probably scoring some brownie points with the Chemistry department faculty as well.

Manfred arrived here Monday. He has looked over the Primate Center's purchasing records and determined that when the school purchased the Philips EEG they also spent several times as much, nearly three hundred thousand Deutsche Marks for the electrodeless receptor and transmitter helmets. These were made by a leading edge medical instrumentation house (Raffiniert Medizinprodukte Gmbh) in Frankfurt. They are merely listed as a Model B transmitter, a Model B receptor and associated hardware. He is pretty sure that Doctor Dietrich Lang designed the interface box. He calls Philips. He thinks he might have met this guy at school once but he can't remember his first name.

It turns out that there is more than one Lang at Philips in Eindhoven. The operator asks what department. As soon as he says Medical Instruments she says you are looking for Doctor Engineer Dietrich Lang.

"Doctor Lang, this is Doctor Bauer here at Heidelberg."

"Hello Manfred, you might not remember me but I was in your lab three years ago fiddling with Professor Baumgartner's interface box. I noticed you because Baumgartner was very proud that you were his student. Congratulations on your Doctor's degree. What ever happened to him anyhow? There were some rumors that he committed suicide."

"I really don't know. He simply disappeared. *(He knows full well that Baumgartner fled to Argentina but Lang doesn't need to know that.)* I have agreed to try to pick up the pieces and keep his work going but I already have a problem with that interface box. I was wondering whether you could make a duplicate."

"Sure, I could duplicate what I sent Professor Baumgartner but did you know that the interface box has a number of customer specified inputs that I don't know. I also think that Professor Eberhardt was some-how involved, although I do not know this for a fact."

"When did you make this equipment?"

"I have to check my records but I think it was ten years ago, maybe eighty five or eighty six. It was right around the time Baumgartner started experiments with the chimps. I hear that you have been quite successful in teaching that chimp a few things. All I know is that there was some extra circuitry and/or additional code inserted by your people in Heidelberg. I have no clue what it does exactly but it is in there. I presume it massages the sig-nal from the receptor helmet and then relays it to the transmitter helmet. I know it has provisions to mix signals into the receptor helmet output before they go to the transmitter helmet."

"Could you figure out what it does if you took the thing apart?"

"I doubt it. We might be able to reverse engineer it so to speak by putting known signals in and seeing what comes out. Hopefully there are some records somewhere of what was done."

"I hope so too. I will look around. Now that I am thinking about this, Baumgartner was always in the lab when we had human subjects. He would unlock the interface box and type a few things on its keyboard before the session started. After the session was over he would unlock the box and type on the keyboard some more. He would then lock the box again. He would leave it in a condition that allowed me to educate the chimps. Will this box work if it was interfacing between two Philips' EEGs?"

"Yes, it can interface with any of the major EEG manufacturers' equipment. I put something analogous to a universal remote for a television in there but that does not help you with the computer your people installed."

"Do you know if this additional equipment may have been as simple as a mixer to mix in particular sound waves with the signal sent to the transmitter helmet?"

"I think that is a good possibility but I don't know for sure. I knew you were using Middle C on the chimp but I really don't know what the extra equipment is capable of."

MEA
San Rafael, Argentina
March 8, 1995

Manny relayed the gist of the telephone call he had with Lang. Siegfried thinks about this for a while. If

Eberhardt was involved, maybe he knew how to get into that computer. Perhaps Basima can hypnotize me and I will 'remember'. Then he remembers something about Oskar saying he was humming something when he was in the lab at Veta Madre.

"Thank you for finding this much out Manny. We will order a duplicate set of this equipment to be sent to Aleman Hospital here in Buenos Aires. Professor Hartmann has a consulting arrangement with the Hospital. He will generate the actual order.'

"Isn't Hartmann the big gun in embryo transplant research?"

"Yes. Hartmann will approve the purchase order as having something to do with embryo transplant research. He already has an agreement between Heidelberg University and Aleman Hospital to do some kind of cooperative research."

"I found the discs with the recordings of the 'source' brainwaves. They were right where they were when I was there. Things are sort of in a state of suspended animation around here. They haven't gotten over the shock of Wilfried's disappearance. How's he doing anyhow?"

"He is doing well. He fit right in at Aleman. We expect he will be very helpful to our effort here."

"How is it going there?"

"They are taking care" of Enos and Ruth but that's about it. Incidentally, these few disks in the lab are the only records that are left. Professor Baumgartner destroyed all the records he had in his home. The police say that someone (presumably Baumgartner) set fire to the place using some kind of time delay device. He was half way to Argentina when the place burned up. All his records were destroyed. I have heard some rumors that some people thought he was a war criminal. Do you need me to do anything else here?"

"I can't think of anything at the moment. I am going to visit with Wig next week. Perhaps we can get together."

"I will be here until the end of next week. Then I am planning on being in Darmstadt the following three weeks."

"I suspect that it will take a month or two to get the duplicate equipment here in Argentina. Could you give us a couple of days with the Heidelberg equipment fairly soon?"

Ludwig Bieber's Office
Heilbronn University MHD Research Station
Neiderhofen, Germany
March 13, 1995 Monday 1000

Zig drove from the Frankfurt airport. It turns out that he has come at a good time. There was a medium sized mishap at the MHD facility Saturday. They will be down for ten to twelve days to fix it. Wig has time on his hands. They talk all morning. They arrange to have lunch with Professor Köhler of the Heidelberg Physics department and Professor Lehman of the Heidelberg Electrical Engineering department. It seems that Kohler and Lehman are about the only people there who believe that magnetic monopoles exist. It is always nice to have lunch with people you agree with. They have a good time. More importantly Zig and Wig learn of some work going on right now at the University which indicates, at least to Kohler and Lehman, that the monopoles may be responsible for the modulation of light in the green to yellow frequency range. They finish lunch at 1430 and drop the Profs off at school.

It is practically 1500. Wig calls Gabby and wants to know if she can sneak out early. She says no but will meet them at Margit's at 1700. They set up shop in Margit's with a bottle of Riesling and two glasses. Zig relates how he has occasionally had these woozy spells which he thinks have something to do with the photolinos. He mentions how he has had similar bouts of wooziness when they have fired off several test specimens in rapid succession. They sketch out a design for a new scintillation counter that Wig thinks can detect photolinos. The brainstorming session continues with empty bottles of Riesling being replaced with full ones as necessary. Optimism abounds. Zig talks Wig into coming to Argentina. Of course he should bring Gabby. Gabby doesn't show up until nearly 1730. By this time they are near the end of their fifth bottle of Riesling and they are both woozy, probably not from any stray photolinos wandering around Margit's. They order another bottle and a glass for Gabby. Wig is suggesting that if they could produce a reasonably steady stream of photolinos, he might be able to modulate them and transmit information. This might rival the amount of information transmittable by fiber optics. By the time they finish the sixth bottle Zig and Wig have talked themselves into believing that this scintillation counter they have sketched on the back of a bar placemat is going to make them into electronics tycoons. Gabby removes the keys from Siegfried's hand and drives them home. The next morning they both get to hear that she is not impressed with their abominable behavior at Margit's.

Baumgartner Laboratory
Heidelberg University
Heidelberg, Germany
March 14, 1995 Tuesday

Bauer, Bachmeier and Bieber are in the lab. Manfred has Enos sedated in the transmitter helmet. They are sending middle C along with a recording of some of Manfred's EEG session with Enos from four years ago. The chimp seems to be smiling. Manfred is explaining.

"We found out that Enos was more receptive when a middle C (512 hertz) note was mixed in with my EEG. On a couple of occasions Baumgartner would deliberately hit the E flat key on the mixer. Enos would stop smiling and he hardly ever seemed to learn anything in a session where this happened. I'll show you."

There is a two octave keyboard on the mixer. Manfred hits the E flat key and Enos face goes blank.

"Well, we might as well put him back in his cage and let him sleep it off. You don't want to be the first thing he sees after you do this. Chimps can be quite nasty when they are angry."

The chimp is in a wheelchair. They simply remove the transmitter helmet and wheel him away. Manfred returns a few minutes later. Siegfried wants to try this.

"Ziggy, I don't think that is a good idea. I have to dope you up a little anyhow and I am not sure what dose Baumgartner used on you. Everyone is different."

"Manny you know something about peoples' brains and chimps' brains. Surely if you gave me the same dose you gave Enos, I outweigh him at least three to one. How can any harm be done?"

"Ziggy, you better stick to your Physics. This is potentially dangerous."

"Do you have an antidote?"

"Schmidt might know. He is the expert on this sort of thing."

"Was he involved in this as well?"

"Professor Schmidt was Baumgartner's protégé. I know that he was seen around the lab here when Eberhardt was here. I think that having the three of them here practically every time you were here Zig was not a series of random events."

"Is he here today? Maybe he can shed some light on this subject."

Manny calls Professor Schmidt.

"Prof, this is Manfred here in the lab. I don't know if you knew but Siegfried Bachmeier is here today. I was showing him how we taught Enos. Now he wants to try experiencing the same recording and see if he learns anything about backgammon."

"You know we use different drugs on people than we do on the chimp?"

"Yes, but not the details."

"Manfred, I do not want to be a party to this experiment. I will give you the dosage to use but this is entirely your and Siegfried's idea. How much does Siegfried weigh?"

"Looks like eighty kilo to me."

Manny gets a 'thumbs up' from Ziggy.

"Give him eighty micrograms of a 50/50 mix of pentothal and Phenobarbital."

"Thank you Prof. We will be very careful. Is there any antidote if something goes wrong?"

"Sometimes Benzylpiperazine works. Aspirin will work but not any time soon."

Now Ludwig is having second thoughts about this too. He has heard Oskar go on about Siegfried not doing this sort of thing.

"Zig, you know Oskar will be bullshit if he finds out about this."

"Wig, we didn't get to square one in Argentina. I am here to learn what I can about this equipment. This is a legitimate part of the learning process. That is what I will tell Oskar if he does find out. I presume you are not going to tell him."

"You presume correctly."

Manny organizes the drugs. They strap Siegfried into the wheelchair. They put the transmitter helmet on him and make the adjustments to the clamps. There is an arrangement in the helmet that immobilizes his head so it can not move relative to the helmet. Siegfried now looks something like a hardhat deep sea diver. Manny administers the drugs which act relatively quickly. They play the recording of the session Manny had with Enos.

When the session is over they remove the helmet and find Siegfried a little groggy but smiling.

"It worked Manny. I have a vision of the backgammon board with the men and the dice."

"Have you ever played the game?"

"No, but I have seen other people play. I was into playing chess blindfolded with my grandfather. Listen, I want to do this again right now with one of the recordings with Eberhardt."

"Absolutely not. Baumgartner told me to never give anyone, including Enos, two doses of the sedatives. We can try again tomorrow. You need to stay away from this stuff for at least twelve hours."

Rancho de la Veta Madre
Provincia de Córdoba, Argentina
March 14, 1995 Tuesday 0800

Oskar has been investigating the provenance of the ranch. He had Hector track back through the land records in Córdoba. They found that the last time the ranch changed hands was in 1932 when a Wolfgang Stauffer purchased it from the Cuarto Rio de la Plata SA (Fourth River Silver Company). The silver company must not have thought there was any useful amount of silver left since Rancho de la Veta Madre was sold only for its value as ranch land. Oskar recognized 'Stauffer' easily enough. He called Benno and told him to see if there is any safe or hiding place that might have any records of the ranch. After two days of searching the ranch house, including drilling holes in the walls and floors and using metal detectors they located a modest Mosler safe behind a boarded up fireplace. Oskar received this news Sunday. Now, he, Basima, Aldrich and Hector are in the ranch house dining room examining the contents of the safe. They find a bible with the family genealogy in it. August Stauffer, Wolfgang and Maria's first child, was born in Munich in 1908. They fled to Argentina in late 1918 after Germany's surrender. They find the deed to the ranch. There is reference to an underground spring which is believed to emit Curie radiation and has highly beneficial health effects. Wolfgang was toying with the idea of building a dude ranch featuring a spa such as the one in Tregano. There is a folder containing numerous correspondences with the owner of the Tregano Spa and a travel agent in Córdoba. These stop in 1934. Then they find a folder with the Nazi Eagle Swastika on the cover. There is a letter from Heinrich Himmler to Wolfgang Stauffer.

17 August, 1934

Dear Wolfgang,

It was good to see you old friend. I must say your hospitality was even better than that on the Graf Zeppelin. I was fascinated with your 'spring of tranquility'. As we discussed, we have a project underway to improve the genetics of our people. One of the things we are trying to do involves improving their minds. I have a Doctor Wilfried Bachmeier who has made some progress in educating rats. He is using some spring water from Tunisia in conjunction with a common chemical on these rats and it seems to make them more receptive to learning. I would like to expand this effort and use your spring water. Both you and your son are chemists. You could help us I am sure.

I will send you two of Baumgartner's assistants to work with you. The Third Reich will compensate you for any and all expenses involved. I am enclosing a bank draft for 100,000 Reich Marks* to cover the losses you will incur by not continuing your present activities on the ranch.

I am looking forward to visiting you again.

Heil Hitler

H. Himmler

Reichsfuhrer-SS

*(roughly equivalent to $40,000 US in 1934)

Then they find a log of the tunnels. There is a detailed map of the tunnel system which is annotated with the dates that the various tunnels which were added after Wolfgang purchased the ranch. They see that there was a flurry of tunneling going on in 1936 and 37.

It looks like there is extensive structure under the terrarium including piping and electrical equipment. Benno is very happy to find comprehensive wiring diagrams for the tunnel network as it was in 1956...

"It looks like we might be able to use some of the existing electrical system. I have been putting all new equipment in working my way down from the surface through the elevator shaft. This is showing the old mains coming from a shed about fifty meters from the elevator. There is no shed there now but maybe the wiring is still there."

He calls Luke and asks him to come over and make a copy of the pertinent part of the wiring diagram and to go see what he can find. This will take a while.

"Benno, I talked with one of the gauchos last time. I would like to talk to him some more. He seemed to know a lot about the history of this place."

"They are not easy to find during the day Basima. This is a three thousand square kilometer ranch. They usually try to get home for their evening meal. I think you talked with Thiago Perez when you were here before. He is the senior gaucho. I will get word to his wife that I would like to see him tomorrow at the ranch house."

Three hours later Luke reports that he found the mains and they have made some temporary connections to one of the generators. It wasn't so easy to find the wiring since it terminated in a manhole which was buried under twenty centimeters of dirt. He has installed appropriate protective circuitry such that no damage will befall the generator if the old wiring has some faults in it. By this time everyone is very curious to see what is under the terrarium.

They have a light lunch and are in the underground laboratory at 1300. Luke made a most interesting discovery. He leads them through the lab, through the right-most door at the back of the lab and down the stairs. They walk to the area beneath the terrarium. He throws one of the switches on the wall. A two meter wide portion of the wall next to the switch recedes three meters. He beckons for them to follow him. They enter a room with two well lit corridors branching off to the northeast and the northwest. They enter the northeast one. There are what appear to be six jail cells on the left. Closer inspection reveals each door opens into the same large room. There are four IBM 650 computers and what appears to be a player piano in there. They walk fifteen meters down this corridor and Luke opens a door on the right. There is a large storeroom with innumerable bottles of chemicals on steel shelving. There is a barely audible whirring sound in this room. Luke says this place has its own fresh air supply coming from the surface. He hasn't found the air intake yet but this fan started when he energized the existing wiring. They retrace their steps and enter the corridor to the northwest. There is a two inch stainless steel pipe cemented into the wall of the tunnel a few meters from the entrance. The pipe terminates in a stainless steel ball valve with a plug in it. Oskar and Benno recognize the Teflon® tape used to seal the plug threads. Oskar is thinking that this must have been done subsequent to 1960. Wilhelm must have wanted this place mothballed after Stauffer and Gruen were killed. They chat a little about what they have found. It will take some time to figure this out….

Baumgartner Laboratory

March 15, 1995 Wednesday 0800

Siegfried has the disk from his last session with Eberhardt. They go through the routine preparing Siegfried as they did yesterday. It is a lengthy session – lasting nearly three hours. There are only the three of them in the laboratory. There are several knocks on the door during this session. Manfred simply tells the grad students that the lab will be unavailable until after lunch. Ludwig and Manfred play careful attention to Siegfried's facial expressions while the session is proceeding. It is 1115 when they finish. Siegfried is not as groggy as yesterday, probably because the drugs had longer to wear off. He starts talking about a mine but quickly catches himself and talks about something else.

"Zig, what's this business about a mine?"

He isn't going to say anything about the Veta Madre. Somehow he has a complete description of how the mine was in the late 1950's. This is fantastic. It seems that he must have needed the visual stimulation of actually seeing the mine before he could recognize what Karl was telling him.

"I don't know. I had a crazy image of a coal mine when I awoke. It was like a bad dream. Maybe I could sense the presence of the helmet. It is kind of claustrophobic in there."

Rancho de la Veta Madre

Provincia de Córdoba, Argentina

March 15, 1995 Wednesday 0730

Oskar and Basima are off to an early start. Señor Perez is waiting for them when they arrive at the ranch house. Benno has prepared a gourd of Mate. They go through the tea drinking ritual. Thiago is honored that the visitors are treating him as an equal. Basima starts.

"Thank you for taking the time to see us this morning. Señor Brandt is most interested in what you know about the early part of the time after his grand uncle Señor Stauffer bought this property."

"When Señor Stauffer bought this property he made my grandfather the chief gaucho. My grandfather spoke a little German and I think that is why they picked him. The property was idle. The silver was all gone and the silver company didn't want it. Señor Stauffer wanted to restore the ranch as a cattle growing operation. My grandfather died in 1950 and my father became the chief gaucho. Señor Stauffer also died about the same time and his son took over the ranch. I remember a little about the son. I worked for him from the time I was twelve until he died around 1960. He was a big German man. He spoke Spanish better than I do. He treated us very well. Everyone who worked here stayed here. Some of the other ranches around here are not such pleasant places to work."

"We are really interested in what your father told you about the ranch. You said you were born in 1942. Did you father ever tell you about much about the ranch before you started working here?"

"He said that the first Señor Stauffer had an important visitor from Germany a few years after he purchased the ranch. After this man came, less than a year later six more Germans arrived and stayed here. Then after that they did a lot of digging. My father said that they brought in copper miners from Chile to do most of the work. My father helped them install the hoist but none of the gauchos were allowed below the surface. My father told me that there were several deaths amongst the imported workers. He thought there might be something below the surface that was harmful. He told me that at first they operated the hoist by having oxen pull the thing up full of the dirt they were digging. They only did this for a few months. There was a deposit of lignite only a kilometer north of this ranch house. They built a boiler and burned the lignite to make electricity. This was the only electricity within fifty kilometers of here. I can show you where they did this if you like."

"Thank you Señor Perez we would like to see that a bit later."

Benno comments that Señor Perez showed him this operation some time ago but it was much easier to bring diesel fuel in and run the generators than to resurrect the old steam plant. Thiago continues.

"After they put in the electricity, many more Germans came. My father said that there must have been close to twenty of them. Señor Stauffer built an office near our cabins and moved the handling of the cattle operation there. He told my father that it would be best if the gauchos stayed away from the main ranch house. My father did stay away but told me that he sometimes watched the barn where the hoist was from a distance with binoculars. Sometimes he saw people come staggering out of the barn. My father said he thought that is what happened to the Chilean miners. Then when the war was over, Señor Stauffer said that it was no longer necessary to stay away from the ranch house but they should continue to stay away from the barn where the mine entrance was. He said that things went back to normal for a few years but just about the time I started working on the ranch a man from the east somewhere near Buenos Aires came for a few days and then we were told to stay away from the ranch house again. I don't know what happened after that because I did what I was told. Señor Stauffer died in 1960. I remember that. He died the same month I was eighteen. This man from Buenos Aires came again. This time I think he shut down whatever they were doing in the mine. He shut down the power station so we had no electricity again in our cabins. They only had a small generator which was used primarily to provide power to the well pump and light in the ranch house. He put a man named Manuel Torres in charge of the cattle operation but other than that we didn't notice much change. I think Torres may have been a veterinarian. I think this man had a ranch closer to Buenos Aires and he was using this ranch so that he could graze more cattle. A truck would come several times a year and bring a few pregnant heifers from his other ranch. These were kept separate from the rest of the herd. He must have kept the bulls at his other ranch. We only had heifers and steers here. Occasionally we would send a male calf from one of these heifers back."

"Did the truck have any identification?"

"No."

This is so like Wilhelm Bachmeier. He kept everything as secret as he could manage.

"Where is Señor Torres?"

"I don't know. He left two years ago and told me I was in charge of the cattle operation."

"Did you ever meet the man from near Buenos Aires?"

"I was never introduced to him. I saw him from not far away though."

Oskar takes a recent picture of Wilhelm out of an envelope.

"Is this the man you saw?"

"Yes."

They probe around a little bit more about the mine but Señor Perez really doesn't know much about the goings on in the mine. They thank him for his time.

They are talking about what they just heard when Prof Baumgartner's driver enters the dining room.

"Please excuse this interruption Kapitän Brandt. I am very sorry to tell you that Prof Baumgartner is dead. When he didn't meet me at the car at 0800 I went to his room. There was no answer to a knock on the door so I went back to the desk and asked them to call him. When there was no answer the manager accompanied me up there and we opened his room. He looked like he was asleep in his bed but when I touched him he was cold."

"That is bad news Horst. Please arrange to have him buried as soon as possible."

(It really is bad news. The consensus is that Baumgartner was keeping some of the drugs he used with human subjects secret. He won't be telling them now.)

John and Henry are listening to Guenther and Mitch who are wound pretty tight this morning. Mitch is talking.

"We have been watching this Bieber guy rather carefully since he went to Argentina over the Christmas break. Siegfried Bachmeier showed up in Neiderhofen Monday. The two of them went to Heidelberg and took a couple of people there to lunch. We are looking into who exactly went to lunch with them. Then Bieber and Bachmeier went to some gin mill not far from the University and started partying. They were a little bit rowdy but not so bad as to get themselves kicked out of the place. Bieber's live-in showed up about five thirty. She had one glass of Riesling out of the sixth bottle they ordered and then suggested she would drive them home while they could still walk to the car because she wasn't going to carry them. Well, that isn't so unusual in those parts. Even I have been known to have done things like that in my youth. Guenther will explain why we are getting excited."

"Bieber and Bachmeier were designing a scintillation counter which could detect photolinos. Bieber was saying he thought he could modulate them in such a way as to transmit information as fast fiber optic cable could. This was done on the back of a paper place mat. They took it with them. One of Mitch's minions managed to get most of the conversation on tape. I listened to it. Henry, you remember when Randy took us to that place? They are getting dangerously close to figuring out how to do what you saw done there."

"I thought Mitch said they were stoned."

"These guys think about this stuff almost subconsciously. Even if they were drunk a discussion of a technical nature is quite likely to be more intelligent than anything most people ever say in their whole lives."

(This is high praise indeed, especially from Guenther.) He continues.

"I talked with Randy at length about this business of modulating the photolinos. This is potentially more dangerous than anything you can imagine. If they were able to teach the chimp to play backgammon by EEE then they already have a means of influencing the brain of any creature that is in the 'subject' transmitter. It doesn't take much of a leap of imagination to think that they might be able to do this on a large scale with a suitable means of modulating the photolinos."

Mitch interrupts.

"That is a long way from what they are doing Guenther."

Guenther comes right back at him.

"I invite you to compare the first British radar installations with the flashlight sized radars every cop in town has now. They appear to be resurrecting Baumgartner's lab. Manfred Bauer, the young man largely responsible for teaching that chimp how to play backgammon has been there since Monday a week ago. He's the one that helped Bachmeier get hold of Baumgartner's recordings. Apparently there is something wrong with the heat in Baumgartner's office. Bauer has the door open all the time to the main lab. This probably won't go on much longer but we are taking advantage while we can. Last Wednesday he had a long conversation with Dietrich Lang at Philips. Lang is the guy who designed and built Baumgartner's interface box and transmitter.

We couldn't hear Lang's half of the conversation but we know that Bauer wanted him to duplicate the interface box. Right after he spoke with Lang, he called Bachmeier in San Rafael. He was talking about buying the receptor and transmitter helmets from some specialty house in Frankfurt. During that conversation we heard that a Professor Hartmann was somehow involved in this. It turns out that he is the honcho of the embryo transplant research at Heidelberg University Hospital. We determined that Hartmann visited Aleman Hospital in Buenos Aires four times last year. This leads me to think that Hartmann went to Argentina to oversee embryo transplants from Siegfried's girlfriend to some surrogates. They are back at it trying to produce 'supermen'. I further suspect that Bachmeier is planning on duplicating everything at Heidelberg in Argentina.

Now we have some good news followed by much more bad news. First, we learned that they always mix a middle C note in with the EEG they send to the chimp. It makes the chimp more receptive. We also heard that if they transmitted a minor note the chimp did not like that and didn't learn anything either, i.e. he became non-receptive. We also learned that they usually use a mixed sedative in the ratio of one microgram per kilo of body mass and that they usually used a common ingredient in 'pep' pills as an antidote.

Siegfried, Bieber and Bauer were in the lab yesterday afternoon and again this morning. Yesterday they had the chimp as the subject for a while and played one of the tapes that came from a session four years ago where Bauer was teaching the chimp how to play backgammon. Then they repeated this act with Siegfried as the subject. They didn't have the CCX-1 in the loop so all we know is what we heard which was all the good news I just told you. Apparently, the tape caused

Bachmeier to think about backgammon. We think that the brain waves can transmit visual information for sure. The interface box in Heidelberg has some kind of gadgetry and/or code installed by Baumgartner et al and it was suggested that the et al was Karl Eberhardt. Bauer and the Philips guy thought this stuff that was installed locally may have been as simple as a sound mixer. The Philips guy is going to do some tests and try to 'reverse engineer' the thing. We know from some of what the CCX-1 picked up that they were playing middle C in both of the chimp's ears and we have reason to believe that this interface box may also be inserting an electronic sinusoidal wave into the signal from the receptor helmet before sending it to the transmitter. We are looking at this matter very carefully. We suspect that this somehow enhances the receptivity of the 'subject', but we don't know exactly how.

Now we come to the really bad news. This morning the 'terrible trio' was at it again. This time they had a disk of an EEE session with Eberhardt as the source and Bachmeier as the subject. They played this disk with Bachmeier as the subject. It took over three hours. When it was over we think Bachmeier was in some sort of trance briefly. He was going on about a mine. Then when they woke him up he said he thinks he had a dream about a coal mine and had some sort of claustrophobic reaction from the transmitter helmet. This sounded like bullshit to me and Randy so I had a couple of people who know about this sort of thing listen to what the CCX-1 picked up. They both think Bachmeier made up the part about the coal mine when Bieber asked him what he was talking about. It is a bit of a stretch but if they have moved their operation to some sort of mine, it is no wonder we are not getting any signals from Argentina."

Rancho de la Veta Madre
Provincia de Córdoba, Argentina
March 22, 1995 Wednesday 0800

Siegfried returned from Germany last Friday. As soon as he learned of the findings at the ranch he wanted to see for himself. He and Oskar and Basima drove to the ranch Monday. Luke and Benno gave them another tour Tuesday. They started in the room with the computers. Siegfried is taking a great deal of interest in all of this. The computers are ancient but they were state-of-the-art in 1958. They find the punched cards used to store the programming code and they find the printed list of the code. These long antecede Siegfried's first appearance on this earth but he has read about such things as punched cards. They get a brief tour of the portions of the #2 tunnel (thirty seven meters below the surface) that have light and power. The source of the 'hot' spring water is at the end of this tunnel. It is almost directly under the terrarium. They also find a large supply of Rochelle salt in this tunnel.. It is badly caked up after many decades, even though it is in plastic lined bags.

Siegfried is expert in Fortran® programming although he works with a much later version. Tuesday evening he duplicates the programming found in the mine on his laptop computer. He thinks that the computers were being used to produce some sort of signal which was being sent to the terrarium.

First thing Wednesday morning he and Aldrich start looking through the chronological file of the experiments in the late 1957 to 1958 time frame. They soon find that Stauffer and his collaborators were trying to duplicate some earlier successes with the player piano using the new computers. There is a cabinet containing many piano rolls. They start looking at these and Aldrich notices that all the music is in C major. It seems that if they placed a subject in the bosun's chair and moved the subject over the island in the terrarium they were able to cause the subject to hum what was being played on the piano. Siegfried wants to test this. Along with Benno and Luke they return to the room with the computers and piano and after a while find out how this equipment is connected to the terrarium. They find that the piano has magnets for every steel string. The electrical impulses generated when the strings vibrate are amplified much the same as in an electric guitar amplifier. These amplified electrical impulses are sent to the terrarium where they are connected to a myriad of micro piezo electric crystals in the honeycomb coral. These in turn vibrate and somehow emit 'something' that the subject in the bosun's chair can sense. The investigators thirty seven years ago had no explanation for this phenomenon. However, they knew how to reproduce it. Oskar is not interested in having Siegfried use himself as a guinea pig to test this arrangement but Siegfried prevails on him to let him try very briefly. Siegfried goes up to the terrarium and positions himself in the bosun's chair above the island. Five minutes go by and nothing is happening. Then he starts humming Beethoven's Mass in C. Then he is silent again. A little while later he starts humming Für Elise but it doesn't sound quite right, then he slumps forward. Oskar pulls him back away from the terrarium.

A few moments later Aldrich arrives. Oskar signaled him to stop playing as soon as Ziggy slumped over and he pulled Siegfried away from the terrarium. Aldrich is somewhat out of breath from the exertion of climbing five meters of stairs when he arrives about forty seconds later.

"Did it work?"

"He was humming Für Elise when he slumped forward. Before that he was humming Beethoven's Mass in C and before that he was quiet."

They help Siegfried out of the bosun's chair to a nearby bench. Basima says.

"Ziggy can you hear me?"

He does not respond so she repeats the question. This time he wakes up and pronounces.

"I see how they do it."

Aldrich picks up the narrative.

"Ziggy and I devised a little experiment. From what we can gather, middle C is of importance in transmitting the emanations. We don't know exactly how yet but the experiment we did strongly supports this hypothesis. First I played Für Elise. That was when the first period of silence must have occurred. Then I put on the piano roll with Beethoven's Mass in C. I played the Sanctus. Is that the part he hummed?"

Oskar answers.

"I think so Aldrich, I have only heard this a few times. It was one of my father's favorites."

"Then I played Für Elise again while the piano was set to play middle C only when I struck the key."

"That is amazing. He was humming something that sounded like Für Elise but it didn't sound quite right, then he slumped over."

Siegfried says.

"I remember that a little. The music was discordant and it made me tired."

Oskar is quite upset by all this.

"That is the last of this experiment using Siegfried as a subject."

Basima interjects.

"You remember Señor Perez' saying that his father had seen people stumbling out of the barn, I wonder."

Wilfried Baumgartner Laboratory

Heidelberg University

March 28, 1995 Tuesday 1000

Henry and Christina are visiting the Laboratory to find out how the Cerebrionics equipment is functioning. They are chatting with Manfred Bauer. The conversation is in English.

"Thank you, Professor Bauer for taking the time to see us today. We knew something changed here last summer when there was a sudden decrease in the data flow."

"Yes. That was when Professor Baumgartner took a leave of absence. He was working with my friend Siegfried there. We got word last Thursday that he died in his sleep."

"I am so sorry."

"Thank you for your sympathy Herr Hartwell. He was a great teacher. We have named the building in his honor."

"Are you running the lab now?"

"I have agreed to work here for the next few months on a part time basis and familiarize Professor Hahn with the operation. Then I will return to Merck."

"We were greatly impressed with what you were able to teach your star pupil. Is he still here?"

"Oh yes, Enos is alive and well. Unfortunately he has not been getting as much attention as he needs."

"We were wondering whether you have any electro-encephalograms of Enos. It would be interesting to compare what his brainwaves look like compared to those of a human being."

"That is an interesting thought. We do have a number of encephalograms of Enos on disc. In fact, I have encephalograms from before I was a student here up through when you were here last time. He only had a vocabulary of forty words when I came here. That is a very interesting idea Herr Hartwell. I can easily see a Doctoral Dissertation coming out of making sense of that."

"Thank you Professor Bauer but I must confess it was Dr. Barton's idea."

"Let me get Felix in here."

Five minutes later Associate Professor Felix Hahn enters the lab. Manfred makes the introductions. They chat a little while. They accept Henry's offer to buy lunch. He says that a friend of his recommended that he try some bar near the university this trip. The bar turns out to be Margit's. The same agent who recorded Bachmeier and Bieber three weeks ago manages to record the four of them while they talk at lunch. The conversation is in German. Henry and Christina manage to manipulate the conversation, as per Guenther's instructions so that Felix and Manfred will say some words that Guenther wants them to say. Henry and Felix have beer and some varied sausages with sauerkraut and potatoes. Manfred and Christina have wine and salads with a plate of cold cuts on the side. Felix agrees that it will be interesting to 'see' what Enos' brain patterns look like. He has a student in mind to work on this. He will finish his undergraduate work in two months. Felix says we can give him a head start by processing these discs before he starts working in the lab. They agree to send half the discs they have of Enos' brain wave patterns to Cerebrionics in Memphis. They will process them and send the 'movies' back to Heidelberg within the month. They will then send the other half of the discs. Felix is already thinking (not out loud of course) about how he might be able to wangle some consulting fees out of Cerebrionics.

The Profs thank Henry for lunch and say they need to walk off some of lunch on the way back to the University. Henry and Christina take two days of vacation before returning to the US Friday. The recordings of everything said in Baumgartner's lab and Margit's are in the Memphis Targeting and Los Alamos computers by 1500 Tuesday.

Rancho de la Veta Madre

Provincia de Córdoba, Argentina

March 28, 1995 Tuesday 0800

Siegfried talked Ludwig into forgetting about Heilbronn and joining him in Argentina. Oskar pulled a few strings and Ludwig and Gabrielle were granted permanent visas in close to a record short time. They purchased all the electronics they needed through MEA and have now constructed something which they think can detect photolinos. Oskar and Siegfried gave Wig a tour of the ranch Monday afternoon. He immediately recognized that Siegfried's comments about a 'mine' after the session in Heidelberg were probably about this mine here under the ranch.

They are off to an early start this morning. Siegfried explained that the experiment where the subject is induced to hum by some emanation from the terrarium has been duplicated on three volunteers in Oskar's organization. It works with the piano rolls which are all in the key of C major and it works with other music not in C major if the middle C note is struck on the piano for every note that Aldrich plays and is non-discordant. The subjects all complained about headaches after the music not in C major and/or discordant was played. Siegfried also continues to have headaches. Ludwig asks the obvious question.

"Have you been able to transmit anything besides musical notes?"

Oskar answers.

"No, I am hoping that you will be able to help us with that. Ziggy said that he thought this gadget you have designed might be capable of modulating the photolinos. He thinks that there is some common ground between these transmissions to the subjects here and to the EEE experiments he participated in at Heidelberg."

Siegfried adds.

"We know that Manny and Prof Baumgartner were able to transmit something besides music to Enos. We are hoping to have the same equipment as the Heidelberg lab installed here in the near future. We have everything on order. We will not have a CCX-1 but we didn't use it last time."

Oskar picks right up on this.

"What are you talking about, 'last time'? Surely you did not endanger yourself again in Germany Siegfried."

"Uncle, we made a fantastic discovery in Germany. We played the last session I had with Eberhardt again. This time I received a great deal of information that I did not recognize before. I could see this mine. I can tell you that there is a safe in the eastern tunnel at the thirty seven meter level. It is carefully camouflaged so I doubt you have found it."

How does Ziggy know anything about the eastern tunnel at the thirty seven meter level? He has never been there. Oskar picks up the phone and calls Benno.

"Benno, how far along are we with refurbishing the thirty seven meter level?"

"We have the room in the southern tunnel rewired."

"What about the east side?"

"We have not started there yet."

"Hold on a second."

"Ziggy, do you think that you can find this safe?"

"I think so."

"Benno, please come here. Bring a couple of flashlights."

Ten minutes later they are in the room on the east side. It is as big as the laboratory at the thirteen meter level. Siegfried goes immediately to the exposed rock face at the opposite end of the room and starts feeling the stone. Right before their eyes part of the wall moves backward. Benno exclaims.

"That is just like the arrangement on the upper level."

Indeed it is. There is a corridor with several more rooms off of it. The safe is directly across the corridor from the hidden door. It is an old Kärcher with a bit of rust on it. Benno says they will have to take it up to the surface to get it open. It is a good sized walk-in safe. Ziggy does some quick mental arithmetic.

"Benno, that safe has eighty millimeter thick walls. It must be close to ten tons."

"How do you know that, Ziggy?"

"I just know. Don't worry about that. There are facilities to move it to and from the elevator shaft. I am sure you can see it has its own wheels. I can move this by myself. I will show you."

To the right of the safe there is a two door metal cabinet. Ziggy opens the doors revealing a large selection of tools. He picks up a spanner wrench, a hammer and a small can of penetrating oil. He walks about five meters into the large room and stops by what appears to be a round metal plate in the floor. He puts some penetrating oil around the plug in the middle and inserts the wrench into the plug. After a few whacks, the plug moves. It takes four turns to unscrew it. There is a thirty millimeter diameter hole in the steel bar. Siegfried goes back to the tool chest and pulls out a thirty millimeter eyebolt which he inserts in the hole. He enlists Benno's aid to help him install the chain fall which they attach to a fixture on the safe and the eyebolt. Benno suggests that he has people with stronger backs and weaker minds than Siegfried to do this sort of thing. Oskar wants a moment to think about this. He chats with Benno briefly about who they will get to move it. Two of the young men who went with Oskar on U-1241 are now working at Veta Madre. They can be relied on to keep their mouths shut. Benno returns in fifteen minutes with the young men in tow. By 1000 they have the safe on the surface in the barn. There is a locksmith in Mendoza who they trust to keep his mouth shut. He will be there shortly after lunch.

Oskar is impressed. It is beginning to look like Siegfried may know a lot more about Karl Eberhardt than they ever thought. They have these recordings of Eberhardt's brain waves. Kessler and Fassbinder are pretty sharp guys and they practically genuflected at the mention of Eberhardt. He is not the only one impressed. Ludwig is equally amazed. He is thinking back. They were doing this experiment in Heidelberg two weeks ago and he has just seen a demonstration that Siegfried really can receive information via this electroencephalographic route.

Ludwig comments.

"So, you have the same equipment we used in Heidelberg coming here?"

"Yes."

"Is Manny getting anywhere with Lang?"

"Lang is busy trying to reverse engineer the thing but if I can get a better read on Karl's thoughts he may have 'told' me already."

The procedure being used in Argentina is really very different from the one in Heidelberg. They have been able to cause a subject to hum a tune with no fancy transmitter helmet or any particular positioning of the subjects head in a receptor helmet and at a considerable distance of two meters instead of the two centimeter separation between the helmet and the subject's scalp.

They have devised an experiment to see if there is any identifiable characteristic of the emanation from the coral. The newly designed scintillation counter is in the bosun's chair and its output is being recorded on disc as well as being sent to an oscilloscope. When they first start the flow of the 'hot' spring water there is a brief burst of white noise displayed on the scope. They start the piano playing a series of middle Cs. This produces a very low level white noise on the oscilloscope. Ludwig and Siegfried have devised a variable frequency band pass filter which controls the radiation that the scintillation counter receives. As the filter slowly transitions from the near infrared on into the visible the oscilloscope suddenly shows a faint sinusoidal wave at 512 hertz (middle C). The band pass filter is allowing radiation at 520+/- 3 terahertz (green-yellow light) to reach the scintillation counter. They walk the band pass filter frequency up and down a few times and get the same response at this frequency. Siegfried is getting excited.

"That is practically the same frequency of the photolinos that my instruments at CERN detected. Of course, there was no middle C."

He goes on to explain to Ludwig the experiment they did last week. It is fairly definitive that information can be transmitted without a high magnetic field to modulate it. Suddenly he exclaims.

"I had a headache after Aldrich played Für Elise with the middle C superimposed. This happened to me several times in Baumgartner's lab. I think he was using middle C or some harmonic as a carrier frequency. He had a much faster computer than these rel cs in the tunnel. Perhaps this is why they could only transmit music. I went over the notes from the late 1950s. They didn't do as well with the computers as they did w th the player piano. There isn't that much information there in the music but the computers were pretty slow then. When I was having those sessions with Karl I was receiving images as well as voice. Now that I am th nking back, I think I could hear middle C sometimes."

Aldrich adds something which will ultimately turn out to be very important.

"Some of the piano rolls have music that has been transposed from the original key to C Major. It will be interesting to see what your efforts at deciphering Baumgartner's recordings bring. It should be simple enough to detect the presence of a middle C harmonic."

Wig gets into it.

"The machine we have at the Heilbronn MHD facility is something of the order of ten million times as fast as those 650s. Possibly if we had a modern computer here we could transmit images. I am sure you could do much better with your laptop Zig than that stuff that precedes your presence on this earth."

"That stuff precedes your presence toc Wig."

After a brief pause he says.

"I wonder whether we could use this technology to cause more than one person to hum the same tune at the same time."

Basima smiles to herself. She found reference to efforts that Baumgartner was making to achieve mass hypnosis in Karl's notes. Apparently Himmler was very keen on this. She has been trying to instill this thought in Siegfried since the third hypnosis session. if this technology can be developed to such an extent that they could more or less hypnotize a crowd at a political speech, for example, it should be possible to seize control of the entire country in a few years.

END OF PART II

Siegfried, Basima and Oskar are in the living room listening to one of the tapes Basima made in a previous session. Siegfried is again speaking in the first person as if he is Karl Eberhardt.

"I must say August, I am glad to be off that horse. When you do as little riding as I do, it gets uncomfortable after a while."

After a brief pause when August Stauffer must have been speaking.

"We must have ridden ten kilometers. You had to drag the timber for the mine the last ten kilometers with horses?"

She stops the tape.

"Is any of this coming back to you Ziggy?"

"I remember seeing that timber in the mine Wednesday long ago. I am trying to think back. This must have been around the time they built that big room we were in. Obviously there were no mine tunnels that wide. This must have been shortly before the war."

He lapses into silence for a moment then he says.

"When will we be able to look at the discs from Heidelberg?"

"Professor Hartmann has some time set up for you in two weeks. He told us he expects to arrive in BA a week from Monday with the Philips interface box. He will supervise the installation at Aleman Hospital the following week. He can use the hospital's machines the following weekend. Unless there is an emergency we can use them six hours both Saturday and Sunday"

"Will that be long enough?"

"I don't think we can get this done in one weekend. First, we have to establish the relationship between your brain waves and the words you say. We are also hoping to get some recordings of how Wig's waves relate to words that he is saying. Then we have to see whether there is anything recognizable in Eberhardt's waves during your joint sessions. We also want to see what at least one of his sessions with Heidi looks like. We have no recordings of Eberhardt's voice. This might be difficult or impossible to do."

"Is Professor Hartmann going to stay for all this?"

"We think he might. He is going to spend some time checking up on the surrogate mothers and your children. He wants to compare Eric's brain waves with some recording of infant boys' brain waves that he is bringing with him."

Eric was born April 11th. Heidi and Siegfried got to hold him within moments of his birth. Heidi went through a lactation inducing regimen at Aleman Hospital the preceding three weeks and was able to nurse Eric immediately. The surrogate mother has returned to Brazil. She was very well compensated for her efforts and said that she would be willing to do it again. Their second child is expected to be born in June. The ultrasound indicates that the child is a girl. They have already named her Karolin. Heidi is going to go through the motions of breast feeding for bonding purposes but will likely have to use some formula or the surrogate mother's breast milk for the next child. She is barely producing enough milk for Eric. At least the one after that isn't due until August. It looks like Hartmann planned all of this quite carefully. They will be able to wean them off after two months if necessary. Siegfried is renting a large house in San Isidro not far from Basima's. They have two nannies and four full time servants. They have a resident dietician who is on the Aleman staff. Supposedly they are going to be able to feed the children food which will aid in keeping them asleep most of the evening. If not, the nannies will worry about it. Nobody wants Heidi getting exhausted tending to all these children. They will know by September how well this plan is going to work.

"This won't hurt Eric will it?"

"Hartmann says he has done EEGs on infants at least two dozen times and none of the children have shown any ill effects. If you strongly object, he will put this off for a year or two. However, he strongly recommends that this be done sooner rather than later. They can detect certain kinds of abnormalities which indicate a tendency toward epilepsy, for example. There are drugs that can mitigate some of these abnormalities which work best the earlier they are started."

Hospital Aleman
Buenos Aires, Argentina
May 23, 1995 Tuesday

Siegfried and Ludwig finished the first part of their effort to deconvolute Baumgartner's disc recordings of the sessions he conducted with Karl Eberhardt and Siegfried. They went through the same procedure that Randy Biggs and Guenther Reinhardt went through and generated discs that have them speaking and then thinking words they think are relevant and recording the output from the EEG. At the same time they also record the output from the Philips interface box. They do not have the Cerebrionics CCX-1 so there is no visual clue as to the output of the 'source' except the traditional electroencephalogram. It will be necessary to repeat these efforts in Heidelberg where they have the CCX-1.

Siegfried made two more trips to Rancho la Veta Madre in April. Aldrich devised a rather clever separation scheme which enabled them to separate the Thorium and Radium in the radioactive spring water relatively easily. They have determined that the strongest emissions from the Rochelle salt seem to occur when stimulated by a 2MEV (2 Million Electron Volts) emission from the radium. This is well within the range of low power particle accelerators including those used for semiconductor doping. Initially they think about manufacturing the Rochelle salt target in a manner analogous to putting phosphors on a television screen. There are certain technical problems with this approach. Zig and Wig decide that it would be simpler to make something more closely analogous to a flat screen display. They will be able to have a physical electrical contact with every pixel on the screen and it will not require operation in vacuum. They intend to repeat the experiments done with the 'coral' using their manufactured emitter.

A serious problem has arisen as a result of the earlier experiments. Two of the three volunteers who had sessions over the 'coral' and were able to receive the emanations causing them to hum the tunes being transmitted have subsequently had numerous headaches. Oskar will not approve more experiments on volunteers. They discuss this matter for some time and then Oskar calls Chief Weiss.

"Good morning Manfred"

"Good morning Oskar. I haven't heard from you in a while."

"Manfred, I have a problem. We are doing some experiments which require human subjects. We think we injured two of our people who volunteered to be the 'guinea pigs'. I was wondering if you might be able to 'disappear' a few people you might not be fond of to help us out in this matter."

The Chief thinks about this for about ten seconds. While he is doing this, Basima whispers in Oskar's ear.

"It would be preferable if these guinea pigs speak German."

"Certainly sir, when do you want them?"

"I will let you know, probably late next month or early in July."

"I will need about a week's notice."

"Do you think you can find some who speak German?"

"That might not be so easy, Oskar."

"I need to talk about whether we could use people who only speak Spanish. I will get back to you Manfred. Thank you for your help."

Basima picks up again.

"I really don't know if this is going to be a problem Oskar. I brought the subject up because I have a passing acquaintance with something called psycholinguistics. There is a field of thought that claims that the language people speak is related somehow to the way they think and vice versa. All our background in this brain wave and thought transference work has been in German. German and Spanish have different syntax and they don't sound much alike either. We may have to repeat the efforts that Ziggy and Ludwig made using people who speak Spanish. I could probably help in this effort but I wonder, since neither of these languages is my native language whether I would have the same brain wave patterns as someone whose native language is Spanish. On the other hand, if the brain wave patterns are associated with visualization of the same concept there might be some similarities. For example, I am thinking that when we say the words, 'casa, haus, house and maison' we have the same concept no matter what the language."

Oskar thinks about this a little while and responds.

"You and Siegfried are fluent in Spanish and German and Siegfried and Ludwig speak some French. You speak all those languages. We can certainly find out what the brain wave patterns look like for any of you saying the same words in those languages. Perhaps we can find out if there are any differences in the brainwave patterns depending on whether a native German speaker or you say the same words. This will have to wait until we have all the EEG equipment set up here – probably at Veta Madre. I can not see you going back to Germany and using Baumgartner's equipment to save a little time. The CIA tried to kill you when you were in Switzerland. Abbo Fassbinder told me that the CIA rented a house not far from him on the German side of Lake Constance. He believes that they attacked your house from across the lake. I know that you have the good sense to stay here in the meantime. My nephew, unfortunately, is long on smarts and not so long on good sense. He is adamant that he and Ludwig use Baumgartner's equipment again sooner rather than later. He and Ludwig are going to do their deciphering efforts over starting next week.

I think that he feels he is short of time. You know that those headaches he complains about seem to be getting worse and Aldrich told me he thought he saw an instance of something that might have been a mild epileptic seizure."

"I didn't know that Oskar."

There is a conference call going on between John and Henry and Guenther and Randy. Guenther is doing the talking at the moment.

"Bachmeier and Bieber went through the same exercise in Baumgartner's lab in the past week that we did in Los Alamos a little while ago. This Bauer guy was there most of the time as well. He knows about the drugs they administer. There is little question that the three of them are very close friends. We gathered from the conversations that the CCX-1 picked up that Bieber and his live-in have moved to Argentina on a semi-permanent basis. Now it looks like Siegfried is trying to get Bauer and his girlfriend to do the same. It sounded like Siegfried wanted him to help conduct the experiments. Apparently they are expecting to have duplicates of the Heidelberg equipment up and running in Argentina shortly. We have receptor and transmitter helmets purchased from Gehirn-Muster-Technologie, a modest sized specialty medical instrument house in Stuttgart. We were reluctant to order from Raffiniert Medizin-Produkt who made the stuff in Heidelberg because we thought this might get back to them. Apparently the patents have run out so there are several people making them.

There was also some discussion about psycholinguistics. Bauer might know something about this but we certainly don't think that this is the sort of thing that technical people like Bachmeier and Bieber would likely be exposed to, yet Bachmeier seemed quite conversant on the subject. He mentioned Oskar Brandt's woman.

We think that this is none other than Basima Karim. We checked up on what courses Ms Karim took while she was studying in the United States. She did have a course where two weeks were spent on this subject. So, it looks like she is alive and well in Argentina and at least in part guiding their efforts. She has a Doctorate in Psychology and is a very intelligent woman. She was Prince Ahmed's mistress and then Rashid's mistress. Now it looks like she has taken up with Captain Brandt. There may be a pattern here. While the first two were extremely rich and powerful, the third one is presumed to be merely rich and powerful. We are beginning to think that she wants to be associated with power as well as wealth.

We think she is making input into the brain wave pattern study because they were speaking and thinking many common words in German, Spanish and English and French. They have already established that the EEGs are closely related to the 'pictures' one has of what tangible things like houses, trees, automobiles, horses, dogs etc are – not the words used. On the other hand the brain wave patterns associated with concepts do appear to have differences between the different languages. We are starting to investigate this latter finding ourselves.

Now we get to the really bad news. They changed the location of the Toshiba MRI for some unknown reason. Monday afternoon they started it up again with the Philips MRI running as well. We are guessing that there must have been something analogous to a 'beat' frequency between the two oscillating radio frequencies. The CCX-1 got totally screwed up."

Randy joins in.

"The electronics we have in there are capable of detecting the very weak electrical impulses sent by striking various keys on the keyboards of nearby computers. We presume whatever they did simply overloaded the CCX-1. They called Cerebrionics yesterday wanting to know what we can do about our machine. I had to play dumb and say I had no idea. I offered to come over and take a look. I fear that much of the circuitry which enables the thing to track the electromagnetic signals floating around in the vicinity has been fried."

"How long will it take for you build another CCX-1?"

"Probably one month but I can't build anything as sensitive that will be resistant to these signals coming from the MRIs. The other thing we all need to remember is that these guys are no dummies. They probably are wondering what went wrong as well as we are. They know perfectly well how far away from an MRI to keep their computers. I can easily imagine that they will wonder what kind of circuitry is in there. This guy Bieber is an expert in signal transmission. I do not want to go there and say anything that he might recognize as bullshit."

Henry pipes up.

"Bauer was talking about moving that thing when Christina and I were there in March. Apparently he thought that a piece of equipment put into the lab next to his was giving the Toshiba some problems so he moved it to the other side of the lab. Randy, if our equipment could only listen to the conversations and handle the EEGs that were input into it could you do that without problems of interference?"

"Yes, Henry, I could. It seems a bit unlike you to be interested in only half a loaf."

"Fuck you very much, Dr. Biggs."

Everyone laughs. It is usually the other way around. Henry wants to go right at it and the other three are the ones counseling a more cautious approach. They decide that half a loaf is a pretty good deal compared to no loaf. Randy says he can put something together in a month.

Basima's residence
San Isidro, Argentina
June 10, 1995 Saturday morning

Oskar and Basima are having breakfast. He is reading the front page article in Clarin detailing the discovery of a potentially huge oil field off the Argentine coast approximately midway between Puerto Santa Maria (in Argentina's southernmost province of Santa Cruz) and the Maldivas (Falklands). Both Argentina and Britain are claiming this particular area is within their sphere of influence.

"This is going to be trouble for sure, Basima."

"You might be able to take advantage of this Oskar. We all know that Governor Sanabria has the reputation of being too accommodating to the British. He is running for President this year. I think you would have an excellent chance of beating him running on your past contributions to fighting the British."

"He is very strong in the southern part of Buenos Aires province and he is the Governor. I am only a Senator – a very junior one I might add."

"President Flores hates him and he can not run again. He likes you so why don't you ask him what he thinks about his party putting you up as their candidate."

"I'll think about it my dear. I suppose you are going to dye your hair blond so you will look like Evita."

Oskar said this in jest but Basima quickly answers.

"You might still like me if I were blond."

Since taking the senate seat, Oskar has had some difficulties with the Governor. The governor is twenty five years older than Oskar. When he was just starting in politics some forty five years ago he was living near San Nicolás and ran for a local office. Siegfried's grandfather and Oskar's father were very much against the party Governor Santabria chose to associate himself with. They actively worked against him and there were a few ugly incidents during his first campaign which he ultimately lost. He moved from the area northwest of Buenos Aires to the area southeast of BA. This happened long ago but Sanabria remembers. To this day the German speaking community around Zarate has never voted for the Governor's party. CCM is a large employer in the area and they have always contributed heavily to the Peronistas and similarly minded parties. The Governor lost this area of Buenos Aires Province to his opponents by large margins in the last two elections. There is a feud going on here that has had a perfectly predictable result. For the past two terms Governor Sanabria has directed essentially all the provincial pork toward the area around Quilmes (where he had a large majority of the vote) while the area northwest of BA has been left to more or less to pound sand.

June 11, 1995 Sunday

Oskar and Basima invited Raphael and Teresa and Hermann and Roberta Schleifenbaum for an afternoon barbecue in San Isidro. Oskar ran the thought of his running for President up the flag pole so to speak. Hermann and Roberta as well as his son and his wife were enthusiastic about this. Hermann offered to take some time off from his construction company and serve as Oskar's campaign manager. They chat about this a while. Oskar will not have the time to do any day-to-day managing of his organization while he is running for office or if he should get elected. He is thinking that Hermann and Raphael should do this. He thinks that he will need a political type to handle the politics.

"My friend, I think we are getting a little ahead of ourselves here. None of this is ever going to happen unless President Flores says this is a good idea. We really don't know what he will do. He and Wilhelm had a good relationship as far as I know but Wilhelm is dead two years now. I have only met the man twice in my life. You remember he was there when we got our pat on the back for sinking HMS Mansfield. I saw him once about eight years ago at a barbecue at Rancho de Mil Robles. I am going to try to get a meeting with him this week. If he thinks this is a reasonable thing to do, you will be the first to know."

June 12, 1995 Monday

Oskar may not know President Flores very well but he is well acquainted with Hernando Lopez who is President Flores Chief of Staff. He calls Hernando and asks if he can arrange a meeting with the President. Hernando asks him what he wants to talk about with the President and Oskar tells him.

Hernando is an astute political operative. He is going to be out of a job (at least a job as important as this one) at the end of the year. What better way to preserve his position than to ingratiate himself to President Flores possible successor. About the only person who thinks Vice President Reyes is going to be the successor is Vice President Reyes. He looks at the President's schedule. He reschedules the President's Wednesday morning mate break. (He doesn't like the guy he just bumped anyway.)

Casa Rosada
Buenos Aires, Argentina
June 14, 1995 Wednesday

Oskar was ushered into the President's office at 1000 sharp. The President has had a recent knee replacement. Nevertheless, he gets up from behind his desk and walks with the aid of a cane across the large office to shake Oskar's hand. He motions for Oskar to sit at the table where the Mate gourd and some pastries are already resident.

"Good morning Captain Brandt."

"Good morning Excellency. Thank you for fitting me into your busy schedule."

'Senor Lopez tells me you covet my job."

He says this with a smile. They both know that he can't run again.

"Well sir, if you thought it was a decent idea I would like to be your candidate."

"I gather that you are having your own set of problems with Senor Sanabria."

(President Flores is well aware of the goings on in Buenos Aires Province.)

"I am. I also feel that he would not be the right man to negotiate with the British."

"I agree with you completely Captain."

This goes on for a while. The President refers to Sanabria as a nincompoop and 'Señor Rendición' (Mister Surrender), amongst other things. They have their tea. The President looks at the clock.

"Thank you for coming by Captain. We will give your proposal our most earnest consideration. I need to consult with others. It will take a while. I will get back to you within the next week."

"Thank you."

They shake hands and Oskar leaves. Hernando meets him halfway down the hallway.

"How did it go?"

"He seemed receptive. I am not sure. I gather he does not want his Senor Reyes to run."

"You gather correctly Oskar."

"He said he would get back to me by this time next week."

"He is meeting with some of the party higher-ups and two of our chief money men this week. I might point out to you although please do not repeat this. He had me schedule meetings with these people shortly after I told him of your request for a chance to talk with him."

Rancho de la Veta Madre

Provincia de Córdoba, Argentina

June 20, 1995 Tuesday

The first group of 'subjects' arrived at the ranch last week. They did experiments with the first two by seating them in the bosun's chair and trying to get them to hum tunes which were impressed on them with the old apparatus. This was successful. By Saturday they had had some success transmitting music using the flat screen transmitter that Siegfried and Ludwig built. They confirmed this with more experiments all day Sunday. After looking over the results Siegfried advised Oskar of these findings Monday afternoon. Oskar was anticipating a telephone call from the President possibly as early as Tuesday evening, certainly no later than Wednesday afternoon. He and Basima chartered a modest turboprop to take them directly from Jorge Newberry to Rio Cuarto. A driver met them at the airport. They arrived at the mine before 0930. They will witness the first attempt to transmit thought of a tangible thing using the flat screen transmitter.

They don't have any luck with the first two subjects but with the third they are able to transmit the images of a house, a steer and an automobile. That is the good news. The bad news is that all three subjects now have splitting headaches. The first two had to be sedated to stop the shrieks of pain. The third one said he had a moderately bad headache and asked for some aspirin.

"Ziggy, you were saying that that happened to you sometimes when you were in Baumgartner's lab?"

"Yes Basima, but not like those two. Baumgartner used to give me a shot of something after the session that would greatly alleviate the pain without knocking me out."

"Do you know what that was?"

"I do not. Manny Bauer probably knows. I will find out if he does."

"Did Heidi also get headaches?"

"She does not think so. You have to remember that Baumgartner was using all kinds of drugs on the subjects. I was always sedated when I had my sessions with Eberhardt. Sometimes I had a headache after them and sometimes I did not. He may or may not have used the same drugs on both men and women."

"That is an interesting thought Ziggy. Did Chief Weiss 'disappear' any females?"

"No. Funny that you should mention that Basima. Aldrich brought up the same subject."

Oskar interjects.

"I will see if Chief Weiss can help us out here."

Oskar is getting much more interested in this exercise now that he has seen a positive result obtained with a 'normal' human being as opposed to someone hyper intelligent like Siegfried or Heidi. He is almost beginning to believe Basima's prediction that they will be able to influence people's thinking on a large scale. He can not imagine that they will be far enough along to have anything useful before the November election. This reminds him that he and Basima need to return to San Isidro this afternoon. If President Flores calls this evening he definitely does not want the answering machine answering.

Basima wasn't just teasing him about changing her hair color. She changed her hair to a reddish blond and also had the salon slightly lighten her eyebrows. Oskar had to admit that she looks good as a blond as well. It turned out that Basima and Rita Flores go to the same salon in Recoleta. They were both there last Tuesday. Senora Flores noticed that Basima was having her hair done over. Then, Senator Brandt had mate with her husband Wednesday morning at the Casa Rosada. At the supper table in the presidential residence in Olivos Wednesday evening Rita explains to Carlos that this is not mere happenstance. She notes a certain similarity between Basima Karim and Eva Peron. She notes that Senator Brandt is a good looking man and he is also Juan Peron's height. She thinks that the Captain is deliberately trying to remind people of the Perons and she thinks that this is a smart move. Senora Flores and the President are beginning to think that running the highly decorated tall and handsome submarine captain with his beautiful woman at his side might just get rid of that jerk Sanabria once and for all. It won't be easy, Brandt is a relative unknown but he is no leftist and he doesn't have any pro-British baggage – indeed, exactly the opposite. They will emphasize Sanabria's record of 'placating' Uruguay in a border dispute last year and they are going to dig up what dirt they can find and possibly manufacture some. They will paint him as the master of appeasement.

President Flores talks this over with a few of the movers and shakers in his party over the next few days. He does not discuss this matter with Vice President Reyes. There is a remarkable amount of enthusiasm to make Brandt the party candidate.

Oskar and Basima arrived home in San Isidro at 1600. At 1645, the phone rang. One glance at the phone revealed that the call was rerouted from Oskar's residence in Zarate. He picked it up. It was President Flores' secretary. The President was on the line shortly.

"Captain Brandt, we think you will have a good chance. We are going to back you. I would like you and your woman to join us for dinner tomorrow evening."

"Thank you Excellency. I will try my best."

On the 1900 evening news there is a sound bite of Governor Sanabria's speech last year suggesting that it is time to take down the billboards proclaiming Argentine sovereignty over the Malvinas. This is followed by reference to a rumor that a highly decorated war hero may be the ruling party's candidate. They show a picture of Oskar entering Casa Rosada last week and a file picture of him receiving the Collar of the Order of the Liberator General San Martin a dozen years ago. The political analyst (talking head) for the station then pontificates for three minutes on how this is an extremely clever move by Partido Conservador National. Governor Sanabria will have a hard time back-peddling away from his statement last year.

Shortly after this, the phone rings again. It is Hernando Lopez.

"Congratulations Captain."

"Thank you Hernando and thank you for helping me in this matter."

"I think President Flores will be helping you with your campaign. He wants me to be your campaign manager."

(Hernando did not get to be the President's Chief of Staff by being bashful. Basima is listening in on another extension. She gives him a thumbs-up. Oskar and Basima talked about how much input they would likely be getting from the party in general and President Flores in particular. There was little to be gained and much to be lost by not just going with the flow. If he got in, there would be ample time to increase his influence.)

"Thank you for this offer Hernando. I would be proud to have you run my campaign."

"Oskar, I will do my best for you. Now that you are going to be in this business seriously, I will say that you need very tough skin. Sanabria plays hardball. If he can find any dirt associated with you, he will use it. He is not above manufacturing dirt where none exists. I want you to examine your past and see if there is anything that might be used against you with devastating effect. If there is, you need to tell me before the convention."

No sooner is he off the phone with Hernando then it rings again. It is a reporter from Clarin. He wants an interview. Oskar says he isn't the nominee yet. If he gets the nomination he will be glad to do an interview. As he puts the phone down Basima shakes her head.

"You may as well get used to this they don't have anything else to do."

Oskar punches a few buttons on the phone. All the calls to Zarate are now going to an answering machine. They plan on having a quiet meal at home. Basima has an excellent chef. They are just sitting down to have their dinner when the phone rings again. Basima's maid answers it. This time it is a reporter from the television station that aired the rumor that he was going to be the nominee. The maid tells him that they went out to eat.

That phone also gets routed to an answering machine and will not ring anymore this evening. They will have to get some more phone numbers that can be used to talk to people that they want to talk to.

They succeed in having a quiet meal and are now sipping port and chatting about Hernando's comments.

"He is quite right about that Oskar. If there is anything that could be harmful to you, there is a good chance that it will come out."

"Well, there have been rumors around the submarine."

"I don't think that will be much of a problem. The US and Israel are not too popular here. It is more likely to be something local that you were mixed up in."

They sit and think for a while. Oskar is well aware that much of what Wilhelm Bachmeier did could cause trouble. His wife was one of Wilhelm's daughters. Then he starts thinking about what he was directly involved in...

(I can not deny that I knew what was done to refit the Maria Morales in CCM Belen. That will come out for sure. Even so, there is little likelihood that anyone will find what remains of that boat. It went down nearly two nautical miles from where people think it went down. On the other hand the Americans must have had some kind of radar that could 'see' U-1241 and Duha Ali in the middle of the night in a driving rainstorm. Maybe they 'saw' something associated with the Maria Morales. I remember Klaus telling me that they clocked forty three knots from the time they left the grave of the Maria Morales until they tied up at their slip in Pinamar. If the Americans were watching any of this, they might have noticed a boat going this fast. Of course, that Bancroft guy was on the Don Martinez. I had him over for a drink after the tournament. I remember that Bancroft was very curious about the SSB. That was the SSB that wasn't an SSB. It was the instrument which sent the signals which lead Maria Morales to her doom. We are nearly certain that Bancroft is CIA. I remember that he wanted to know how much power the boat had. Could the Americans have possibly known that this boat was involved? I must get rid of that boat....)

"You are lost in thought Oskar."

"I think we have to get rid of the Don Martinez. The more I think about it, the more it worries me."

Manfred Bauer knew enough about the drugs Baumgartner used to solve the problem of the subjects' headaches. Since then Siegfried and Ludwig have discovered that the subjects are more receptive if they are playing the C Major triad as opposed to simply Middle C (512 hertz). At Basima's suggestion they have also played the C Minor triad during several experiments. This diminishes the amount of information that the subject can recall but they make an important observation. The subjects are expressing 'dislike' of the images that they sent them while playing the C Minor triad. They have repeated this experiment several times. It looks like they can instill 'like' sometimes and 'dislike' nearly all the time, even if the same image is displayed. This is exactly the result that Basima is looking for. They run EEGs on several of the subjects after these 'like' 'dislike' sessions. They show many similarities with the EEGs generated by people under hypnosis. If they can achieve this on more than one person at a time, say a theater full....

This gets Siegfried to thinking.

"Wig, I have an idea. Try this major/minor thing on me."

"Ziggy, you know that you are not supposed to be a subject."

"Nobody is going to find out. Just try it for fifteen seconds."

They run the experiment for fifteen seconds. When this is done, Siegfried just sits there a while. Then he turns to Aldrich, who has been observing this.

"Aldrich, do we have any quality control samples here?"

"You mean for the Selenium tubes?"

"Yes."

"You remember how we could 'hear' a burst of white noise if we were near the firing of the test specimens?"

"Yes."

"I think I just 'heard' something very similar."

"Was that with negative or positive feelings?"

"Negative."

It is the culminating moment of the Partido Conservador National (PCN) convention. President Flores is delivering the nominating speech for Captain Oskar Brandt. It is in part praise for Oskar's contribution during the Malvinas War and in part excoriation of the opposition for many things. The situation with the oil field and the British is not improving with the passage of time. The British have dispatched an aircraft carrier group to the Falklands with much ado. The Argentine media are fanning the flames of nationalism, much to the benefit of the National Conservative Party. Ricardo Sanabria was named as the Partido Socialista (PS) nominee last week. He is already calling Senator Brandt a Nazi warmonger. This is not setting very well with much of the populace who rather think of Captain Brandt as a native Argentinean War Hero of German extraction. For their part the NCP is comparing Sanabria to Neville Chamberlain and is suggesting that he may have been involved in a sex scandal involving under age women recently. President Flores finishes his nominating speech to thunderous applause. When Oskar walks to the podium he is accompanied by Basima. It is the first time most of the party faithful have seen this beautiful woman. Her hair is now a reddish blonde, she is tall and slender and she is wearing a beige pants suit – a color favored by Eva Peron. This has all been carefully orchestrated by Rita Flores. None of this is lost on the crowd. Legend has it that Luna Park is where Eva Duarte and Juan Peron met. The applause increases as the President embraces each of them in turn. After perhaps forty five seconds, President

Flores starts trying to quiet the crowd with hand gestures. They will have none of that. It takes nearly another minute before the faithful quiet down. President Flores and Basima sit down and Oskar starts.

"Thank you. Thank you. Thank you. It is four months to the election. My opponent has been politicking since before I was born. We pretty much know what he stands for,

This provokes many boos from the faithful.

at least for the moment."

(*Laughter and applause*)

"I hope to become known for not standing for such nonsense."

There is standing applause. When it dies down, Oskar continues.

"We will not indulge in cat and mouse games."

This is a thinly veiled reference to Governor Sanabria's concession of Isla del Gato (Cat Island) to Uruguay last year. The Uruguayans promptly built a resort hotel on this island which sets in the northernmost bay of Rio de la Plata – a little closer to the Argentine shore than the Uruguayan shore. Now there is more applause and much laughter.

He speaks for only eleven minutes but it takes nearly twenty because of the interruptions by applause. He finishes up.

"Thank you again my friends. With your and God's help we will prevail."

Basima rises and stands on his right while President Flores stands on his left. He takes their hands and raises them overhead.

The faithful rise as one and give them another thunderous ovation. They exit the stage to the last stanzas of the Argentine national anthem with the original martial lyrics.

John and Henry are talking with Guenther. Guenther is mildly upset.

"Did you see what happened in Argentina last Friday?"

"No, what happened?"

"They nominated Oskar Brandt to run for President."

"Well, at least he won't be running submarines around sowing death and destruction."

"I wouldn't expect him to be doing that again Henry."

"You know that the Brits and Argentines are at it again?)

"I heard something about that."

"This National Conservative Party that is running Brandt has a plank that says the Brits will never get one drop of Argentina's oil."

"Parties have all kinds of planks."

"I am sure that even if they can not exploit that oil field themselves, the Argentines will be quite capable of denying it to the Brits. You remember they used that V-3 speedboat to hit New York?"

"Yes."

"The Argentines could probably build several of those a week if they were of a mind to. These things can easily carry a ton or more of high explosives. They can take then down south by truck and then launch them from damn near anywhere within two or three hundred miles of the field and no doubt hit any drilling or production platform there. They are stationary targets, you know."

"The Brits are not entirely helpless. They have radar controlled guns. It might not be so easy to get next to them with anything on the surface."

"Argentina has five submarines now. They only had three when the Falklands thing got out of hand and the only one they used was the one Brandt captained that sank one of the Brit's destroyers. As soon as this current business started heating up two months ago, they started reinforcing the sub pen at the Puerto Belgrano naval base. Early last month they resumed tunneling into the side of a hill on the coast near Santa Cruz. They started doing that during the previous war but stopped it. Now, they have restarted this thing less than a week after the word was out that Brandt was going to be nominated. The current President, a guy named Flores, is backing Brandt. Brandt is an able tactician – much more of a military type than Flores. We think as soon as the deal about the nomination was done that they asked Brandt what he thought about what they were doing. We think that he suggested that they complete this second bombproof for the submarines closer to the oil field and Flores acted on it. There is every indication that they are preparing for a fight. The Brits have nothing short of nuclear weapons that will be able to penetrate this tunnel in the side of the hill. I don't think they have the will to use nuclear weapons. There is water deep enough for a submarine to fully submerge less than two hundred yards off shore from this potential submarine pen. They could pretty well come and go as they please without our satellites noticing."

"Of course, Brandt might not win the election. The other guy is diametrically opposed to messing with the Brits again. The problem is that this is not selling very well with the population. The election is probably going to be close. We are thinking that perhaps we might leak some of the story about the Maria Morales."

"How do you intend to go about doing that Guenther? I think that if it ever got out that the United States had anything to do with such a leak we would assure Brandt's election."

"John, didn't you say that the Don Martinez was tied up at CCM Belen when your friend Bancroft took his boat to the yard?"

"You have a good memory Guenther."

"We think there is an opportunity here. You may not know that this guy, Ricardo Sanabria, that Brandt is running against has had a running feud with those Nazis for a long time going back to right after the Second World War with Wilhelm Bachmeier and Otto Brandt. We found out that he, Sanabria, used to do a fair amount of sport fishing in tournaments like you participated in Henry. We aren't quite sure where he got the money to compete in this sort of thing but that isn't relevant. He has a boat which costs the better part of two million. His son now captains his sport fisher which he runs out of a marina south of Buenos Aires that is just as posh as the one in San Isidro where you were. We have been nosing around and found out that in addition to the political rivalry, Sanabria and the Nazis have had a few run ins out on the water. Riding over the other guy's lines and that sort of thing. The long and the short of it is that Sanabria would likely be most cooperative in spreading any and all dirt about the Nazis that he can find. We are just going to give him a map and a shovel. It took a little doing but we have managed to extract from Gerbert Bachmeier a complete description of how the Nazis managed to destroy the Maria Morales and the fifty seven people on board. We have forged a 'ship's log' for the Don Martinez. Therein there is a page which describes the last moments of the Maria Morales. After they destroyed that boat they took off toward the fishing tournament. They stopped overnight in Pinamar. There was a drunken party. There were some women involved. The story is that Gerbert took some broad back to his boat. After a while he had had too much to drink and fell asleep. She stole some of his money and the log. She was intending to blackmail him but she knew that this was a very dangerous thing to do. She gave the log to her sister for safe keeping. Two weeks later she disappeared. This log is going to show up in Sanabria's campaign office in Bahia Blanca soon."

"I suppose you want Henry to hand it to them?"

"It would be a nice touch John. Who knows what Brandt will do if he finds out Henry has visited again?"

They bat this around a little. Henry suggests that it might be somewhat more realistic to drop the log off in Mar del Plata (much closer to Pinamar than Bahia Blanca) if the Sanabria campaign has any presence there. They were going to include the location of the boat or at least the last observed location but after some further discussion they decide that they don't want to make it too easy. Sanabria will believe this nonsense better if his minions have to do a little work to assemble the puzzle. They know that the boat had some decidedly non-standard electronics on it. Possibly some vestige of these is still there. This will worry Brandt. Maybe this will provoke some kneejerk reaction....

Ministro Pistarini International Airport
Ezeiza, Argentina
July 13, 1995 0837 Thursday

United Flight 743 landed right on time. Henry, traveling as Hudson Mark complete with a gray wig and mustache had no problems getting through immigration and customs. He rented a full sized car with an automatic transmission from Hertz. The same agent who was there two years ago was at the desk. The agent noted Henry's height and long legs but because of all the make-up it only rang a faint bell.

Henry drove the three hundred eighty five kilometers or so to Mar del Plata. Sanabria's campaign office was in one of the meeting rooms of Hotel San Martin. Henry simply pulled up near the front door and handed the parking valet a twenty dollar bill to watch his car for a few moments while he delivered his package. Five minutes later he was back in his rent car heading back to Ezeiza.

Sanabria a la Presidencia
Campaign Office
Hotel San Martin
Mar del Plata, Argentina
July 13, 1995 1430

Manuel Ruiz is in charge of Governor Sanabria's campaign in the southern half of Buenos Aires Province. He has just returned from lunch with a major local donor. His secretary hands him the envelope that is marked to his attention. She doesn't know anything else about it. All she could find out was that a rather tall gray haired man brought it to the hotel front desk less than an hour ago. The clerk on duty was pretty sure that the guy was from the US. His Spanish was just okay – definitely not his native language. The clerk said he noticed that the guy's voice sounded younger than he looked. He noted that the guy gave the parking valet a big tip for doing essentially nothing.

Manuel takes the envelope into an area partitioned off in the large room which serves as his private office. He opens the envelope and finds what looks like a ship's log. He skims through this and soon finds the horrifying description of the last moments of the Maria Morales. He isn't quite sure what to do with this. He calls Ruben Gutierrez, who is Governor Sanabria's campaign manager and tells him what he has. Five minutes later, Gutierrez calls back.

"Is there any identification of the boat that this paper you have is supposed to be the log for?"

Manuel has been reading his 'find' rather carefully since his first phone call.

"I think the boat is called the Don Martinez."

"Does it say who owns this?"

"I have not found anything else."

"But it describes the sinking of the Maria Morales?"

"Yes."

"Manuel, lock this up someplace. This might be useful to us. I will have someone do a little homework on this."

Gutierrez is back on the phone.

"Manuel, this boat belongs to Gerbert Bachmeier. He is another one of those fucking Nazis. We think we can link him to Brandt. The boat is at the Salida del Sol marina in Puerto Rosales. We want you to go there and see what you can see."

(There is a ton of road construction going on south of Mar del Plata. This is probably a six hour drive. It can wait until tomorrow.)

"It is too late to get to Bahia Blanca today Ruben."

Ruben brushes this aside. Manuel can be there in an hour if he charters a flight.

"Use Sanchez Aviation."

"There won't be anyone there at this hour in the middle of the winter."

"So much the better."

(Ruiz is not making much progress at avoiding this trip.)

"How late can I call you back?"

"Call me at home."

Gutierrez Residence
Quilmes, Argentina
July 13, 1995 2240

"Ruben, there is no boat named Don Martinez in that marina. I looked around. There was no one there so I went to a local bar and asked if anyone knew anything about the Don Martinez. It turned out that the boat

was well known and that someone thought that someone named Bachmeier owned it. But, it is nowhere to be
found."

"So, you established that there was such a boat but
it is not there?"

"I guess you could say that."

"Where are you now?"

"I am calling from my room at the Hotel Tamarisces
in Villa del Mar."

*Manuel does not mention that he has his secretary
along for what he expects will be an extended weekend.*

"We need to find that boat. I will call you tomorrow
morning."

Hotel Tamarisces
Villa del Mar, Argentina
July 14, 1995 Friday 0745

Ruben is on the phone.

"Find out whatever you can. I suggest going over the
newspapers in Bahia Blanca. Ask around. Maybe some-
body knows something."

*That morning, Ruiz goes through similar motions
that Henry and George Ramos went through two years
ago. He and his secretary pose as reporters from Clarin
who are reinvestigating the disappearance of the Maria
Morales. They find a ready source of information in the
librarian who is still grieving over the death of her uncle.
They determined that the Maria Morales was refit in the
CCM Belen yard. The librarian shows them the newspaper photographs of her uncle's previous boat, the Jose
Salazar, down at her dock. She says there was a rumor
around that this boat was deliberately sabotaged so that it
would sink. It was old and it was wood but she thought that
her uncle maintained it well. She has talked with her aunt*

Maria (who the Maria Morales is named for) many times. They think that Oskar Brandt, the owner of CCM, showed up in Bahia Blanca a little too shortly after the Jose Salazar went down. Her aunt said that her husband kept telling her he got a really good deal on the boat. It was worth at least half again as much as he paid for it. Manuel and his secretary gather up quite a bit of incriminating circumstantial evidence that Oskar Brandt had something to do with the disappearance of the Maria Morales.

What they don't know is that they have been under nearly constant surveillance since they left the hotel this morning.

(One of the employees at CCM Bahia Blanca was in this bar where Manuel was asking questions. This employee was one of Wilhelm Bachmeier's grandsons. In fact, he was the man who installed the deceitful GPS on the Maria Morales. Senor Ruiz's inquiries were promptly reported to Raphael Brandt. Raphael immediately suspects that the CIA is somehow involved in this. They presumably have been able to piece together what happened to the Maria Morales by interrogating the people they captured at Rancho Don Martinez. He starts a search to see if anyone they recognize has entered the country recently.)

By noontime Raphael et al have the phone in Manuel's room tapped. When Manuel calls Gutierrez to report the day's findings, Raphael Brandt is listening and recording the conversation at CCM Belen. Shortly after this phone call, Rolfe Dietz the Hertz agent who rented the car to Henry returns Raphael's call.

"Raphael, this is Rolfe here."

"Yes Rolfe."

"I think Henry Magnuson was here yesterday. He came in on the plane from New York. I just had a funny feeling like I'd seen this guy before – especially after you called. As you know, we take pictures of everyone we rent to. I went back and looked at the pictures I have of him and his buddy from two years ago. I think that this guy yesterday had a wig and false moustache but he couldn't fake his height and his long legs. He rented the car in the morning. This morning, after the morning rush was over I checked to see where the car was. He put down "Crown Plaza, Buenos Aires" on the rental sheet. He returned it last night barely in time to catch the plane to New York. He put nearly eight hundred kilometers on the car in the ten and a half hours he had it. It looks like he just drove someplace four hundred kilometers away and turned around and came right back to the airport."

"Could you send me copies of your pictures?"

"Yes. I will drop them off at the TASA office if that is okay."

"Thank you Rolfe."

Raphael pulls out a map of Buenos Aires Province. About the only direction this stranger could have put on eight hundred kilometers in ten hours was heading south. He takes a scale and measures the distance to Mar del Plata. It is about four hundred kilometers. He calls Hernando Gomez.

"Hernando, this is Raphael Brandt here."

"Good afternoon Raphael. What's up?"

"Do you know anyone named Ruben Gutierrez?"

"Of course, he is Sanabria's campaign manager."

"Some guy named Manuel Ruiz called him this afternoon from Villa del Mar."

Hernando has files on many of the people in Sanabria's campaign organization. He quickly finds that Manuel Ruiz is the local campaign chief for the southern half of Buenos Aires Province.

"And?"

"It sounds like they are planning to spread some dirt about my father."

"What kind of dirt?"

"Some cock and bull story about this party boat that went down with most of the CCM Bahia Blanca employees a few years ago."

"Is there any truth to it?"

"No. My dad looks bad but there nothing but circumstantial evidence."

They go around about this a while. There is a lot of circumstantial evidence. Hernando suspects that Raphael has probably obtained this information in a clandestine manner. He does not bring that subject up and neither does Raphael. Raphael says that he has reason to believe that the CIA has a hand in this. Hernando remembers the big hoo-hah which followed the American raid on Rancho de Mil Robles. It led to severance of diplomatic relations with the US. Hernando immediately seizes upon this and suggests that they launch a preemptive counterattack on the CIA before Sanabria can even leak this thing out. He will have to clear that with President Flores and Oskar.

He does just that and Flores and Brandt agree that a preemptive strike is the right course. By the time the evening news programs come on mention is being made of a rumor. The pro-conservative stations are describing it as an unconscionable smear against Captain Brandt set loose by the CIA. The pro-socialists stations have dredged up file footage from two years ago of their talking heads pontificating on the disappearance of the Maria Morales and are stating that these rumors about Senator Brandt have surfaced again. They make a point of stating that Senator Brandt was and is the owner of the CCM shipyard where the Maria Morales was refit.

Governor Sanabria's residence
Buenos Aires, Argentina
July 14, 1995 Friday 1917

Governor Sanabria is having a heated telephone conversation with Ruben Gutierrez.

"Ruben, how did this leak out?"

"I have no idea Ricardo."

"Do you trust Ruiz?"

"I think he is trustworthy. I think he is very loyal to you. I can not believe that he had any hand in this."

"We can not allow this bullshit to go unanswered. Put out the word that Brandt's campaign spread this rumor. They are doing the same thing the Nazis did after the Reichstag fire."

Ludwig, Siegfried and Aldrich have been investigating the effects of the 'white noise' which the subjects 'hear' in their brains but which is not detectable with exceedingly sensitive microphones. The subjects often report painful levels of white noise when the test specimens are fired off in a nearby soundproof room but it is not audible. They have found that whatever is being emitted from the test specimens can penetrate considerable distances through certain sound insulating materials in much the same way as cell phone transmissions do. They have gone to considerable lengths to insulate the subjects from the audible noise so that they can be certain that the emissions caused the subjects' reactions, not the audible noise. They can induce dislike of whatever is on the television that they are having the subject watch about seventy percent of the time. They have had all fourteen of the unfortunates that Chief Weiss 'disappeared' in the same room watching the same television at once. Typically ten or eleven of them 'get the message'.

Siegfried is relaying this news to Basima who has become, at the least, Oskar's co-campaign manager.

"We are achieving around seventy five percent."

"That is wonderful Ziggy. Do you think that you could do this on more than fifteen people at once?"

"Possibly. We might have some trouble keeping everything as quiet, in the physical sense, as we are able to do here under controlled conditions."

"We have a debate with Sanabria three weeks from tomorrow."

"Where?"

"Luna Park."

"Is this place close to a road?"

"Oh, yes. It is surrounded by roads."

"We might be able to fire off the test specimens inside a soundproof truck. They don't seem to be attenuated much with distance. When is the debate?"

"Three weeks from now."

"I mean what time of day is it?"

"It is not certain yet but I think it will be before the evening news. It is going to be on every channel as far as we know."

There is a conference call going on between Guenther, Mitch Rogerston and Randy Biggs. Mitch is doing the talking. Apparently, Henry's visit to Mar del Plata has stirred things up. Both campaigns are hurling all kinds of charges at each other. This is having the unintended side effect of giving Oskar Brandt a great deal of publicity. Merely seventeen days after his nomination, Brandt has almost as much name recognition at Sanabria.

"It isn't that surprising. The Conservatives are outspending the Socialists by three or four to one. They are making a big fucking deal over some twenty acre mud flat in the Rio de la Plata that Sanabria negotiated away to the Uruguayans last year. It seems that one of his wife's relatives was in the back row on this deal. The conservatives have an ad campaign going with a partial anagram of Sanabria's name preceded by no. I believe it is 'no sana rabi' which loosely translated is 'unhealthy rabbi'. In other words, this deal is not kosher. It is kind of silly but it is politics. It must have rattled Sanabria. He was on some talk show Tuesday and apparently his microphone was on when it wasn't supposed to be on. He was heard to say."

"What the (expletive deleted) does that (expletive deleted) Nazi know about kosher?"

"This merely added fuel to the fire. By Friday afternoon some wag in Brandt's campaign had something vaguely resembling Boggle® out with all the letters of Ricardo Sanabria in it. They are having a ball with it."

"So Sanabria hasn't had much luck trying to tar Brandt as a Nazi, has he?"

"Apparently Nazi isn't as bad a word in Argentina as it is here Hank and, of course, we had no idea that he would try to twist this thing in that direction."

The remote broadcasting truck from Córdoba is parked with the other media vehicles in the area reserved for them on the north side of the Luna Park arena. The outside of this truck is festooned with antennas very much like the surrounding vehicles from the other television stations. The umbilical cables running off to the building are providing power and the sounds and images from inside the arena to the technicians in the trucks. There, the similarity ends. The truck from Córdoba has very effective sound insulation inside. It also has two heavily shielded machine guns in fixed mounts aimed at the side of the truck closest to the arena. Aldrich has produced two thousand cartridges containing his version of Plodamax with the Selenium-containing fibrils embedded. These are essentially 9 mm blanks which generate the transmission when they are fired. The guns have highly effective silencers. In conjunction with the sound insulation in the truck, the noise is reduced to nearly inaudible levels outside directly outside the truck. As an added precaution they are playing some rather loud music into the side of the truck directly in front of the gun. Although the Nazis don't quite understand how this works they know it does because they have tested it many times. The firing of the test specimens produces some kind of white noise in the brain which is highly disturbing. The brain, in its wisdom, promptly associates this unwelcome noise with whatever information the eyes and ears are receiving at the time.

Senator Brandt won the coin toss and he is going to speak first. He and Sanabria will have four minutes for opening statements. There will be a commercial. Then there will be eighteen minutes of questioning by the Moderator interrupted half way through by one more commercial segment. The place is packed with every seat taken and many standees. The Conservatives are seated on the south side and the Socialists are on the north side. It is fairly noisy. The Moderator cautions the crowd that they will be using up their candidate's speaking time with their applause. With that he gestures to Brandt to take the podium. Each candidate was allotted the same number of seats but Luna Park is in a strongly pro-Sanabria section of Buenos Aires and most of the standees are pro-Sanabria. When Brandt gets to the podium he is greeted with a chorus of boos from the standees. The Moderator informs them that he will take away speaking time from their candidate second for second while these interruptions go on. After another five seconds or so the standees quiet down.

"Good evening my friends and those of you who I hope to make my friends."

This provokes a few seconds of applause from the conservatives and another warning from the Moderator.

"Your choice is clear. I will not be negotiating any further loss of Argentine territory or our territorial rights. It is hard to tell with my opponent."

He continues along these lines for two minutes, alluding to the questionable circumstances surrounding the ceding of Isla del Gato to Uruguay without actually saying that Sanabria is a crook. He does not call him Señor Rendición but there are large billboards all over Buenos Aires to that effect. He says something about the futility of a policy of appeasement. He reminds the crowd that he did the best he could for Argentina during

La Guerra de la Maldivas unlike his opponent who even wants to remove the billboards stating that the Maldivas are Argentine territory. This provokes the conservatives to stand and applaud. The applause consumes the last twenty seconds of his four minutes. (This is not a coincidence.)

Governor Sanabria takes the podium. He must have been on a crash diet the past few weeks because he definitely looks thinner than he did when he appeared at the Socialist Party Convention, or maybe he has a corset on. Either way he looks pretty good for a man in his mid seventies. He starts talking about all the public works that are going on in Buenos Aires Province under his leadership.

This is when the folks in the truck ostensibly from the Córdoba television station get into the act. They are watching the speech and they fire multi round bursts of these weaponized test specimens at the mention of any specific. They are getting feedback from several cameras trained on the crowd. The conservatives are all frowning and many of the Socialists are too. A number of people put their hands over their ears. They zoom in on the standees. There are a number of frowns here too.

The Governor touches on the need for moderation in dealing with the British. The folks in the truck manage to fire four bursts while he is trying to sell a joint venture with the Brits to develop the oil field. There is very little applause on the Socialist side of the arena as he finishes. They all stand up but there doesn't seem to be that much enthusiasm.

The two 'question and answer' periods that follow are relatively uneventful. The folks in the truck manage to fire short bursts during many of Sanabria's answers.

The candidates are escorted from the arena by their security people at roughly thirty eight minutes after the hour but the station talking heads who are not in the arena manage to consume the rest of the hour with instant analysis. The crowd reaction does not get much discussion because the talking heads are mostly leaning toward the Socialists. It is clear that the Socialists were not pleased with their candidate and had a certain lack of enthusiasm, especially toward the end of the question and answer period.

The Conservatives did some polling prior to the debate and they now manage to do a little 'exit' polling after the debate. It is very encouraging. The people who identify themselves as Socialists are now only about six in ten in favor of Sanabria. Before the debate it was nine in ten. For the first time, the polling shows that a majority have a favorable view of Senator Brandt.

There is an unintended consequence. There were a few fifteen round bursts from the machine guns which took roughly three quarters of a second each. During these bursts every cell phone in use in the area produced static for three quarters of a second. This was not noticeable inside the arena because the audience (roughly 99.7% of the people in the building) had been repeatedly admonished to shut their phones off during the debate. However, there were many people outside in the general area. Shortly after the last burst, a number of people were calling Argentina Telefono wanting to know what was going on here. Of course, no answers were forthcoming. Ramon Moreno, a trouble shooter for the telephone company was amongst the people outside who listened to the interference. (He had been in Luna Park for two hours prior to the start of the debate to fix up the cell phone system inside the arena so that the public couldn't use it but a number of people on both candidates campaign staffs could. A few of these people also experienced the interference.) He was walking to his car while on his cell advising his girlfriend of his imminent arrival at her apartment while Sanabria was giving his opening speech. The interference came over his cell loud and scratchy, just like everyone else's. He remembered that there had been a number of unexplained interferences in San Rafael last year. These were essentially 'clicks'. The present interference was much more extended. He has some recordings of these earlier disturbances in his office. Since then, he has had a number of recording stations installed around Buenos Aires, Rosario, Córdoba and Mendoza that monitor this sort of thing. The one thing he knows for sure is that he is not going to alter his plans for his ski weekend with Elena. He will compare the recordings that his stations made this evening with the old ones first thing Monday morning. He calls his office and leaves a message regarding his observations on his office phone.

Ramon Moreno's Office

Argentina Telefonos

270 Avenida Rivadavia

Buenos Aires, Argentina

August 14, 1995 Monday 1010

Ramon has not shown up for the Monday morning staff meeting which started at 1000. The General Manager Geraldo Montez calls him. Moreno's secretary answers on the second ring.

"Ramon is not here, sir. I made his flight reservations two weeks ago. He and his girlfriend were going skiing in Bariloche this weekend. He was scheduled to return yesterday evening."

"Please track him down."

This is very unlike Ramon. He is punctual to a fault. She thinks he might have left a message if there was a problem. When she checks his messages the last one pertains to some cell phone disturbances Thursday evening. There is nothing else.

The phone company has received all kinds of flak about cell phone service interruption since Thursday – particularly from both campaign staffs. Not surprisingly, this is the first thing on Montez's agenda this morning and Ramon is the big gun in this area.

Maria calls Ramon at home – no answer. She calls the airline.

"My boss hasn't shown up this morning. Can you check and see if Ramon Moreno and Elena Romero were on the flight from Bariloche yesterday evening."

"Let me check."

Forty seconds later.

"They did not fly with us yesterday."

After a few moments hesitation the agent adds.

"I don't want to alarm you but did you know there was an avalanche in Bariloche Saturday?"

"Thank you. I hope Ramon is not involved in that."

Twenty minutes later Maria goes to the staff meeting and gestures Montez to come outside. She tells him the bad news. Ramon and Elena were last seen Saturday morning at the breakfast table. They had a dinner reservation but they did not eat at the hotel Saturday evening. She notes that he sent himself a message Thursday evening to look into the cell phone interference. Montez tells the rest of the people at the meeting to carry on without him. He will be back shortly. He accompanies Maria back to Ramon's office and listens to the last message.

This cell phone interference is a matter of great concern to the phone company. By noon, Montez is mounting a full court press on this subject. By early afternoon they have tracked back through their records. There was some sort of cell phone interference in the San Rafael neighborhood for a little over a month in late 1994. The first reported instance was November 1994 and the last one was New Years day evening 1995. There is a note that the last instance of interference may have been caused by this mysterious lightning strike that destroyed the equipment in MEA. They have the recordings. A comparison of the recordings from Thursday evening with the ones from last December have a great deal of similarity but it looks like whatever it was, it was repeated many times Thursday. Montez orders a thorough going over of the recordings from Thursday night. There were twenty seven interruptions between 1835 and 1910. They have some means of massaging the raw data so as to triangulate where the interference came from. By 1600 they have the source located within two hundred meters of Luna Park. Montez calls Benedicto Soto, his next door neighbor and the local police chief in the area of Buenos Aires where Luna Park is.

"Beni, we are catching hell here because of all that cell interference Thursday."

"You should. Those phones are way too expensive."

"Pricing is not my department. Look, I was wondering whether your people noticed anything unusual Thursday."

"You know that there was a little bit of a riot after the candidates had their say?"

"No. What happened?"

"It was kind of weird. There were maybe thirty people involved, mostly from San Nicolas. They started squabbling amongst themselves. We didn't have to arrest anyone but it was weird because as you know, the vast majority of people in San Nicolas are pro Sanabria. As best we can tell some of them got into a heated argument with the others about whether Sanabria knew what the hell he was doing and that Brandt was probably a better choice. It seemed like they changed their minds as a result of the debate. My people sent them home in different directions. These political things are a pain in the ass. I have to be very careful to be and to be perceived to be neutral. You do not want to get in the middle between Flores and Sanabria. Like they say, when the elephants fight the ants get trampled."

"Thanks Beni. We are looking into this matter very carefully. My expert on this sort of thing went off and got himself killed in an avalanche in Bariloche Saturday. The last message we had on his answering machine was going on about the cell phone interference Thursday."

"Don't hesitate to call me if you need anything else Geraldo."

CIA Headquarters
Langley, Virginia
August 14, 1995 Thursday

Carpenter, Magnuson, Reinhardt, Biggs and the new Secretary of the NSA, Lawrence Cooper, are in a modest conference room next to Mitch Rogerston's office. Cooper has only been on the job two months and the only one of these people he has met before is Mitch. They need to 'bring him up to speed' on the goings on in Argentina. Guenther is doing the talking at the moment.

"We think that they have figured out how to make a primitive mind control weapon with the Plodamax-type explosive they have. If you have been following the news in Buenos Aires, which I have, you will find that there was a 'mysterious transmission' a week ago that was focused on Luna Park where the first Presidential debate was going on. We were fortunate to have one of our polar orbiters capable of detecting such 'transmissions' flying over Buenos Aires at the time. It didn't detect anything while it was north of or directly above Buenos Aires but when it was south of the city and still in range, it detected nine bursts. This in and of itself would not be cause for alarm but the Argentine media is reporting that there were numerous instances of cell phone static in the same time period as these bursts we detected. The bursts were of significant length, varying between about one third and three quarters of a second. We are postulating that they have something resembling a machine gun which can fire several discrete charges in rapid succession.

The Argentine phone company is saying that they think that there is some similarity between the interference that happened in San Rafael last December and the interference that happened in Buenos Aires last week. We know this for a fact. The material that MEA was making last year before we made our contribution to their efforts *(Guenther is smirking as he says this.)* was producing similar emissions."

Mitch interrupts.

"These are the first emissions we have detected since last December?"

Randy Biggs answers.

"Yes."

"What about that new factory they built in Rojas?"

"We have not detected anything."

"Maybe they have someplace else?"

"No doubt about that."

Guenther goes on to explain how one can cause unpleasant sensations by irradiating someone with the emissions at very low power levels. If the power is raised, the subject being irradiated sometimes loses his sense of balance. At higher levels the subject may get severe headaches. He says that we obtained most of this information from Baumgartner's records. He does not say if we generated any of this from our own experiments.

The other men in the room are not overjoyed at the prospect of having to deal with Lawrence Cooper. He is a career bureaucrat who has held various positions in the government over the past twenty years. He tends to act more like someone from the State Department rather than the Defense Department. He recently found out that the CIA and ONI had an installation on East Gorham. Apparently Simmons told him that 'he had no need to know anything about East Gorham'. President Simmons more or less put this guy up as a sop to the doves in the Senate when he saw that he couldn't get

Grainger approved. Naturally, the leaders of the doves were the very two senators who Whitworth pointed out were responsible for defunding SOSUS. They and others are still upset about the raids on Argentina and were threatening to filibuster the appointment of anyone as 'pugnacious' as Harold Whitworth. Rogerston has already complained to the boss man about Cooper and was told to 'deal with it'. Rumor has it that Cooper complained to his two backers on the Senate Defense Committee that he was being 'shut out' of several things that he thought he should be involved in. Apparently they complained to Simmons who pointedly reminded them that the NSA Secretary served at his pleasure not theirs and that he was thinking about appointing a series of temporary 'acting' secretaries until the next election. If one is good at reading tea leaves inside the Beltway, one can surmise all this. He asks his first question.

"How long has this been going on?"

Guenther answers.

"These folks have been working on this thought transference stuff for sixty years starting in pre-WWII Germany. They even had the guy who started it working for them until recently when he died. They have been successful in transferring thought under certain highly specialized conditions for at least twenty five years. Tell him Henry."

"They taught a chimp how to play backgammon and how to read at least two hundred words in German."

"Do we know how to do this?"

Randy answers.

"Not as well as they do. We have a better understanding of how to cause the emissions than they do but they are learning fast. Our efforts have been more along the lines of creating beam weapons."

Guenther picks up again.

"What they are attempting to do is extremely dangerous. During the early work before and during World War Two, they killed a few hundred people using them as guinea pigs to try to transfer thought. We decline to do such experiments because of the harm it inflicts on the subjects."

Cooper interrupts.

"I thought I was just told that they have been successful in teaching a chimpanzee."

"We know of only the chimp, a prodigy nuclear physicist named Siegfried Bachmeier and his girlfriend, one Heidi Freud. They were all in Professor Wilfried Baumgartner's laboratory in Heidelberg. Without going into the technical details of how we know this, I can assure you that there is a lot more to this. We know that they have had very limited success. It seems that there are very few people who can act as either the source or the subject – at least so far. Now, Mitch will get to the really bad news.

"We had two people from our embassy in Buenos Aires who attended this debate last Thursday. They reported that they had numerous instances of negative thoughts about Governor Sanabria's statements. This was particularly so when he was talking about a joint venture with the British to exploit this oil field they have a ways out in the South Atlantic. We asked them what they thought when Senator Brandt was talking. They said they were predisposed to not like this guy because it looked like he was advocating another war with the Brits."

Cooper comments.

"Yes, I have heard that too."

Mitch continues.

"Well, they didn't get any negative thoughts from what he was saying at the moment. They did notice however that there were a number of people frowning while Sanabria was speaking. Each candidate was given the same number of seats in the arena and all the Socialists sat on the North side and all the Conservatives sat on the South side. Sometimes these South American politics can get pretty heated, like some of the soccer matches down there. Anyhow, our people noted that there were nearly as many Socialists frowning at what Sanabria said as there were Conservatives. Of course, there were many frowns on the part of the Socialists when Brandt was speaking but there were no frowns on the part of the Conservatives when Brandt was speaking."

"So, you think that these emissions or transmissions or whatever, were affecting what people thought of the speeches?"

"We don't know, but it is a distinct possibility."

Geraldo Montez's Office
Telefono Argentina
270 Avenida Rivadavia
Buenos Aires, Argentina
August 16, 1995 Thursday

Señor Montez has considerable assets available to him to prevent people from damaging the phone system. He has had them working overtime on this static problem since Monday morning. They have established that the transmission which caused the static came from an area within seventy five meters of the north side of Luna Park. They suspect that the transmissions came from the area designated for the television trucks. Security was tight around Luna Park last Thursday because of the mucky mucks in attendance. Chief Soto provided the list of the license plates of all the vehicles that were parked in this area. They check each one out. Soon enough they find that the TV station in Córdoba that the license belongs to did not send any truck to Buenos Aires to cover the event. They used the pool feed. Half an hour later the television people call back and say that the license is where it should be on their truck. Presumably, the license on the TV truck at Luna Park was a counterfeit.

The police have also taken increased interest in this matter for another reason. Since Monday morning, Chief Soto has personally interviewed every one of his patrolmen on duty around Luna Park on the day of the debate. He has found that there was an abnormally high incidence of what first appeared to be drunken behavior on the part of the people exiting the arena. There was no alcohol served in Luna Park that evening until well after the debate. But several people who left early were reeling as if they were drunk. His men offered to help a few of these folks to nearby benches. Strangely, none of them had any alcohol on their breaths and they all claimed to have not had anything to drink – they just felt a little dizzy.

There were fewer than forty cell phones switched on inside Luna Park during the disturbances. Two of these, both on the north side of the arena, have been reported to have stopped working. It is beginning to look like there was some mysterious transmission coming from the mystery truck.

This is not happening in a vacuum. The news media is following this sequence of events closely and noisily.

Basima, Oskar, Hector and Siegfried are sitting on her veranda contemplating their next move. The 'trial' last Thursday was a great success. They can see the numbers in the polls. There was even one high ranking Socialist who openly broke with Sanabria on Saturday. Not unexpectedly the interference with the cell phones has been widely reported. The phone company says that they detected similar interference in San Rafael last December. Basima is talking.

"Ziggy that was great. I'm not sure that we can pull off an encore now that everyone is looking for cell phone interference. Can you do anything about that?"

"I don't think so Basima. The shielding we had protected the people in the truck but we obviously had to let most of the emission out in the direction of the arena. Speaking of the truck, we need to thank Hector for making the truck disappear."

Hector responds.

"The counterfeit plates did the trick. We removed the decals and put the truck back in Rosario where it came from Friday."

Then Siegfried resumes.

"You said that you and Oskar didn't feel anything out of the ordinary even though you were subjected to the emissions."

Oskar answers.

"We talked about that Ziggy. As far as we can tell the emissions made no difference in our attitudes toward Sanabria."

"When is the next debate?"

"It is supposed to be the thirty first in Luna Park."

"Supposed?"

"Sanabria is already trying to wriggle out of it. His polling numbers must be showing the same things ours are. He wants the ground rules changed. All the changes would be in his favor – naturally. Flores says we are not going do that, period."

"So, there may not be any more debates?"

"I don't know."

"What is Flores saying about the numbers?"

"He is happy."

"He doesn't know anything about our involvement in the emissions?"

"He does not know and we have no plan to tell him. The next thing you know he would want you doing this for every Conservative running for anything – including dogcatcher."

"What about Hernando?"

"I think he might suspect that something strange is going on but he doesn't know anything for sure and he is too smart to ask me. He surely is not going to make any fuss about this as long as we are doing so well against Sanabria."

After more negotiations and some input from President Flores, they have agreed on a format for the next debate. Governor Sanabria insisted that his supporters sit on the south side of Luna Park this time. The Sanabria campaign has reached the conclusion that Brandt's people did something that only acted in the north side of the arena during the first debate. They can't prove anything but they are insisting on a careful inspection of Luna Park to find whatever it was. The Brandt campaign had no choice but to participate in this charade, if for no other reason than to assure that Sanabria's people didn't find something that was not there.

There is another problem. Oskar and Hector are telling Basima and Siegfried about this. Hector is doing the talking.

"There is a problem with Hernando. At Oskar's request, I have had two detectives following him for the past few weeks. He has been seen with the same woman, probably half his age, several times at every place within driving distance of Buenos Aires that Oskar has made a campaign speech. We are fairly certain that this woman is Ricardo Sanabria's grand niece. At the least, this will not be good for us if it just comes out that he is having an extra-marital affair. One can imagine far worse things that could happen if he is confiding our plans to her."

This is the first that Basima has heard of this business with a niece. She and Oskar have noticed that Hernando has this pretty gal with him quite often but if she is a relative of Sanabria, this just won't do. She is also a little hurt to find out this bit of information in this forum. Then she remembers that Oskar and Hernando go back quite a ways. They have been team mates on the same amateur football team for many years. Probably, he wanted to be sure before he brought anything up. She asks.

"Does Flores know about this?"

"We don't know. You would think that he must."

Now Oskar changes the subject.

"Ziggy, did you and Wig figure anything out last week? You told me Wig had some ideas about focusing the irradiation."

"We learned how to focus the beam fairly well. It should be possible to irradiate only the half of the arena where Sanabria's people are. We will have to use an aircraft to do this. It has to be fired from nearly directly overhead. We think we can bounce a laser off the building and use that as a reference aiming point to keep the beam on target. The focusing is good enough such that we can maintain a five meter zone of influence at one kilometer range. The exposure time must be very short. The focused beam is nearly three orders of magnitude as intense as our previous best effort. I must note that we killed three of our guinea pigs in the process of finding out an appropriate exposure time. We need Chief Weiss to get us some more."

This gets Oskar's attention. All he had heard earlier in the week was that Siegfried needed some more guinea pigs. Now he is finding out why.

"You won't hit me with this will you?"

"We can focus it so that it gets no closer than ten meters to the stage. It is likely that Sanabria's most important people will be in this area in disproportionate numbers. They will likely escape any irradiation."

"What about the people next to fence?"

"We will stay five meters away from the fence unless you approve going closer."

"I talked with Chief Weiss about the additional guinea pigs. He told me that it may take a few weeks. They may have to get some people from Chile."

"We can not do any more experiments with the few we have left. They have all been damaged to some extent."

Hector asks the same question again.

"You think you can do this from an airplane Ziggy?"

"Yes."

"How big an airplane?"

"I think the plane that Oskar hired to take us to Bahia Blanca would be big enough."

"We will rent another plane for the campaign. Can you bring the equipment you need to install to Rosario, Siegfried? TASA has a small hangar there where we can do the work in secret. We can get a campaign banner which the plane can drag through the air above Luna Park during the debate. This will be a convenient pretext. No one will be the wiser."

They agree that this will be perfectly feasible. The next debate is two weeks away. Then they start talking about dragging these banners around wherever Sanabria is giving a campaign speech. He is going to be speaking in Mendoza on Saturday. This is perfect if they can get a banner organized. He will be speaking in the stadium which has been renamed after the Malvinas. They will drag some banner reminding everyone that Oskar served Argentina with distinction during la Guerra de Malvinas. Meanwhile Señor Rendicion (Mr. Surrender) will be trying to sell his plan to negotiate with the very same British. They will put an ad in the

Mendoza newspapers for Saturday. Basima suggests that they say that when you negotiate with the British, the British position is always clear. Just buy a small ad to appear on the front pages of all the papers Saturday.

The British Negotiating Position
"What's mine is mine and what's yours is negotiable."
(Ad paid for by Patriots for Capitán Brandt.)

Then she adds.

"Oskar, are we going to tell Hernando any of this?"

"No."

Oskar has been taking this all in. His associates have plenty of ideas about how to help him, whereas Hernando does not seem to come up with anything useful. Why?

Later that Evening

They had supper at the la Ostra Sonriendo returning home around 2200. Basima is trying to find out what Oskar knows about Hernando without actually asking him – and of course, there was no opportunity at the restaurant. Oskar must sense this because he brings up the subject by himself.

"I don't know what is going on with Hernando. Flores must know that this is going on with the woman and he probably knows that she is a blood relation of Sanabria. All I can guess is that Hernando or possibly even Sanabria knows something about Flores that he does not want known. Flores is quite protective of Hernando but Hernando is in the business for Hernando. I think he thinks that I will win and give him a political plum of some sort."

"Are you?"

"Mein Schatz, this is not a suitable subject of conversation at this hour. I will want you to take over as my campaign manager as soon as I can figure out a way to get him out of the way."

He does not elaborate on this subject.

The aerial banner and front page ads in all the newspapers in Mendoza completely flummoxed Sanabria. He was so angry that it is rumored he wanted the Provincial Police to arrest the plane's pilot. Someone pointed out to him that he was the Governor of Provincia de Buenos Aires not Provincia de Mendoza. By the time he left the stadium there was a crowd lining part of his route back to the airport. They were all waving little white flags.

Basima and Oskar are watching the afternoon news show which is featuring a live interview with Governor Sanabria. First they show some footage of the airplane and the banner. Then they show the newspaper ads. Then they show the crowd with the white flags.

"What do you think of this Governor Sanabria?"

"I think Senator Brandt's tactics are very similar to those that Adolf Hitler used to gain power."

"We have noticed that you have accused Captain Brandt of being a Nazi several times in the past. Do you have any evidence that this is the case?"

"I have been having trouble with the Brandts and the Bachmeiers for decades. They are up there in Zarate where you will hear more German spoken than Spanish. They even teach German in the elementary schools there."

It goes on like this for a while. The Governor says they better not try that stunt in Buenos Aires Province. Oskar comments.

"We may have some trouble with the banner over Luna Park next week."

Basima answers.

"Flores can probably help you there my dear."

"Yes, but will he?"

After the show, Oskar calls President Flores at home.

"Mr. President, can he interfere with our aircraft?"

"It is not clear. The Buenos Aires Police have a few helicopters and a few small planes, mostly they worry about traffic. I have to be careful here. The lines of authority are not clear. Have you talked with Hernando about this?"

"No sir. This is the first I have heard of this threat to our aircraft."

What Oskar doesn't say is that it will be very difficult for anyone to talk to Hernando – or his girlfriend for that matter. They were 'disappeared' yesterday evening. By Monday it will come out that they were having an affair and that by a great coincidence they were connected to opposing political groups, rather tangentially in the case of Sanabria's grand niece. By Wednesday it will further come out that Hernando Lopez apparently embezzled several million dollars from the Conservative Party's Presidential Campaign war chest (funded in no small measure by the ten million dollars that Basima has contributed). Speculation is that they ran off some place.

Basima is taking Hernando's place as Campaign Manager.

Luna Park

Avenida Madero 240

Buenos Aries, Argentina

September 7, 1995 Thursday

The second debate was postponed one week so that it would not conflict with an important football game. It turned out that President Flores had more stroke in Buenos Aires than Governor Sanabria did because Buenos Aires is the federal capitol. Airplanes will be allowed to drag campaign banners around as the various campaigns see fit.

The arena is packed for this second debate. There will be no standees except for the one hundred or so police. All seating is assigned. Because of the increasing animosity between the two factions, a fence has been erected in the middle of the central aisle to keep them apart.

Governor Sanabria speaks first.

"Good evening. The last time we met here there were a number of cell phone interruptions. These were carefully investigated by the phone company. They found that the interruptions were very similar to some interruptions they had experienced last December in San Rafael. Some of you may recall that there was a strange lightning strike in San Rafael on New Year's Day. The lightning hit an electronics company named MEA, essentially destroying their electrical system. There were unverified rumors of some radiation leakage caused by this strike. The important thing here is that there have been no further instances of cell phone interference since that date until four weeks ago when it happened during the first debate. MEA rebuilt their factory in Rojas and it went into production in late July. Shortly thereafter we had this cell phone interference here. Incidentally, the founder and principal of MEA is Doctor Siegfried Bachmeier who happens to be Senator Brandt's nephew."

He moves on to complain about the dirty campaign that his opponent is waging. Finally he ends up calling for negotiations with the British again. When he is finished, all the Conservatives are frowning and about half the Socialists are frowning. The airplane has been zapping the Socialists every few seconds in ten millisecond bursts. It is dragging a considerably less provocative banner simply proclaiming

Las Malvinas son Argentinas

(The Malvinas are Argentine)

No one will mistake this for Sanabria's airplane because his position that these signs, which are ubiquitous around Buenos Aires, be taken down is well known. Now it is Oskar's turn.

"Good evening my friends. The ad that my opponent is so unhappy about merely points out that the British negotiating position is "What's mine is mine and what's yours is negotiable." This isn't news to anyone but my opponent."

(There is standing applause and gales of laughter on the Conservative side. The moderator docks thirty seconds of his talking time.)

"You may have noticed that there is quite a bit of new construction from here to Quilmes. My opponent continuously uses your taxes to pay off his cronies. Then they contribute some of your money back his campaign coffers. Remember the Montoya scandal. My opponent's major contributor put up a housing project which promptly fell down. *(The apartment building stood for three months and was fully occupied when it collapsed. There was considerable loss of life.)* This building was built with matching federal grants so the Feds had some interest in this event. After they found numerous building code violations, they decided to provide him with some of their housing." *(Señor Montoya presently resides in Cárcel de Caseros (the federal slammer in Buenos Aires).) Again the Conservatives stand and applaud and laugh. Oskar sits down.*

The format is similar to the first debate. There is a commercial after the opening speeches then there are two brief question and answer sessions separated by one more commercial. The moderator reads all the questions. It is slow pitch softball. There are a number of reporters trying to ask Oskar about the cell phone interruptions while he is making his way to his limousine. Oskar is having none of this and does not even break stride. One of the reporters, in his eagerness to put a microphone in front of Oskar, accidentally bumps into Basima. He is rewarded with a right fist to the temple which drops him to the ground. The fist belongs to Roberto Santiago who is now one of President Flores' bodyguards but was the light heavyweight champion of Argentina from 1987 until 1992. This incident is duly reported in the Socialist press as "Brandt's goons terrorize innocent reporter."

Brandt Campaign

Hotel Intercontinental

Avenida Moreno 809

Buenos Aires, Argentina

October 24, 1995 Tuesday evening

There is a large and boisterous crowd in the hotel ballroom. Oskar is wearing a suit which is the color of the Argentine Navy dress uniform. Basima has a pants suit to match. They are all smiles. They arrived at the hotel about 1600 and have been in the ballroom since 1800. The exit polling they have is showing Oskar is slightly ahead everywhere except the southern part of Buenos Aires Province. Shortly after the polls close the television stations start announcing their latest results. There are numerous cheers for almost all of them. By 2130 it is clear that Senator Brandt is going to be President Brandt.

Hilton Hotel

Less than a mile away this is also apparent to the gathering in the ballroom of the Hilton. They are expecting their candidate to make a concession speech but Sanabria is no where to be found. His campaign manager goes up to his room. The door is locked but he has a key. He finds Sanabria sitting on a sofa, apparently unconscious. It doesn't take long to figure out that he is not unconscious, he is dead. There is an empty bottle of Morphine Sulfate tablets and a half full glass of water on the table.

Enrique Medrano has been with Sanabria for nearly ten years. He knows that his boss has been taking morphine the past five because of back pain. He also has watched Ricardo become increasingly dispirited the past two weeks as the polls have turned against him.

There is no help for the situation. He returns to the ballroom and informs the media people that he has an important announcement.

"I regret to inform you that Governor Sanabria is dead. I found him in his room upstairs moments ago. As most of you know, the Governor has had problems with his back for a long time. He takes pain killers to alleviate this. These pain killers are potentially very dangerous even when taken in prescribed amounts.

It is not my place to concede the election but I congratulate Senator Brandt on his victory."

It has been slow going for the reporters in the room. Most of the attention has been on Brandt's party. Now, they all start immediately asking Medrano about the drugs and how long has Governor Sanabria been addicted. Did the Governor commit suicide? This action infuriates several of Sanabria's supporters who start shoving the reporters. Someone has the presence of mind to turn the lights out in the ballroom. At least there will not be any television of the scuffle. When the lights come back on, order has been restored.

END OF PART III

La Quinta de Olivos
Olivos, Argentina
December 1995

Oskar and Basima have settled into the Presidential Residence. It is less than four kilometers from her home in San Isidro. In deference to her neighbors they stay away from San Isidro because they are accompanied by his security people and the media people and the scandal sheet paparazzi etcetera. Oskar doesn't like all this attention anymore than Basima's neighbors do. He has had a number of streets made one way and instituted 'no loitering' areas on all the streets immediately surrounding the Presidential residence. This has been some help but does not completely solve the problem. He travels back and forth from Quinta de Olivos to Casa Rosada almost exclusively by helicopter. They organized some 'doubles' in the hope that they might be able to slip away unnoticed for an evening occasionally. This worked for about half an hour the first and only time they tried it.

Oskar ordered that the construction of the submarine bomb-proof at Santa Cruz be carried out around the clock 24/7. This has been duly noted by US satellites and relayed to the Brits. It is already having some effect on the British. They realize that there is no way that they can keep track of or bottle up the Argentine submarines when this new sub pen is completed. There have been several discussions in the UN about this situation. The Argentine position is perfectly clear. The British are occupying Argentina's property (Las Malvinas, aka The Falkland Islands) and now they are trying to parlay this illegal occupation into an ocean bottom grab based on the distance from these illegally occupied islands. The

British for their part are claiming that they have legally settled and continuously occupied the Falklands for one hundred and fifty years. The Spanish UN ambassador vigorously supports the Argentine position and gets a plug in for the return of Gibraltar to his country. There is a certain amount of 'piling on' in the UN as several other countries take a whack at the British – after all, for nearly one hundred years 'the sun never set on the British Empire' – much of which was taken by force. This is more or less a side show as far as Oskar is concerned.

He sees Raphael, Hermann, Hector and Siegfried at least once a week. He named Siegfried the head of the Argentine Nuclear Energy Administration the first week after he was inaugurated and Hermann Minister of Defense a few days later. Siegfried wants to relocate the next Argentine nuclear power plant from Provincia Buenos Aires to Provincia Córdoba. Oskar approves this right away because it will be seen as a 'thank you' for their support during the election. Siegfried says that he knows a place in Germany that can build the steel portion of the reactor containment system in a matter of weeks. He says this outfit is in Mannheim. Oskar thinks this is far into the future but gives his reluctant approval for Siegfried to visit Germany again.

Oskar has other things on his mind. He is mindful of how successfully they were able to influence the people in Luna Park.

"Siegfried, can you zap something from several kilometers away?"

"It is a line of sight weapon uncle. Of course the intensity declines more or less as the square of the distance but we can certainly reach ten kilometers."

"I was thinking more along the lines of one hundred twenty five nautical miles."

"I will have to chat with Wig about that. What do you have in mind?"

"I am thinking that we might be able to disable the crew on the British Petroleum exploratory rig they have sitting on the Martinez Macizo (Martinez Massif), clearly in our territorial waters. (The westernmost part of the massif is located one hundred and twenty five nautical miles off the closest Argentine shore. Not surprisingly this is very nearly the same distance as the easternmost part of the massif is from the closest Falkland Islands shore.)

Siegfried pulls out his pocket calculator and shortly announces.

"If we could put the weapon in a balloon we could 'see' something one hundred twenty five nautical miles away at an elevation of a little over three kilometers."

Raphael spent a year at the University of Miami as an exchange student in a cooperative program with the University of Buenos Aires. He comments.

"The Americans have some balloons about twenty miles east of Key West that they use to watch the water around the Florida Keys looking for drug runners and people trying to enter the country illegally. I know that they can see Cuba from there when it is a clear day. How much would something like this weigh Ziggy?"

"How big are these balloons?"

"I never got that close to them. I don't know. I do know that in the afternoon you could see them in Key West. They were less than half as long as the moon is wide, if that is any help."

Siegfried punches his calculator a few more times.

"Something which appeared to be half as long as the moon is wide at a distance of thirty two kilometers would be of the order of one hundred meters long. Back to your question about how much something like this would weigh, the answer is I don't know. The weapon we had in the truck at Luna Park weighed possibly thirty kilos but it didn't have the focusing coils. They are pretty heavy. I have to check with Wig but I will venture that we would end up around four hundred kilo. Then you have the power supply for the coils and a few thousand rounds – we are probably getting close to a ton."

Oskar thinks the youngsters are getting far afield here.

"Why don't we just use the airplane like we did before? There is no way we are going to be able to hide this blimp."

The boss has spoken. They will use an airplane.

La Quinta de Olivos
Olivos, Argentina
December 19, 1996 Tuesday

Siegfried knows very well that following the usual procedures will not result in any new nuclear power in Argentina before the turn of the century. Despite his bouts with whatever it is that is the matter with him he retains his amazing ability to concentrate upon occasion. Perhaps these thoughts are also in his dreams. Either way, he thinks that in one session at Heidelberg Eberhardt told him several things about power reactors. He is in the library of the large residence. All the curtains are drawn. Basima is going to try to coax this information to the forefront so he can say what it is. After the usual preliminaries, she has him hypnotized. She suggests that he play a game of chess with her. They move over to a table which has the board all set up. They start playing. They have played several times when he is in a trance and he always starts with the Ruy Lopez opening. She counters. Shortly he is talking in the first person as Karl Eberhardt.

"You are not the only one in Mannheim who knows how to deal with that opening Georg."

Basima asks the first question.

"What are you doing here?"

"I am looking at this crazy scheme to look directly into the pile."

They have talked about some of his previous sessions. He has prepared a list of questions that he wants her to ask when he is in his trance. She asks.

"Where are you?"

"I am in Rostock."

"Why are you mentioning Mannheim?"

No answer is forthcoming. She tried to explain to Siegfried that she did not think a straight question and answer period would work. She notices his eyes are blinking open and shut. He may be coming out of it. She sits quietly. After a while he yawns.

"That was a terrible train ride. It took two days from München. The engine was destroyed by enemy aircraft. I was lucky to get here with the parts we need."

He rambles on some more. The Q&A session simply is not going to happen. She has been going over Karl's floppy discs dealing with the reactors. She doesn't know what she is looking at. All she remembers is a photograph of Karl and some other man in front of a large building with the letters KF on it. She prints the letters KF and hands the paper to Siegfried. There appears to be some recognition. She takes a big chance and brings him over to her computer. In a few moments she has the photograph up on the screen.

Siegfried looks at this for a while.

"You did well to fix the damage so quickly Georg."

There is a pause. Georg must be speaking.

"So, you can have another two forgings for us in one month?"

He lapses into silence. After a few minutes he gets his familiar facial tic which invariably indicates he will soon awaken.

Krueger Faber GMBH
Mannheim, Germany
January 9, 1996 Tuesday

After the last hypnosis session, it did not take long for Siegfried to pinpoint what 'Karl' was talking about.

He flew to Frankfurt yesterday and is now in the office of Franz Faber the president of KF. Faber is about sixty with steel gray hair. Siegfried notes his diplomas on the wall. He has a Doctorate in Mechanical Engineering from Karlsruhe. After an exchange of pleasantries Siegfried gets right to the point.

"Herr Doctor Engineer Faber, it is my understanding that you produce reactor pressure vessels."

"We can but we don't Herr Doctor Bachmeier. We have a proprietary process which we choose not to reveal. The authorities will not approve our products for use in the nuclear industry without knowing exactly how we make them. Our business is almost entirely with the chemical industry."

Siegfried knows how they do this because he and Basima found Karl Eberhardt's reference to this manufacturer and building up heavy sections by explosively cladding many layers of steel plate. They found out what they could about this company which was primarily that the Faber family owned it. Basima remembered that there was a Faber in Karl's list of contacts. When they looked it up, they found it was Georg Faber.

"I can appreciate your position. We in Argentina have no objections to using explosively bonded fabrications."

"How do you know that?"

"A friend of mine knew your father."

Siegfried opens his attaché case and produces a drawing. The vessel will be a two piece spherical shell two thousand millimeters inside diameter and six hundred millimeters thick.

Franz immediately recognizes the unique flanging arrangement. This is all the information he needs. He knows that his father produced reactor shells during the war. His father and Professor Eberhardt invented this explosive bonding technique since it was the only way they could produce these large heavy pieces. All the conventional forges in Germany at the time were working overtime producing armament. He makes a mental note to find out how Bachmeier is associated with Eberhardt. In the mean time he will extract the highest price he can. He punches his computer keyboard a few times.

"We are fairly busy at the moment. We expect to finish the task in the shop this week. After that we have some fractionating tower heads for Dusseldorf Refining."

Siegfried interrupts.

"Our needs are very time sensitive. We would be willing to compensate you for any penalties associated with this customer if you are a little late fulfilling your contract."

Siegfried just said the magic word. They soon reach an agreement. Krueger Faber will start on the capsule Monday. Siegfried hands Franz a disc with the instructions for the KF numerically controlled plasma cutter and a check for ten million Deutsche Marks.

"If we started next week and we worked three shifts every day we could have this on a barge ready to go the fifteenth of next month."

Guenther Reinhardt's Office LANL
Los Alamos, New Mexico
January 20, 1996 Saturday

Guenther is leafing through a weekly intelligence report on European Reactor Technology. He notices in the summary of material orders that Krueger Faber placed an order for 275 tons of a specialty alloy steel plate. This material is very expensive and is used exclusively for reactor containment because it is comparatively highly resistant to neutron embrittlement. It is also always sold as ingots to specialty forging houses. This order is for twenty five millimeter plate. The longer he looks at this the more curious he gets. He calls his librarian and asks him to find out what he can. Fifteen minutes later the librarian walks into his office.

"Good morning Guenther."

"Good morning Andy."

(The librarian is Geoffrey Carnegie but everyone calls him Andy.)"

"Krueger Faber is a specialty house that makes high pressure vessels for the chemical industry, primarily the German chemical industry."

"Do they do anything for the nuclear power folks?"

"Not that I could find. They are privately held. There isn't much to find."

Guenther is thinking back forty years.

"Where are they?"

"They are in Mannheim on the river."

He is thinking Krueger Drexler not Kruger Faber.

"Andy, please spend an hour and see what you can see."

When he returns it is lunch time. Guenther buys in the Lab's main cafeteria.

It turns out that Guenther's memory is very good. The outfit was founded in the mid twenties as Krueger Drexler. Drexler's daughter married Georg Faber in the mid thirties. We don't know what they did during the war but they came through in good shape. In the early sixties they changed the name to Krueger Faber. The Fabers also own a machine works that builds large forges.

After lunch, Guenther calls Tom Stevens at home.

"Tom, did you ever hear of a Krueger Drexler or Krueger Faber?"

"Yes. We sold a very early version of Plodamax to Krueger Faber about fifteen years ago."

"Do you know what they were doing with it?"

"No. But, at the time we were trying to drum up some business for Plodamax by flogging it as an excellent material to use for explosive cladding. Wally went over there once. Let me check our records. *(This doesn't take that long since they keep digitized records of all sales of their proprietary explosives and Tom is on the GSE LAN with his computer at home.)* They ordered a total of one hundred kilos of Plodamax between 1980 and 1984. Then we stopped making that version and the feds prohibited us from exporting the new material. I think they were using Hexogen before they tried the Plodamax and went back to using Hexogen."

"You tried using the Plodamax for cladding?"

"Yes. It works fine but so does Hexogen for most alloys. Of course, if you want to fool around with hard material, you can do better with Plodamax.'

Comandante Roca Aeropuerto
Provincia Santa Cruz, Argentina
January 29, 1996 Monday 1215

The Argentine Air Force C-54 transport touched down after a modest flight to the coast and back. It is one of fifteen such craft that Argentina purchased from the US Army Air Force as military surplus in 1945. This one is a little different from the others. It has a recently added external fuel tank under each wing. The one under the starboard wing contains the apparatus which produces the radiation beam. Since the meeting in December Siegfried and Ludwig shrunk the focusing equipment to the point where they were able to fit the entire apparatus inside a seven hundred millimeter diameter drop tank. They also improved the focusing such that the beam is only five meters in diameter at a range of two hundred fifty nautical miles. An important part of this rapid progress was due to the use of an improved scintillation counter. They didn't need any more guinea pigs to determine the strength of the signal. The equipment was brought in an unmarked truck to the military side of the Córdoba airport. The C-54 had the two drop tanks installed prior to its arrival at Córdoba. Once the hangar doors were closed, the starboard drop tank was removed and the drop tank assembled in the Belen yard of CCM was installed. Comandante Roca was chosen because it is well removed from the Atlantic coastline. In fact it is closer to the Pacific. They don't think the comings and goings of any planes from this airport will attract any attention. As part of the overall deception, the Argentine Air Force is flying several reconnaissance missions around the BP rig every day. Purportedly, this is an effort to demoralize the crew. What they are actually doing is lulling the British into a false sense of security. There are also 'training exercises' involving C-54 transport aircraft delivering various cargos to Santa Cruz and Deseado, the airstrips closest to Martinez Macizo. There is speculation in the press that there is a big buildup of weaponry going on in Santa Cruz and Deseado. Oskar's administration has had no comment on these speculations. Collectively, all these aircraft are creating lots of blips on the British radar screens in the South Atlantic and the Houses of Parliament.

Anything to do with the radiation beam is only known to a very few of the Nazis, some of whom are in the Argentine Secret Police. If it were ever found out, it would probably make for very bad publicity with respect to the strange things that went on in Luna Park this spring.

Ludwig and Siegfried are delighted to be back on the ground. The flight was uneventful but somewhat noisy. They zapped the BP rig for five minutes as they were approaching Santa Cruz and then the aircraft actually landed in Santa Cruz for a few minutes. It then turned around and came back to Comandante Roca. A brand new Argentine Air Force Embraer ER135 is waiting to take them back to Córdoba. They are not expecting to hear anything about the results until something appears in the media – if something appears in the media. The Embraer Pilots greet them at the steps to the aircraft.

"Senor Bachmeier did you hear that the BP platform is on fire?"

Ludwig and Siegfried are hard pressed to not to show any emotion.

"No, what happened?"

"One of our reconnaissance planes was in the area when they picked up a Mayday from the platform at 1115.

The copilot was fluent in English. He said it sounded like the guy issuing the Mayday was drunk. They flew around once again to see what was going on. Suddenly there was an explosion and a large fire appeared. They heard some British response to the Mayday to the effect that there would be a destroyer there in two hours. We are monitoring the situation with constant surveillance."

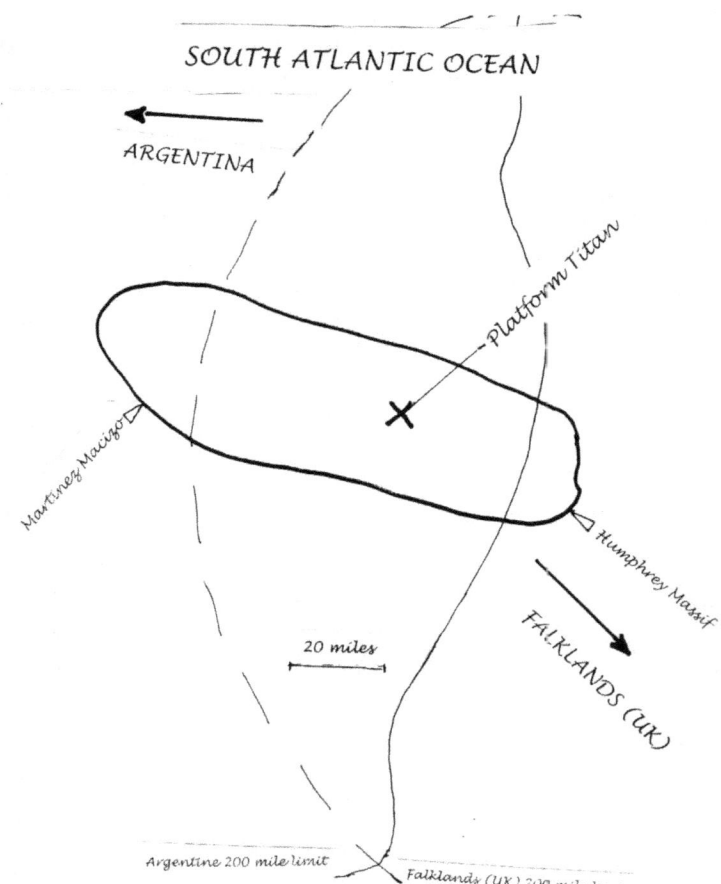

SOUTH ATLANTIC OCEAN

ARGENTINA

Platform Titan

Martinez Macizo

Humphrey Massif

FALKLANDS (UK)

20 miles

Argentine 200 mile limit

Falklands (UK) 200 mile limit

BP Platform Titan

South Atlantic Ocean

January 29, 1996 Monday 1412 Zulu

Doctor Lawrence Jones (the resident physician on the rig) is on the phone with Mark Johnson, the Manager of Operations.

"Mark, have we got a gas leak or something?"

"I don't think so. Why do you ask?"

"I have four people in my office complaining of splitting headaches."

"I have a bit of a headache myself Doc. Oh shit!"

"What's going on there?"

"Big trouble, Dan Murphy just keeled over and hit some buttons he should not have on his way down. I gotta go."

As he runs across the control room to help his chief operator the platform shudders violently. He looks out the window. There is a geyser of fire pouring out of the hole. It is impinging directly on the local control panel which is wide open for some maintenance. He reaches for the panic button which is supposed to activate the 'doomsday' valve but to his dismay this part of the control panel is opened up and there is no power to it. What is supposed to be a redundant system has been rendered useless. He really does not understand the intricacies of the wiring in the control panel. He grabs the microphone and asks for an instrument man right now. Fortunately one of the instrument men is on the other side of the control panel and is about the only person who hears him. The roar of the gas is all anyone outside can hear. The instrument guy is a quick study. He perceives the problem and manages to restore power back to the panic button. It was forty five seconds of hell.

They practice disaster drills fairly often. About ten seconds after the 'doomsday' valve closed the fire died. They have a head count in five minutes. There are three men on deck dead. There is one missing, presumably blown overboard by the explosion and presumed dead. The rig's helicopter is badly damaged. Many of his crew members appear unsteady on their feet, just like Murphy.

Two hours later the Sheffield class guided missile destroyer HMS York arrives on the scene. It is deemed prudent to evacuate the rig leaving only a volunteer skeleton crew. It is a five hour run at flank speed to the hospital in Port Stanley. It was windy and raining at the time of the explosion but now the sea is calm on this beautiful summer's day. There is no further excitement.

DCAC
Woburn, Massachusetts
January 30, 1996 Tuesday morning

Guenther is on the speaker phone with Henry and John.

"You saw that the BP rig had a problem yesterday?"

"Yes."

"There is a good chance that that was not an accident."

"Why?"

"As best we can tell the attack occurred between 1350 and 1415 Zulu. That is right in the middle of the time between successive satellite passes. Our friends in the Royal Navy told us that a number of the people they evacuated from the platform were staggering around like they were drunk. There is no alcohol permitted on the platform. I am beginning to think that they zapped the platform with something similar to what they did in Buenos Aires."

"You would think the Brits would have seen anything in the neighborhood on their radar."

"I agree John."

"Are you suggesting that they have some sort of stealth capabilities?"

"We don't think so. There is another equally unsettling speculation going around. Randy says they wouldn't have to have made much progress in focusing to have been able to zap the rig from a considerable distance, possibly even while over land. Listen, I want to go there and personally see what's what. You get to ride the whole way in Gulfstream luxury Hank."

"Can Christina come?"

"Sure, we have plenty of room."

"When is all this going to take place?"

"I will be landing in Manchester at 1000. We will have to make stops for fuel in Miami and again in Sao Paulo. It is a long way to Port Stanley."

Henry calls home and soon finds out that Christina prefers to go skiing rather than shag nearly a third of the way around the earth to 'nowhere central'. When Henry gets to Manchester, he finds Randy, Guenther and a Sam Hoover in the General Aviation lounge. It soon transpires that Sam is a world class statistician who teaches at Harvard. He is about 5'6 with a grey crew cut and is sporting reasonably thick glasses and a bow tie – definitely a candidate for Nerd of the Month. He must have gone to another well known campus on the Charles River. When they get to Miami they are joined by two Navy Techs and a bunch of boxes.

January 31, 1996 Wednesday

It takes nearly eight hours to get to Sao Paulo and another four to get to Port Stanley. Several people including Henry manage to get some sleep along the way. Shortly after dawn they board a Royal Navy helicopter for the hour and one half journey to the platform.

The Techs deploy the instruments in the boxes as per Guenther and Sam's directions. Mark Johnson is their guide on the tour of the rig.

"I was here in the control room when it happened. Doc Jones called me wondering about a gas leak. He said there were four guys in his place complaining about headaches. I was listening when my control room operator keeled over onto the control panel. He tried to break his fall by putting his hands out and hit several buttons on his way down. Then there was this blast. The floor shook under my feet. I immediately ran to the window to see what was going on. You will get to see this all up close a little later so I won't go into detail twice."

Henry asks.

"How did you feel?"

"I had some sort of unpleasant feeling about the weather. It was a bit weird but rain depresses me somewhat anyhow."

"You didn't feel dizzy?" "No, but I did talk with enough of my crew to get the impression that if you were on the west side of the rig you were more likely to feel dizzy than if you were on the east side."

Sam and Guenther already read the preliminary report which was faxed to the Gulfstream and they are nodding in agreement. Sam asks.

"Would you venture a guess about the relative rates of dizziness?"

"My SWAG *(Silly Wild Ass Guess)* would be maybe twice as many on the west side as the east side, but don't hold me to it. There were plenty enough dizzy people to go around."

Henry has an ear for such things.

"That sounds something like an Oklahoma guarantee."

"Yes, I grew up in the Panhandle and spent some time in the oil patch there before coming to work for BP."

At this very moment three sheets emerge from the fax machine in the Control Room. Mark looks at them quickly and hands them to Guenther. There is a summary of the debriefing of everyone on the rig separated by location. While Guenther and Sam are looking at the fax, Henry is looking around the control room. He is pointing to an outdoor thermometer on the other side of the western window.

"Mark, what is that?"

"It is an outdoor thermometer."

"Has it always been there?"

"I have only been on this platform for two months. II think it was there when I got here."

"Can you bring it here?"

"That will take some doing. I don't have any Maintenance people at the moment."

"Who is helping the Navy Techs?"

"Oh, I forgot about them. When the Techs finish I will have them get it."

They go on a tour of the platform. When they get to the lunch room, they see that here on the west side only windows separate them from the great outdoors. Guenther notes that the fax indicates that essentially everyone in the lunch room had bad headaches and/ or was dizzy. On the east side there is less than ten percent. The rig is made entirely of steel and the various compartment walls are all one quarter inch plate, or heavier. On the east side there is easily an inch of steel between the western side of the rig and the interior of the compartments on the east side.

The Navy Techs finish whatever it was that they were doing. They pack everything up and take the helicopter over to the HMS Ajax which has assumed station about half a mile west of the rig. There is a chat with Captain McMillan which reveals that there were no unusual radar contacts reported by the HMS York on Monday so there is no evidence that an Argentine aircraft was involved. He notes that the Argentines are generating nearly thirty contacts a day but they don't venture more than sixty miles offshore, still more than one hundred miles away from the platform, so they are assumed to be non-threatening contacts.

Randy and Guenther huddle privately with Captain McMillan for half an hour. The Navy Techs will remain on HMS York for another three days. They will install the equipment arriving from the US on the platform tomorrow. HMS Ajax and its successors on station will provide constant Marine guard for the equipment on the Titan.

The visitors sans the Navy Techs return to Port Stanley. After supper with some of the local brass there is private meeting in Henry's room. There is a bottle of 25 year old Ballantine and three liters of Perrier Sparkling water on his coffee table. Guenther starts talking.

"We installed some detectors on the rig today. If there is another attack we will see it. All this hoopla about the marine guard has to do with the weapon which will arrive tomorrow. We have decided that it would be best to put the weapon on the rig as opposed to the escort ship because the escort ships come and go about every week. Nobody here knows anything about this weapon. They have received instructions from the highest level that that is the way it will remain. We have another problem. If this incident was indeed caused by the Argentines, they would almost certainly have needed a signal from the rig to home in on. They presumably took their shots from close to two hundred nautical miles away from an aircraft that was over the mainland. We think the shot was taken from either Puerto Santa Cruz or Puerto Deseado. While we are sitting here drinking scotch Sam is hard at work trying figure out from the pattern of ills suffered by the crew of the Titan which place is more likely."

"So you think there is or was someone on the rig that sent the signal."

"We are not certain. The Argentines could have brought some swimmers in a submarine and planted the device."

"Did either of you notice that funny looking outdoor thermometer?"

Randy responds.

"I noticed that Mark looked a little uncomfortable when you wanted to take a closer look at it."

"So did I. He said he has only been on the rig for two months and he thought it was there before him."

"Where was he before that?"

"I have not a clue. Let's call BP and find out."

"Guenther, it is 2300 in London, presumably they are not there at this hour."

"That is the first order of business tomorrow morning."

Henry continues.

"I noticed that you can not see the portion of the control panel where the panic button is located from Johnson's office."

Randy agrees.

"I noticed that too, Hank."

"So this doesn't agree with his description of the event where he is talking on the phone with Doc Jones and watching his control room operator fall down."

"You are right."

Port Stanley Airport
Falkland Islands, U.K.
February 1, 1996 Thursday 0800 Zulu

Guenther is patched through from the Gulfstream via MILSAT to BP Headquarters in London. He has reached Reginald Hopkins, head of BP Production.

"Good Morning Mr. Hopkins. This is Guenther Reinhardt calling from Port Stanley."

All Mr. Hopkins knows is that the 'accident investigation team' sent from the US might try to contact him and that he should extend them every courtesy.

"Good Morning Mr. Reinhardt. You are three hours behind us if I remember correctly."

"Yes, it is dawn here. I don't want to appear abrupt sir but I need to find out a few things about the Manager of Operations on the Titan. He told us that he has only been here two months. Where was he before that?"

Hopkins has chapter and verse about the Titan spread out on the large table in his office. This is the most exciting thing going on in BP at the moment. He has Guenther on the speaker phone so he walks over and picks up his file on Mark Johnson.

"He was on the Leviathan for six months before he moved south."

"Where is the Leviathan?"

"I am so sorry. How stupid of me. The Leviathan is one of our platforms off southern Brazil. It is fairly close to Porto Alegre."

"How long has he been with BP?"

"Thirteen years. He is a rising star in this end of the business. We are likely to offer him a position here in London in the not far distant future."

"Thank you Mr. Hopkins. This is most informative. I may be in touch again soon. Have a good day."

Guenther is gone as suddenly as he appeared. Hopkins is wondering "What the hell was that all about". Then he remembers that BP has a continuous monitoring of the control room on the Titan. His recent caller probably should know this. He buzzes his secretary and tells him to find out who he was talking to and get him back. The secretary manages to trace the call back to the Army Signals Group in Feltham. An answering machine instructs him to punch in his pass code. Pass Code? Ten seconds later the machine announces that calling this number even by mistake is not viewed kindly by the authorities.

This information has Guenther thinking. Those Nazis building the Brazilian patrol boats are in Porto Alegre. He is going to see what he can see about this but it will be a few hours from now. He goes back to the hotel. The four of them sit down for breakfast at 0600. Sam starts.

"While you were partying last night a few of us were working. As best we can figure from the ills suffered by the crew, they took the shot from somewhere around Santa Cruz which is nearly directly west of the platform. There is less than a twelve percent chance that they took the shot from Puerto Deseado, which is to the north. I also considered Puerto San Julian although that was not on the list. I can not tell with any confidence whether they took the shot from Puerto San Julian or Puerto Santa Cruz."

Guenther says.

"I am sure our hosts have all the radar contacts cataloged. As I understand it, there isn't much of an airport at

San Julian so this suggests that Santa Cruz is the place. Sam, I didn't spend the morning as a slug abed like some others. I have already been out to the airport and I chatted with BP in London an hour ago. It turns out that Johnson was working in Brazil near Porto Alegre before he got this assignment. We know that there is a strong Nazi presence in Porto Alegre and we have reasonable suspicions that this boat building outfit has connections to the Nazis in Argentina. This is just an aside, but the Bachmeier boat is gone from its slip near Bahia Blanca. We can't find it and neither could some other people who would have liked to have found it. If they took it out of the country, as opposed to a little ways offshore and sinking it, they may have well taken it back to Porto Alegre where it was built. It was a perfectly nice boat."

Henry gets his two cents in.

"My friend who is into that sort of thing said the boat probably cost two to two and one half million US when it was new. Why sink a perfectly good boat? They probably can still get the better part of a million for it now."

Guenther and Randy are planning on supervising the weapon installation today. They thank Sam for his contribution. He gets to go home in a P3 Orion waiting at the airport. The Gulfstream with its invaluable communications systems stays here with Guenther. Henry wants to go to Porto Alegre and take a look but is dissuaded as soon as Randy points out that he does not have a current visa to get into Brazil. Henry will be going back to the platform.

When they get to the Titan they are greeted by Royal Marine Captain Michael Thomas.

"He gave us the slip. We sent a few men at 0100 to pick him up but he was gone. There was a radar contact some three miles north of here at 1147. We sent a launch there at first light. They came back dragging an inflatable. We think he rendezvoused with an Argentine sub."

There is nothing to be done about that situation at the moment. The Captain's hand held marine radio crackles.

"Thomas here."

Captain McMillan of HMS York is on.

"Captain Thomas, please hand the radio to the big guy with the white hair."

"Doctor Reinhardt, I have a message from a Reginald Hopkins in BP London. He says there is a tape of the control room which may help you."

"Thank you Captain."

Several shipping containers arrived by air into Port Stanley during the night. They were accompanied by two millwrights with advanced weapons clearances. All have been transported to the Titan by HMS York. The largest part of the system is the steering mechanism which can control the aim to +/- one ten thousandth of one degree in both Azimuth and Altitude while automatically compensating for the minute motions of the platform as modest waves impinge on it. It takes all morning to install it in a storage shed on the west side of the platform. At 1300 they test it by shooting at a drone one mile west of the platform. The drone promptly falls out of the sky. It has flotation so the launch waiting below has no difficulty retrieving it. By 1400 Guenther and Randy have determined that the test was successful. Since there was no way to conduct this test in private, the cover story given to the various spectators was that the weapon jams the drone electronics. The folks on the launch think that the damage to the drone looks like more than typical electronic warfare countermeasures could possibly inflict, but they know better than to pursue this matter. In the mean time, it has been discovered that the tape of the goings on in the control room is not there. This is very bad news. This tape has their photographs in it. There is some good news though. The funny looking outdoor thermometer turned out to have a GPS in it. They soon figure out how the Argentines managed to zero in on the rig. When they send a signal to the device, it responds with a signal giving the GPS coordinates. They now have the GPS coordinates of the aircraft and the platform. These are close enough to be both 'seeing' the same set of satellites so they are presumed to have the same errors. They are then able to calculate the bearing between the aircraft and the platform with sufficient accuracy to raster the irradiation over the platform. Now that Guenther and Randy see what is going on they devise a means of hunting the hunter.

When they return to Port Stanley Randy heads off to HMS Invincible. There is a sizable staff of electronics experts on the aircraft carrier. They are already well along building what Randy faxed to them from the Titan.

Guenther and Henry call Mitch Rogerston. Guenther does the talking.

"Good afternoon Mitch. We are in need of your able assistance."

"Where are you?"

"We're in Port Stanley but I need your help in Porto Alegre. Please send someone down there and find out what you can about Bachmeier's boat. We are speculating that they may have sent it back there to sell."

"What happened down there anyhow?"

"They made a fifteen million dollar mess. BP says they will have it put right in a month or so."

La Quinta de Olivos

Olivos, Argentina

February 4, 1996 Sunday

There is a lively discussion about the Titan going on in the dining room. All the higher ups are there, to wit, Oskar, Basima, Siegfried, Ludwig, Raphael, Hermann, Hector and Aldrich. It seems that the fire and explosion were not part of the game plan. Oskar does not want the Titan dead. It will cost Argentina the better part of one billion US to replace when they push the British out. He hopes to buy it at a distressed price. If the thing is sunk or destroyed, Argentina will lose a bargaining chip. Oskar had one of his minions in Argentine Naval Intelligence debrief Mark Johnson yesterday. He has the report and the control room tape. As soon as he heard about the control room tape he asked Benno Weber to come to the Presidential Residence today. They watched a few minutes of the tape.

Benno immediately comments.

"That is Henry Magnuson."

Oskar asks.

"Do you know any of the others?"

"No sir."

Basima has something to say also.

"The big older man may be Guenther Reinhardt. He works with Magnuson."

Oskar says.

"Judging by their expressions and body language, I would guess that he is the leader. I am also wondering who that very tall man is. Ziggy, didn't you say something about a very tall man being the man who designed this machine that made a movie of brainwaves or something like that?"

"I never saw him but Heidi did. I will ask her to come over and look."

Fifteen minutes later Heidi is there looking at the tape. She points to Randy and Henry.

"I have seen both of these men in Professor Baumgartner's laboratory. They both work for an American company named Cerebrionics. The taller one is Doctor Randolph Barton and the other one is Mr. Robert Hartwell. Manny has also seen these people."

They thank Heidi for coming over on such short notice. She knows that Siegfried has many meetings with his uncle and she has never been present. As soon as she is gone Ludwig speaks up.

"I wouldn't be surprised if that contraption they installed in Baumgartner's lab had some surveillance capabilities. You remember Ziggy when the thing cratered. It was right after Manny moved the Toshiba MRI."

"Yes, Manny and I talked about that a little. They were not using the EEG machines that day. He says he wasn't paying much attention to it so he doesn't know exactly when it went down. As luck would have it, that is the week that Manny decided to accept my invitation to come to Argentina. We are out of the loop as far as Heidelberg is concerned."

This is the first that Oskar has heard about this. He makes a note to find out what he can about what the Americans may have learned listening to the conversations in Baumgartner's Laboratory. Maybe his nephew will wise up a little. How many times have I warned him about going back to Germany? He needs some answers right away.

"Ludwig, Ziggy, I want you to think hard about this. Do you remember ever mentioning anything to do with your development work on this zapping capability?"

Siegfried answers.

"I know we talked a little about our efforts at Aleman Hospital but we never said anything about the work at Rancho de la Veta Madre. Ludwig did not know that that place existed until we took him to see it. Furthermore, we had not yet done any testing with humans at the time the CCX-1 went down."

Oskar is not letting go of this surveillance stuff.

"What about that instrument you have Aldrich? Wasn't that made in Massachusetts also?"

It is quite clear that Oskar is getting angry. Aldrich does not point out that the CCX-1 was made in Tennessee.

"Yes."

"I want that thing gone over with a fine toothed comb. If there is any question at all about whether there is surveillance equipment in it, destroy it."

Siegfried's and Aldrich's shoulders slump almost simultaneously. The Wardnor Mark V is the finest Spectrometer in the world.

Wig comes to the rescue.

"Captain *(Oskar prefers his former title in the presence of his close associates)* we might be able to use this thing to advantage to send false information to the Americans."

Oskar thinks about this for a little while.

"That is a decent idea Wig. Where is it now?"

Siegfried answers.

"It is in Rojas, mostly gathering dust. We use it occasionally for quality control."

"Quality control of what?"

"Our version of Plodamax."

"So if this thing is actually a bug it is presumably sending whatever it knows to some satellite. The Americans can probably watch our progress very nicely. We will do well to assume it is bugged. Maybe you and Aldrich can figure out some things to analyze with it that will totally confuse the Americans without them knowing what is happening."

They agree to look into this matter carefully. Oskar resumes.

"It looks like the explosion was not caused by the zapping – probably. I say probably because Johnson said his control room operator could have hit some wrong buttons as he was falling down and he fell down as a result of the zapping. Johnson thinks it was a real accident."

Raphael speaks.

"What do you want to do with Johnson?"

"Let's hold off on any decision for a while. He may be of further use to us. That was quite a risk he took snatching the tape. I want to be sure we have every bit of information we can get about this 'accident investigation team' that showed up. It is already clear that these other two men are closely associated with Magnuson."

John and Henry are having their first coffees of the day.

"Christina was right. That is 'nowhere central'."

"How much damage was done?"

"I heard numbers like fifteen million US to the rig. They were talking about one month to put it right again. They had forty men working on it when we left. All the heavy stuff has to come from Sao Paulo which is nearly two weeks away by ship. Randy and Guenther cooked up something which they think can prevent this from happening again."

"Did Mitch's crew come up with anything?"

"Yes, they hit pay dirt. The boat was in the Barco Fazendo Porto Alegre yard. They didn't make an appearance at the yard. They took a bunch of pictures from a helicopter."

"How do they know it was the Don Martinez?"

"It was the only sport fisher there and he had the pictures we took a couple of years ago at the fishing tournament to compare against. Everything else there belongs to the Brazilian Navy."

"Speaking of pictures, the bad guys have our pictures."

"Yes. Randy will not be participating in any more visits to Heidelberg. We need to pick up the CCX-1. You and Christina handled the business arrangements with the University. I am sure you will have better luck getting her to accompany you to Heidelberg than you did to Port

Stanley. Presumably you will be talking to the guy you made the deal with."

"Yes, Schmidt is the head of the department."

"Try to get a feel for what this Schmidt guy knows about this whole show."

The crew fixing the Titan is having a tea break. Most of the men are drinking Coca Cola®. It is nearly thirty degrees Celsius (eighty six Fahrenheit) in this freakish heat wave. There is a loud report. Walter Rodman is the only man on the west side of the rig. He is busy trying to haul in what feels like a good sized codfish. He turns around just in time to notice a port on the mysterious box close.

Four miles above
Puerto Santa Cruz, Argentina

Everyone aboard the transport is dead. All the electronics have been fried. The plane noses over and crashes into the sea two miles offshore. News of the loss of the aircraft soon reaches Casa Rosado. Oskar has direct control over the recording of any conversation on this very private line. The recorder is shut off.

"I am glad you were not on that plane Siegfried."

"Me too, Wig wasn't so lucky."

"I wonder whether they put any kind of defense system on the platform."

"All the actions of the electronics on the aircraft are recorded. If we can retrieve the recording we might be able to find out."

"How far down is it?"

"We think that it went down in fifty meters of water. The aircraft was observed on radar until impact so we know where it struck the sea."

"I will have the Navy go get the recording."

La Quinta de Olivos
Olivos, Argentina
February 25, 1996 Sunday

Navy divers recovered the recording from the air-craft yesterday afternoon. It is useless. They do have a little more information. The airplane crash was on the front page of the local newspaper Thursday. There was a request that anyone who saw anything to advise the authorities on what they saw. Friday morning an amateur photographer who saw the aircraft came forward. He was fishing close to the shore somewhat north of the aircraft at the time of the event. He heard the airplane coming and he was looking up at it through stabilized binoculars. He is quite certain that the underside of the aircraft was lit up for an instant just the way his flashgun lights up what he flashes it at. Admittedly it was late morning and the sun was shining, but not on the underside of the aircraft.

"It was a long shot that anything survived the crash Ziggy."

"The electronics in the recording device were defi-nitely fried by something electrical in nature Uncle. I saw something after that disaster at MEA that looked like that. Every computer in the place was fried. I am begin-ning to think that they have a countermeasure for our device."

"Well, the report from the fisherman might be the straw in the wind. You said that it takes a few seconds to get the device aimed?"

"Yes. We send a signal to the transponder on the platform. When it sends back its GPS coordinates, we make the final adjustment to the direction we are firing and then we fire."

"How long does that take?"

"Three seconds unless we don't have the airplane pointed within five degrees of the target. In that case it might take another three or four seconds."

"So, even if everything is working right it is at least three seconds."

"Yes."

"So, if they have some kind of laser or who knows what, they would have three seconds after they sense your signal to aim and fire."

"Yes."

"I was hoping to save the platform but we are not going to allow them to take our oil. I am going to get Abbo Fassbinder to come here. When he was here two years ago he showed me plans for a very long range torpedo. We will destroy that platform."

39.41 South 61.93 West

5 Nautical Miles South of Isla Trinidad

Bahia Blanca, Argentina

March 5, 1996 Wednesday

The recently commissioned navy salvage ship Ciudad de Zarate has been anchored above the ill fated Devilfish for a week. Abbo suggested shortly after the Devilfish was sunk that the reactor might well be undamaged. Wilhelm Bachmeier et al did not have any use for this reactor at the time, but now Oskar does. The Argentine navy is going to try to retrieve the reactor. The hope is to retrofit one of Argentina's existing turbo-electric drive subs with the nuclear heat source. They have excellent logistic support here. The Devilfish is within forty nautical miles of Puerto Belgrano Naval Base. Aldrich and Siegfried devised a plastic explosive which is quite flexible. This has been formed into long 'sausages' some twenty millimeters in diameter and fifty meters long. In the past three days, the submersible tethered to Ciudad de Zarate has managed to stick several lengths of 'sausage', a total of about sixty five kilograms, onto the Devilfish's hull. This morning a three hundred ton barge crane was tied up to the salvage ship. The plan is to explosively cut the outer hull of the Devilfish into bite sized pieces, so to speak, and haul them off to one side. Once they have a clean shot at the pressure hull they will methodically open it up as well.

The detonators are in place. The mini sub is safely out of the water. Minister of Defense Hermann Schleifenbaum arrived an hour ago in a fast patrol boat and he gets to push the button. There is an enormous explosion. The water turns white for almost three hundred meters around Ciudad de Zarate. The ship is nearly lifted out of the water by the blast. The shock wave breaks the ship's back. The barge was built to work in rivers and harbors, not the open sea. It is comparatively flimsily built compared to a ship this size and it fares much worse. The bottom is ripped like tissue paper and it vanishes into the sea in a few seconds.

Ciudad de Zarate immediately sent off an SOS. The water tight compartments were all secured prior to the detonation and this bought a little time. The ship took nearly ten minutes to go down. That was plenty of time for an orderly evacuation to the lifeboats. The destroyer Rosario showed up forty five minutes later and picked up the crew of the Ciudad de Zarate and their distinguished visitor. Three of the five men on the barge were lost.

This is the fruition of Operation Possum. Almost immediately after the Devilfish went down the US Navy anticipated that the Argentines might attempt to salvage her reactor. Knowing the construction of the boat, they had the inside track on how the Argentines would proceed in their efforts to gain access to the reactor vessel. Two years ago the USS Georgia devoted an entire mission to placing ten tons of C-4 in the starboard ballast tanks of the Devilfish complete with shock sensitive detonators.

Hermann is telling Oskar his account of what happened Tuesday.

"It was a hell of a blast. Our people said they only had about sixty five kilos of explosives down there and they were spread out over an area of probably one hundred fifty square meters of hull. There is no way that those explosives did what happened. The Americans must have booby trapped the sub Oskar."

"That is a nuclear submarine. They may have breached the reactor core."

"We should know that very shortly."

They continue chatting. His old friend keeps asking Oskar to speak a little louder. He hopes the blast didn't damage his hearing or at least it is only temporary. A few minutes later the phone rings. Oskar put the caller on the speaker phone.

"Capitan Brandt, Minister Schliefenbaum."

"Yes Admiral."

(Admiral Lucas Mendez is the commander of the Puerto Belgrano base and an old friend.)

"I have just spoken with our people on the scene. There is significant radioactivity in the vicinity of the submarine. I am told that the radioactivity at the surface is easily detectable but not dangerous for short exposure times. We sent a camera down. The pressure hull has been completely destroyed. What we think is the reactor shell is badly dented and probably leaking. We can't be sure that the shell has been breached, but as

I understand it, there are a number of pipes connected to the shell. Nothing could have withstood this blast. I wouldn't be surprised if there are many broken connections and missing pipes at this point."

"Thank you Lucas."

The Admiral speaks softly. Hermann didn't hear much of the report. Before he plays it back at much higher volume Oskar asks Basima to join them. As soon as it is over, she asks.

"Do the Americans have nuclear mines or torpedoes?"

"I think they have very small nuclear warheads on some of their torpedoes."

"We lost our salvage ship there. We could claim they hit it with a nuclear torpedo. That would explain the radioactivity we detected."

La Quinta de Olivos
Olivos, Argentina
May 23, 1996 Thursday

Basima is orchestrating a reasonably effective propaganda campaign against the British and the Americans. After the booby trap incident in Bahia Blanca they decided that they couldn't sell the US nuclear tipped torpedo story but they cooked up one just as good. They are not mentioning anything about any radiation leak because they don't want the UN inviting themselves to help them with the additional ecological problem. The story that they are telling is that a monster British mine had been placed in the sea lane normally used by their warships traveling to and from the Puerto Belgrano Base. That was an act of war but instead of destroying one of their warships the mine destroyed a non-combatant navy hospital ship that was returning from a mission of mercy at San Antonio Oeste. This is playing very well at the UN.

On the second of May, the fourteenth anniversary of the sinking of the Belgrano, Oskar held a highly publicized memorial service. There was world wide coverage when he spoke of the three hundred twenty three Argentines that were killed. He also alluded to the seventeen men women and children killed the fourth of March. Later in the month there was a highly publicized 'leak' about a forthcoming joint naval exercise with Brazil. This will involve all of Argentina's submarines and numerous surface vessels. At the end of the exercise there will be a weekend leave in Rio de Janeiro for many of the participants.

The 'leak' does not include mention of the fact that all the Argentine submarines will be highly visible at dock at Castro de Silva, the Brazilian submarine base near Rio de Janeiro or that there will be no Argentine naval vessels south of Puerto Belgrano or anywhere near the Titan platform.

Abbo, Raphael and Rudy Kleist are in the shed that housed U-1241 for nearly fifty years. The six torpedoes are in wheeled cradles. Rudy is taking Polaroid® photographs of these finished products. The pictures will be on Oskar's desk this afternoon along with the final progress report.

Each of the torpedoes is eight meters long, five hundred millimeters maximum diameter and tapered fore and aft. Each has a fifteen kilowatt (twenty horsepower) electric motor powering a high volume low velocity axial flow water jet drive. The arrangement is similar in concept to a high bypass fan jet. The electric power is provided by a high temperature solid oxide electrolyte fuel cell operating on Perhydrol (stabilized hydrogen peroxide) and methanol. The torpedoes have extremely low drag coefficients that Abbo estimates at 0.037. They have a range of two hundred nautical miles at a modest twenty knots or three hundred and fifty miles at ten knots. They have gyroscopic guidance as well as magnetic homing capability. Each can carry up to a one ton charge. They will be most suitable for destroying stationary targets like the Titan Platform or any anchored ships 'riding shotgun' for the platform.

As soon as Rudy is finished four of them in their cradles are loaded into a trailer and secured. These will be taken directly to Santa Cruz. They are armed, fueled and ready to go.

Tomorrow morning there will be a 'live' test of the other two. They will be dropped into the water off

Necochea and aimed at a ship that CCM Bahia Blanca will have waiting off Monte Hermoso. They will surface at the end of their scheduled seven hour run and this ship will retrieve them. They will be refueled and armed when they get to Santa Cruz.

The plan is to launch the torpedoes from the Santa Cruz sub pen. They will attack the escort ship the first day and the platform the next day. The Argentine Navy is flying reconnaissance missions daily. When a reconnaissance aircraft is in the disputed airspace (within two hundred nautical miles of both the Argentine mainland and Islas Malvinas) the Air Force provides fighter escorts. They have established the British rotation schedule. HMS York stays one week and then the Ajax stays by the platform the next week. They change on Saturday mornings which allows the crew to be in Port Stanley for the evening meal. The British sunk an ocean going ferro-cement barge one kilometer west of the Titan and are using it as a permanent mooring anchor. The attack is planned for the morning of the twenty second. HMS York will be there if the present schedule holds. This ship is relatively fragile compared to the Ajax. They will use a two hundred fifty kilo shaped charge which will hopefully greatly damage but not immediately sink HMS York. It was decided that it would be much easier to deal with the British if there is minimal loss of British life. Oskar is hoping that the British will evacuate everyone from the area after the escort vessel goes down. They will send reconnaissance aircraft to see what is going on after the HMS York sends a distress signal. They will send two more torpedoes to sink the platform as soon as it appears that the platform has been evacuated. Since nobody has torpedoes that have this range, the British will be left to wonder what hit them.

END OF PART IV

BP Platform Titan
South Atlantic Ocean
June 22, 1996 Saturday 1115 Zulu

HMS York cast off from the mooring half an hour ago and is now barely visible as she heads east toward Port Stanley. At 0815 local, 1115 Zulu, the platform shudders. A few seconds later the ocean surface barely thirty meters east of the platform erupts. Something has gone very wrong at the wellhead. The 'doomsday' valve assembly must have been damaged. A huge amount of gas is leaking out. Fortunately there is a westerly wind blowing the gas further away from the rig at the moment. Robin Greenville orders an immediate evacuation and radios an SOS. This is received by everyone within eight hundred nautical miles. HMS York turns around and races back toward the Titan. Ajax is still three hours away. She increases her speed to thirty two knots.

Comandante Roca Aeropuerto
Provincia Santa Cruz, Argentina
June 22, 1996 Saturday 0819 local 1119 Zulu

Master Sergeant Antonio Garza is discussing the SOS with Colonel Jose Menendez.

"Coronel, el mensaje proviene de la plataforma no es un barco." (Colonel, the message came from the platform not a ship.) There was an immediate answer from some British ship to the effect that they would be on the scene in thirty five minutes. What I presume was another British warship sent a message that they would be there in three hours."

"These were in the open?"

"Yes sir."

The Colonel telephones Santa Cruz and orders a search plane up.

Thirty five minutes later that plane is three miles west of the platform. It is at barely three hundred meters elevation. The British destroyer is approximately one half mile west of the platform. There are several inflatables approaching the destroyer. Suddenly they detect that they are being illuminated by fire control radar. This is promptly reported. They have seen what they were supposed to see. They turn away to the north and are instructed to loiter two miles further west and observe. Thirty minutes after than it looks like all the survivors have been picked up.

They flew through some isolated thunder storms shortly before reaching the platform. The first of these is over the platform now. They watch in amazement as a huge smoky flame erupts from the ocean, seemingly right around the platform. Soon, the platform is enveloped with smoke.

The Argentines are not the only observers. As soon as the thunderstorm passes the smoke attracts the attention of the NSA. They are receiving real time video of what the particular satellite in the neighborhood sees. It will be the same story when the next satellite is within range in ninety minutes. Contemporaneously a Russian satellite also picks this up.

BP International Headquarters
1 St. James Square
London, United Kingdom

It is difficult to tell who set this information loose in the world but by 1650 Zulu there are one hundred protesters, mostly from the Maritime Environmental Congress, (a well known Communist front organization) with freshly printed posters walking around in front of the BP building on St. James Square.

BP = BOTCHED PRODUCTION
HOW MANY FISH DID YOU KILL TODAY BP?
BP = BUNGLING PETROLEUM

On the evening news several prominent Socialists call for the immediate nationalization of BP to put a stop to its disdainful attitude toward the environment. The British public, particularly the left, is not unanimously in favor of this adventure in the South Atlantic. Soon one hears on the talk shows "What the hell are we doing in Argentine waters anyhow".

This is the second catastrophe on this rig in less than six months. BP has been in constant contact with the Royal Navy since the mishap this morning. At 1800 Reginald Hopkins issues a brief statement.

"A serious explosion followed by a large fire occurred on our exploratory platform Titan at approximately 1115 this morning. Maintaining safe working conditions is the top priority at BP. We hold frequent disaster drills and this constant emphasis on the safety of our people paid off this morning. There were no injuries and our people are now all safely aboard. HMS York and HMS Ajax. We are constantly monitoring this rapidly changing situation."

BP doesn't have a chance. First the BBC newscaster wants to know where Sir Charles Hampton Rogers, the big gun at BP, is. The newscaster, obviously one of Socialist leanings, more or less implies that Hopkins is some kind of flunky for Sir Charles. He goes on to answer his own question that Sir Charles is fox hunting on his estate in Devonshire. Half an hour later an evening comic is having a blast with the 'disaster drills' comment.

"They don't have enough disasters so they have to drill to find new ones."

"Should we refer to these as drilling disasters or disastrous drillings?"

"I heard that the drills run backwards in the Southern Hemisphere."

Oskar is talking to Siegfried Raphael and Abbo who are in CCM Belen.

"What is going on here? I know the ship moved unexpectedly but how did the torpedo get 150 meters down to the well head?"

Abbo answers.

"I don't know Captain. I have a thought but it is just a thought. Most of those offshore rigs have cathodic protection. That may have neutralized the magnetic effects of the steel in the platform legs. Possibly, there was a large mass of steel at the wellhead. I understand that these underwater emergency shutdown valves are very heavy. The torpedoes have gyroscopic guidance. I am suggesting the following might have happened.

The torpedo was running at ten meters and set to get close to the ship with the gyroscopic guidance. Once it was close the magnetic homing was supposed to take over. The ship wasn't there but the ship was essentially on the line between Santa Cruz and the platform. When there was no ship, the torpedo continued on past the outer structure of the platform legs without hitting a leg or a cross member. It is a very open structure. Once inside the zone bounded by the legs it 'found' the wellhead. That shaped charge could easily have penetrated four hundred millimeters of steel."

"Well, whatever the reason, it looks like the rig is going to be destroyed. No one is putting that fire out anytime soon. It is merely a question of time."

The time turned out to be three days. The wind shifted from time to time so the fire was hotter on various different parts of the rig at different times. There was a great deal of ethane, propane and butane in the methane i.e. the gas was very 'hot'. These heavier hydrocarbons all burn hotter and faster than methane. By Tuesday morning the rig was sufficiently warped and twisted that it was declared a total loss. This still left the gas burning and completely unknown amounts of crude gushing onto the Humphrey Massif (Martinez Macizo).

Tom Stevens has come to visit DCAC for the first time. The first thing he observed was that the intersection of I-93 and Route 128 (the major highway encircling Boston) was a nightmare. It took him forty seven minutes to shag the eighteen miles from the New Hampshire border to 128 at seven in the morning. John says that he makes a point of being through that intersection by six thirty at the latest. They get their coffees and migrate to John's office. Tom immediately notices that the windows are very thick. Copies of the drawings of the BP well closure device are spread out on John's table. (Guenther managed to extract the drawings of the 'doomsday' valve from BP. That took intervention by the Royal Navy. BP apparently considers this valve is one of the company jewels and was not eager to share them.) John asks Linda to put the conference call together. Shortly they have Guenther and Randy on the line. Hellos are said all around. Randy starts.

"I went back over those recordings that Baumgartner was so kind as to lend us. In the last session with Eberhardt and Siegfried there appears to be mention of a torpedo. I am not one hundred percent certain but it looks like Eberhardt had drifted off some place and was thinking about the 'küfer torpedo' while he was in the middle of his thoughts about shaped charges. This translates as cooper torpedo. I talked with Guenther about this and he pointed out, that Fassbinder translates literally as 'barrel binder' which is a cooper."

It is Guenther's turn.

"We think Fassbinder fled Germany to South Africa."

Henry interrupts.

"We should have killed that SOB when we had the chance."

Guenther continues.

"We have no way of knowing if he went all the way to Argentina. Let us suppose for the moment he did. We are beginning to think that there may have been a very potent shaped charge used to damage the well head. We went around with BP about this and they said they doubted that anything could damage their 'doomsday' machine. When all else fails, this thing which is something like a monster Guillotine ball valve, simply rotates one quarter turn. This shears everything running through it, like the pipes carrying the oil, the drill stem etc. You shut the well but you effectively put yourself out of business with the push of a button. The long and the short of it is that this thing is built like a battleship – massively thick high alloy steel – the whole nine yards. You can set a five hundred pound bomb off on this thing and nothing will happen – it weighs something like ninety tons. They activated this thing during the problem in January. They have not figured out how they are going to salvage the situation but they needed to repair the platform in any event before they could try."

They launch into a discussion of what they can do about this oil spill. The Royal Navy has already sent a mini-sub to look at the wellhead. There was 'a lot' of oil and gas coming out of the hole. The gas bubbles made it practically impossible to get decent pictures. The guys who went there said the leak seemed be coming out the east side of the top of the 'doomsday' gizmo. This further confuses the issue because if it was indeed a torpedo that did this, one would think it was launched from Argentina and would have hit on the west side.

"How much is 'a lot'?"

"Understandably, no one wants any numbers leaking into the press. They are quite capable of manufacturing absurdly high numbers all by themselves. What we know is that back in January before they closed the wellhead, they were showing something like fifty two hundred psi. This might produce a maximum leak of roughly one barrel per second for every square inch of hole. That is about one hundred thousand barrels per day per square inch. Of course, to the extent that the gas is also trying to get out through the same hole this could be considerably diminished. On the other hand BP was using heavy walled five inch drill pipe which is four inches inside diameter. Under the worst circumstances there might be a completely open pipe. The oil they have already found is two thousand feet below the wellhead."

Guenther starts mumbling. They can't see him punching his pocket calculator.

If the 5200 psi number is characteristic of the pressure two thousand feet below the well head, then there will be a significant pressure drop for the oil flowing through the drill pipe. I ball park that number as a little bit less than two barrels per second if it were all oil and no gas."

John responds.

"This will no doubt be reported as more than seven million gallons a day."

"Exactly. So much for this nonsense. Tom, tell us what you think."

This is the major reason Tom is here. He has extensive experience dealing with oil well problems, particularly offshore platforms.

"BP has already retained Soileau and Guidry out of Morgan City. They have experience dealing with this sort of thing. I have worked with S&G before. They like to say that they practice Cajun Engineering on the grand scale. You might take at look at these folks and quickly reach the erroneous conclusion that they are a bunch of hayseeds. Then you find out that they have a ship which has a three thousand ton lift capacity – roughly half that of the Glomar Explorer. I understand it cost the Navy two hundred million to build but then they didn't need both of them and they sold this one off as surplus for something like thirteen million. I got involved with them when PEMEX had a similar problem in the gulf a few years ago. They also have a five hundred foot long fourteen foot diameter pipe. This thing was a cement kiln shell in its previous incarnation. They bought that for scrap prices at the time. Anyhow, they have added some floodable compartments and anchor points and some other stuff."

"The Titan is in four hundred thirty feet of water. What do they do with the extra seventy feet?"

"They have a couple of flanged connections so that they can adjust the length a bit. They also have an ocean going tug which they drag this thing around with. It is very impressive. I am going down there to watch them do their thing. Then the Navy and I will do our thing.

I am proposing that we come straight down on the 'doomsday' gizmo. The Navy and I will prepare a shaped charge which will penetrate into the inside of the ball but not all the way through it and out the other side. Having gained access, we will pump in some well sealant that reacts with sea water producing a rather stiff paste. We will then chase this with a proprietary material which I can not talk about."

"Are you sure you can punch through this thing Tom."

"Yes Randy. We built a few eight inch shells with shaped charge warheads for the Navy a few years ago.

They used a South Dakota class battleship that was on its way to the scrap yard for target practice. We fired these shells from a cruiser three miles away. Two out of the three shots penetrated through the forward armor of one 16" gun turret. That is very nearly two feet of alloy steel. At the time I was trying to get them interested in using Plodamax® to make reactive armor. We made a twenty square foot section of reactive armor which we put on the other forward turret. The eight inch shell penetrated this too, but just barely. This is all academic now. Nobody is building armored ships anymore. There is no doubt that we can punch through that thing from the top."

"Isn't the existing platform there?"

"Yes. We have to remove it first. We are going to sever the legs with explosives and then just topple it over to the east."

They don't know what the Brits are going to do. Guenther has been in touch with his 'source' (as he puts it) in the Royal Navy. He knows that they are plenty steamed about this.

"The Brits are inclined to just go and kick some ass but they have no evidence that Argentina was involved. They sent another fleet carrier south yesterday. We reckon it will take a week and a half to get there.

Here is another interesting tidbit. The Argentine and Brazilian navies held a first-ever joint anti-submarine warfare exercise that ended last Friday. We have photographs of all five of the Argentine submarines. They were in Rio de Janeiro from Friday afternoon until Sunday afternoon. In fact, the Argentine Navy was conspicuously absent from the Atlantic Ocean anywhere further south than Bahia Blanca, some seven hundred miles to the north."

"Do you think they might have used something like they used to bomb New York?"

"Doubtful. That was easy to see on radar and it was designed to run on the surface."

"I thought the interrogations at East Gorham indicated that the thing was built to operate tc two hundred meter depth."

"Yes, but it was attached to the submarine at that point. Once they launched it, it was strictly a surface craft. I am certain the Brits would have noticed anything on the surface. The closest surface contact at the time of the explosion was eighty five miles west of the platform. We confirmed that this was some kind of monster container ship that doesn't fit in the Panama Canal and has to go around."

"So the oil is leaking and there is not much to be done about it until the drill ship arrives?"

"Correct."

"What about the gas fire?"

"Maybe you should come down and watch this show too Hank."

Guenther continues.

"This is not to imply that we are going to sit idly by in the meantime. We have three more of the gadgets which destroyed their aircraft under construction. The plan is to put one on the drill ship and one on each guard vessel. USS Georgia is going to deploy passive sonar buoys in a thirty mile radius around the Puerto Santa Cruz sub pen. We will have two attack subs in the neighborhood as will the Brits. One of the attack subs will poll the sonabuoys daily. There are several people reviewing the documents we captured after the war to see if there is mention of any super long range torpedo work. My gut feeling is that this will be a dead end. We know so much more about fluid dynamics now than we did then...."

John interrupts.

"Excuse me please Guenther. Would you mind if I got Fred in here for a moment. You remember he has this fraternity brother in the Korean shipyard."

Before he can go any further Guenther responds.

"That is an excellent idea John. Please take the drawings off the table and we must not mention anything about zapping anything by anybody."

Two minutes later the resident computer guru is there. They introduce him to Tom Stevens and then it is back to work. Fred is the guy who originally made the connection between Fassbinder and the Italian submarine base at Ancona. They explain that there is a possibility that Fassbinder is in Argentina and there is a possibility that they have a very long range torpedo which conceivably may have made that mess in the South Atlantic.

"Is there any way to find out if Fassbinder did any torpedo related work for the Italians?"

"Maybe. Give me half an hour."

He goes back to his machine. His office is bigger than John's but he is crowded into one corner. Most of the office is occupied by a huge array of computer equipment and data storage equipment. Everything is on disk.

Guenther resumes.

"We have one of our geosynchronous satellites continuously observing the area from the Chilean border to the Falklands. We believe that the plane that we zapped came from some base west of Santa Cruz. We had the good fortune to pick up some of the zapping they did in Luna Park because our satellite was in the right place at the right time − pure happenstance and they were shooting north to south which is the way the satellite travels. Here they are shooting west to east with, we think, much better focusing capability. We have no way to detect this unless it is aimed right at us.. ."

They take a break. Fred returns and has a little bit.

"They do their torpedo research near Taranto. They have excellent cyber security which I can not hack – at least not anytime soon. Things are not so secure at Ancona where we have placed Fassbinder a few times. I found some mention of water jet drives powered by steam turbines but we already knew that. You are implying that the Argentines have a battery powered torpedo which can travel one hundred forty nautica miles? I am no authority on batteries but I don't think you could do this with batteries. My uninterruptable power supplies have the very best batteries available and they are only good for half an hour tops. You could achieve much higher energy density using fuel cells. I am just a computer nerd, what would I know?"

Guenther pounces on this.

"Excellent thought Fred. I will have someone look into this."

John finishes up.

"Thank you all. Any other thoughts? Anyone?"

It is nearly lunchtime.

"Let's go before the mob gets there."

"You and Tom go ahead. Save me a seat."

Henry and Tom head for the dim sum and John makes another phone call.

Bob Stockbridge is head of torpedo research at the US Naval Ordnance Laboratory. John recounts selected portions of the conference call without mentioning anything which will identify what he is talking about.

"Yes, John, you could use a fuel cell. We have done this. The performance is perfectly acceptable but no where near the range you are talking about."

"Suppose you ran the torpedo at twenty knots."

"You would have a snowball's chance in hell of hitting a ship at over one hundred miles at twenty knots. We can get that kind of range if we fly part of the way, but not with a prop alone."

"No, this has to be completely underwater. Suppose the ship was anchored."

Bob Stockbridge was near the head of the line when the Good Lord was handing out brains.

"You mean like the Titan?"

"You didn't hear that from me."

"Well, if you used a fuel cell and an electric motor and you went only twenty knots, and you did some other things which I am not supposed to talk about, you could do that."

"Like water jet drives like I have on my Blackfin?"

"Definitely you could use the most efficient propulsion."

"Thanks Bob. Are you going to manage to get up here for Tuna season?"

"I will let you know. Have a good one."

Forteleza Submarina
Puerto Santa Cruz, Argentina
July 10, 1996 Wednesday 0943 local 1243 Zulu

The newly constructed submarine fortress now has two of Argentina's submarines in it. They traveled directly from Rio de Janeiro after the naval exercises and the weekend of leave. The subs have been taking on fuel for more than a day. This is taking some time because the (essentially home fuel delivery) trucks they are using each carry only two or three tons of diesel. The permanent fuel storage and delivery facilities are still three months away from completion. Most of the crewmen are in the base cafeteria or recreation hall while fueling is proceeding. The attractions of Santa Cruz, a city about one two thousandth of the population of Rio are approximately in proportion to their relative populations. This is why most of the crewmen are here on the base.

Senor Alfonso Ramos, the owner of the only oil delivery company in town, is chatting about how slow this delivery is with Capitán Fidel Herrera when his phone goes dead. He feels a slight vibration under his feet. About twenty seconds later he hears a muffled whoomp. He delivers diesel directly from his trucks to the fishing fleet here in Santa Cruz. He has a marine radio on all the time he is in the office to arrange dockside deliveries etc. He hears a lot of chatter about some huge explosion on the coast. Someone says the new submarine base just blew up. Then he hears sirens.

The sub base was hacked out of the side of a seaside cliff. There is roughly eighty meters of hard rock above the roof of the pen. The Argentines, mindful of the accuracy of smart bombs, have constructed the shafts communicating with the surface in two segments. All the utilities go down halfway then sideways for twenty meters and then down the rest of the way. There are two lifts with a twenty meter horizontal hallway between them for transport of men and materiel. There is a blast door in this hallway which is closed unless someone is actually passing through the hallway.

The first people on the scene soon find that the lower elevator is inoperable. Two marines descend via the emergency ladder. When they open the door at the bottom, they are looking at a raging fuel fire. They quickly shut the door and climb back up. There is smoke coming out the seaside entrance. There is no way to get fire fighting equipment in there from land-side. Puerto Santa Cruz has an eight meter boat for the Harbor Master who happens to also be the Police Chief. It doubles as a fire boat and has one small water cannon on it which would be challenged by an out-board motor fire. Four marines, the fire chief and the Police Chief/Harbor Master get aboard and motor out to the coast. Smoke is still billowing out of the entrance to Forteleza Submarina.

Thirty minutes later, divers with SCUBA gear appear on the scene. The smoke has substantially abated. They bring their boat into the shadow of the cliff only a few meters from the entrance and three of them swim in. The two men remaining on the boat are not taking any chances. They too are using their SCUBA gear. They have a carbon monoxide sensor on board. After ten minutes on station they are satis-fied that there is no appreciable amount of CO around at sea level and they take their SCUBA gear off. There is still plenty of smoke but the wind is blowing it shore-ward. A few minutes later they hear from the men who are inside that they haven't found anyone alive.

The pilot, who is also the dive master, enquires as to whether they are using their SCUBA to breathe. When they answer in the affirmative, he tells them to come back and change tanks.

HMS SOVEREIGN
50.55South 68.28West
South Atlantic Ocean (about 6nm southeast of sub pen)
July 10, 1996 1244 Zulu

Captain Hargreaves is looking at the flat screen display of what the camera in the periscope is focused on. The time since launch is displayed in the upper right and Zulu in the lower right. This is all being recorded for posterity but not likely to see the light of day for many decades.(The self propelled Big Max was expressed to Port Stanley by fleet carrier HMS Illustrious at an average speed in excess of thirty knots. Big Max is powered by electric motors and has inertial and GPS guidance systems. It also contains a forty metric ton RDX warhead. It can travel about fifteen nautical miles at fifteen knots while submerged. It was mounted on the submarine in a floating drydock in Port Stanley where it was well shielded from curious eyes on the ground, on the sea or in the sky.)

Approximately twenty four minutes after launch there was a flash. The sonar man wisely placed his ear-phones on the counter in front of him when he saw the captain's 'thumbs up'. The sub shook noticeably about eight seconds later. Half a minute after that the micro-phone on the periscope picked up the boom. There is a great deal of black smoke pouring out of the entrance to the sub pen. He has instructions not to 'linger' there. He lowers the scope and orders the nuclear sub to proceed east at twenty knots.

USS Georgia
45South 68West
South Atlantic Ocean (about 300 nm north of the sub pen)
July 10, 1996 1249Zulu

The sound of the blast is picked up by USS Georgia's sonar about five minutes later. They haven't a clue what is going on. It sounds like a ship's magazine might have blown up. Captain Elliott Reagan orders the boat to one hundred feet and has an antenna sent to the surface. There might be a newscast on the MILSAT system. Patience is rewarded. At 1307 there is a coded transmission that there has been an explosion at the Argentine sub pen in Santa Cruz.

Casa Rosada
Buenos Aires, Argentina
July 10, 1996 1320 local 1620 Zulu

Oskar was informed that there was an enormous explosion at the submarine pen in Santa Cruz twenty minutes after it happened. Now he has been informed that there are no survivors. There were one hundred thirty five men in the pen and they have all perished, if they were lucky from the blast or not so lucky from the fire and lack of oxygen. Both submarines were docked bow in. They are both down at the stern, one slightly, the other resting on the bottom.

He suspects that the British sent a very large weapon right into the sub pen. He remembers his father telling him of massive British bombs used against the submarine pens during the war. They have not completed installing the netting to prevent underwater intrusions. They did well to get this far in the time allotted, but now this. He has his secretary call General Aguilar.

"When is the incident investigation team going to be there?"

"They are scheduled to be on the ground at 1435. They will be on the scene by 1500."

"Is there any evidence about the British having any unusually large conventional weapons?"

"Our intelligence people have not found anything of that nature yet, Señor Presidente."

"Keep me informed."

"Yes sir."

Oskar has two high resolution satellite photographs on his desk. These came from the Russian Embassy. They both show the British aircraft carrier next to a floating drydock which has been identified as the USS Morgan City. There is a tarpaulin or something over the interior of the drydock so he can not see if there is anything in there. There is a box on the carrier deck. In the second photograph the box is gone.

Forteleza Submarinas

Puerto Santa Cruz, Argentina

July 13, 1996 Saturday

The Argentines were all over the sub pen Thursday and Friday. Oskar, Hermann, Aldrich and Siegfried arrived late yesterday afternoon.

They are in the sub pen doing their own inspection. As best they can figure, ground zero was the southernmost of the four finger piers. Siegfried spent Thursday afternoon and Friday morning looking at one of Eberhardt's floppies dealing with conventional explosives. Karl had a list of things to look for as measures of damage and Siegfried took this all in.

The Navy has restored electric power and ventilation to the man made cavern. The preliminary investigation showed that a little sea water was blown up as far as the hallway between the two elevator shafts. More importantly they found significant amounts of Aluminum oxide and Magnesium oxide everywhere. There must have been a large quantity of these metals in powder form in the explosive. This suggested something similar to Torpex (an explosive sometimes used in British torpedoes) may have been used but the markers they found did not appear to correspond with those of any known explosives producer.

Oskar comments.

"My father told me many times that the British used Aluminum powder in the bombs they used against the U-Boat pens."

Siegfried agrees.

"That is mentioned in Professor Eberhardt's notes that I was reading."

They are standing on the south west side of the cavern where the cafeteria was. There is a three meter metal pipe with a hemispherical head flanged to it some four meters above the floor. There is a one and one half meter pipe beneath which is also flanged to the head. There is a large dent in the three meter pipe up near the ceiling. Siegfried asks.

"What's this?"

Capitán Rodriguez, their tour guide, answers.

"That was our practice evacuation station Doctor Bachmeier. We practice evacuation from our submarines if they are in no more than thirty or forty meters of water. This simulates what the crew will encounter."

He leads them around to the other side. There is an eight dog automatic door attached to the lower pipe, as well as several small pipes and rising stem valves. Capitan Rodriguez starts to explain this thing to Siegfried but Oskar wants to move on.

"Why are you interested in this?"

Siegfried has seen something like this before.

"We had something like this in Bremerhaven."

Oskar and Aldrich both give Siegfried a double take. Oskar tries to snap him out of it.

"Ziggy, didn't you take a cruise out of Bremerhaven three years ago?"

Siegfried returns from wherever he was.

"There are tables of blast over-pressures versus distance from the detonation Uncle. If we know the strength of the particular structure, we can estimate how much pressure would be required to deform it."

Now that Oskar sees what he is up to he tells the captain to help Siegfried as much as he can. Oskar and Hermann chat briefly while Siegfried and Aldrich get the particulars about the pipe and an air compressor against the south wall. The compressor reservoir has also been partially crushed. They establish that the rescue practice pipe and the air compressor reservoir are nearly sixty meters from the estimated ground zero location. Siegfried writes it all down in a notebook he keeps in his shirt pocket.

They talk with the people who were first on the scene. Most of the dead were in the rec room, the gym or the cafeteria – all are on the south side of the pen. They found a few men dead in the aft torpedo compartments of both boats. They were probably involved in the fueling operation. Two men were missing and presumed to have been close enough to the explosion to have been effectively obliterated. They postulated that the fire burned as long as it did because the fuel truck was simply discharging fuel by gravity from atop the cliff down through the fuel line in the utility shafts and tunnel. The driver was found dead in the cafeteria. (Possibly this is just as well for him.) It had been necessary to severely limit the fuel rate out of the truck because if the truck discharged fuel faster than the submarine was taking it on board, the fuel simply accumulated in the piping – there was nearly a one hundred meter difference in elevation between the submarine fuel tank and the top of the cliff. If this line was full, there was something of the order of ten atmospheres pressure on the hose connecting the piping to the submarine. There was another valve immediately upstream of the hose which also served to limit the rate of fuel flow and prevent this from happening. (The more this gets explained the angrier Oskar gets at this ridiculous procedure.) The explosion destroyed the hose but the fuel continued pouring from the pipe at

something of the order of three hundred liters per min-
ute. The truck wasn't emptied until twenty minutes after
the blast. The blast damaged the port side fuel tanks of
the submarine closest to it. Several thousand liters of
this diesel also leaked out and contributed to the gen-
eral conflagration. Essentially all the air contributing the
oxygen necessary to sustain combustion had to enter
through the seaside entrance to the pen. The portion of
the pen above the water was approximately one hun-
dred twenty meters deep into the cliff by forty meters
wide at the entrance and ten meters high to the roof.
There were overhead cranes to bring material and parts
to the submarines – in fact the thing was very nearly
a copy of the Hamburg submarine pen that U-1241
started its journey from years ago. In essence, all the
combustion was taking place near the water with the
smoky exhaust traveling back to the entrance near the
roof. They estimated that there was a total of fourteen
thousand liters of diesel consumed. Completely burning
this would have required nearly ten times the volume
of air in the pen. A great deal of the fuel ended up as
greasy, carcinogenic-laden soot covering every surface.

They returned to Olivos in time for the evening meal.
Basima got a blow by blow description of their tour.
Siegfried estimated that the bomb was possibly as large
as forty tons TNT equivalent. There is a long discussion
about how to play this at the UN. Oskar has had a time
scheduled Wednesday morning for Argentina to have its
say. He shows the others the photographs of the British
carrier next to the American drydock. His intelligence
people told him that they have an excellent length mea-
surement. The aircraft on deck are Harriers and they are
14.4 meters long. Therefore the box is 19 meters long
by 2.5 meters wide. They assume that it contains a mas-
sive torpedo somewhat over two meters in diameter and
perhaps eighteen meters long. They believe the British

probably used some doctored up RDX. The density of RDX is about the same as sea water. They could fit this in a cylinder thirteen meters long by 2.2 meters diameter with room for the necessary air to maintain neutral buoyancy in the sea water. Oskar goes on to say that he talked with Abbo about this as well. Abbo said this was perfectly feasible and the size of the box is about right.

They want to spin the story at the UN to maximize its impact. Basima feels that the environmental damage done by the spill will generate at least as much world-wide sympathy and indignation as the loss of the one hundred thirty five men. They will save this information they have about the box for some other time. Oskar's focus is on getting the British off the Martinez Macizo. He will work on getting the Malvinas back later. He wants her to make the speech at the UN. A woman will be better received than a man – especially about the environmental stuff. To bolster the environmental argument, Rudy Kleist ginned up two photographs of oil soaked turtles which were delivered to Olivos in early afternoon. If anyone challenges the bit about the turtles they are going to say that these hapless creatures were picked up by some Argentine fishermen fishing seven miles west of the rig.

United Nations

New York, New York

July 17, 1996 Wednesday morning

The President of the General Assembly, Ramon Garcia of Venezuela is introducing Basima.

"Good morning ladies and gentlemen. As you all know, there is an ecological disaster taking place in the South Atlantic....Please welcome the Argentine Foreign Minister Doctor Basima Brandt."

There is scattered applause primarily from the delegates representing the southern countries of the Americas. Basima walks to the podium. She is wearing a black pants suit. She addresses the Assembly in English. They had some discussion about whether to use Spanish or English. They thought the English would get to the English speakers better than Spanish would, especially about the environmental part.

"Thank you President Garcia. We have come to this assembly seeking justice. There is a massive amount of Argentina's crude oil gushing into the ocean off our coast since the twenty second of June. What is particularly galling is that this Argentine oil, which is being spilled in Argentine territory, is being spilled as a result of a disaster on a pirate oil platform put there by British Petroleum with the active aid of the British Military. This platform is thirty nautical miles inside Argentine Territorial Waters."

She shows several photographs taken from Argentine reconnaissance aircraft. She points out the British ships guarding the platform.

"I will recount the salient events in chronological order.

On May 24, 1995 the British towed this pirate platform to the Martinez Macizo. The Argentine government protested this move most vigorously. The initial British reaction was to send two warships to guard the platform. In August, they sent one of their four aircraft carrier groups to Islas Malvinas. On January 24, 1996 there was some sort of mishap on the outlaw platform. We don't know what happened. Then on June twenty second, barely three weeks ago, the British suffered yet another catastrophe. Their platform caught on fire. Argentina responded to the SOS sent from the platform by dispatching search aircraft and coastal patrol vessels to render aid. The British response was to illuminate our reconnaissance aircraft with their fire control radar."

She shows a photograph showing the HMS York in the foreground and the platform further away. There is a lot of fire and smoke. The time of the photograph is displayed in the upper right hand corner.

"In yet another example of British saber rattling, a second Fleet Carrier was dispatched to Islas Malvinas on June twenty fifth. This carrier arrived at Islas Malvinas the seventh of July."

She shows a photograph of HMS Illustrious which was clearly taken from the surface.

Walter Bevan, the British Ambassador to the UN notes to himself that this substantiates the Royal Navy's finding that the Argentines have one or more of their submarines in the vicinity of the Falklands most of the time. He is under strict instructions to not get into any kind of discussions with this woman – simply categorically deny any and all accusations she makes if asked.

"One week ago an Argentine installation in Puerto Santa Cruz was bombed. One hundred thirty five of our sailors and civilians perished. We have conducted an investigation of this bombing. We can show beyond doubt that the British struck our installation with a massive bomb. I have the results of our chemical analyses of the residue from the explosion here. This is an Act of War."

She pauses for fifteen seconds to let that sink in.

"They have not only declared war on our military, they have declared war on our homeland and our food supply. They have stolen our national resources drilling for oil on our territory and then spilling it on our territory killing our marine life. You will eventually hear the British say that this rig is in their territory. This is a completely absurd position. They illegally occupied Islas Malvinas some time ago. The only people there were from the nearest land which was then and is now Argentina. Those people were Argentinean. Islas Malvinas were Argentinean then and are Argentinean now. They are attempting to parlay one illegality on top of another.

Argentina is a peaceful country. We choose to spend our resources helping our people, not building a huge military. We recognize that we cannot dislodge a thermonuclear power from trespassing on our land by force. We hope that bringing their unconscionable acts to your attention will produce the general opprobrium that they so richly deserve. We hope that you will pass a resolution condemning these acts. We hope that you will pass a resolution banning the British from interfering with our efforts to clean up this mess.

We filed a suit with the International Court of Justice in The Hague earlier today seeking fifteen billion dollars reparation from British Petroleum to help us clean up this mess.

"Gracias Presidente García y gracias señoras y señores por su atención."

There is polite applause. She has no plan to stay in New York one moment longer than necessary and leaves the room quickly. Copies of her speech in English and Spanish including the surveillance photographs and Rudy Kleist's oil soaked turtles have been made available. After a short break, what might pass for a spirited debate in the General Assembly ensues. The most casual analysis will reveal that this debate has a decidedly anti-British theme. The same crowd piles on the British until they quit in mid afternoon – a typical day's farce at the UN.

BP Headquarters

1 Saint James Square

London, United Kingdom

July 17, 1996 Wednesday 1630 Zulu

The Maritime Environmental Congress has more than one hundred protesters milling about St. James Square. Not all of them are MEC people Forty seven of them are professional protesters hired this morning. The MEC received an anonymous one million pound donation Monday. The check was drawn on a bank in Liechtenstein. They don't know that these funds came out of one of Basima's accounts. All the posters have four inch square photographs of Rudy Kleist's turtles in the upper right hand and left hand corners. Several of these two foot square posters have enlargements of these photographs with the comment.

Biological Poisoner

None of this is going unnoticed by the media. The BBC and Sky News have people on the scene, but they are outnumbered by the folks from the US, France, Germany, Brazil, Japan and Russia. A BP marine biologist on his way to the car park comments to a protester.

"Excuse me sir, do you know that that picture you are carrying around is that of a fresh water turtle."

The protester responds rather loudly.

"Why don't you mind your own fucking business, guv?"

Some of the demonstrator's colleagues are coming this way. A London Bobbie is not far away and he heads in that direction too. The biologist turns around and heads back to the BP building.

The powers that be in BP are having a meeting in the third floor conference room which overlooks the small park to their west. It is normally tranquilizing to look at the beautiful trees especially in the late spring and summer. Today they have the heavy curtains drawn so that people on the street cannot see them. Sir Charles is speaking.

"I am not sanguine about our chances of fixing this mess."

Reginald Hopkins answers.

"The Shirley Danforth will be there tomorrow. We expect to have her anchored by Friday afternoon."

"How can we do that with all that gas leaking?"

"Our Navy says that they can plug this thing with some gadget the American Navy has."

"Yes, I heard something about that but they will still have to put the Shirley Danforth over the well to fix it. We could have another catastrophe if something else goes wrong."

Sir Charles turns to Patrick Harmon, head of BP's legal department.

"What's going on with the lawsuit Pat?"

"There won't be any lawsuit if we can prove the well was sabotaged."

"And in the meantime?"

"We are going to get a lot of bad press."

There is a knock on the door and Sir Charles' secretary walks in with Harold Farnsworth in tow. Everyone in the room knows Harold because he has found some rather clever relatively inexpensive solutions to several of BP's environmentally related problems.

"Excuse me gentlemen. I thought you might be interested in the fact that the posters my 'sponsors' are wandering about St. James with have a photograph of a freshwater turtle on them. *(Dr. Farnsworth was hired two years ago at an enormous salary in direct response to all the hassling BP had received from the environmentalists. He was promptly denounced as a 'turncoat' by his former colleagues at Imperial College. He mischievously adds.)* I don't know where the oil came from."

Reggie speaks.

"Thanks Harry. I gather you went out there recently. What is happening?"

"The usual kooks. I think they might have some hired help out there as well. I happened to bump into a particularly ugly individual. You might want to think about organizing some help from the Police to get out of here."

50.8 South 64.7 West

Humphrey Massif

South Atlantic Ocean

July 17, 1996 Wednesday 1430local 1730Zulu

The Shirley Danforth not only has a three thousand ton derrick, it is probably the world's largest catamaran. She is anchored approximately one thousand feet west of Platform Titan. The gas leaking from the wellhead continues to burn slightly to the north of the platform. There is a slight subsurface northerly drift across the massif. This is carrying the crude nearly half a mile off to the north as it slowly rises to the surface. The Royal Navy guided missile destroyer HMS York is steaming in a north-south screening pattern approximately two miles west of the platform. Forty miles to the east HMS Illustrious is launching and retrieving Harriers. The aircraft are armed for anti-submarine warfare. There are two British nuclear attack submarines in the area. They are equipped with transponders which will identify them as friendly if any aircraft dropped sonabuoy detects them.

Henry and Tom Stevens are on the port side leaning on the guard rail and taking in the passing scene. At 1500 S&G detonate the shaped charges cutting the platform legs off at the sea floor level. Fifteen seconds later they set off the second set of charges which sever eighty feet of the two easterly legs. A few seconds later the platform keels over to the east. What was once one point two billion dollars disappears into the sea. The erstwhile cement kiln shell is connected by steel cables top and bottom to winches in the bows of the Shirley Danforth and at the top to a single winch in the stern of the Cajun Lady. It has a metal flotation collar at the top and four legs and a flexible flotation collar at the bottom. The tug now proceeds on a counter clockwise circular route around the Danforth from the south to a point east of the wellhead. A modest amount of air is released from the lower flotation collar. They now have the kiln shell positioned such that as they pay out the cable on the Danforth that is attached to the bottom, the bottom of the kiln descends until it and its appurtenances are being held up by the flotation collar at the top end. The four legs appended to it at the bottom broaden its stance to eighty feet. No one had any illusions that they could balance a four hundred foot high contraption on a fourteen foot wide pipe. After a bit of fancy dancing by the Cajun Lady, they have maneuvered the six hundred ton contraption, which is now vertical, into position directly over the wellhead. Two of the crew of the Danforth motor over to the device and work a chain valve allowing air to escape from the flotation collar. They have some rather elegant gyro stabilized surveying equipment on board the Danforth. They see that the kiln flotation collar is now down to right about where they want it and radio the two men on the scene to stop bleeding air. Henry remarks.

"That looks a bit more dangerous than the business I used to be in. I am sure that is not an OSHA approved operation."

"Yes, I have mentioned that more than once. It seems that they tried with some radio controlled valves which didn't work right and the whole damn thing sank. It took a while to fish it back up."

They watch a little longer. The gas fire on the sea has gone out. One of the crew in the motorboat shoots a flaming arrow which passes near the top on the south side of the floatation collar. Voila, a new and hopefully more controllable gas flame appears. It is quite impressive in the gathering dusk.

Oskar, Basima, Hector and Siegfried are having a quiet supper.

"We need to hit the British where they live. I don't think rendering that platform useless got their attention."

"Surely you are not thinking of bombing Britain."

"No, I am thinking that if Siegfried could coax a little more power out of his irradiator, we could zap the south and east coasts of Britain from a ship transporting a normal item of trade. We ship a fair amount of beef to the Netherlands. On the return journey the sea lanes pass within fifteen miles of the British south coast."

"I think if I just ca'copied the one we used on the pla'platform we could do this uncle."

Siegfried stuttering is getting worse. Oskar does well not to let on that this is quite noticeable this evening. They have had to let Hector in on the knowledge that all is not well with Siegfried.

"How long will that take Ziggy?"

"I think we ca'can do that in three weeks. We have to make some m'more material."

Later that evening

"Did you do any good in New York?"

"It is hard to tell."

"Can you do anything about Siegfried?"

"I am not a Psychiatrist Oskar."

"Maybe if you hypnotize him again you could do something."

"We can try. He has his own set of problems. Two of those surrogate children or whatever we call them are not right and he knows it. He and Heidi have both spoken to me about that."

"And?"

"I don't have any answers. I told them to see what Professor Hartmann has to say."

"Well, I am glad you are home mein schatz."

"Show me."

Basima's residence
San Isidro, Argentina
July 20, 1996 Saturday afternoon

Siegfried, Manfred Bauer and Basima are in her study. Manfred is well attuned to some of the stranger things that have happened to Professor Baumgartner's subjects. He has spoken to Basima several times about Siegfried's behavior. Basima has Siegfried under hypnosis now. He is sitting in an over stuffed chair which is high enough that his feet do not touch the floor unless he deliberately bends his toes down. She read a text on hypnosis that mentioned that when the subject's feet are not touching the ground it is easier to produce a condition where the subject thinks he or she is weightless. She and Manny are discussing the situation.

"Basima thank you for obtaining the mephirazol sulfonate. It is not an approved drug in Germany. We used to synthesize it on campus for Professor Baumgartner. I have observed that the 'subjects' are generally less fidgety when we use this in conjunction with the Dilantin®. It definitely is useful in stopping any grand mal seizures."

"You haven't seen any of those with Siegfried, have you?"

"It is only a question of time in my mind Basima."

He is right. It is only a question of time. They try to never leave him alone and they do limit his contact with the outside world particularly one-on-one with strangers. He wouldn't have gone to Santa Cruz last week if not for Oskar's insistence. The remark about Bremerhaven convinced Oskar that Eberhardt must have implanted all kinds of information about submarines that Siegfried

*had heretofore never spoken about. Manny injects him
with the drugs. While they wait for these to take effect
Basima is looking at Siegfried very carefully. He has
blond hair but it certainly looks like he has some gray in
front of both ears.*

"Manny, how long have you know Siegfried?"

"About five years."

"Do you notice that he has a few gray hairs?"

He looks and confirms her observation.

"Those are recent Basima. He didn't have any when
he was in Heidelberg."

*Now she is studying his face. There are the begin-
nings of some wrinkles. It has been five minutes. They
start.*

*Soon, Siegfried is talking in the first person as Karl
Eberhardt. He appears to be talking about the nuclear
pile in Rostock.*

"Willy, that is very dangerous. Why do you think
you must have someone look inside the pile? We have
instruments to do that."

*There is a pause. Probably, Willy, whoever he may
be, is responding.*

"Look, if you must do this you need to look through
three or better yet four meters of schweres wasser
(heavy water). Use mirrors. Definitely do not allow anyone to be directly exposed."

*She probes some more. 'Karl' is now talking about
the sub pen in Scharbeutz. He is talking about putting
the material from Rostock on a U-Boat in Scharbeutz.
Basima guides the conversation around to 'his' experiences in Bremerhaven. They find that the cylinder in the
Santa Cruz sub pen that was partially crushed by the
blast was the same diameter as the evacuation training*

rig the Nazis installed in Bremerhaven in the late thirties. They find that 'Karl' was toying with the idea of capturing the heat from a breeder reactor and running a steam turbine to power a submarine. They didn't know enough about materials to have any way of confining the pile other than using so much graphite that they could not transfer any useful amount of heat out of it.

After about an hour, Siegfried develops a noticeable facial tic. He is not stuttering but his speech starts getting jerky. Basima decides that this is enough for today. She snaps him out of the trance by calling him Ziggy. He returns from where ever he was complaining about being sleepy and having a little bit of a headache.

John and Henry are on a conference call with Guenther Randy and Mitch. S&G with some help from Tom Stevens and the US Navy managed to plug the leak from the Titan wellhead Tuesday. BP is not going to get one drop of oil out of this formation as long as Oskar Brandt is calling the shots in Argentina. The destruction of the airplane with the irradiation device and the damage to the sub pen have had the effect of stopping any further attempts by the Argentines to eject the British by force but they have intensified their efforts on the propaganda front. BP, Britain in general and the Americans make excellent targets, especially to people who speak Spanish. Oskar released the Russian photographs of the disappearing box on the British aircraft carrier lying next to the American drydock. There was also a very public memorial service for the one hundred and thirty five sailors and civilians that were killed.

The British caught an Argentine spy not far from Port Stanley but not before the damage was done. Apparently he saw the arrival of HMS Sovereign and its entrance into the drydock. This information was transmitted to his homeland before the British located his transmitter. It was easy enough for the Argentines to put this all together into a virulent anti-British and anti-American campaign in the world's media. Henry had plenty of time to think about this while he was on the Shirley Danforth. To make matters worse Exxon had another VLCC (Very Large Crude Carrier) run aground last week. The fact that this happened half a world away and that the ship had a double bottom and that no crude leaked out was conveniently missing from media accounts.

BP made some effort to discredit the photos of the fresh water turtles as Argentine propaganda. MEC responded that that was irrelevant. The point was that BP has plenty of turtle blood on its hands. It seemed like every movie ever made about the life and times of every kind of turtle imaginable was running on half the television stations in Western Europe and the US.

Henry had plenty of time to think about these sorts of things during his ten day stay on the Shirley Danforth. It turns out that S&G also does marine salvage work but their equipment is so expensive to hire that they are almost exclusively confined to things related to the petroleum industry.

"I chatted with Leroy Deslatte the captain of the Shirley Danforth about whether they could pick up the Maria Morales. He said there would not be a problem if they could find it and it was a metal boat. What I am wondering is whether if there was lots of obvious damage we could pin this on Brandt – for sure he was in on it."

The Maria Morales is believed to be down in somewhere between seventy and two hundred fathoms. That doesn't really make any difference as far as the Shirley Danforth picking up something this small. The party boat is down in a recognized sea lane. There should not be any problem with Argentine jurisdiction, unlike the situation on the Humphrey Massif (Martinez Macizo) where the oil is inside both parties' claimed two hundred mile limits on mineral rights. (In all fairness to the Brits, it should be noted that normally, when the zones of influence conflict the boundary is equidistant from each country. The Titan platform was on the British side by a few miles.) Nevertheless, this Three Hills formation

*where the Maria Morales went down is barely sixty nau-
tical miles from a major Argentine naval base. The US
Navy will have to ride shotgun if the Shirley Danforth is
going to go there. They bat this around a while. Mitch
says that he thinks that the President will go for this.
He is thoroughly pissed off at the Argentineans again.
They will send selected NSA satellite data to the Bahia
Blanca newspaper and the Socialist Party – if they can
get it declassified.*

*The plan is to use one of the newly refit spy subs to
locate the Maria Morales. They will then bring the Shirley
Danforth to the scene which is conveniently located
close to the route back to the US from the Humphrey
Massif.*

*By the time they get through thrashing this out, they
decide that a US Navy presence there would appear
less provocative if there were a convenient cover story.
They call Fleet Admiral Richard Stone. It takes a few
minutes but Guenther pushes the right buttons and he
gets through to Admiral Stone.*

"Good morning Admiral."

"Good morning Doctor."

"Richard, we have an assortment of misfits on this
conference call. I believe that you know Randy Biggs,
John Carpenter and Mitch Rogerston. John's assistant
in mayhem, Henry Magnuson is also on the line. Now
that the problem with BP has been mitigated somewhat,
we are trying to get rid of this guy in Argentina."

The admiral interrupts.

"Guenther, you know that the Navy does not 'get rid
of' civilians. Talk to Mitch about that."

Guenther continues.

"We believe that now Argentine President Brandt
was involved in the murder of a number of Argentine

civilians in February of 1993. His organization destroyed a party boat with fifty seven people on board. If we can find the boat, which we feel that you can do without too much trouble, we would like to pick it up and examine it. We believe that we will find ample evidence of foul play. Our plan is to present this evidence to the news media and the opposition party in Argentina. We expect that they can do the 'getting rid of'.

This is not all fleshed out yet but you know that big lift ship is down there. What we are hoping you can help us with is providing some assets to ride shotgun while we pick the thing up. It is only sixty miles from the Belgrano base. We are also wondering what is in the immediate future for the USS Morgan City."

"The Morgan City is scheduled to be towed to Pascagoula for some refitting work. The nuclear powered tug USS Samson will be doing the towing. It is Navy policy to provide armed escort for unarmed nuclear powered vessels. The tug and the drydock will have at least one guided missile destroyer as escort."

"We are hoping that if the thing can be timed right, we can pick the party boat up with the Shirley Danforth and somehow get it into the drydock where we can examine it at our leisure."

They end up telling the Admiral about the satellite evidence and the circumstances surrounding the sinking that they know about. Eventually it comes out that Oskar Brandt is suspected of having had a hand in the sinking of the USS Devilfish.

As soon as he hears about the Devilfish his tone changes.

"Work out the details. We will provide a destroyer and a cruiser along with the Morgan City. I think we can say that we are looking for the Devilfish if anybody asks."

"Thank you. Looking for the Devilfish will provide the convenient cover story if anyone asks. We are trying to recover the submarine. We have the second largest lift ship in the world and a large floating drydock. I don't think they will touch this with the proverbial ten foot pole. What are the Argentines going to say? 'The Americans are looking for their submarine forty five nautical miles from where we sank it.'"

John and Henry are on the phone with Guenther and Mitch. President Simmons gave approval in principal to the plan two weeks ago. They are going to send all the Argentines back from East Gorham. On the second day of the month, they started feeding them very well and seeing that they got plenty of sunshine and exercise. No US Military will set foot on Argentine soil. It will be carried out entirely by DCAC and the CIA. The Navy will provide the Special Ops submarine USS Georgia for transportation. Former SEALS, now nominally in the CIA will be violating Argentine territory, hopefully undetected. They have decided that the evidence will be most effective if it is presented in Bahia Blanca.

Two CIA operatives resident in the US Embassy in Buenos Aires visited Bahia Blanca last week. They were posing as a reporter and a photographer for the Buenos Aires news magazine Grafico Noticias. They made some interesting findings. The tragedy of the Maria Morales has not been forgotten in Bahia Blanca. Maria Morales Guzman built a small shrine on her dock to honor her husband and the entire staff of CCM Bahia Blanca. As soon as it became known that she was building a shrine, many men and women who worked near the harbor catching and processing fish started donating a few hours a week of their spare time helping her. Their employers contributed money to hire the skilled craftsmen needed to complete it. Maria goes there daily to pray. She is often joined by other women who have lost their men to the sea as well as those whose men went down with the Maria Morales. There is a one tenth scale reproduction of the Maria Morales at the foot of a three meter high cross. There is a semicircular wall behind the cross. Photographs of everyone who disappeared that day are in cabinets mounted on that wall. The windows protecting these photographs from the elements are cleaned at least once a week.

They talked with the librarian who was Ricardo Guzman's niece. She wanted to know if they knew the other two reporters from Clarin who came here last year. No, they didn't know very many newspaper people. She showed them the microfiche of the pertinent editions of La Provincia. Yes, she did visit the shrine at least once a month to pray for her uncle's soul.

Guenther starts.

"We want to get on with this sooner rather than later."

Mitch says.

"We are thinking about sending the three Argentines back together."

Henry gets his two cents worth in.

"The CCM yard is only half a kilometer from the Maria Morales slip where the shrine is. I think we might do better to drop Gerbert off at the shrine and the other two off in the CCM yard. I am sure that they know we have had these guys captive. What can they tell them? They have been on some tropical island for the past three years?"

John agrees with this.

"Gerbert's the guy with the blood on his hands. Let's not confuse the issue with the others."

40.7651 South 60.7627 West

South Atlantic Ocean

August 30, 1996 Friday 1100 Zulu

The crane operator on the Shirley Danforth is watching his flat screen monitors as the tines of the giant clam shell bucket close around the party boat. He has to jostle the bucket a little so that the tines go into the sandy bottom under the boat as opposed to through the hull. They had some good luck. Two days before the little armada arrived, the Maria Morales had been found lying upright more or less along a north-south axis in one hundred fifteen fathoms (690 feet) two miles west of Tres Colinas. The location is known within one meter. They actually have a very nice day for late winter in these parts. There is a two foot sea and the wind is barely ten knots. The Shirley Danforth's thrusters can easily keep the ship within a meter of the horizontal coordinates and the crane has a gyro computer controlled luffing feature which compensates for the rise and fall of the sea as long as there is less than a five hundred ton load on the derrick. The Maria Morales is ten feet out of the water at 1115 Zulu. They position a modest forty meter long barge under it and deposit the Maria Morales into the barge. By 1225 Zulu, the barge is in the Morgan City. Shortly thereafter two Argentine guided missile destroyers take up stations approximately five miles to their west. They were a little late to see the Maria Morales whose superstructure was considerably higher than the sides of the barge. Once the boat was in the drydock it was covered with a tarpaulin to keep it out of view of any Argentine reconnaissance aircraft.

Tom Stevens and Henry are on the Morgan City along with Commander Donald Whiting a US Navy accident investigator who happens to be on Admiral Stone's staff and in the Office of Naval Intelligence. The most cursory of examinations reveals that the six holes cut in the hull were not accidents. There are a number of fully clad skeletons in the cabin. The denizens of the deep have had ample access and time to pick the cabin occupants clean. A number of the skeletons still have wedding rings on. They collect these as well as two inscribed pocket watches. They notice that there is no glass inside the cabin. The cabin windows are all broken outward. They take numerous photographs. Tom has a technician cut some samples from the edges of the holes. He says that metallurgical examination will confirm that these holes were cut with shaped charges mounted inside the boat. Henry and Commander Whiting are going to visit East Gorham on the way home. They want to talk to all the captives some more now that they have seen the scene of the crime.

They thank the captain of the Morgan City for his hospitality and radio a well done and thank you to Captain Deslatte on the Shirley Danforth. The dry dock launch takes them to a Grumman Albatross. Originally the plan was to fly to Sao Paulo but the Brazilians have become markedly less cooperative with the Americans since the bombing of the sub pen at Puerto Santa Cruz. Later it will be found that the Argentine and Brazilian navies were running something akin to an 'exchange student' program. There were five Brazilian sailors in the rec hall in the sub pen. Plan B is to fly to Montevideo which is much closer but still the better part of four hundred and fifty nautical miles the way they have to fly. That will take close to four hours. There will be a Navy Gulfstream waiting in Carrasco to take them to East Gorham. Tom will not be getting off the plane in East Gorham. He gets to ride to Boca Chica (Key West Naval Air Station). The Navy is providing him a less comfortable but speedier ride the rest of the way. He gets to sit in the back seat of an F-18 Hornet all the way to Manchester New Hampshire. Of course, all these wonderful plans are contingent on having a relatively calm sea. The Albatross can not take off in much more than a four or five foot chop without JATO rocket assist. The present two foot chop is perfect. The twin Wright cyclones are more than sufficient. The aircraft is into the air in well under a half mile.

East Gorham Island

ONI Detention Center

August 31, 1996 Saturday 1000 Zulu

Don and Henry are talking to Gerbert Bachmeier. He has been on East Gorham since May 1993. Sometime in August of that year his black hood were removed but he remains in solitary confinement. Gerbert's cell is padded. He tried running head first into the door two years ago. He got a nasty headache from that but that is gone and he is now in a padded cell. There is no way he can harm himself in his present environment. It turns out that Don Whiting is a psychiatrist. He thinks that Gerbert might respond to a good cop bad cop routine. He is going to be the good guy while Henry can just be himself. The guards transport Gerbert with his hands cuffed behind his back to the garden of the facility. It is very nice day and the first time Gerbert has seen the outside world in a long time.

Whiting is fluent in German, Henry less so but competent. Whiting starts in German.

"Guten tag Herr Bachmeier. If you behave yourself, I think we can remove these cuffs for a while."

There is a sniper with a tranquilizer dart loaded and ready should he do anything untoward. Gerbert can't see him but assumes that there must be something like that. He turns around and Whiting cuts his cuffs off. He sits down on the bench offered to him. It is Henry's turn.

"We raised the Maria Morales yesterday you prick. How could you do such a thing? I thought you might like to admire your handiwork."

Henry removes several photos from a large envelope. They are the ones of the boat's cabin taken yesterday. He hands them to Gerbert. Gerbert's first instinct is to throw them on the floor but he heard sometime back that Magnuson is an extraordinarily violent man and he appears to be in very good shape. It is probably better to go through the motions, so he does. Whiting picks up.

"Herr Bachmeier, we know that you were acting under orders from your father. You really didn't have any choice in the matter. This in no way renders you innocent of course, but it is a mitigating circumstance."

Gerbert is beginning to wonder if they are finally going to put him on trial. Whiting continues.

"We killed your father three years ago this month."

Henry interjects.

"I was there. He had couple of slugs in him and he apparently was too close to a fragmentation grenade."

This does not get a rise out of Gerbert. They have some rather clever electronics around here. They are remotely sensing his pulse and the temperature of his forehead. Whiting notes this and continues.

"We think that your father was a very bad man. You know he was in the Waffen SS?"

"Of course."

"You are a Nazi too, aren't you?"

"Yes. I was brought up that way."

"And you passed this on to your son?"

"Siegfried was closer to my father than he was to me. I could never figure that out. He spent more time with my father than he did with me."

"What about his mother? How did she fit into the scheme of things?"

"My wife died in childbirth. She was not there for him."

"Do you know that Siegfried is not your son?"

"Impossible."

"It is not impossible. We ran DNA tests on you, your father, Siegfried and Fritz Schroeder. There is a zero probability that you are Siegfried's father and *(Whiting ostentatiously looks in his notes.)* and a 0.9993 probability that Fritz Schroeder is his father. Surely you noticed that Siegfried has blond hair and your hair is dark? Blond is a recessive gene. What color was you wife's hair?"

They talked about this before this interview for quite a while. Henry wanted to tell Gerbert that Siegfried was Wilhelm's son and really piss him off. They know Gerbert is sterile. They would have thrown that at him too. Whiting thought 'maybe later'. Gerbert's head is starting to roll around ever so slightly from this verbal pounding. He answers very quietly.

"Gisela was blond."

"Did you ever meet Fritz Schroeder?"

"I am not sure, possibly when I was very young. My father spoke of him often."

Henry butts in.

"We dug that prick Schroeder up and took a few samples. We got Siegfried's samples from the apartment he rented when he was in Heidelberg. That is my apartment now. Do you know he is tied up in this shit at least as deep as you are?"

Whiting intercedes.

"We are not certain of that Herr Magnuson."

They work the discussion around to his early years. His father sent him to a community college in Rosario. His father sent Siegfried to Germany to Karlsruhe and eventually for his doctorate at Heidelberg. He starts remembering how many times his father called him dummkopf. Henry butts in again.

"We figure that Schroeder knocked your wife up a day or two before she came to Argentina. The kid appeared at the right time. Nobody was the wiser."

Gerbert's pulse is quickening and his cheeks are nearly a degree warmer than they were. He is starting to sweat. Whiting signals the guards who are a good fifty feet away. They walk back and escort Bachmeier back to his cell. They will give him some time to think about what transpired today.

They follow the same routine they have used every time at East Gorham. Recordings of the interrogation are transmitted to interested parties in the CIA, NSA and Los Alamos. They go over them and if there is something that someone thinks might be useful to ask during the next interrogation they send back their suggestion(s).

By next morning they have received requests from Los Alamos and Langley to find out anything Gerbert knows about Oskar Brandt, specifically how, if at all, he was tied in with the Maria Morales atrocity.

Whiting leads the discussion again. Henry is beginning to think that one of the reasons he is here is to learn about interrogation techniques from a master. Again they speak German.

"Guten tag Herr Bachmeier."

Bachmeier responds in kind.

They recount the events of the fishing tournament up to and including Roger Bancroft's visit with Oskar Brandt on board the Don Martinez. Yes, Gerbert did meet Bancroft. He was the guy from Torre Bermeja, wasn't he? He had a fifty four foot Striker. It was named ALICALLA. They add a little fib here and there. They tell

Gerbert that Bancroft was a CIA agent. When he was on board the Don Martinez he noticed a peculiar looking single side band radio. When he asked Oskar what it was, Oskar gave him some total bullshit. They lead Gerbert to believe that their initial suspicions about the Don Martinez arose during that visit. There is the unsaid message that Oskar's bullshit answer somehow brought Gerbert to his present situation. It works perfectly.

"What was your relationship with Oskar Brandt?"

"My father and his father were close friends. They were both on the U-1241 when it came from Germany before I was born. I would see Oskar at various get-togethers a few times a year, usually at my father's ranch. CCM did all the work on my boats."

"And Oskar was the head of CCM?"

"Not when I first met him. His father was the head of CCM. He became the head of CCM after the Maldivas war."

"Did CCM install this radio that attracted Señor Bancroft's attention?"

"I presume so. They had the CCM Belen instrument guy on board the day the Maria Morales went down. I was piloting the boat but he was operating the electronics. I don't know anything other than that."

"So Oskar probably knew about the strange electronics?"

"He must have."

"We understand that he did not invite you to the U-1241 send-off party."

"He told me to continue the search for the American listening devices we thought were there in Bahia Blanca."

"And did you?"

"Yes."

"Do you think if you had been at the send off party you would be sitting here now?"

"I would not be here because I wouldn't have been at Rancho Don Martinez Monday night."

That is exactly what they want to hear. Gerbert will soon have himself convinced that it is all Oskar's fault. There has been some talk about trying to convert Gerbert into some kind of an assassin ala "The Manchurian Candidate". No decision has been reached to date. When they examined the Maria Morales, they found a number of pocket watches and wedding rings on the victims. All the rings and two of the watches had the owners' initials engraved on them. These were gathered up for future use. Henry noted that the silver pocket watch of the skeleton at the helm was engraved.

MM y RG

19 de Junio 1965

It doesn't take long for him to figure out that this was a twenty fifth anniversary gift from Maria Morales to Ricardo Guzman. Depending on how this effort to expose Oskar as the mastermind behind the atrocity goes, they think that it might be useful to return Gerbert to Argentina with a few of these artifacts on his person.

La Quinta de Olivos
Olivos, Argentina
August 31, 1996 Saturday

Oskar is on the phone getting a blow-by-blow description of the American visit to Tres Colinas (Three Hills) yesterday from the captain of the St. Martin, one of the guided missile destroyers sent to see what was going on. Things have been going very well for the Navy ever since Oskar took office. They try especially hard to please him.

"Señor Presidente."

Oskar likes himself referred to as Capitän Brandt especially when he is speaking to his former brethren in the Navy.

"Captain Brandt please."

Captain Castillo responds.

"Yes sir. This is what we saw. We first noticed them at 1045 Zulu on the Belgrano Base radar. Nobody thought anything about that since our reconnaissance aircraft had been tracking them since they left the Martinez Macizo. They were ostensibly taking the drydock north, probably all the way to the US. At 1145 Zulu we noticed that three of the five American vessels were stationary. Two destroyers including the St. Martin were dispatched to observe the scene and find out what was going on. We arrived at Tres Colinas at 1300 Zulu. Almost immediately the Americans started moving north again. That is what I know for sure.

When I returned to base I heard that our reconnaissance aircraft had observed that the Americans had a tarpaulin over whatever they had in the drydock. They said that they couldn't get close enough to get a good look. The American guided missile destroyers had the aircraft illuminated with their fire control radars. We know that the Americans are using a nuclear powered tugboat and that they are very protective of it. The pilots decided to not push their luck and stayed three miles away."

"Yes, I heard about the tarpaulin too. Thank you Captain."

"Thank you sir."

"Oh, Captain, before you go. Where were the Americans as best you know?"

"One moment please. *(Captain Castillo looks in his log.)* We were over the central peak of Tres Colinas. The lift ship was showing two point one five nautical miles to the southeast and the drydock was no more than a tenth of a mile west of them. There was also a seaplane there. The plane took off shortly after we arrived."

"Thank you Captain."

He thinks about this a while. The more he thinks about the big lift ship, the more he thinks they were looking for the Maria Morales. That boat only weighed forty one tons with the fuel and water tanks full.

He has a problem. He can not very well tell the Navy to go find the Maria Morales. Very few people know what happened and for sure a lot of people will know what happened if the Navy did find it.

USS Georgia
Offshore of Bahia Blanca, Argentina
September 7, 1996 Saturday

The Georgia is lying on the bottom in one hundred feet of water slightly south of the sea lane into the harbor. The Special Ops folks are almost finished assembling the utility module to the command module. Each element is thirty three feet long and six feet in diameter. The command module has accommodations for twelve. The utility module has a two hundred kilowatt fuel cell. Three quarters of this power goes to a two hundred horsepower electric motor which is driving an axial flow water jet. The rest of it goes to the command module for air quality management, gyro stabilization, instrumentation and a modest selection of tools which the co-pilot of the sub can operate.

They finish the assembly task at 2117 Zulu. The men board the command module through the port side hatch. The three Argentines are heavily sedated. It takes some effort to get them through the hatch to their seats. Henry and five former SEALS now nominally in the CIA make up the rest of the compliment. The not-so-mini (now sixty six feet long) mini sub departs from the USS Georgia at 2139 Zulu. They have a twenty mile run to the inner harbor. This takes the better part of two hours. It is dark and raining when they arrive near their first stop. Henry has been here a few times in the past in the daytime. The mini sub surfaces. He opens the hatch and takes a look. There were a few dress rehearsals a week and a half ago. They had a one quarter scale mockup of this portion of the Bahia Blanca waterfront in East Gorham at that time – it is gone now. Henry is now acquainted with what this scene looks like through night vision equipment and quickly locates the Maria Morales Shrine only eighty yards from where they surfaced. The sub motors over to the dock and they tie it up there with light lines which are not strong enough as to impede any hasty departure. Two of the former SEALS manhandle Gerbert Bachmeier up through the hatch. The dock is only about three feet above the top side of the sub. Someone has thoughtfully covered the cylindrical mini sub hull with anti-skid material in the immediate vicinity of the topside hatch. The SEALS have no difficulty putting Gerbert onto the dock. As expected the place is deserted at this hour. They carry Gerbert around the wall to the front of the shrine. He is still unconscious and handcuffed behind his back. They secure him to the replica of the Maria Morales with a line that passes through the aft starboard hawse. Then they remove his pullover revealing a nearly one foot square body artwork on his torso. The decal for this body art was derived from a photograph of the cabin on the Maria Morales taken the day she was raised from the depths. They place a lanyard which is holding Captain Guzman's pocket watch around his neck. Finally they leave a water tight zippered pouch with several more photographs and several wedding rings propped against the cabin of the replica.

Fifteen minutes later they drop Helmut Vogel and Fritz Wexler off in front of the CCM Bahia Blanca dock. They each have life jackets on and their hands are cuffed behind their backs. They are both tied to the same cleat and they won't float away. USS Georgia has a stealthy radio antenna floating at surface level. At 0015 Zulu she receives a transmission from the mini sub 'all's ashore that's going ashore'. The Georgia dutifully relays this information up into the heavens. The mini sub is broken down and back in its launch tubes by 0220 Zulu. At 0225

Zulu, USS Georgia sans the one way passengers rises off the bottom and heads northeast.

Maria Guzman's residence
Bahia Blanca, Argentina
September 7, 1996 Saturday 2120 (0020Zulu Sept 8, 1996)

The phone is ringing. Her son Mario picks it up.

"May I please speak with Senora Guzman?"

By this time his mother is at the phone. She asks who it is. He does not know.

"This is Senora Guzman. Who is this?"

"I have a report of some disturbance at your husband's shrine."

The phone goes dead. They don't have call tracing but it wouldn't matter if they did.

Mario drives her to the shrine with his flashing lights on but not his siren. Shortly after they arrive, a reporter and a photographer from La Provincia show up. Mario reported the incident as soon as he saw the shrine. His mother immediately notices her husband's watch dangling from Gerbert's neck. Then she notices the body art. She screams in anguish. She fumbles around in her purse and produces a pair of scissors. Mario gently holds her hand restraining her. Her screams have awakened Gerbert.

"Mom, I called this in. We will have help momentarily. We need to get some photographs and I don't want you in trouble for injuring or killing this bastard. Help is on the way."

Two more police cars are on the scene in another few minutes. All the flashing lights have a predictable effect. El Pescador se Extiende (The Lying Fisherman) bar is barely fifty meters down the road. Soon there are numerous patrons of the bar and a nearby restaurant on the scene. Another five police show up in a van and cordon off the area. About the same time a reporter from UPI arrives. He is forcibly restrained from crossing the cordon. The folks from La Provincia offer to share their photographs they took earlier with UPI for a modest fee.

Dolf Ackerman was having a drink with his girlfriend at El Pescador se Extiende. They have joined the crowd at the shrine. He was a night watchman for CCM Belen for several years but since he has completed his community college studies he is now a foreman and the chief engine mechanic at CCM Bahia Blanca. He recognizes Gerbert Bachmeier who he has not seen in three years. This can not be good. He calls Benno Weber on his cell but only gets his answering service. Something tells him to go take a look at the yard. When he gets there he finds the night watchman asleep. He walks outside.

"Hilfe."

"Hilfe."

He walks to the edge of the dock and sees two men with life jackets. One of them is conscious and is softly crying 'Help', 'Help'.

Dolf is close to two meters (6'7") tall and exceedingly strong. He unties the men from the cleat and gently pulls them over to a ladder. He reties them to a cleat next to the ladder and then descends down the ladder until he is waist deep. He grabs the strap on the life jacket of the man who is conscious with his left hand and climbs back up the ladder. He then repeats the process for the other guy. He thinks he has seen the one who is conscious before. After a few moments he realizes that this is Helmut Vogel, the former manager of CCM Bahia Blanca. His picture is on the wall in the front office. He has a pocket knife which he uses to cut off their cuffs.

"Are you Herr Vogel?"

"Yes."

"I am Dolf Ackerman. Who is this other guy?"

"His name is Fritz Wexler. Where am I?"

"You are on the CCM Bahia Blanca dock."

"Thank you for getting us out of there."

"No problem. How did you get there?"

Helmut launches into a tale of woe which has a lot of speculation in it because he doesn't know exactly what happened to him. He finishes up.

"I need to talk to Captain Brandt."

"He is the President of Argentina."

Obviously this is news to Vogel. He hasn't seen a television or a newspaper for three years. They manage to wake Fritz up. Dolf's girlfriend does not speak a word of German and hasn't a clue as to what is being said. He whispers to her to go back to the watchman's shed and wake him up. He will be toast if one of these guys sees him sleeping.

A few minutes later when they get to the watchman's shed, he is awake and the wine bottle is no where to be seen. He tries to call Benno Weber again but all he gets is an answering machine.

Dolf is beginning to suspect that the incident at the shrine and this incident are somehow connected.

"Herr Vogel, when is the last time you saw Gerbert Bachmeier?"

Helmut shudders and says quietly.

"It was a long time ago when we were captured at the ranch."

"I don't know what to do Herr Vogel. It is getting late. I think the best bet is for you and Herr Wexler to stay here in the yard tonight. I need to talk to Herr Weber."

The yard provides work clothes for the men. They have a modest supply of clothing in the storeroom. They find a few things to wear and some overly large shoes. Overly large is better than no shoes and much better than too small. The clothes have the distinct advantage of being dry. The best he can do is to offer them a couch and a chair in the front office. There is an ample supply of sparkling water in the refrigerator. He will bring them something to eat from an all-night diner not too far away.

His girlfriend is getting increasingly antsy but he takes her with him back and forth to the diner. After they deliver the food they proceed to his place.

La Quinta de Olivos

Olivos, Argentina

Sept 8, 1996 Sunday Morning

Oskar is looking at Clarin with disbelief. There on the front page is a picture of Gerbert Bachmeier tied to the replica of the Maria Morales and another picture of the cabin of the Maria Morales taken after the boat was raised. Shortly his private line rings. It is Raphael.

"Dad, Helmut Vogel and Fritz Wexler were found floating off our dock in Bahia Blanca last night."

"Alive?"

"Yes, they were all doped up."

"This is obviously the work of the Americans."

"I am sure that you are correct but that doesn't make it any less of a problem."

"Get them out of Bahia Blanca now."

"I will see to it. What about Gerbert?"

"He is no doubt in jail at the moment."

"We do not have much influence in Bahia Blanca and the whole place is in an uproar this morning. Our people report that they are picketing our yard. What are you going to do?"

"I don't know. I have to think about this.'

He is dazed. The whole thing is blowing up right before his eyes. He doesn't think about it very long. This is not going to get better. He gets up from the breakfast table and kisses Basima on the forehead as he normally does on a work day.

"Oskar, it is Sunday, you are not going to work."

"I feel a little woozy I am going to go upstairs for a little while."

Half an hour later she goes up to check on him. He is sitting looking out the bedroom window at the olive trees. He is not breathing. There is a half empty glass of water and a half empty bottle of 80mg oxycontin tablets on the table next to the chair.

She calls Raphael. He says that she should call the Supreme Justice to La Quinta and get sworn in immediately. There will have to be a special election, probably in November or December but she is the lawful successor. They will explain his death as a heart attack. There will be no autopsy.

Basima was sworn in as President of Argentina at noon Sunday. She asked all of Oskar's direct reports to meet with her yesterday. Their allegiances have been with Oskar. She got assurances that they will follow her lead. Raphael will remain as the head of the Nazis in Argentina and they will try to carry on Oskar's policies.

There is a fair amount of noise coming out of Bahia Blanca about the Maria Morales. The death of the President has overshadowed this, but not completely. People pointing the finger of blame at Oskar are getting a lot of front page, lead story bad press in much of the conservative news media. The Socialists are accused of planting the most damnable lies about the fallen hero. It is well established that Oskar's policies have pushed BP off the Martinez Macizo. All the members of his, now her, administration are spouting the party line in every television news interview. Polling indicates that most people are praising Captain Brandt for evicting BP and furious at the lies coming from the Socialists in Bahia Blanca. The Maria Morales affair is not selling newspapers in Buenos Aires by Tuesday afternoon.

Metropolitan Cathedral of Buenos Aires
September 4, 1996 Wednesday

The funeral procession started from La Quinta de Olivos and followed Avenida del Libertador to Retiro. It proceeded along Avenida Reconquista almost into the very shadow of the cathedral. The choice of Reconquest Avenue was duly noted by those who note such things.

The last three kilometers of the route were strewn with rose petals. The caisson carrying Oskar's coffin was drawn by four black horses. It was followed by an open carriage with Basima, Raphael and Hermann Schleifenbaum – also drawn by four black horses. In front of the caisson and behind the carriage were four cavalrymen dressed in the uniform of 1880 (the year General Jose de San Martin's mortal remains were returned to Argentina). Fully half of the Argentine navy submarine service marched the last kilometer to the cathedral. A televised high mass was celebrated by Cardinal Gaspar Vargas. Basima delivered the eulogy. Oscar's coffin was placed in a crypt not far from General Jose de San Martin's sarcophagus. The cruiser Córdoba, one mile away in the Rio de la Plata fired a twenty one gun salute at the close of the service.

438

Javier Rojas makes the long drive from Buenos Aires to Bahia Blanca twice a month. He doesn't have to be in Bahia Blanca until 0700 Monday morning but nobody in Buenos Aires knows that. There is a tavern a few miles east of Bahia Blanca which also has seventeen seedy cabins next to it. These are rented exclusively to the patrons of the bar. This is very convenient since the patrons can walk as opposed to drive to the evening's accommodations after their sessions at the bar. They are usually accompanied by a senorita they met at the bar by this time.

This particular evening, the senorita who accosts Javier is one of the higher priced hookers in Bahia Blanca. She has been bought and paid for to get Javier drunk. She even buys him alternate rounds. By 2215 she has accomplished her mission. Roberto Drescher and Julio Braun who are yard mechanics from CCM Belen have been watching these proceedings while nursing a few beers. They help (carry is probably more descriptive) Javier out. They are just a couple of friends helping their friend off to his cabin. They take him to his truck. One of them will drive the truck. The hooker wants a ride back into town. She can go with the guy driving the car. He gallantly opens the door for her to get in. As she is getting in she gets a whack with his sap which renders her unconscious or worse. Javier's Isuzu has an automatic transmission – which is why he and it were selected. They drive into town and park in an alley on the east side of Avenida Solieri. They move

Javier to the driver's seat and transfer the hooker from the car to the passenger side of the cab. Julio positions the hooker so that her head is under the steering wheel. They empty the last of a half liter bottle of cheap whiskey into Javier's mouth spilling half of it on his shirt. There is a slight downgrade from the alley to Avenida Solieri and a little more of a downgrade on the way to Avenida Harbor. The truck crawls along very slowly out onto Avenida Solieri. Both doors are open. Roberto is standing on what will have to pass for a running board steering with his right hand and holding onto the door with his left. As soon as they have the truck pointed straight down the street toward the water Julio shoves the hooker causing her shoulder to lean on the accelerator pedal. They both jump off and slam the truck's doors. The vehicle is a mere thirty meters from the Maria Morales when it starts accelerating. The truck is heavily laden with building materials but manages to reach thirty kilometers an hour before it crashes into the Maria Morales. The replica, the cross behind it and much of the semicircular brick wall behind it are pushed into the harbor along with the Isuzu. Everything sinks in three meters of water. There will not be much in the way of a crowd visiting the shrine Sunday.

The pilot boat cum tug met USS Georgia some two miles out of the lagoon. Henry said thank you and good- bye to Captain Johnson and the SEALS. He was able to get from the sub to the tug via a short gangway without getting wet. USS Georgia headed northeast and shortly disappeared beneath the surface. Henry was on shore twenty minutes later. He is going to check up on Werner Runkel. Now that the other three have been returned to Argentina, there is strong sentiment to let Werner go. Nobody seems to have any good ideas about where. Tom Stevens is willing to take him on as a GSE employee. Tom does a lot of highly classified stuff. The folks in DARPA aren't too sure about the wisdom of that idea. There is some talk of letting him go home. That isn't popular either. Suppose he ended up working for another set of Saudis? Henry was instructed to spend a day or two here trying to sort this out.

Werner was transferred to another part of the deten- tion center three years ago. His cell has a window facing the ocean to the north. There are blinders underneath the window and on both sides which preclude him see- ing the ground or very much to the north or south. There is a small library at the facility and he has availed himself of it. Largely through his own efforts with a little help from the guards he has become fluent in English. He really was in it for the money. He has never committed a war crime or any kind of atrocity.

Henry gets there in time for the evening meal. They eat outdoors next to the garden. The walls are high enough such that one cannot see what is outside. Werner had always been highly receptive to the drug the French used on him. He really does not remember his early interrogations and he certainly has no clue that Henry was involved in a few of these.

September 18, 1996 Wednesday

Commander Donald Whiting joins them for breakfast Wednesday morning. Don and Henry lay it out for Werner. Donald starts. The conversation is in English.

"Werner, we are thinking about letting you go. If we do, you can never return to Germany. Your brother is well as far as we can tell, but I am sorry to inform you that both of your parents died while you have been here."

He hands Werner some copies of their obituaries that appeared in the Hanauer Anzeiger in 1993 and 1995. His face twists a bit as he reads them. Doctor Whiting is making mental notes. They sit in silence for about a minute after he has finished reading.

"I can never see their graves?"

"That is correct Werner. Quite frankly, we would worry that you might take up with other Saudis if you returned to Germany."

"I could work in the family business. I will never return to Saudi Arabia."

Henry picks up.

"I am sorry Werner but this is not negotiable. Let's move on.

After a moment's pause he continues.

As I am sure you recognize we also know something about making explosives. We think you could help us. We have in mind to offer you a job working for the US government at one of our explosives research facilities.

We are leaning toward a relatively sparsely populated area in the western part of the country. You can apply for citizenship, you can find a suitable woman, you can raise a family and you can live out a normal life there. You won't get paid as well as the Saudis paid you but you will get paid as well as our engineers do."

"When would this happen, if it happens?"

"Conceivably you might leave this place with us later this week."

"What happened to the others in Argentina?"

"The other three that were captured when you were, were sent back there recently. We expect that Gerbert Bachmeier will be dealt with harshly by the Argentines in Bahia Blanca. The other two were minor players. We don't know and we don't care what happens to them. Did you ever meet Wilhelm Bachmeier?"

Henry knows damn well that Werner has met Wilhelm at least a few times from previous interrogations but all these interrogations were done with the magic drug. Werner says the right thing.

"I met Bachmeier several times. He is the head of the Nazis there in Argentina."

"He **was** the head. We caught up with him and Prince Rashid three years ago."

They take a break for lunch. Henry polishes his club sandwich off in less than five minutes and leaves to make a phone call. He has done his thing which was to find out if he thinks Werner can be trusted to live a free life in the US without causing any more trouble. It turns out that Werner has a most powerful and unlikely ally. Guenther Reinhardt was highly impressed with the engineering that went into refitting U-1241. He has read the transcript or listened to the tape of every one of Werner's interrogations. Guenther wants the young man to work in a government lab, probably Los Alamos but possibly north Texas where one will occasionally find Tom Stevens.

"Good morning Guenther."

"What do you think Hank?"

"I think he will be okay. I left him with Don at the lunch table. Later this afternoon you will get a chance to hear his opinion."

Don has reached the same opinion. They throw Werner softballs all afternoon. When they sit down to dinner, there are two bottles of an excellent Californian red wine on the table. Werner hasn't had a drink in three years. He feels it shortly, but he is a happy drunk. Nobody seems to mind. They manage to get one after dinner brandy into him and then they pack him off to bed. Don and Henry have an impromptu celebration of the day's events which ends with the brandy bottle empty.

September 19, 1996 Thursday

Henry gets to be the chaperone for the rest of the week. Werner leaves East Gorham the way he came, to wit, with his head in a black bag. When the Gulfstream has been up for about an hour and a half Henry removes the bag. They land in Boca Chica (NAS Key West) long enough to let Dr. Whiting switch aircraft on his way to the Pentagon. They spend part of Thursday and all of Friday in Houston where the local FBI office manufactures a new identity for Werner. They let him keep his first name but from now on he is Werner Wurtzberg. He has a complete set of credit cards, a social security card, and a New Mexico driver's license. He does not get a passport nor is he ever likely to.

Los Alamos National Laboratory
Los Alamos, New Mexico
September 21, 1996 Saturday

Guenther met them at the airport and had them in his office half an hour later. Werner is surprised. He has heard of Guenther Reinhardt. This is the guy who was with Henry in Jizan.

Guenther greets him in German before switching to English. He is introduced to the people he will be working with. About five pm Guenther takes them to meet Gregor Boehm. They eat at a local steak house. Greg is going to put Werner up for a week or so until he can find a place and get settled. Greg has already lived the life that they are offering Werner. There is probably no one better suited to put Werner at ease. Henry stays at Guenther's Saturday night.

September 22, 1996 Sunday

Guenther doesn't sleep much. His day starts between 330 and 4 am. Henry's alarm goes off at six. By the time he has showered and dressed, Guenther has his breakfast cooked except for the eggs. Henry opts for scrambled. Guenther suggests his house specialty omelet. That's what they have. There is some hot sauce on the table and Guenther cautions that he makes this stuff himself and it is hot. Henry learns the hard way.

"Guenther, what have you got in here?"

"I drop a few Scotch Bonnets into the blender along with a little salt, olive oil and vinegar and push the button."

Henry manages to brush most of it off. The cheese in the omelet puts the fire out a little.

They go to Greg's place to see how Werner is doing. All is well. Guenther is going to see Tom Stevens this afternoon, he wants to get going. Henry is all in favor of this. He hasn't seen Christina in three weeks. They arrive in Manchester New Hampshire at four. There are two Jimmies waiting. Henry is home by four forty five.

Henry was instructed to not show up before ten this morning. He knocks on John's door just to tell him he is alive and well. Linda tells him that John is in the conference room. That door is closed as well. He knocks.

"Come in, Hank."

He is amazed. Guenther, Randy, Lieutenant General Art Woods, Fleet Admiral Dick Stone, Mitch, Henri Drouhin, General David Cometz (Israeli Defense Minister), George Maxwell (head of MI-6) and Lawrence Cooper the new head of NSA stand up. There is a polite round of applause. Guenther hands him a plaque. He notices President Simmons' signature at the bottom.

"Congratulations. We got the major players in the bombings of New York and Tel Aviv and you got most of them. That's the good news. The bad news is that you will not be having such an exciting life in the future."

John picks up.

"Hank, I have been diagnosed with lung cancer. It is hard to tell how much longer I will have any decent quality of life so I intend to enjoy the rest of it while I can. You are the main man at DCAC starting now."

Tears start rolling down Henry's face. After a moment he regains some of his composure and says.

"I trust that you know that the consumption of cognac and sparkling water is a highly recommended regimen for treating respiratory problems."

"You will have to come to the Keys to do that in a month or so."

"What about your place on the Annisquam?"

"I make you and Christina a good deal, if you want it."

Every man comes forward, offers congratulations and shakes his hand. He and John embrace for at least ten seconds. John has become his older brother in these past five and a half years.

Guenther picks up.

"Despite the nice plaque and the heartfelt thanks we all have given you, all is not sweetness and light. I guess you heard that that woman is now Senora Presidente."

"I did."

"They are going ahead with a nuclear power plant sixty miles southwest of Córdoba. This plant was originally scheduled to be constructed someplace south of Buenos Aires. There is no way they can be up to any good."

"And?"

"If you have a big enough electromagnetic accelerator, you could use this in conjunction with the not-so-good Plodamax that they are making to punch holes in satellites. This thing will take a lot of electricity. The civilian demand for electricity is in Buenos Aires. Why are they going to build another power plant out in the sticks?"

"Córdoba isn't exactly the sticks Guenther."

"You are right but you can find them sixty miles south west of Córdoba. They may be going to build it inside a mountain."

"Building that sub pen inside the cliff didn't work out so well for them."

"That was the largest conventional weapon in the world. We can not deliver that by air."

Cooper speaks.

"She is beating the war drums as loud as Brandt was. They are condemning the United States for holding prisoners without trial at some unspec fied location. They are condemning the Brits for helping us. They are claiming that we mounted an unlawful salvage operation in Argentine territorial waters. Then they added some complete bullshit of their own. They took some of the wreckage from the UA-63 raid in May of ninety three and claimed to have pulled it out of the sea near Bahia Blanca last week. They are claiming that the US Navy pulled the same stunt last month that they did three years ago – and they lost some equipment and here it is. As you are well aware, nobodies comprise roughly three quarters of the nations in the General Assembly. They are spreading rumors that we hit an Argertine salvage ship with a nuclear torpedo. They are passing all sorts of resolutions condemning us and the Brits for everything from causing malaria to sun spots. We and/or the Brits are vetoing at least one resolution a day. We have formed a small group of Psychologists and Shrinks to try to figure what she might do next. This woman is a Doctor of Psychology and a master propagandist."

This goes on a while longer. Around noon, everyone departs for their aircraft waiting in Boston or Manchester or Bedford. John had Linda organize a huge Chinese spread. Everyone in DCAC is there to partake. This is an appropriate forum to announce that Henry will now be running the show.